# DISPLACED – PART TWO

Cover artwork by Stephanie Tunnell
Interior artwork by Zoe Price

Manufactured in the United States of America

Library of Congress Control Number: 2023920971

First Edition (print on demand)

ISBN (hardcover): 979-8-9889635-3-0
ISBN (paperback): 979-8-9889635-4-7
ISBN (ebook): 979-8-9889635-5-4

# Displaced – Part Two

SCOTT G. SKINNER

A novel

For Greg and Carolyn

# Key Characters

MARS, 2314 (NEW EARTH)

RESISTANCE FIGHTERS
Atwood "Old Man" McCarthy, leader of the Freedom Contingent Brigade
Susie Walker, McCarthy's trusted top lieutenant
Albert "Dixon" Dixon, lieutenant
Rosalina "Rose" Martínez, lieutenant
Leonard Debussy, lieutenant
Samara Jones, lieutenant
René de Rooij, lieutenant

SECOND STRINGERS
García García, reformed shuttle driver
Keith Sargent, long-haul truck driver
Jeff Hawkins, venture capitalist
Gary Underwood, baseballer and model
Johnny Cardellini, supermarket manager
Eric Adams, gay men's chorus director
Barbara Purkey, Army wife

ABDUCTED TEENS AND YOUNG ADULTS
Pete Dimkowski, 18
Josh Brewer, 18
Shauna Robinson, 18
Tiffany Cantrell, 18
Brandon Sayers, 18
Dana Golding, 26
Steve Myerson, 27

RESPONSIBLE ADULTS
    Gwendolyn Pierce, seamstress
    Fred LaChance, restaurant owner

BAD GUYS
    Dorian Ross, chancellor of New Earth
    Donovan Barstow, commander of the Loyalist Army of the
Republic of New Earth
    Lucien Reynolds, informant
    Marcus Brown, corporal, Ross's Army

TECHNICIANS AND OPERATORS
    Gustav Greene, control room operator first class
    Colm O'Malley, control room operator first class
    Lymott Banks, control room operator second class
    Andrés López Peña, control room operator second class
    Vanessa Marquez, technician first class
    Abraham Singh, technician second class
    James Maxwell, technician second class

# Key Characters

CHICAGO, 1987 (EARTH PRIME)

THE TEENAGERS
Robert "Bob" Wilkinson, Jr., 18
Lorraine "Lori" Rainsmith, 18
Becky Dimkowski, 15

THE PARENTS
Robert Wilkinson, Sr., four-term U.S. senator
Gail Wilkinson, Bob's stepmother
Stanley Dimkowski, ceramics factory foreman
Dolores "Deedee" Dimkowski, hairdresser
Charles Rainsmith, dean of admissions, DePaul University
Helen Rainsmith, housewife

THE AUTHORITIES
Harold Washington, mayor, city of Chicago
David Orr, deputy mayor, city of Chicago
Alton Miller, press secretary, mayor's office, city of Chicago
Leslie Barnes, chief of police, city of Chicago
Marshall Bennett, captain, Chicago Police Department
J.D. Mayotte, detective lieutenant, Chicago Police Department—Missing Persons Division
Martin Heinbrenner, detective, Chicago Police Department—Missing Persons Division
Terrence Morgan, SWAT commander, Chicago Police Department
Oscar Ramirez, SWAT officer, Chicago Police Department
Reginald Hunter, captain, United States Air Force

Dale Ramsey, captain, United States Air Force

RESPONSIBLE ADULTS
Gerald "Gerry" Kirchner, PsyD, Bob's psychiatrist

BAD GUYS
Wesley Arendt, CEO of Chicago Genetics Center, Inc.
Miles Myrick, senior technician, CGC
Balthazar Garrett, technician trainee, CGC
Christopher Gilman, technician trainee, CGC
Mark-Lin Chang, Ross Army Loyalist

PETS
Molly, Lori's golden retriever
Max, Detective Lieutenant Mayotte's tuxedo cat

# Part Two:

Hot Tubs, Cold Cuts, and Things That Blow Up Real Good

# Chapter 1

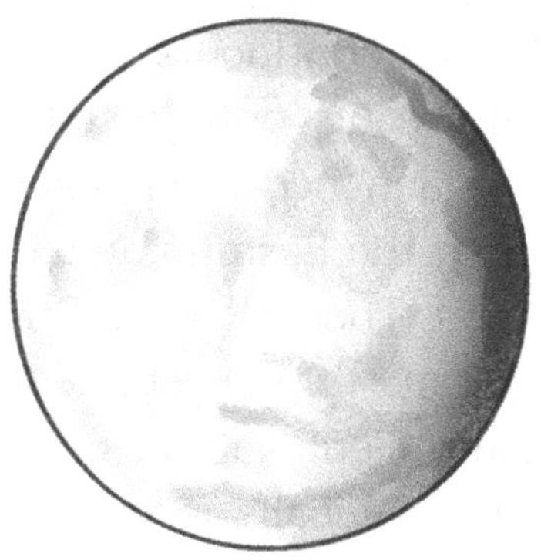

1

The instant 18-year-old Pete Dimkowski disappears from Chicago in 1987 is represented by a horrible *WHOOSH*. The sound is gone almost as quickly as it arrives, replaced by a roar that lasts 30 seconds but seems like 30 years. The roar represents his body being whisked through Earth's atmosphere. This aural assault is similar to the noise one hears during freefall when skydiving. It is surreal, but not as surreal as the image that follows when Pete dares to look down. His body appears to float in oxygenated nothingness—a micrometeorite-resistant, waterless amniotic sac, if you will—yet his molecules have disassembled. They spin in place, discombobulated but resembling the shape of an adolescent male *Homo sapiens.* Impossibly, his heart beats in place and his lungs are visible where his chest would otherwise be, pumping air from the nadir. His eyeballs also remain whole, as do his ear canals—how else could he see and hear? *What is this madness?* Pete's brain ponders, but the horror has only just begun.

His disassembled body slowly turns to offer a 360-degree view of the cosmos as he passes beyond Earth's atmosphere. Pete will never forget the image of Planet Earth rotating to offer a view of all seven continents and a blue so iridescent it practically sears its beauty onto his retinas. But something happens. Missiles are launched and nuclear winter slowly destroys the Earth. First, the Eastern United States goes up in flames. Then, the West. Then, Western Russia. Then, a miniscule blot of green that may or may not be the British Isles.

China and the Korean Peninsula are next, followed by Japan. Then, three consecutive fireballs appear in place of what, from this vantage point, could be Paris, Berlin, and Vienna just as easily as they could be Brussels, Hamburg, and Geneva. Further west, Cuba and Hispaniola go next, then the Great Lakes region. Then, a series of fireballs, each one larger in size, explode across all of Asia Minor, vaporizing everything from Saudi Arabia to Turkey to Iran. Eastern Canada follows suit.

More nukes fly, and equatorial nations fall like fiery dominoes. Venezuela and Colombia are next, followed by Peninsular Malaysia, the Indian subcontinent, and much of Central Africa. What did these impoverished nations do to piss off the rest of the world? Pete, whose favorite subject in high school was geography, is unsure where the next explosions occur; Earth retreats further into the distance while he floats closer to Mars and a fallout cloud the size of an entire planet blankets the globe from north to south. He *thinks* the final explosions happen in the Southern Hemisphere—Australia and South Africa are his guesses. Equally horrifying, however, is what comes next: The cloud dissipates to reveal Antarctica's white mass shrinking in size as the ice caps melt and the oceans consume all.

The destruction of Mother Earth takes just 42 seconds in Journey-time, and Pete wonders how long it will take in real time for all the nuke-wielding countries on Earth to destroy each other along with anyone thoughtful enough to finger-wag about their actions. *Not long at all*, he thinks.

Mercifully, Earth soon recedes from view, and the ear-splitting roar is replaced by a vacuum of silence so different from the previous din that it defies description. The silence is anything but peaceful, however; the hollowness of it often leads to delirium. Stars and orbs within the Milky Way wage a trippy, high-speed assault from hundreds of millions of miles away. Finally, a reddish-orange orb comes slowly into view, and a few craggy rocks, strays from the planet's asteroid belt, streak past.

The deafening roar returns and Pete floats closer and closer to the planet he'll find was rechristened "New Earth." Countless canyons, valleys, and craters appear as pockmarks and scars from afar, and it is of little wonder astronomers believed Mars to be a dry planet. Remarkably, rivers flow through some of these canyons and provide farmable land *à la* the Nile River Delta. Strangely, they don't feed into anything except underground aquifers. Lakes and oceans are nowhere to be found.

Pete, whose nausea has finally abated (makes sense—his stomach literally disassembled itself), isn't sure *what* he sees. The final seconds of his Journey feel rushed, as if his consciousness is being sucked through a pneumatic tube. There is that awful *WHOOSH* sound again, then blackness.

2

He awakens untold seconds later in a sterile room awash in screamingly bright overhead lights. He's woozy and disoriented and is unsure what to make of the commotion in the next room, except that it sounds like someone going into labor.

"*Push! Push!*" a voice—that of time chamber Technician First Class Vanessa Marquez—yells.

"*She's lost a lot of blood,*" another voice—Technician Second Class Abraham Singh—states.

"*I know. Grab her shoulders so she stops fighting,*" Marquez replies. Then, to the expectant mother: "*Push!*"

Pete's head is pounding, and he has that unmistakable sensation in his gut of nausea forthcoming. He swallows to delay its arrival. He sits up and finds himself on a padded bench in a sort of interstellar waiting room—the orientation bay—behind a transparent door off to one side of the time chamber.

The fluorescent lights above are blinding. Pete looks around and sees three dozen additional benches, all unoccupied and each featuring a drain on the cement floor beneath. *I'm alive,* he thinks. *I made it!*

Alas, the vomit can wait no more. Pete positions his head between his legs and unleashes a torrent of spray that splashes the cuffs of his jeans. He stops, wipes his mouth with the back of his hand, then vomits again, more the second time. A few chunks stain the *Hard Rock Cafe* T-shirt he borrowed from his best friend, fellow high school senior Bob Wilkinson. The vomit eventually gives way to dry heaves, and he gradually finds his center of gravity.

"*Breathe!*" he hears from the next room. Marquez again. "*In! Out! And push!*"

"*I see something coming,*" a third voice—Technician Second Class James Maxwell—announces. "*I think it's the head!*"

"*Switch places, she's cresting.*" Marquez's voice again. The shift in tone suggests she is addressing the mother-to-be. "*What's your name?*"

A new voice: *"D-Dana."* The voice squeals with labor pains, made worse by nausea and dizziness courtesy of the Journey its owner completed just moments before.

*"You're doing good. Almost there . . . steady breathing . . . and . . . give us a big push!"*

*Dana!* Everything rushes into focus for Pete. He stands up, wobbly, his knees shaky. He makes his way to the glass door, careful to sidestep the mess he left behind and registering at the last possible second that the "glass" is not glass at all, but transparent laser.

Through the laser pane he observes 26-year-old Dana Golding from behind, legs spread and splayed on her back on a counter, the contents of which have been hurriedly shoved to one side. Singh pins down Dana's shoulders as Maxwell watches from the sidelines and Marquez reaches for the newborn, now halfway out. "C'mon, you're halfway there, give us one more push."

Dana bars her teeth and screams at the top of her lungs. With a final push, she gives birth to her four-pound, eight-ounce miracle baby. The newborn doesn't make a peep, sending Dana into a panic. "I-is she okay?! Why isn't she crying?! What's happening?!" Fifteen interminable seconds later, the baby cries, and so does her mom—tears of joy.

"Congratulations, it's a girl," Marquez marvels.

"Lemme see her. Give her to me."

Pete watches from the next room, happy and angry at the same time. "Give her to her, you bastards," he says, under his breath.

Dana reaches for her daughter, but her arms are weak and Marquez has to lay the infant down on Dana's chest. "Here you go," she says, with surprising tenderness. "Let's get you two cleaned up and in front of a doctor. You're both lucky to be alive."

Marquez turns to Singh and Maxwell. "You, call the hospital. You, find something we can use as a gurney."

"What about the . . ." Maxwell points to a motorized cart used to transport corpses.

"Don't be ridiculous." She rifles through drawers beneath the counter until she finds a roll of 24th-century paper towels and a bottle of hydrogen peroxide. She rolls up the sleeves of her lab coat, runs across to the opposite wall, and rubs her hands beneath the tap at a sanitizing station. "I'm just going to clean her a bit," she tells the new mom, but Dana's attention is focused on her child, who has stopped crying and who stares at her mother's blurry visage with inquisitive brown eyes. Marquez tears off a wad of towels and dampens it with water and a dose of hydrogen peroxide.

Dana's eyes widen when Marquez reaches for the infant. "It's okay, I'm just cleaning her. Water and a dash of peroxide for sanitary purposes."

"No, lemme hold her!" Dana cries out as Marquez lifts the newborn.

"As you wish." Marquez releases the child and dabs her on the head and all over. She must pry Dana's fingers away for a thorough cleaning, but does so for only a moment. "There there, all set."

"Look at you, so clean and beautiful," Dana coos to her daughter. A coughing fit prompts Dana to turn her head and cough away from the baby. The coughing returns her to reality. She looks at her daughter, then at Marquez, then around this strange, strange room. "Where am I?"

As a mother herself, Marquez chooses her words carefully, lest she traumatize new mom Dana. "You're not ready for that yet. I don't have you on my list. Neither one of you."

Dana looks away from Savannah and discovers Pete is watching from some distance. She doesn't realize the door is translucent laser, and wonders why he isn't approaching. "Pete?" she half-asks, half-coughs. "Where are we?"

Pete is elated that she recognizes him. "Dana. How are you feeling?"

"W-weak. Scared. But also happy. Look at my little girl. She's so tiny and beautiful."

"She's precious," Pete says.

"Don't you wanna come see her?!"

"I can't," he replies. His eyes fill with tears.

"W-why not? What's going on?"

Pete swallows and slowly raises his hand to the all-but-invisible door. He folds in all digits except his pinky, and inches it toward the laser field that comprises the door. He hears the static charge just before a pink spark flies and his pinky is shocked with a hideous cracking sound. He flies backward and Dana screams. "Pete!" she cries out. Her daughter cries anew.

The outside doors open as Singh enters with a table on wheels. Gustav Greene, control room operator first class, charges in beside him. "What's going on in here?" Greene bellows.

"Someone decided to play hero," Maxwell replies. He motions to Pete, who gets to his feet and blows on his burnt pinky finger.

Greene is a lackey like everyone else in the room, and is as terrified of Donovan Barstow as the rest of them. Nevertheless, he's prone to asshole tendencies of his own when the highest-ranked person around, as he is currently. Dana cowers in his presence and protectively holds her baby tight against her chest.

Greene, to Pete: "We'll get to you in a minute." To Dana: "Well well. Remarkable. The chancellor will be pleased."

"Ch-chancellor?" Dana asks. "W-what ch-chancellor? Where am I?"

"Should we tell her?" Maxwell asks.

"Can she handle it?" Greene asks in return. Seeing Marquez's lab coat stained with afterbirth, he says, "I take it you helped with the delivery?"

"Yes. It was something of a miracle."

"It was, wasn't it?" He nods. "Tiny little thing. But look at those eyes. Already so alert."

"She's a beautiful child."

"What about the mother? How did she come to be here?"

"We're not sure, but she's a fighter."

"This is highly irregular all the same. Let's get her and her daughter to the hospital. Take the tunnels."

Marquez nods. She motions for Singh to roll the table closer and help transfer Dana and her daughter to it so they can be wheeled to the hospital, one quadrant away but connected by a maze of subterranean tunnels. "Lay your coat on the table," Marquez suggests. "It's cleaner than mine." Singh nods and removes his lab coat.

3

The comely Vanessa Marquez, who finds herself being regularly hit on by the aggressive Gustav Greene, has already changed her lab coat once during her shift. Earlier in the day, the head, arms, and torso of the late Gavin Berringer, inventor of JourneyTech, materialized on the arrivals side of the time chamber. She and Singh lifted the partial corpse onto the motorized cart. She covered the body with her original lab coat and drove the cart to the transport bay for disposal.

Much like Dana, Marquez is a single mother doing a job in which she doesn't have all the facts. She wants to believe that people who perish during their Journey—or due to some freak accidents beforehand that result in their bodies being disposed of by *literally* being sent to a different time and place, such as was the case with Gavin—are given proper burials, and that the transportation bay's foreman is responsible for having their bodies interred in a cemetery somewhere. The one time she agreed to have a drink with Greene, however, he told her corpses are sent instead to an unpleasant place known only as "the Pit." She was disgusted to learn this, and was mortified because Greene appeared to be bragging when he told her, as if he was proud to have come upon this disturbing information.

Cosmo Jenkins, the foreman of the bay, has always been amiable and professional toward Marquez—and never overbearing like the aforementioned Greene. *Surely Cosmo wouldn't casually dispose of a body without giving it a proper burial,* she thought. She acquiesced to his request that they blitz their contacts on Earth Prime, circa May 1987, and in a *communiqué* sent that afternoon, asked her Earth Prime counterparts to vaporize their own corpses going forward.

"Maybe they're running low on plasma magazines?" she posited to Jenkins.

"Maybe," he replied. "At any rate, I'll take care of this. Meanwhile, blitz 'em three times if need be. This is the second one of these in as many days. Whatever the hell's going on down there, they need to clean up their own messes."

She drove the moto-cart back to the time chamber, dodged Greene's innuendos once more upon her return, and donned a new lab coat. *Why, of all possible colors, are these coats white?* she asked herself while Singh mopped the blood trail leading off the arrivals telepad and Maxwell logged the corpse's unexpected arrival.

Marquez skipped lunch, having lost her appetite following the arrival of Gavin's legless body. She had just regained her appetite when the alarm blared to announce the arrival of 16 new abductees. Everyone made it to the orientation bay without vomiting, and to the holding pen from there once they regained their sea legs. "I'm cabling Earth Prime," Marquez said while Singh tidied up and Maxwell recalibrated the time chamber.

"Whatever for?" Maxwell asked. Although he hadn't worked in the time chamber as long as Marquez, he (like the boorish Greene) was a company man through-and-through.

"To tell them not to send us their garbage anymore."

"Legless Leopold from earlier?"

"Don't be crude, Jim."

"I'm with you," Singh interjected. "That was disgusting."

"Thank you, Abe."

"Do as you will, but keep my name off the correspondence," Maxwell remarked.

Marquez no sooner logged into the messaging program at her workstation when the arrivals alarm sounded a second time.

"What the heck?" Singh said.

"I see two inbound," Marquez stated, "but none on the roster."

"I concur," Maxwell added.

It was then that Pete and Dana materialized on the arrivals telepad, the former on the verge of vomiting from his Journey and the latter moments away from giving birth.

4

Greene turns to Dana, who trembles. He raises his hand to convey that no harm will come to her. "No need to be scared," he says, unconvincingly. "I just wanted to see what the fuss was about. Your first child?" Dana nods. "Have you decided on a name?"

"Savannah."

"Savannah. Like the city in your United States? Or like the prairies of your African grasslands?"

"Neither. Just Savannah."

"I see. I'm merely a layperson in the control room next door, but I imagine your Savannah will come to be known as quite the miracle baby. Nothing like this has ever happened before." Greene's bullshit humility doesn't fool Dana. She erupts in another coughing fit and turns her head to cough away from her daughter.

"Ma'am, hold tight to your child," Marquez says. "We're going to move you."

"Um, okay." Dana looks around and sees Singh holding the table still while Maxwell grabs her shoulders and Marquez grabs her legs. "Hold tight, my darling," she coos to Savannah, who has fallen asleep. Moving Dana and Savannah from the counter to the table is seamless.

Greene, a full-on creeper, looks Marquez up and down. "Marquez, I am impressed. Have you ever delivered a child before?"

"Only my own." The time chamber tech is afraid Greene's about to ask her out again. She redirects the conversation accordingly. "Why don't you accompany Singh to the hospital? They may need your clearance for no questions asked."

"You're taking me to the hospital?" Dana asks. With her daughter sleeping peacefully, the subsiding adrenaline rush of time travel, and the exhaustion of childbirth, she is fading fast.

"That's right," Marquez replies. "They'll cut the umbilical cord and examine you both."

"Aren't you gonna tell me where I am?"

"You're in the Central Command Complex of District 1A, Zone Alpha, New Earth."

"Y-you mean Mars?"

"I mean Mars, yes."

Dana's eyes widen as she fights sleep. "So it's all true then? Pete?"

Pete looks on from the transition bay, helpless. "Looks that way."

Dana's heart sinks. "*NOOO!*" Greene snaps his fingers and Singh wheels Dana out. Greene follows close behind.

"I-is that a baby?" Greene's colleague, Banks, asks from the control room. He is late to the party.

"Yes. *This one* you'll wanna tell Ross about. There's another one in there you can get the story from."

"On it."

Greene and Singh wheel Dana and Savannah into the CCC's main corridor. They choose a downward-sloping exit ramp to the lower level, where another ramp leads to a series of tunnels and Clara Barton General Hospital.

5

Marquez approaches the transparent door to the transition bay. Pete, feeling defeated after seeing Dana wheeled away, slouches on a bench close to the door. Marquez swipes her magna-card, revealing a panel in the wall. She turns a knob and the sound of rushing water startles Pete. He turns to see a faucet pour water from the back of the bench in front of where he was sitting earlier. The water washes Pete's vomit into the drain beneath the bench. Marquez turns the knob the other way. The water stops running and a spray of something not unlike Lysol sanitizes the bench and purifies the air.

Pete decides to stop questioning what he is seeing. He approaches the translucent door and sees two technicians and a control room operator sizing him up. "Is my friend gonna be okay?"

"She'll be fine," Marquez says. "She and her daughter are lucky to be alive."

"So am I. That was . . . earlier when I . . . that . . . Earth was destroyed, wasn't it?"

"Our annals confirm Earth has been unable to support human life for approximately 260 years."

"Jesus. Just like Arendt said."

"He knows Wesley," Maxwell whispers to the others. Pete isn't supposed to hear that, but he does.

"I shot him in the arm," Pete replies. "Too bad my aim sucked."

"What's your name?" Banks asks.

"Pete."

"Pete, I'm Lymott. I work over there in the control room. I-I was actually born in St. Louis, but, uh, my folks moved to Hyde Park when I was ten." Chatty for a bad guy.

"You're from Chicago?!" Marquez and Maxwell marvel at this factoid as well—they were unaware of their colleague's birthplace.

Banks nods. "C'mon. We need to get you processed and over to orientation—there's a session that's just started."

"How are you feeling?" Marquez asks.

"You mean aside from *that?*" Pete motions to the drain below his arrival bench—little more than a scant trace of water currently, but a literal vomitorium just moments ago.

"The nausea's quite common," Maxwell explains. "What do you think of our drainage system?"

Pete shrugs. "Uh, it's fine, I guess. Do you have any Tylenol though? My head is pounding."

"Headaches are normal, too. They'll come and go for the next several days. It's best you learn to live with 'em."

"Great." Sarcastically.

"Why did you and your friend come here? You two obviously aren't from Ross's Army—"

"Obviously." More sarcasm; Bob would be proud.

"Hey, answer his questions," Banks commands. His words lack the bark one might expect.

Maxwell addresses Marquez, who has turned her attention away from Dana to check her workstation monitor for new messages at his workstation. "Did we miss anything, Vanessa?"

"Nothing. Not a word on these two. Or is it three?"

"So what gives, Pete from Earth Prime?"

"I plead the Fifth."

Maxwell walks over to the other side of the laser door. He swipes his magna-card and the door opens pneumatically. Pete is fascinated by the door, which, like the time chamber itself, reminds him of *Star Trek*. While he is distracted, Maxwell sucker punches him in the gut. Pete doubles over and sits down, lest he lose his balance. Although he would vomit under normal circumstances, he does little more than dry heave this time. His post-Journey nausea has left him empty inside.

"If we can't break you, maybe Barstow can."

Marquez and Banks shudder at the mere utterance of Commander of the Loyalist Army of the Republic of New Earth Donovan Barstow's name, and it doesn't go unnoticed by Pete. Banks extends a hand. Pete takes it and is yanked to his feet. "Jesus!"

"Sorry, you won't find Him here." Maxwell motions for Banks to escort the prisoner. "Need a hand?" he asks the St. Louis-born control room operator.

Banks shakes his head. "Just log their arrival. His and the woman's. The baby's too, I guess." He unholsters a plasma pistol from his belt and jams it into Pete's back. "Move."

6

The holding pen for new arrivals is immediately north of the time chamber, accessible via a pair of interior corridors branching off both the northwest and northeast corners of the room housing the chamber itself. The two corridors meet north of the corridor itself as it widens in front of the double doors that mark its soundproofed entrance.

Banks's magna-card grants him access to the holding pen, and he pauses before scanning it in front of the card reader.

"We had a small group come in about 90 minutes before you. There were s'posed to be more—our roster had 28 names—so we just kept 'em waiting until it seemed clear no one else was coming. Then you two showed up. So now we're behind. Barstow *hates* when that happens. He's in there now I'm sure, getting all riled up. Don't think you'll like him very much." He scans his card and opens the door.

Sure enough, Barstow is in mid-speech, his cloak billowing as he makes exaggerated arm movements. He pauses at the beep that precedes the doors opening, and turns to see who would dare interrupt him. "Ahem, I'm in the middle of my speech, now *DO YOU MIND?"*

"So sorry, Commander," Banks replies, meek. "We had a late arrival."

Barstow lets out an overdramatic, irritated sigh. "Show him in."

Banks motions for Pete to enter the staging room and make his way toward the cell in the back. A table in the center of the room plays host to a covered cage of some sort. The cage is rattling. *I don't wanna meet whatever's inside there*, Pete thinks, and trips over an untied shoelace.

One of the soldiers standing beside the cell's transparent laser door aims his plasma rifle at the door while the other scans his magna-card so the cell door slides open. Banks motions for Pete to step inside. Pete complies, dejected. "I'm sorry," Banks says, not without sympathy.

*"NO TALKING! THIS IS MY SHOW!"*

Pete looks around and sees 16 other new arrivals, many of whom are crying. The front of one person's shirt is stained with vomit, more than Pete's. Another person's shirt is splashed with blood, though they themselves appear otherwise uninjured. Four or five new arrivals mill nervously about and shuffle their feet. Most, however, sit on the concrete floor, backs against the wall, in various states of distress. Pete joins them.

"You look like hell," one of the new arrivals, Johnny, whispers.

"I just puked my guts out."

"So did I—that was messed up. He managed not to throw up, though." Johnny points to Eric, the new arrival seated beside him.

"No, but my head's pounding," Eric whispers. They exchange nods but do not shake hands, for fear of Barstow's wrath.

Barstow resumes his welcome speech, and since the smaller crowd of new arrivals doesn't offer up any volunteers, he manages to show off his replacement belly beater without any blood being shed.

7

The nurse administering Pete's blood test is of East Asian ancestry. Under different circumstances, her black hair, slender figure, and calm demeanor would almost certainly tempt Pete to offer up one of his usual, inappropriate comments. *"How 'bout your shoes throw a party and invite our pants down later?"* is one such oft-recited *bon mot*. *"You must be exhausted, because you've been running through my dreams all night!"* is another. *"Are you from Tennessee? Because you're the only 'ten' I see!"* is a third. (He learned that one from his uncle in Sevierville when he was nine, and it's one of his only fond memories of those dreadful Dimkowski family summer vacations.)

Pete is tired, angry, and scared; cheesy pick-up lines are the last thing on his mind. "All set," the nurse says. She carefully withdraws the syringe and dabs the injection site with a cotton ball before applying medical tape to secure it in place. Little has changed in this regard over 300 years.

"Didn't hurt at all," Pete replies.

"We know what we're doing here," Nurse Li replies. "Just keep that covered overnight and it should be healed by the time you shower tomorrow."

"Do you have anything for headaches? Some Tylenol or something?"

"I don't know what Tylenol is, but we do have an opiate. It's in short supply for the time being, however. For now, I recommend you stay hydrated, don't over-exert yourself for the next few days, get as much sleep as you can, and avoid alcohol."

"I'm not 21."

Nurse Li looks at him quizzically, then motions for him to complete his intake form. "You gave us your measurements and answered the questions about your medical and sexual history. All we're missing is your age in Earth Prime years, and your full name in two more places—*here* and *here*. Then you'll head over there to queue for the shuttle, where we'll have your dorm assignment."

Pete completes the intake form in silence. He queues for the shuttle in a line marked by a sign reading MALES. Johnny and Eric line up behind him. "You look like you're feeling better," Johnny observes.

Pete waves his hand in a seesaw motion. "Little bit. I still wanna barf, but there's nothing left."

"Same here. Is it true what he said in the other room about where we are? Because if so . . . holy sh—"

"It's true."

"Man. I . . . just . . . Jesus."

"I know." Pete is uncharacteristically terse. Johnny's ashen expression reminds him of the pale faces of his friends Bob, Lori Rainsmith, and the late Vinnie Modigliani after they viewed Wesley's time chamber trial videos.

A panicked new arrival is dragged, kicking and screaming, to the queue. A pair of soldiers stand on either side of him to ensure he doesn't try to run—it happens sometimes, and never ends well for the runner. Although Johnny and Eric look suitably mortified, Pete simply stands there, expressionless. "How can you be so cavalier?" Johnny asks.

"I-I'm not, I just . . . I sort of expected this."

"W-whadoya mean?"

"Long story."

"No talking, now move!" one of the soldiers barks. He motions them forward. Pete boards the shuttle and clutches his stomach in anticipation for another round of nausea.

Johnny and Eric sit across from him. "You okay?" Johnny asks.

Pete holds up one hand in a *"one moment, please"* gesture, and covers his mouth with the other hand. He lurches as if to vomit, but the urge passes. His upraised hand gives a thumb's up.

The shuttle is full as it pulls out of the CCC transport bay. "Better now?" Johnny asks. Pete nods. "Name's Johnny, by the way. Lincoln Park. And this is Eric. From . . ."

"Boys Town," Eric volunteers, referring to the famously gay enclave in East Lakeview, not far from the Belmont "L" station Pete, Bob, and Lori walked to less than 24 hours (and 300 years) ago. "Sorry 'bout the 'nasty.' "

Pete waves a dismissive hand. "I'm Pete, from Glencoe."

Eric responds with catty sarcasm—his usual default setting. "Ooh, Richie Rich."

"Hardly," Pete scoffs.

The shuttle crosses the Century Bridge and the mood on board changes. The passengers marvel at the canyon and Red River below. "Would you look at that?" Eric says.

Pete, who is afraid of heights, instinctively grabs the *oh, shit* handle built into the seatback in front of him.

# Chapter 2

1

Lori catches up with Bob, who is on all fours in the middle of Kilbourn Avenue, tears running down his cheeks and washing away the soot. She is teary-eyed as well. "Bobby, I'm so sorry." She voices concern about his knee, which bleeds from when he stumbled and tore his jeans.

"Forget my knee, those assholes took him!" He brings one trembling hand down hard on the asphalt, like a judge's gavel.

"Don't do that!"

"But it's my fault! I didn't gas up yesterday before I came and got you. Lines were too long. Today I saw the 'LOW FUEL' warning, but goddamn ignored it. So stupid. *Sooo* stupid."

Lori extends a hand and offers him this reassurance: "Remember what I said this morning? It's not your fault."

"Oh, stop it with that!" Bob barks in reply. Lori retracts her hand, as if in response to a viper strike.

"You know what I mean." Softer, like walking on eggshells.

Bob nods. He clenches both fists and takes several slow, deep breaths before apologizing. He gets up on his own, wincing as his knee cracks.

"It's okay," Lori says. "You have it real bad sometimes, don't you?"

"I guess." Bob looks away. "I hate when others see me like this."

The *babushka* Bob almost hit with his car catches up to them. She passes on the far side of the street, still dragging her grocery cart behind her. She gives Bob and Lori the evil eye as she passes, adding a curse in Polish for good measure.

"Let's get out of the road," Lori suggests. Bob nods and walks gingerly to the sidewalk. She attempts to cheer him up. "Maybe Pete'll be okay?"

"Yeah. He's so overbearing they'll probably let him go just so he stops talking."

Lori chuckles despite her emotions. She's glad to see Bob's hands no longer trembling. "C'mon. If anyone's watching, I totally don't wanna know what they're thinking."

"Good call. Maybe there's a payphone on the corner there. We can call that detective. Lemme grab his card." He motions back in the direction of Fullerton Avenue, a major east-west street sure to be blockaded further west, near the suburb of Elmwood Park. "We'll figure out the car situation afterwards. I really hate to leave her here, but I guess she'll be okay for a little while."

"She? Your car's a girl?"

"All cars are girls." Bob limps to his fuel-deprived Trans Am and fishes the detective's card from the glove compartment. He is about to close the door when he espies something in the back seat—the AK-47, stashed there by Lori. He chuckles.

"What is it?" Lori asks. Bob points to the back seat as he walks around behind the car to pop the trunk. "Yeah, someone would steal that for sure," she says, adding a chuckle of her own.

Bob hands Lori a blanket. "Here, cover it with this and we'll hide it in the trunk for now, I guess."

"Good idea."

Deed done, Bob closes the trunk and limps to a gas station on the corner. Plastic bags are wrapped around the pumps and secured with rubber bands—not a good sign. Bob notices a payphone in the lot. Alas, the handset's cord has been severed. The metal on the payphone acts as a mirror, and Bob sees how disheveled he and Lori appear. His shirt collar is covered in blood while Lori's hair is tousled and her face is peppered with soot.

"We look terrible," he says. "Well . . . I look terrible. You look great. But we can both stand to wash our faces. And . . . well . . ." He points to his filthy Bugle Boy T-shirt and to the fresh tear in the knee of his jeans. "Hang on." He turns around, modest, and flips his shirt inside out so the bloodstains are less pronounced. "There. C'mon." She brushes dirt from her face as he leads her into the gas station. He grabs a Mountain Dew from the cooler and sets it on the counter.

"Hey, what's up with the gas pumps?" Bob asks the greasy-haired attendant, whose tank top is caked with pit sweat.

"Out of gas since yesterday," the attendant replies. "Dunno why everyone made a run. Not like they can go anywhere."

"When's the truck come?"

"Wednesday. If it can get through."

"Aw, man."

"Tell me about it, kid."

"In that case, can we use your phone?"

"Phone's outside."

"It, um, doesn't work."

"Then I guess that's a 'No.' "

"O-kay, can we use your bathroom at least?"

"Don't have one."

"Where do *you* go?"

"In my pants. You gonna pay for that?"

"Yeah, one sec." He waits for Lori to set a bottle of water on the counter. "This too."

"Two twenty-three." Bob hands him a twenty from his wallet. "Got anything smaller?"

Bob snaps. "Hey man, what's your problem?!"

"Alright kid, Jesus! Don't have a cow." He swipes the twenty and makes change. "Seventeen seventy-seven is your change. And kid, I'm sorry. It's just . . . my own kid was taken a couple days ago. She was at that thing at the Art Institute, you know?" He gestures to a photograph of his daughter, an attractive brunette in her early 30s. The photograph is taped to the glass partition between his booth and the entrance. "She was doin' good, you know? Making everyone proud, nothing like me at all. Gets that from her mother. I sure do miss her."

"I'm sorry about your daughter," Lori says, compassionate.

"Me too," Bob points to Lori. "She and I are missing friends, too."

"Crazy times." The attendant fidgets with a sheaf of receipt paper.

"Hope you find your daughter," Bob says.

"Hope you find your friends."

"Working on it." Bob holds the door for Lori. They step into the late afternoon sun, where he takes an enormous swig of Mountain Dew and offers Lori a sip.

She shakes her head and gives her bottled water a flick of the wrist.

"Cool. Don't finish it, though; we can use what's left to wash our faces. We sorta stick out like sore thumbs." He grabs a wad of paper towels from the windshield washer station by one of the pumps and dabs water on some of the towels. He hands the rest to Lori and washes his face, neck, and arms with the wet towels.

Lori takes a good-sized swig, then douses the remaining towels with water. She washes her face, neck, and arms. "I feel better already."

"Me too. Sure you don't want any of my soda?"

"I'm sure, Bobby."

Bob finishes the last of his Mountain Dew and looks away while belching. " 'Scuse me."

"You've been hangin' around Pete too much."

They toss the empty bottles and soiled blue towels into a curbside trash bin and walk aimlessly down Fullerton Avenue. "Hey look," Bob says. A motel beckons them from up ahead and across the road.

2

The Fullerton Arms Motel features a sign boasting AIR-CON * POOL * H0T T B * HOME B X FF1CE on the top row and VAC NCY on the bottom row. A 1983 Chevette and a late-'70s Bonneville suggest the place is open. The Chevette is parked beneath the *porte-cochères* awning, while the Bonneville occupies the last spot in the lot, and is adorned with a coating of bird poop thick enough to imply it's been there for a while.

"Whadoya think, Bobby? Should we check in? I can certainly use a shower. And maybe they have a restaurant." Lori's hair is a hot mess, but she rinsed the soot out of it with the water bottle and combed it back with her bare hands as best she could.

"I doubt they have a restaurant, but, uh, we should probably get off the street, yeah."

They enter a nondescript lobby and walk up to the front desk. A young clerk, barely out of his teens, emerges from the office after Bob rings the bell. "Afternoon, kids. Need a room?"

"Two, if you have 'em," Bob answers.

" 'If we have 'em.' That's funny. We have 62 of them, as a matter of fact. Well . . . 61."

"Yeah, I saw a car in the lot, plus what I'm guessing is yours right outside?"

"Yvette the Chevette, my pride and joy. The other car belongs to the guest in 237. He, um . . . well . . ."

"Did he disappear like so many others?" Lori asked.

"Not exactly. He's a traveling salesman and he's been staying here a few days, but, um . . . I think he may have shot himself last night." The clerk lowers his voice when delivering the news.

"That's terrible!" Lori says.

The clerk shrugs. "I'm not sure. I heard what sounded like a gunshot. His car was still in the lot so I knocked on his door, but there was no answer."

"You didn't go in or call anyone?"

"Honestly, I was too scared to go in. I'm sure he isn't the first person to have killed himself since this thing started."

"It's only been like three days!"

The clerk shrugs again. "He's paid up through the night. I guess I can deal with it in the morning if he misses checkout. Anyway . . . tell you what: I'll give you adjacent rooms on the ground floor, opposite end. Does that work?"

"Sounds fine," Lori says through a yawn.

"Great. With tax that'll be . . . let's see here . . . $143.60."

"Okay, just a sec." Bob forks over eight twenties from his wallet. The source of the double sawbucks he grabbed after returning home from last night's regrettable boat trip is a cookie jar his stepmom, Gail, stashed in a cabinet above the fridge for emergencies.

"Thank you," the clerk says. "Normally we'd make you sign the register, but I think we can skip that. I'm mostly just concerned you're okay. You both look . . . well . . ."

"Like shit?" Lori asks.

"I wouldn't phrase it quite like that, but yes. Everything okay?"

"We're fine," Bob remarks.

"I think I'd like to hear it from the young lady, if it's all the same."

"We're fine," Lori says.

"So that's not blood on your collar?" The clerk motions to Bob's shirt, turned inside out but stained all the way through.

"Transmission fluid," Bob fibs. "Car broke down a couple blocks from here."

"We're glad you're open," Lori says. "Concerned about the new curfew."

"This is all pretty crazy," the clerk replies. "Wish they had curfew two nights ago. That way my cousin wouldn't have disappeared."

"I'm sorry," Lori replies. "We're missing friends, too."

"Well, I hope you find them. Here's your change, $16.40 to be precise. And your keys. Rooms 104 and 106, just around the corner where you make a left. They'll be on your right, all the way down past the pool."

"Thanks," Bob replies. "Pool's not open, is it?"

"Until ten."

"Oh wow."

"Enjoy your stay."

As they round the corner, Bob immediately remarks about the pool room. "Check it out, they've got a hot tub." He's unsure why he said that, as neither of them brought swimwear.

"Don't you wanna shower and eat first?"

"Of course. I was just saying." They stop outside their adjoining rooms. Lori holds out her hand for her room key. "Here you go. Speaking of which . . ." He hands Lori his spare change. "I need to make a couple phone calls real quick. Go ahead and grab something from the machine there for both of us. We can eat in my room later if you want and, uh, maybe figure out what to do next."

"Sounds good. What time?"

"Maybe seven o'clock?"

"Okay. Hopefully they'll have those mini-pizzas. I'm starving."

"That does sound good." Bob enters his room and tries the phone on the nightstand. No dial tone. "Damn," he whispers, and steps back into the hall at the same instant as Lori. "Phone doesn't work," he explains as she heads to the vending machine. "I'm gonna try the one in the lobby."

"Good luck. Lemme know if you get ahold of the detective."

The clerk is working his way through a book of crossword puzzles at the front desk when Bob re-enters the lobby. "Hey," he asks, "does this payphone work?"

"Off and on," the clerk responds with a shrug. "The ones in the office and at the counter here have been on the fritz all afternoon; they make this weird clicking sound, and then the call either goes through with static or it doesn't go through at all. Strangest thing."

"I've seen stranger." Bob picks up the handset and is relieved to get a dial tone. He dials the pager number of his law enforcement confidant, Detective Lieutenant Mayotte, but stops halfway through. He hangs up and the coin drops into the return. *I should let him know what happened, but I'm not ready to actually speak with him,* he decides. He deposits another quarter and dials the general precinct number from the card, certain the ardent detective will be out and about and not at his desk.

A CPD operator picks up on the first ring. *"Central District. How can I direct your call?"*

"Uh, yes, Detective Mayotte. Er, um, Detective *Lieutenant* Mayotte."

*"One moment, please."*

Rather than hold music, Bob is subjected to the following loop: *"This is a public service announcement from the First Lady of our United States, Nancy Reagan: Just say 'no' to drugs."*

The operator returns. *"I'm not getting an answer at that extension. You can try him later."*

"No, that's okay. Can you leave him a message?"

*"Whenever you're ready."*

"Tell him, 'Bob and Lori are safe, but Pete and the woman were taken.' Tell him, 'There's a mess at her place that'll need cleaning up.' "

*"Anything else?"*

"That's it."

*"I will relay the message. Thank you for calling the Chicago Police Department."*

The call ends and the quarter drops. Bob marvels at how impersonal the operator was, considering the ominous nature of his message. He deposits another quarter and dials Dr. Kirchner, his therapist of four years, not knowing that the doctor's daughter, Stacy, perished in the Blockade and Occupation. Instead of ringing, the phone makes an obnoxious clicking sound for several seconds. The dial tone returns. Bob furrows his brow and dials the number again. As with his two previous attempts, he gets the doctor's answering machine.

*"Hello, you've reached the office of Dr. Kirchner. If this is a life-threatening emergency, please hang up and dial 911. For all other issues, please contact me during my office hours, which are 8 a.m. to 3 p.m. Monday through Thursday and 9 a.m. to noon on Fridays, or leave a message after the beep."* BEEP!

"Doctor Kirchner, this is Bob Wilkinson again. I left you a couple messages already about phoning in my refill. Are you back in town? I really need to speak with you about some other stuff as well—it's about what's been going on in the city. Uh, I'm actually not home right now, so I guess I'll try you again later. Don't forget to phone in that refill. Bye."

He hangs up and the quarter drops. He dials a third number—his politician father's direct, toll-free Capitol Building office number, no quarter needed. He knows it will be one of his dad's secretaries or aides who answer, not his father straight-away. Still, it'll be good to hear his baritone voice. He actually misses the man.

Rather than ringing, the receiving end makes that awful clicking sound again, the dial tone returning after several seconds. "Damn," he whispers again, and redials the number. This time it rings through . . . but no one answers.

3

The life of a four-term United States senator can be hectic, but today is busy even by normal Congressional standards. Robert Wilkinson, Sr. hurriedly sifts through paperwork as he crams documents into his attaché case. His aide, Candice, rifles through a file cabinet. In his outside office, Elaine, his secretary of many years, is on one phone with military brass while a young Senate intern, eager but out of her depth, is on another phone. She speaks with Gail, who is at home in their Georgetown condo, gazing out the sliding patio door as she often does.

"Candice," the senator asks, "Where are my notes for the Mayor Washington meeting?"

"I already packed them, sir," Candice replies. "Along with your Daytimer. You're good to go. I can tidy up here."

• • •

From the outside office, Elaine barks into the phone with the urgency of 30 years as a Washington, D.C. secretary. "Sergeant Miller, are you sure there's room not only for the senator but for Mrs. Wilkinson as well? . . . No, I understand, weight is a factor, but the missus might weigh 110 pounds soaking wet . . . Yes, I understand. The senator is on his way out the door as we speak, and we're getting in touch with Mrs. Wilkinson as well . . ."

"Mrs. Wilkinson," the intern says from a different phone line, "we're leaving now. The senator's secretary is confirming seating arrangements as we speak. His driver can call with an ETA while we're en route. I just wanted to give you the head's up . . . I'm sorry, one moment, ma'am." She turns to Elaine, who mouths something the intern can't decipher. The intern shakes her head and mouths, "*What?*"

"One moment, Sergeant," Elaine says, and addresses the intern. "Tell her to pack light. Carry-on only—there's a weight limit. And tell her to hurry."

The intern nods. "Did you hear that?" she asks Gail. "Yes? Good. We're on our way . . . Yes, Mrs. Wilkinson . . . You too. Have a safe flight."

Robert, Sr. and Candice emerge from his private office. A Capitol guard in military dress hovers in the doorway. "We set here?" Robert, Sr. asks.

"There's another call coming in," the intern announces.

"Let it go to his mailbox," Elaine commands. She hangs up on Sergeant Miller. "The senator has to get going."

"Yes, ma'am," the intern replies, knowing her place in the grand scheme of things.

"Did you get ahold of my wife?" Robert, Sr. asks.

"I believe Miss Rosenbaum was handling that," Elaine says.

"Yes, Senator Wilkinson," the intern, Tulane University political science major Emily Rosenbaum, responds. "She understands she's to pack light and knows you're on your way to her."

"Terrific Emily, thank you." Robert, Sr. addresses the room. "Team, we're behind the curve on this. The junior senator left with the governor by train for Illinois 36 hours ago. He's working out of the capitol building in Springfield. But the people of Chicago need real leadership, actual boots *on* the actual ground *in* the actual city. I am unavailable for press comments until you hear otherwise." He turns to the capitol guard. "Mark, are we ready?"

"Ready and waiting, sir."

"Great." To the others: "I'm told phone service is spotty in Chicago, but I'll try and send word when we land."

"Good luck, Senator," Emily the intern offers.

"Good luck, *Chicago,*" Robert, Sr. corrects. He steps into the hall, accompanied by Candice and Mark, the steadfast capitol guard. "Candice, brief me on the latest while we ride to the airport. I'll have the driver take you home afterwards."

"Thank you, sir," Candice replies. She and Robert, Sr. follow Mark as he walks with the urgency of a man prepared for emergencies such as this one.

The phone rings again from the senator's office. Elaine and Emily, who have put in 14-hour workdays since this ordeal began, look at each other and let the call go to their boss's mailbox.

In January, 2016, Mark will retire with a full pension and a Distinguished Service commendation. Five years later, he will watch the news in horror as animals—humans technically, but we're reaching here—raid the building in which he worked for four decades to stop the vote certification following the most tumultuous presidential election in his lifetime. *I should've been there,* Mark will think. But by rushing Senator Wilkinson to a car that will bring him to a plane prepped to fly the senator and others to the Windy City, a flight with the most terrifying landing any of these passengers will ever endure, Mark does his own small part to help in this earlier emergency. While he doesn't know it yet, he is one of countless heroes in what is already being called the Blockade and Occupation of Chicago.

4

Miles Myrick calibrates the time chamber for the next group of Journey passengers, 18 to be precise, these unwitting time travelers hand-picked by a sextet of soldiers targeting the Bridgeport and Pilsen neighborhoods and expected to materialize on the arrivals telepad within the next 15 minutes. Miles's less-seasoned colleague, Balthazar Garrett, mops the floor of Pete's vomit and Dana's amniotic fluid. Mark-Lin Chang and Merritt Dawson, the driver and navigator who delivered Pete and Dana to CGC-Meigs in person, hover nearby, awaiting orders and fearing retribution for "allowing" their colleagues to get killed and their 12 other captives to escape.

"When do I get to plead my case with Commander Arendt?" Chang asks.

"He's indisposed at the moment," Miles replies, miffed. "And at any rate, 'Chief' Arendt is a more appropriate title than 'Commander' Arendt."

"Understood. No disrespect intended."

"Why don't the two of you go back to your preassigned offloading center and wait for reinforcements? I'm sure we'll have more for you to pick up for processing in due time."

"And you'll explain what happened? You'll explain how I choose the pregnant woman over the others as being the more valuable target?"

Miles sighs. "Of course. Now if you wouldn't mind . . ."

Chang takes the hint. He and Dawson make themselves scarce.

Balthazar calls out from midway between the holding cells and mop sink. "Hey boss, I just peeked in on Mr. Arendt. He doesn't look so hot."

"I'll go check on him. Watch the board for me."

Balthazar wheels the bucket to the mop sink and returns to the bank of workstations. Miles walks over to the holding cells. The ailing CEO slumbers in his cot in the fetal position, rasping and shivering. Miles unlocks the cell—locked for his boss's safety should Bob and Lori return—and steps inside. He places his hand on Wesley's forehead. It's warm despite his shivering, and the blanket is drenched with sweat. "Let me get you a fresh blanket, sir," Miles whispers. As he grabs the blanket, Wesley bursts into a particularly violent coughing fit. Even in the low light, Miles can clearly see blood droplets staining the mattress cover.

Wesley Arendt is on borrowed time, and the excuses of someone like Mark-Lin Chang are the *least* of his worries.

# Chapter 3

1

The Freedom Contingent Brigade's recruitment raid, four days after Pete and Dana's jarring arrival on New Earth, is a success. If nothing else, it features something of a rarity: zero body count! Led by the tireless Susie Walker, resistance fighters Josh Brewer, Dixon (first or last name unknown), Rose Martínez, and Jeff Hawkins visit one of the male dormitories to free as many willing new arrivals as they can. They scope out the dorm from afar over three consecutive days to establish a pattern and a schedule, and agree it makes sense not to move in until the first work crew departs for its morning detail. Once the crew makes its leave and the dorm captain heads to the lower level to shower, they enter in plain view. Susie and Rose wear the same stolen Loyalist uniforms they wore to the canal extension jobsite raid that gave them Josh and Hawkins. Hawkins borrows reformed Ross Army driver García García's old uniform while Josh and Dixon wear civilian clothes, Dixon's fatigues having been given a 21-gun salute after his previous adventures left them tattered and torn. To play their costumed roles convincingly, Susie, Rose, and Hawkins tote plasma rifles while Josh and Dixon strap smaller plasma pistols to their belts, shirt bottoms untucked to conceal the weapons.

. . .

Pete, Johnny, and Eric have become fast friends despite Pete being ten years younger than his colleagues; Pete acclimatized quickly aside from some stomach issues. In telling his story about the fact-finding visit to CGC-Meigs and about his and Dana's abduction the next day—he neglects to include any humorous anecdotes about Katie, the purple-haired, North-western University grad student who chauffeured him and his friends, as it'll be another year before he focuses on the humor of the situation, rather than the horror of it—Pete morphs into quite the storyteller. The three *amigos* are discussing amongst themselves how dire their predicament truly is when Susie and her fellow lieutenants enter the dorm.

"We're here to rescue you," she announces. "Anyone who doesn't want to work against their will, come with us." The immediate reaction is not the elated, mad dash she had hoped for, but one of confusion. Some of the more timid new arrivals hide under the covers, frightened by the sight of Susie and Rose entering the all-male dorm bearing arms. A few claim they are too sick to leave, and one even professes not to speak English, although he is fibbing; his language skills were vetted during post-Journey processing.

"What's going on?" Eric asks.

"Dimkowski?!" a familiar voice cries out.

Pete looks up and sees his high school classmate and towel-snapping tormentor, Joshua Richard Brewer, standing at the front of the room and holding his plasma rifle like a born-again hero. Neither can believe their eyes.

"No way," they say, simultaneously.

"Have you been here since prom?" Josh asks. Pete shakes his head.

"There's no time for small talk," Susie interrupts. "If you're coming, let's go."

"Right," Josh says. To Pete, Johnny, and Eric: "Come with us. There's good news in the works, but it could all go belly up. We're here for if it does."

"Hold up. Where does your barracks commander bunk?" Dixon asks. Pete points to a corner bed. Dixon spots the C.O.'s uniform laid out. He slips into it. The uniform is baggy, even over his civvies. "Is he a big guy?"

"Put it this way: He hasn't skipped many meals," Pete replies.

"You guys coming?" Josh asks.

Pete and his new friends nod at one another and follow Josh's cue. They follow Susie, Josh, Dixon, Hawkins, and ten other new arrivals out the door and into broad daylight. Several of the more depressed new arrivals opt to stay behind. Pete swears he hears someone sobbing on his way out. Rose brings up the rear. She closes the door behind them. Her hair is in a bun. "Act normal, *joven,* like we're escorting you on a detail." She settles in behind Pete and the others for the long walk to the FCB barracks.

*This is exciting,* Pete thinks, gears turning inside his head. *Maybe I really can make a difference—especially since I failed to make one back home.* He eventually catches up with Josh. "Where's the women's dorm?" he asks.

"Dunno, why?"

"Can you find out?"

"Hang on." Josh speed-walks to the other lieutenants.

Johnny walks up to Pete. "What'd you ask that for? I don't think they're gonna give us dates."

"I'm worried about Dana," Pete replies.

"The pregnant chick?"

"Yeah. Well . . . she's not pregnant anymore."

Susie motions for Rose and Dixon to take the lead to maintain the illusion of a Ross Army work detail. She stops walking so Pete can catch up to her and Josh. "There are two female dormitories I know of," she says. "Why are you asking?"

"I have a friend who I assume is in one of 'em. She and I were brought here together."

"If you've each been here four days, she's most likely to be in one of the west dorms. Those are in a different quadrant. Last we checked, they weren't fully occupied. Are you wanting to send her a message?"

"No, I wanna get her out of there. Her and her kid, if possible."

"They brought her *and* her child here? That's highly unorthodox."

"She . . . she was pregnant. She gave birth as soon as she arrived."

"That's remarkable. I've never heard of such a thing!"

"You *saw* this?!" Josh asks, mouth agape.

Pete nods. "It was beautiful . . . but also disgusting."

"That *is* disgusting," Josh agrees, earning an uncharacteristic glare from Susie.

"This changes things," Susie says. She hurries to Dixon to share the news.

"Hey Josh, where's she going?"

"Beats me, Dimkowski."

"So we're gonna get her, right?"

"Beats me, Dimkowski." With a chuckle this time. Then: "Hey, I've been dying to ask: Do you know if Lori's okay? She never made it to prom."

"She made it, alright."

Dimkowski grabs Pete by the collar. "What do you mean, she made it?"

"Josh, take it easy!"

"Whoa," Johnny adds.

Josh, whose assumed leadership position with the FCB comes with a sense of maturity his role as football captain did not, dials it back. He lets go of Josh's collar. "Sorry. We cool?"

"We cool," Pete replies. He takes a step back regardless. "And don't worry. Lori made it to prom, but it was after you guys were taken. She's fine."

"Tell me the rest later. We're here."

Dixon, who set the pace courtesy of his knee injury, pulls aside the aluminum slats and motions the new arrivals inside. Josh and Hawkins escort them to the sub-basement barracks. Susie, Dixon, and Rose linger on the street, weapons out to suggest to any nosy, surface-level eyes that they are Ross Army Loyalists sending these workers on a task.

"Are they finally going to finish that building?" someone living across the street from the never-finished residential high-rise asks a neighbor. The rumor spreads like wildfire, and only seamstress Gwendolyn Pierce, ever-watchful from her tailor shop on the next block, knows what's really going on. She recognizes the faces of Susie, Dixon, and Rose, and realizes the FCB is recruiting once more.

2

"This is a miracle."

Susie addresses her usual contingent of civilian freedom fighters in the commissary about the hope that news of a successful, post-Journey birth could bring to the masses. She concludes by hinting at the political capital such news could lend to her cause. Just in time for the peace talks, natch.

New arrivals Pete, Eric Adams, and Johnny Cardellini are among those in attendance. Pete sits beside Susie and tells his story from start to finish, beginning with his late arrival to prom and ending with his van ride to CGC-Meigs. His audience, particularly Josh, is rapt. In the telling, Pete is careful to avoid any mention of possible sparks flying between Bob and Lori.

"Let's get your friend Dana then," Josh says. "I say we go now." Susie's heart leaps, and her slight head nod in response to Josh's enthusiasm doesn't go unnoticed by those who realize she's in love with Josh—basically everyone.

"Pete, how was her health after the delivery?" she asks.

"Uh, fine, I think. That baby was awfully tiny, though."

"The child has no doubt been placed in an incubator. If it's to have a fighting chance, it'll need to stay there awhile. Those of you here who have children know our atmosphere doesn't provide the same level of oxygen the mother's umbilical cord provides while the child is in the womb."

Hawkins, one of the only ones among them with kids (two girls, aged five and seven), looks down. The others nod.

Susie continues. "But yes, I agree we should rescue the mother. Getting her involved in our movement will distract her from post-partum depression, and she's almost certainly recovering in the women's medical dorm, which won't be heavily guarded."

Pete jumps to his feet. "Let's go then." Josh, happy to meet another brave soul, raises his hand in a high five motion. Pete slaps him some skin. If his high-five isn't as convincing as it would normally be, this is because Pete was not expecting to find an ally in the form of his high school nemesis.

"Tomorrow," Susie says.

Pete's heart sinks. "T-tomorrow? Why not today?"

"Because it's far. A longer walk than today's. The sun sets early during this calendar cycle. And you need your rest."

"Don't tell me what to do."

"It's 'Pete,' right?" Pete nods, and Susie shoos the others away with a flick of her wrist. "Pete, I want to thank you for sharing your story. The Freedom Contingent Brigade thanks you. But we need to strike early, like we did today. These raids we do . . . we've been taking bigger and bigger risks. The one that gave us your friend Josh . . ."

"He's not really my friend. We went to the same school, is all."

"Whatever your relationship is, the raid that gave us Josh didn't go off without a hitch. We bit off more than we could chew that day, and if not for the bravery of people like Josh, things would've turned out different."

"But they *didn't* turn out different."

"We were lucky this morning. We staked out your dorm for three days before acting, and managed to get away unscathed and unseen. As a saying—from your world I believe—goes, lightning seldom strikes twice."

"But you said it won't be heavily guarded."

"It won't, that's correct. But that doesn't mean we shouldn't be careful."

Pete nods, disappointed. "I'm worried about Dana, is all."

"I know you are."

"She played an unknowing role in all of this, and she deserves our protection. If there's a way to get her home—her *and* her daughter—we owe her that. For starters, let's get her the hell out of their clutches."

"We will. Tomorrow."

"What's the story with this medical dorm, anyway?"

"It's on the outskirts of Zone Omega, a klick or so south of the Red River. It's where they send new arrivals with complications—headaches lasting longer than ten days, fecal incontinence, an irregular menstrual cycle after the Journey, things of that nature."

"And you're sure she'll be there?"

"If she gave birth immediately *after* the Journey, she'll be there. The good news is that the tunnels will take us much of the way there unseen. We'll still need to be careful, of course."

"Her baby will still be in the hospital, right?"

"For certain. All newborns are kept in the incubator for seven days regardless. If what you said about the child being born premature is true, she'll be there for at least 21 days, maybe longer."

"It's true. Any way we can get word to the mother about how the baby's doing?"

A lightbulb illuminates as Susie remembers her upcoming exchange with Lucien Reynolds. "I might know a way, yes."

"Great!"

"Right now, let's find you a cot to sleep on. Later, you can dine with the lieutenants and we can go over tomorrow's plan. I know better than to ask whether you'll want to tag along."

"Are you kidding me? Does a bear shit in the woods?!"

Pete *must be* feeling better if he's cracking jokes. This one goes over Susie's head and she merely shrugs; she knows neither what a bear is nor what woods are.

3

Susie was wrong. In the case of the FCB's raid on the women's medical dorm, lighting really *does* strike twice. She isn't there to see it, however; she sends Rose, Josh, Pete, Samara Jones, and García in her stead while she prepares the agenda for her meeting with Reynolds near the side barracks entrance. Dixon chomps at the bit to join Rose and the others, but Susie requests he accompany her to the handoff instead. His ankle and knee, injured during the canal extension jobsite raid, are better, but Susie doesn't want him overdoing it. As it is, he already logged a few klicks during yesterday's mission.

"If I'm sitting out the medical dorm raid, I'm at least coming with you to check out this mystery grove," he counters. "Be nice to finally find it."

"Up to you."

"You know I'd feel better about the raid if you and I were there."

"It's pretty low risk. Besides, our meeting with Reynolds gives the Brigade—or at least you and I—a natural alibi. And as long as they limit their liberation to no more than two civilians apiece, they should be good."

. . .

The medical dorm is the same size as the other worker dormitories, but has one-fourth the number of beds. For one thing, there are no bunks. For another, each bed has extra space on either side for an IV stand or food cart.

It's been a quiet week at the dorm. The influx of new arrivals has slowed to a trickle due to Wesley Arendt's incapacitation on Earth, and Dana is one of just three residents. She makes fast friends with Barbara Purkey, who is the same age and who is almost fully healed from a tear in her C-section scar, which reopened as a result of her refusal to stand still as gold light washed over her on the departures telepad. The two women have a good cry after Dana coos over her miracle birth and Barbara reveals that her only child, baby Lucas, perished of SIDS at just five months of age.

The third resident is none other than Shauna Robinson, close friend of Lori and girlfriend of the late Curtis Jackson. Shauna has kept her distance from Barbara and Dana not because of racial differences, but because she's been in too much pain. Her appendix burst within 48 hours of arrival following her prom night abduction. She ignored the pain . . . until sepsis set in. Her dorm captain rushed her to the hospital, saving her from certain death. Shauna spent a week in intensive care and was finally discharged to the medical dorm for an additional ten days of bed rest and a diet of water, legumes, egg whites, and skinless chicken.

Shauna is finally feeling better; lately she's been attempting longer and longer walks around the dorm (always escorted, of course), and the only thing delaying a complete recovery is crippling depression. She misses her parents, her younger brothers, her friends, and her left tackle boyfriend, the latter of whom she has no idea perished.

The rotating dorm captains are trained in anti-matter weapons use and hand-to-hand combat, same as everyone else in Ross's Army, but they consider themselves nurse practitioners first and soldiers second. The captain on duty during the raid is Nurse Noakes, and she is dozing at her duty station, 24th-century stethoscope around her neck, when the raid commences.

Rose makes the first move, and opts for a different strategy than her usual approach of kicking in the door—she simply knocks. The nurse stirs but doesn't fully awaken, and it is Dana who peers out the window and recognizes Pete's familiar face. Her eyes widen and she motions for Barbara to distract Nurse Noakes. Barbara grabs a towel and prepares to tie the nurse's hands together as Dana opens the door.

"Pete!" Dana cries out. She runs toward him as he waves his hand in a lower-your-voice gesture. "Sorry." She lowers her voice and hugs him. He returns the hug with one hand and motions for his new friends to enter the dorm.

"How are you?" he asks.

"Missing my baby girl, but good. Did you see how beautiful she was?"

"I did. She's precious. Right now, I need you to wait here while we grab the others."

"There're only three of us."

"Still. Wait here." He motions for her stay. She is reluctant to remove her embrace. Pete enters the dorm when she finally relents. Nurse Noakes has fully awakened. She writhes in her chair; the resourceful Barbara ties her arms to the back of the chair with a towel and uses the stethoscope to bind her ankles. Rose, armed and dressed in Loyalist garb once again, stands guard while Samara searches for a rag to use as a mouth gag. Josh tends to Shauna while García keeps watch, playing the part in his Loyalist fatigues, his regular uniform until not long ago, when he realized he was fighting for the wrong side.

"Josh, is it really you?" a disbelieving Shauna asks.

"It's really me, Shaw. These people helped me escape, and now we're here to help *you* escape."

"Where's everyone else? Where's Amber? Where's Tiffany? Where's Lori? My God, Josh, where's Curtis? Where's my boy-friend?"

"Lori's safe. I haven't seen Tiff or Amber. I was hoping maybe you had." Shauna shakes her head, and Josh ends his response with a lie. "Uh, I don't know where Curtis is. Thought I saw him when we first got here, but it was someone else."

"Where are you taking my patients?" Noakes barks. "They're in no position to leave!"

"We'll let them decide, *Capitana,*" Rose says. She gets right up in Noakes's face.

Barbara tries to the use rag as a mouth gag, but it isn't long enough. She motions for another towel. García hands her one, thick enough and long enough to gag Nurse Noakes and stay securely tied in the back.

"Don't you dare," Noakes begins, "don't you *frbbrrbg drrbg.*" The towel cuts off the last of her words, and she seethes with rage so different from her usual bedside manner.

"That was exciting," Barbara says. She speaks with an exhil-arated smile that suggests she's never stepped up in such a way before but will eagerly do so again.

"I like her," Rose remarks.

They leave, single file, with Noakes left behind to be untied by her relief, Nurse/Corporal Wang, in a few hours' time.

Shauna shuffles her feet. Josh breaks the single-file line to walk beside her. "Some prom, huh?" he remarks.

"It was great until . . . you know. I was rooting for you and Lori. I still can't believe she'd skip our senior prom."

"I appreciate that. Dimkowski there says she was on her way when we were taken. I don't remember much except for calling her on the phone and begging her to come. Said I'd save her the last dance."

"How does *he* know?" Shauna points to Pete. Cheerleaders and nerds don't travel in the same social circle, and she doesn't deem his name as one worth remembering—not even after he made a fool of himself at Vinnie's.

"You know, I'm still not sure I follow it all." Josh throws up his arms and chuckles. Shauna joins in; her chuckles rapidly turn into a coughing fit.

"Need some water?" He unscrews the lid of his canteen, but she shakes her head.

"It's just the last of the"—she coughs twice—"sepsis. I'll be okay."

Pete breaks the single-file rank as well. He walks alongside Dana. "How are you feeling?" he asks.

"Hurts to pee," Dana replies. "They told me I have a bladder infection. Guess I'm okay, though. What about you? I thought I'd never see you again!"

"I'm okay, except for this this monster headache."

"I have one of those, too. They said it'll pass."

"Did they tell you anything about your daughter?"

"No. That's been the hardest part. The not knowing is killing me!"

"So, Susie—she's not here right now and I guess she's sort of the boss—she says she'll try and find out."

"I don't understand. She doesn't know me! And I certainly don't know *her.*"

"I told her what happened. She thinks it's something of a miracle that can, like, bring everyone together."

"Really?"

"Really."

"I'm not sure how to feel about that. My daughter shouldn't be used as a bargaining chip."

"I don't think that's what she meant, but I dunno." He shrugs. "You should meet Susie tonight. I only just met her yesterday myself, but she seems like the real deal."

4

Reynolds waits beside the graffiti-tagged blast door that represents the side entrance to the FCB barracks. He chuckles knowing that while no one would dare spray graffiti along major thoroughfares such as Haile Selassie Boulevard, taggers are more fearless in alleyways and on side streets such as this one. The most overt political graffiti is generally erased soon after its first appearance, but Chancellor Ross knows he has to let the occasional tag slide, lest Susie and the FCB become martyrs of censorship. Reynolds recalls a rare, anti-revolution tag he saw a few weeks ago. Meant to be someone's representation of Susie, it was drawn with what looked like a child's hand and featured a boxy frame, crazy hair, and fangs for teeth. Today's art is nothing political in nature, just an imaginative tag of a belly beater walking upright, hand in hand, with a large-breasted woman.

News of the morning raid on the women's medical dorm has yet to enter the Ross and Reynolds orbits when Susie, accompanied by Dixon and fellow lieutenant René de Rooij, opens the side door for the hand-off. Reynolds greets them with a nod and a duplicitous smile. "I'm surprised Rose wasn't chomping at the bit to come along and rip my head off," he says.

"We thought it best she remain inside," Susie replies.

"Are we doing this or what?" Dixon asks. He extends his hand. Reynolds waits a few beats before shaking it. This is ultimately quite telling, but no one picks up on it.

"Dixon. Whether first name or last name, who can say, right?" Reynolds flashes his pearly whites in a shit-eating grin.

"Certainly not I," Dixon responds.

Reynolds shakes René's hand next, and Susie's last. "I trust you prepared a rough agenda?"

Susie nods. "Did you bring the map?"

Reynolds pats his breast pocket, but delays handing it over in favor of asking an incriminating question: "Yesterday, several new arrivals went missing from one of the male dorms. You wouldn't happen to know anything about this, would you?"

"I'm afraid not." Susie shakes her head. She turns to her colleagues, who shake theirs as well.

"You wouldn't be pulling my leg?"

"Any dead bodies? That seems to be our calling card of late, although it's seldom by choice."

"No dead bodies. No witnesses. And no one's talking. Seems they just walked away while their dorm captain was in the shower and their dormmates were asleep."

"And you didn't find them hiding in the tunnels, or frozen in an alleyway this morning?" Susie is thinking of two unfortunate young men, liberated during her crew's aforementioned raid on the canal extension jobsite. The men escaped the warmth of the FCB barracks during the night but froze to death on the surface within minutes.

"No. Which means one and one aren't adding up to two. Someone's giving them shelter."

"That does sound like something you'd do, Suze," Dixon points out for dramatic effect.

"It does, that's fair," Susie admits. "But with these peace talks coming up, you know we wouldn't do something stupid to jeopardize things."

"Actually, I *don't* know that," Reynolds replies.

"Lucien, it's what we've been fighting for," René explains.

Susie can't resist getting the last word. "I suppose I shouldn't say this, but if they escaped and found refuge . . . good for them."

"*There's* the Susie Walker that's gotten the chancellor to finally see reason," Reynolds remarks.

"So we're doing this, then?"

"It's up to you. All of you. I'm sure you'll have trouble sitting still for the next several days, but hopefully your Great Gourd Expedition: Final Chapter This Time—that's what I've been calling it—will offer enough of a distraction. And of course, I believe you and Diego—"

"Don't say his name."

"I believe you and your ex-lover were the last ones to embark upon such a quest. I doubt you can resist another go."

A roving Sauron passes by and shines its ever-watchful, motion camera eye in their direction. Reynolds removes his magna-card and holds it up in the air to be scanned. Susie tenses up. René grabs her hand and caresses its three remaining fingers.

"It's okay," René whispers. Susie nods and wipes away a tear with the knuckles of her other hand, which is still clenched in a fist.

A beep is heard as the card is scanned and the Sauron moves on. "I hate those things," Dixon says.

Susie echoes Dixon's sentiment; her hatred of Saurons runs especially deep. She takes slow, calming breaths. "You're going to reroute those away from the grove, yes?"

"I give you my word. Or rather, Chancellor Ross gives you his."

"And I suppose you'll want to review the agenda before handing over the map?"

"Just to eyeball it and make sure it isn't a haiku on the subject of how our beloved chancellor can, shall we say, blow it out his anal cavity."

"It isn't." Susie hands Reynolds the agenda, hand-written in a notebook resembling a college examination blue book. "And the Old Man's release is non-negotiable."

"So it reads here, item three right on the first page," Reynolds says. He scans the page one entries, then randomly thumbs through the others. "You've put a lot of thought into this."

"There's a lot to think about."

"There is indeed. Have you chosen your seconds?"

"I'm one of 'em," Dixon says.

"And the other?"

"Not sure," Susie says. "Maybe one of our newer recruits. I'll make sure they know the rules."

"Just make sure it's not Rose." Reynolds removes the map from his vest pocket and stashes the agenda in its place. The map is drawn on parchment that's been sprayed with a sealant to prevent it from being blown to tatters in a strong wind— of which New Earth has plenty. As he unfolds the map, Susie interrupts with an unrelated question.

"Reynolds, there've been whisperings on the street about a 'miracle baby.' Do you know what that's all about?"

"It's disconcerting how quickly rumors fly, but yeah, there's truth to this one."

"And that is?"

"We scored a first: A woman in the late stages of pregnancy gave birth immediately after her Journey."

Susie and the others feign surprise. "That's incredible. And the baby's okay?"

"It's a little girl from what I understand, and she's doing fine. A real fighter."

"Wh-what about the mother?" René asks.

"Sent to one of our care dormitories, but doing fine and also a fighter, from what little I know."

"That's incredible," Susie says again.

"It's exciting," Reynolds says, "and it's one more reason to go forward with these peace talks, don't you think?"

"Yes, let's give this child a hopeful future." Susie turns to Dixon and René for their assent; Dixon nods and René mouths her approval.

Reynolds unfolds the map. He rotates it until its coordinates face Susie, Dixon, and René. "Very well then. You know where District Nine is, I assume?"

Susie nods, and Reynolds points out the route from the edge of the district, the westernmost in Zone Omega. It ascends a gentle ridge, then passes around a mountain and a cave where they can overnight after visiting the grove, perhaps two klicks from the cave and at the bottom of a cliff previous scouts assumed had nothing to offer when they scanned it from the rim above. Reynolds reiterates that the route will be safe from Saurons and asks only that—for now—she not make any public announcements of the grove's existence beyond her "own little motley crew." With that, they shake hands once more and agree to meet in the middle of the Century Bridge in five days' time.

Reynolds told the truth when he guaranteed the FCB's safety from Sauron sightings during the expedition. The trip is not without danger, however; Susie and her friends will see and experience horrors along the way they won't soon forget. Was Reynolds holding out in that regard? Susie will never find out . . . and neither will we.

The following day is dangerously windy; a violent sandstorm essentially closes street level businesses in Zones Alpha and Omega to the outside world. Though it's nothing like the Great Sandstorm of 2277 that claimed a thousand lives, set New Earth living back to the Stone Age, and led to the eventual election—years later—of Dorian Ross as chancellor, it still knocks out power in several districts and keeps street sweepers extra busy.

The storm delays the Great Gourd Expedition: Final Chapter This Time by three days, but Susie reasons that if the trip takes one day there and another day back, the FCB will still have a full day to finalize security for her meeting with Chancellor Ross for supposed peace talks. Word about the talks has spread like wildfire, and despite storm damage, there is a general air of good cheer among ordinary civilians. Repair crews are out and about, and the sound of drilling and hammering can be heard on every block.

Susie's usual A-team (Dixon, Rose, Samara, and Leonard Debussy) joins her on the expedition. She is delighted when Josh, Pete, García, and Hawkins volunteer as well. The final person to join the quest happens to be the FCB's newest member, a 24-year-old roofer and one-month resident of Zone Omega named Underwood.

6

Gary Underwood approached Leonard, García, and Hawkins on the street ten days or so ago while they were purchasing foodstuffs in bulk from a local wholesaler grocer—one of the only grocers who agreed to work with the rebels (for a cash surcharge, of course). Underwood abandoned his position in line and was tailing them for three blocks when Leonard called him out. "What do you want?" he asked, punctuating the last letter of each word for cautionary emphasis.

"You three . . . you're with her, right?" Underwood asked.

"I don't know what you're talking about," Leonard replied.

"Get outta here, man," Hawkins added.

"No, it's okay guys, you see . . ."

"You heard him," García said, referencing Hawkins's order to am-scray and unzipping his coat enough to reveal he was packing heat.

Underwood put his hands up in surrender. "It's cool, it's cool. I just . . . I heard about the peace talks and wanted to know how I can help. In case, you know, you guys all get a say, you know, in whatever happens."

Leonard, García, and Hawkins exchanged glances and decided this tall, husky interloper didn't pose much of a threat. "What's your name?" Leonard asked.

"Underwood. G-Gary Underwood."

"How'd you know who we were?"

"I-I've s-seen you at the store before."

"You work there?"

"I'm a roofer actually, but I've only been here a few weeks. So as low man on the totem pole, I go there every day to grab lunch for the rest of the crew. I've seen you there a few times, e-every four days or so. I'm good with faces. Well, you I've never seen before"—he points to Hawkins—"but I've seen you" —García—"once or twice and I've seen you"—Leonard—"a few times. You usually come with a woman."

"Her name's René. She's one helluva good cook. Today's her . . . well, she's not feeling well."

"Her time of the month?"

"Don't be crude, Gary."

"Call me 'Underwood.' All my friends do."

"Alright, Underwood. I'm Leonard. This here's García. And the guy you don't recognize is Hawkins, new to our ranks."

"Hey Gary, I'm Jeff," Hawkins said. He extended his hand.

Leonard knew Susie could sometimes be too trusting for her own good. As such, he refused to allow Underwood to accompany them all the way to the barracks, and instead arranged for Susie and Dixon and Rose to meet Underwood for a debriefing later that day at a secure location in the opposite direction so as not to reveal their current hiding place. "You know we're gonna have to move again soon," Leonard lamented. "We're on borrowed time here."

"All the same, let's wait and see," Susie replied. She and Dixon decided almost at once that Underwood's intentions were genuine, as did Josh, who Susie insisted join them for the debrief instead of Rose. ("She distrusts everyone," she explained to Leonard later, who assumed Susie simply preferred Josh's company over Rose's.)

When Underwood was first herded into the holding pen following his interstellar jaunt and his brief visit to the orientation bay, he immediately spotted his talent agent on the women's side of the divide. She told him the last thing she remembered before the Journey was seeing their client vaporized for attempting to flee the Union Station Great Hall where they were accosted. Of the director and camera crew, there was no sign.

The beefy roofer is in tip-top shape ("athletic" is how he has always described his build). He didn't have the acclimatization issues that plague most new arrivals, and was given expedited placement on a work detail as a result. His work on a roofing crew ever since has kept him fit as a fiddle. He told Susie, Josh, and Dixon during their first meeting that despite his relatively good fortune compared to other indentured workers, he ultimately believed Ross's idea of forced labor, in particular his method of remedying workforce shortages by recruiting from a different planet in a different century, to be morally wrong. He said he wanted to do what he could to help Susie's cause, starting with finding the time chamber.

"You're very brave," Susie said. With that, he was as good as in. He volunteered for every assignment and chore on the books, including the Great Gourd Expedition. Even Rose was impressed.

Susie was surprised scrawny newcomer Pete volunteered for the expedition while seasoned lieutenant René did not. Pete admitted he needed to atone for failing to prevent Dana's abduction, while René said someone needs to stay behind and cook for the others. She added that Keith Sargent, who was hobbling on crutches due to a broken leg, wasn't mobile enough to handle KP duty on his own.

Hawkins, a venture capitalist in his Earth Prime life, had the same FCB tenure as Josh, and more than Pete or Underwood. He was fascinated that Pete and Josh knew each other from Earth even though their Journeys took place on different days.

Susie, in turn, was fascinated by Underwood—he lacked Josh's natural leadership skills, but as a Chicago White Sox slugger and part-time model in his Earth Prime life, he was tough. *No wonder he quickly found work as a roofer,* she thought. Susie knew nothing about baseball but was sure Underwood's size would make him an asset in battle. *Hopefully these peace talks are the real deal and there* are *no battles,* she amended.

7

If Gary Underwood is tall and husky, then Jeff Hawkins is short and stocky. He makes up for his stature with personality and drive; the five-foot, four-inch partner at Kettner and Goldstein, an investment firm with offices in Chicago's One Illinois Center, was the youngest member of his firm to make partner. For him, attending the "40 under 40" event at the Art Institute's Chicago Stock Exchange Trading Room was easy, logistically— he took the South Shore train into the city from his suburb of

Hammond, Indiana, knocked out a few hours' worth of paperwork, then strolled the five easy blocks to the Art Institute.

Married to his college sweetheart, Sarah, and raising two beautiful toehead girls in their quad-level house complete with dog, cat, and white picket fence, Hawkins epitomized the American dream. *Casa de Hawkins* was within walking distance of both the train station and the local Catholic parish, where he was named deacon after turning 35 last autumn. He attended PTA meetings and was on the neighborhood watch committee—all this in addition to working 55 hours/week with a 40-minute commute each way.

After the power was interrupted and weapons were fired into the ceiling to get the crowd's attention during the museum gala, Hawkins knew it was best to remain calm. He shouted for his boss, there to honor him, to stand still. Instead, the man, who had traces of cocaine powder on his nose, bolted for the exit and was made an example of. Hawkins resisted the urge to fight back during a moment when Ross's goons were distracted; he didn't want to orphan his children or make his wife a widow. He second-guessed his decision once on Mars, so when the opportunity came to fight back during the struggle for control of the transport shuttles coming back from the canal extension jobsite tour, he didn't hesitate to act.

Cool under pressure, Hawkins is the perfect addition to Susie's rough-and-tumble crew. He hopes the opportunity will arise to make a return Journey so he can see his wife and daughters again. Volunteering for the Great Gourd Expedition isn't a direct path, but a means to an end. He figures the more he learns about the lay of the land on Mars, whether in the CCC complex or out in the remote Martian Outlands, the better positioned he'll be following the peace treaty, especially if the treaty leads to a literal changing of the guard. And if that positioning is inside the CCC complex itself, where he can force someone to escort him to the time chamber, so much the better.

8

The group sets out for the grove on a sunny, balmy day—about as perfect as weather gets on Mars, and a far cry from the brutality of the storm just three days prior. Before setting out, Susie asks Pete to join her in relaying Reynolds's news about young Savannah to Dana. The young mother suffers one of those debilitating, multi-day migraines that never seem to go away, and has been distracting herself by cleaning the barracks. She falls to her knees over Susie's good news; Pete grabs her by the arm to prevent an all-out face plant. Her joyous wail is so loud others rush to see what is the matter.

"Thank you," she tells Susie through tears. "Thank you thank you thank you thank you thank you."

"No, thank *you,*" Susie insists. "Thank you for this miracle."

Dana turns to Pete and mouths the words, "*Thank you.*"

"We'll be back tomorrow," he responds.

"Take care."

"I'll take it any way I can get it."

Dana laughs in response. On Earth, Lori described Pete as "a bit much." Dana wishes to give Pete the benefit of the doubt. In her opinion, a bit of blue humor is more than a fair trade-off for being a genuinely decent human being. So far, Pete has shown ample evidence of being just that.

9

The sound of post-sandstorm hammering dissipates as the ten gourd seekers follow an unpaved access road from the outskirts of District Nine over a rise that, in turn, becomes the western foothills beyond Zone Omega. They dress in layers;

it's pleasant now but will turn dangerously cold come night-fall. In addition to the canteens fashioned on straps running diagonally across their chests, they wield backpacks filled with hand warmers, jerky, protein packs, flashlights, blankets, sleeping mats, and oxygenators. Later, assuming they find the gourd grove, they'll transport the contents of their backpacks to their pockets in order to fill the packs with as much of the rare fruit as they can manage. There is little room for weapons, though they are not entirely unarmed; Rose totes a full-sized rifle, Susie and Josh wield anti-matter pistols, and Underwood wears a knife sheathed in a scabbard tied around his right thigh; no telling where he found it. Susie and Josh lead the pack while Rose brings up the rear, looking back every few paces to make sure no one—man or drone—is tailing them.

The terrain changes after a few klicks. A series of boulders, approximately waist-high, materialize along the left shoulder of the road. They disappear when the road descends through a sandy wash, where the only evidence of the path are a pair of wheel ruts. The ruts turn into a gravel road that climbs out of the wash, and the road curves to the right at the next rock sighting—this time a cluster of five giant boulders, most of them larger than a person is tall. The road continues in a northwest trajectory, climbing over the distant hills. A fence-line in the distance suggests this road leads to government land, closed to the public.

Susan checks her map, hand-drawn by Reynolds but re-markably detailed, against the landmarks. "Looks like we leave the road and just continue west from here."

Samara points to the fenceline. "What do you think that is? Should we check it out?"

Leonard answers with certainty in his voice. "Landfill."

"Have you been here before?" Samara asks him.

"Remember Quinn's Gully, when we all had to scatter?" Leonard's question refers to a skirmish in the FCB's earlier days, when the resistance, whose numbers were far fewer, went on a scouting mission for medicinal orchids, said to grow only on western slopes, and were ambushed by a pair of Saurons. They blasted the Saurons from the sky, but the weapons fire alerted a shuttle of Ross Army soldiers, on a nearby scouting mission of their own. The chancellor's men were killed and Susie's rebels escaped with only minor injuries, but things looked hairy for a while when the group became separated.

"Ah, good times," Rose interjects.

"I won't go so far as to call 'em 'good times,' but I remember what happened," Samara replies. "That wasn't here, though. That was in District Six, southeast of here."

"There's a landfill in each district though, right?" Leonard asks.

"Yes."

"Let me explain: At Quinn's Gully, I shot one of Ross's guys in the ass," Leonard begins. "Saw a big red hole materialize where his butt used to be, then I ran for my life. There was a fence just like this one over there. Made it all the way there before I realized no one was chasing me and headed back, catching up to the rest of you and the shuttle."

"And it was a landfill?"

"The fence was too tall to scale, but it had an access road leading to it, same as this, and the gate said, 'DISTRICT SIX LANDFILL—NO TRESPASSING.'"

"That explains the road," Dixon says.

"No time for detours," Susie interrupts. She pulls out a compass. "Let's keep heading west and hope we don't lose the way. There's a cave we can have lunch in. According to the map, the grove's only a couple klicks from there."

Scattered "okay's" and "sounds good's" from the others.

"Pete, you doing okay?" Susie asks.

"I'm good."

"How's your breathing?"

"Better than Darth Vader's." The males in attendance chuckle.

"*Pinche* Stars Wars, *osh!*" Rose remarks. Susie furrows her brow, unfamiliar with the pop culture reference. "They think their *pitos* are lightsabers," Rose explains, as if that clears everything up.

They resume walking, unaware the gentle hill they're about to ascend is made of magnetic rock that will throw off their compass.

**10**

"You did good, Sergeant."

"Thank you, sir." Reynolds sits across from Chancellor Ross inside the chancellor's office. They drink hot tea as Ross thumbs through the agenda prepared by Susie. "What do you think of her demands?" Reynolds asks.

"I was going to ask you what *you* thought. I assume you read it?"

"I flipped through it quickly at the handoff, just to make sure she wasn't wasting our time. It *seemed* well organized at a quick glance, but I wanted you to be the first to really see it."

"Let's go through it together, shall we?" Ross turns to the first page and reads: "Agenda for peace accords of day 12,140 on the planetary calendar. Talking points prepared by Susie Walker of the Freedom Contingent Brigade on behalf of the citizens, naturalized and otherwise, of New Earth."

"That's a mouthful right there, sir."

Ross continues to read aloud. "Objective: Find common ground on matters including civil rights, labor laws, health and welfare, recruitment, women's issues, and natural life expectancy, with particular focus on infrastructure improvement and the cessation of indentured servitude.

"Item #1: All incoming migration from off-world must cease immediately. Time chamber to be decommissioned and bricked off, as before the Great Sandstorm. Compliance committee created to perform routine inspections of the site.

"Item #2: Safety officer present on every terraforming work detail. Coordinated rest and meal breaks for all workers. Minimum number of labor hours logged for all foremen and supervisors performing the tasks they are overseeing. Required number of hours to be negotiated.

"Item #3: Atwood Jedediah McCarthy to be released immediately. All charges against him to be dropped henceforth and forever more."

"I'd have figured she'd make that item #1," Reynolds remarks.

"Indeed."

"Sir, do you think knowing he wasn't her top priority might loosen his lips a bit?"

"I spent enough time with the Old Man to deduce he told us all he was ever going to, but it might be worth a shot. Good thinking, Sergeant. Come with me."

"Should we get Barstow, too?"

"No, he'd snap the Old Man like a twig just for looking at him the wrong way."

Both men shudder at the thought.


## 11


Ross and Reynolds ask Corporal Brown, the soldier guarding the cell of Old Man McCarthy, leader of the resistance movement, to leave the room. Ross drags the young man's chair to the front of McCarthy's cell door. Reynolds scans his magnacard to power down the electrified, translucent force field between soldier and inmate. He sticks his arms between the iron bars and spreads his legs into a comfortable standing position.

"Lucien. Dorian." McCarthy, who had just begun to doze off in his cot, a tattered Mark Twain novel folded over his chest, addresses his Judas first and his chancellor second. "To what do I owe this rare honor, gentlemen?" Calm and smooth, his greeting could be mistaken for diplomatic if not for the slight of not addressing Ross and Reynolds by their government titles.

Ross's blood boils, but he tries not to show it. "Tides are changing, Atwood," he says. "We've decided to change with them."

"Is that your way of saying you're seeking gender reassignment surgery?"

Caught unawares by McCarthy's unexpected burn, Ross is slow to respond. Finally: "Well, you know the law prohibiting such things better than most people. Isn't that one of your brigade's points of contention? Says in here that it is. Page seven, I believe." He holds up Susie's agenda.

"I don't know what that is you're holding—and apologies, for my remark was not particularly couth—but yes, putting an end to the policing of gender preferences is one of our talking points. Not at the top of the list, but on the list regardless."

"Sergeant Reynolds and I have some good news for you, then. This booklet, hand-delivered to the sergeant here by your very own Susie Walker, is the subject of peace talks set to take place five days from now."

McCarthy rubs his aching back and asks, "Why do I suspect my leg's being pulled?"

"It's no bullshit, Old Man," Reynolds says.

"I'd like to hear it from your boss, if it's all the same."

Ross turns to page one and reads the title and objective. "Shall I continue?" he asks.

"You've piqued my interest, sure."

It takes eight minutes for Ross to read through the agenda items. He speaks slowly, allowing his prisoner a few seconds to process each item before moving on to the next. At the end, he asks McCarthy for his thoughts.

"If Susie prepared this herself, I suppose I should be quite proud," the Old Man replies. "Her list of demands or bullet points or what have you is quite comprehensive. I dare say, she covered everything we've been fighting for better, perhaps, than I could have. Frankly, I find myself feeling rather redundant."

"She's one helluva bright young woman," Ross says. "And tough as hell."

"I couldn't agree more."

"You and me, we're dinosaurs. It's people like Susie and Lucien here who are the future."

"Beg pardon, Dorian, but the only thing Susie has in common with Officer Reynolds is her age."

"Hey now, watch it!" Reynolds enters McCarthy's cell and raises an arm as if to strike him. Ross restrains him.

"None of that now, Sergeant," Ross says. "You *did* betray him and kill another man in his presence, after all."

"And I'd do it again in a heartbeat!"

"Gentlemen!" Ross raises his voice, something he is wont to do. Reynolds backs off and retreats from the cell.

It is the Old Man who takes the high road. "We all lose our heads sometimes. It's fine."

Ross stares at Reynolds until he takes the hint and apologies. "I'm sorry I lunged at you." McCarthy raises at hand to dismiss the apology, but Reynolds continues. "As for my actions in the tunnel, just know I was only doing my job."

"Your actions cost Schaeffer his life. The man had a daughter."

"There are always casualties in war," Reynolds responds. "If he had a daughter, why the hell wasn't he home with her, instead of hanging out with the likes of you and I?!"

"He wanted to help. That's it. That's always it. We want to help, things escalate, and we find ourselves in too deep. May the gods help us, we find ourselves in too deep."

Ross reels the conversation back to its original purpose. "Which leads to why we're here, Atwood. Do you think it'll work?"

"The peace talks? I'd say that's up to you and your army more than it's up to Susie Walker and the Freedom Contingent Brigade."

12

Susie and her friends have been walking for two hours. They have yet to make any forward progress.

"I swear, we're going in circles," Dixon says. "Didn't we pass that rock formation 40 minutes ago?"

"Sun's still directly overhead, so that doesn't help," Samara observes. "What's the compass say?"

Susie checks the compass, which dangles from her belt loop. "It says . . . this can't be correct." They stop walking while she shows the compass to Samara.

"That's not good," Samara states.

"What is it?" Dixon and Josh ask, simultaneously, as they come in for a closer look.

The compass needle is spinning randomly. It appears to stop and point in a westerly direction, then spin in both directions again. "This happened to Diego and I on our last expedition, too," Susie says.

"Did you drop it?" Dixon asks.

"No, I know what this is," Samara says. "I was a Girl Scout once upon a time—"

"Three hundred years ago," Dixon jokes. He massages his knee while they stand idle.

"Something like that," Samara continues without laughing. "We did a camping module and part of it was on how to read a compass. I remember reading that if it was near anything magnetic, it could go haywire. Just . . . like . . . now."

Pete, Hawkins, and Underwood join the huddle while Rose keeps watch. There isn't a Sauron in sight. "You mean we're lost?!" Pete bemoans.

"I do think we got turned around for a bit. It's midday, so it's too early to navigate by the sun. But it'll be alright."

"How?!"

Samara looks around and notices a prominent peak to their left. "There. Someone needs to climb to the top, scan the horizon for their bearings, and see if the needle provides a stable reading from up top."

"Good thinking, Sam," Susie remarks. "I need someone in peak physical condition to make the trek. I can offer an extra protein pack as an incentive."

"I can go," Underwood volunteers.

"Thank you, Underwood, but I haven't seen you in action yet. Anyone else?"

"But I can do it," Underwood insists.

"Fine, but I'll need someone else to go with you."

Dixon steps forward, but Susie quashes the notion. "Not with that knee of yours. I debated even letting you come along today. I want someone who's armed."

Underwood taps the scabbard on his thigh. "With a firearm," Susie clarifies.

Dixon opens his mouth to protest, but Josh speaks first. "I'll go."

"Thank you, Josh," Susie responds. Her admiration for the quarterback-turned-resistance fighter continues to grow.

Dixon turns the statement of protest into a simple expression of gratitude. "Thanks, Loverboy."

Josh dismisses the remark and turns to Pete. "Dimkowski, why don't you come, too?"

"Uh . . . I . . . uh . . ." Pete is floored.

"Are you up for that, Pete?" Susie asks. "How's your breathing?"

"Uh, fine, I guess. I, um, I'm a bit scared of heights, but, uh, I can go if you want me to. Just wasn't expecting it."

"Be honest, kid, you weren't expecting any of this, were you?" Dixon remarks.

"Weirdest two weeks of my life."

"Are you *sure* you're up for this?" Susie asks.

Pete nods after a moment's hesitation. "It'll be good for me."

With that, Susie unzips her pack and removes a protein pack along with her homemade periscope. "Can anyone else spare a protein pack for our explorers?" Leonard offers up his to Underwood and Hawkins offers up his to Pete. "Thank you, boys," she says. She pulls Josh aside and hands him her protein pack, periscope, and compass. She leans in close. "Be careful, okay?"

"We'll be fine," he replies. "It can't be more than 20 minutes to the top."

"Stay alert for beaters. Where's your weapon?" Josh pats a visible bulge on his jacket that is the anti-matter pistol stowed inside. "Hurry back." She steps aside and he heads up the steep hill toward the rocky summit, with Pete and Underwood following closely behind.

13

Aside from a class-3 scramble near the summit that requires the use of all four limbs for purchase, the climb is non-technical. Josh, Pete, and Underwood ascend quickly, stopping to rest just once. Josh breathes easy and has barely broken a sweat, whereas Pete's back is sticky as he finds himself gasping for breath. Underwood's early lead flags after he stumbles, tripping over his size 12 feet. Josh and Underwood are eating from their protein packs when Pete, who was lagging, catches up to them. He wipes the sweat from his brow and brushes away that pesky lock of hair.

Josh takes a swig from his protein pack, which resembles an elementary school milk carton, but with pureed meat-and-veggie foodstuffs instead of *leche*. Filling, but vile. "Pop a squat, get some food in you," he says to Pete.

"No thanks, eating anything now would just make me barf." Pete bursts into a coughing fit with the last syllable.

"Drink some water at least."

"Man, this is high," Pete remarks, uneasy. He unscrews the lid of his canteen with hands shaky from exertion.

Underwood remarks at the specks that are Susie, Dixon, Rose, Leonard, Samara, García, and Hawkins. "They look like ants from up here."

"Did you really play for the White Sox?" Pete, gasping for breath, asks the gentle giant after downing a hearty swig of water.

"I do. I'm their designated hitter."

"You *do*. Right. I guess present tense still applies"—gasping —"until we know for sure we can't find a way out of here."

"I hope we can find a way." He swallows the last gulp from the protein pack and crushes it with one hand.

"That stuff any good?"

Underwood shrugs. "It's about as good as any of the supplements I took back home. Some of them are just nasty. Your friend here"—he points to Josh—"probably knows. He looks like he takes care of himself."

"No supplements, just a good workout and lots of carbs," Josh responds. "C'mon let's go, we're almost to the top."

Pete takes one more swig, then stows his canteen for the rocky scramble that follows. Ten minutes of careful climbing brings him to the true summit—and a bone-chilling gust of wind. He unfolds his jacket collar so it covers his earlobes, which are raw in less than a minute. Josh and Underwood hunker together on the summit's high point; they've stacked rocks into a cairn as a makeshift barricade against the wind. The gusts are reduced by two-thirds from behind the cairn.

"C-c-c-cold," Pete says, teeth chattering.

"Should have eaten your protein pack," Josh replies. "It gives strength."

"L-later. W-what are we l-l-looking for?"

"Orientation landmarks so we know we're on the right track. Like that . . . over there . . . Holy shit."

Pete is careful not to crawl too close to the edge. He and Underwood follow Josh's gaze to the southwest horizon. Their eyes behold the distant red cliffs of an Outlands canyon that looks like something out of Utah's desert southwest. In the foreground, before the canyon walls, the hills crest gently toward their current vantage point.

"Wow," Pete marvels. His breathing stabilizes. He foresees himself never forgetting this stunning vista.

To their right, the giant fenceline they saw earlier is visible, zigzagging every which way. A plume of black smoke billows from whatever is there—perhaps not a landfill after all.

"Whadoya think that is?" Josh asks.

"Beats me, guys," Underwood replies.

"Maybe a controlled burn at the landfill?" Pete surmises.

Josh shrugs. "Looks like we weren't so far off after all. I'm guessing the grove's on the side of that canyon closest to us. Can't be more than a 90-minute hike."

"I'm up for it if you are," Underwood says. The others nod.

"How's the compass?" Pete asks.

"Stable," Josh marvels. "Would you look at that?"

"Huh."

Josh pockets the compass. "Let's head back. This is a beautiful spot, but you ain't wrong, Dimkowski—it's cold up here!"

Underwood is fastest on the descent. He stumbles once on a patch of scree but is otherwise undeterred. He waits for Pete and Josh to descend the rocky class-3 scramble. They catch up at the halfway point, and Josh motions for him to continue his descent. "We're right behind you." Underwood gives a thumb's up. Josh turns to Pete. "Hang back a minute, Dimkowski."

Pete unscrews the lid from his canteen and takes another gulp, this one a sip rather than a swig. "What's up?"

"I've been hanging out with Susie's team for a while now . . ."

"The two of you look tight."

"It's not like that. You know Lori's waiting for me."

"Chill out, I didn't mean anything by it. There aren't any towels around here to snap my ass with again, are there?"

"Anyone ever tell you you've got quite a mouth?"

"I might have been told that a time or two. And again, Josh—and for the record—I'm sorry for the thing at Vinnie's with Lori."

"Forget it. My question is—and I'm asking you this before I ask the others—what if we don't go back?"

"You're joking, right?"

"Hear me out. Send back a few people, the ones with health issues like Shauna or families like Hawkins. But otherwise and afterwards, the rest of us stay. We stay and destroy that thing."

"We'll be stuck here!"

"Dimkowski, did you not see what happened to Earth on our trip here?! It's a dead planet! I don't wanna go back to that!"

"Yeah, Earth's screwed, sure. We learned that in junior high anyway. Remember Mr. Bayer teaching us about the hole in the ozone layer and shit? But that's not for like another 40 years! And who knows? Maybe the forecast was wrong. Maybe it doesn't happen 'til our friends back home have long since died of old age."

"Maybe—"

"Besides, what about Lori? You just said she's waiting for you."

"Yeah, if your friend Wilkinson keeps his hands off her. But . . ."

"But what?"

"But she's too good for me, anyway."

"Don't say that! You're playing the part of hero! She'll totally throw herself at you when you return. Especially once she finds out all the amazing shit you've done here."

"I just happened to be in the right place at the right time. Or the wrong place at the wrong time. Not sure which."

"Dude, you saved my life. I'm not cut out for slave labor! You saved Dana's life, too. And Shauna's!"

"You helped with the girls."

"Yeah, but I'd only been here like five days. My head was pounding. I didn't know *what* was going on. Trust me: It was all you." Pete's uncharacteristic singing of Josh's praises is something he doesn't realize he's doing until the next afternoon, when he's back in the warmer, more-oxygenated environs of the FCB barracks.

"Have I been wrong about you all these years, Dimkowski? Are you not the pantywaist I always thought you were?"

"No, you were right. Also, that might be the nicest thing anyone's ever said to me."

Josh chuckles and shake his head in disbelief. "Fucking Dimkowski. Who knew?"

"C'mon dude, let's beat feet. Underwood's almost at the bottom."

14

The group makes good time; Susie's glad to hear they aren't as far off course as she initially feared. Pete finally samples a protein pack as Underwood slows his pace to match. "Whadoya think?" he asks.

"Tastes awful," Pete says. "But I swear I can feel it coating my insides. These work fast; I see why people drink 'em." He takes another gulp. His face cannot mask his revulsion.

"Say, what were you and him"—he points to Josh, who leads the pack alongside Susie and Rose—"talking about?"

"We were talking about a couple mutual friends back home."

"I miss home. Feel like I'm letting the team down. If they didn't cancel the whole season over what happened, that is."

"Uh, they said on the news before I was taken they plan on postponing as many games for August and September as they can."

"Oh good. Double headers, I'm guessing?"

Pete, a movie geek and not a sports geek, shrugs. "My friend Bob—he's one of the dudes Josh and I were talking about—his whole family are huge Sox fans. He'll shit when I tell him I met you."

"Well, when we get back, I can put you guys in touch with our PR office. I'm sure they can send some tickets his way."

"He'd like that."

Despite his claim of missing home, Underwood seems to be the only member of the expedition to genuinely be enjoying himself. He bounds past Pete toward the head of the pack. Pete picks up the pace, lest he miss out on any 24th-century gossip.

Susie and Josh walk, side by side, in relative silence. Josh goes with the flow and Susie is mindful not to talk his ear off. Underwood catches up, barely winded. "I have a question," he says.

"You're in remarkable shape," Susie responds. "What's your question?"

"So, you brought me up to speed on the stakes when I first joined your team, but there's still one thing I'm unsure of."

"And that is?"

"How did this all get started? You and the FCB, I mean."

"Good question," Pete remarks, out of breath once again, as he catches up. Josh rolls his eyes. *Fucking Dimkowski,* he thinks.

"A while back, two or three of your Earth Prime years ago by now, a group of civilians were peacefully demonstrating after Ross mandated a price hike on the cost of meat and eggs," Susie begins. "He also added a hefty surcharge any time our goods-and-sundries cards needed to be topped off. Soldiers, of course, were exempt from this fee. Have I told you about my mentor?"

"The Old Man?" Underwood asks.

"That's right. He was protesting the loudest and the most passionately. Things turned violent when one of the protesters tripped and stumbled into a squad of soldiers tasked with keeping the peace. Someone—and no one evens knows who, or which side they were on—overreacted and everything spiraled out of control. One of the soldiers went for the Old Man, and I threw myself in front of him to block the charge. Don't know what I was thinking, I—"

"You just did it," Pete interrupts.

"Exactly. Anyway, a lot of the protesters were able to run away, but those of us up front were arrested. They spread us around different lock-ups to weaken our resolve, but the Old Man and I were housed in the same facility. They sentenced us to 30 days, and whenever the guards were away—tobacco breaks, shift change, what have you—we started talking about creating a larger movement."

"I'd love to meet him," Underwood says.

"He's a great man. You don't know how relieved I was to learn he's still alive. Even more than when Reynolds offered coordinates for today's excursion, knowing the Old Man isn't dead was what gave me hope that maybe he—Reynolds, I mean —can be trusted after all."

Rose hears this and frowns. *Careful* mujer, she thinks.

15

The group continues toward the cave and the grove, but the plume of black smoke comes into view 15 minutes later.

"We saw it from up high," Josh says. "Dimkowski there thinks it's from the landfill."

"That doesn't make sense," Leonard says. "The dumps are lined with canvas. There's no need to burn trash this far out. Something's up."

Rose, vigilant as ever: "Should we see?"

Susie sighs and checks her compass, which has indeed stabilized. She checks its accuracy against the position of the sun. Although it has moved westward, the sun is still high in the sky—by Mars standards, anyway. "How far?" she asks Josh.

"We've made good speed. Can't be more than a couple miles."

Susie turns to Leonard for translation. "Three-point-two klicks," he says.

After a brief discussion, the group agrees to check out the source of the blaze. They set ground rules: Split into two groups, assess the situation, and act or retreat. Susie suggests they *may* have safe passage since their journey was pre-approved by Chancellor Ross. "Or so I was told," she adds, prompting titters from the others.

They head in the direction of the fire, and the source of the burn comes into view once they crest another rise: A pit of charred earth, several football fields in size, is set back one-half klick from the fence. It is lined with boulders to block the view from anyone immediately next to it, but the group's elevated position offers a disturbing view that will grow even more disturbing upon closer inspection. They descend to the fence, stopping halfway down to pull their shirts over their noses as the smell hits—a putrid repugnance that turns even the strongest stomach. Later, when the war is over and word spreads across both zones of how little respect Chancellor Ross had for the dead, the survivors of today's expedition will refer to this place simply as the Pit. It would surprise none of them to learn that even belly beaters avoid the Pit. There is nothing for them to feast on anyway . . . except ashes.

"Are you sure this is what you saw before, Leonard?" Samara asks.

"No, this is something else."

"Whatever they're burning, I don't think it's just garbage," Pete says. He pulls his shirt away from his nose and mouth to throw up. Others do the same.

"That's not garbage," Hawkins says, "that's bone."

"*Oye,* how do you know?" Rose asks.

"My cousin worked in a slaughterhouse. I told you that before, I'm sure."

"*¡Guácatelas!*" Disgusting!

"Let's check it out," Susie orders, "but quickly and carefully. Two groups like we agreed."

They reach the fence. Josh draws his anti-matter gun and fires it in a downward angle at several pieces of chain-link, driving the plasma charges into the ground. He manages to peel back a section of chain-link large enough for them to squeeze through, but winces from the plasma-heated temperature of the fencing. He is the first to climb through. Susie waves the others through as she brings up the rear. Samara, Leonard, Pete, and Underwood accompany Josh while Susie, Dixon, Rose, García, and Hawkins comprise the second group. Susie glances at Josh for a moment, disappointed they aren't in the same group. *At least each group has a marksman,* she concedes. Josh leads his group toward the manmade rock wall in one direction, Susie toward the other. They crouch low.

"It's getting worse," Samara says, referencing the smell.

"Shhh!" Josh points to a break in the rock wall. He disengages the safety and Underwood unsheathes his knife. They squeeze through the rock wall . . . and immediately regret doing so. The eastern half of the Pit is a landfill, sure enough, but the western half is an open-air crematorium. Flames make way to black smoke over a burning pyre of corpses. The fire crackles and something—an aorta, perhaps—pops like a New Year's Eve party favor. Everyone jumps. The sound of a moving vehicle is heard. The two parties of five turn to see a tractor hauling a cart filled with more dead bodies, some naked and some clad in whatever clothes they perished in. Pete averts his eyes and observes similar, mortified reactions on the faces of his colleagues. Even Josh, his high school's star quarterback and jock *extraordinaire,* is pale.

"How horrible," Hawkins remarks.

"*Dios mío,*" Rose adds.

Pete's lip quivers. He steels himself and looks back at the Pit. The tractor stops along the rim of the Pit. The driver looks into his rearview mirror and engages a lever. The cart spills its contents into the Pit. A mass of bodies tumbles to the ashy ground below. The driver engages the lever again and the cart uprights itself. He changes gears and the tractor pulls away, driving to the westernmost end of the Pit, where the driver makes a U-turn and returns via a higher road. A smaller truck pulls up and stops where the tractor paused to unload its contents. Two men, both in 24th-century hazmat suits, exit the truck. One unfurls a hose from the back of the truck and pumps gas over the side and into the Pit. He finishes and rolls up the hose, stowing it safely. He gives a thumb's up to his colleague, then steps backward. His colleague removes what appears to be a flamethrower and ignites the bodies below.

An enormous flame leaps into the air and the flamethrower's operator immediately steps back, lest he be consumed by the initial flame. He turns off his flamethrower and returns it to the truck bed. He motions for his colleague to join him. They don goggles, step forward, and gaze into the Pit, either admiring their handiwork or wishing the victims a peaceful voyage into the afterlife.

"How could they?" Samara cries. Underwood turns to comfort her, but she runs off. "Don't, it hurts my eyes."

Underwood starts after her, but Pete grabs his arm. "Leave her."

The truckdrivers on the other side of the Pit apparently can't see Susie's team through the smoke and haze. Rose, whose vision is back to 20/20 after nearly losing her sight during the canal extension jobsite raid, aims her rifle in an unauthorized act of vengeance against the dozens of corpses burning in the Pit.

"Rose, what are you doing?" Susie asks.

"I can take out both of those *putos*. Maybe the one in the tractor, too."

"Don't do it. That's not what we're here for."

"Why do you care? Those *bastardos* have lost their humanity."

"Don't lose yours, too," Leonard cautions. "This place'll do that to you."

"*¡Mierda!*" Rose says after thinking on this for a spell. She refuses to lower her weapon, however, so Dixon puts an arm on her shoulder.

"*Amiga,*" he says in a cautionary tone, "don't."

Rose stares at the ground and sighs, long and deep. "*Vamos.*" She lowers her weapon and doesn't utter another word until they reach the cave. Normally one to lead the pack, she brings up the rear this time as the others retreat, several of them in tears, across no man's land and through the tear in the chain-link fence. She stops halfway up the hill and turns toward the smoky crematorium of the Pit. From afar, she raises her weapon again and sights the two men through the haze as they gaze upon on their ashy handiwork.

Susie and the others stop and watch from further up the hill as Rose appears to bide her time for the right moment. Dixon steps forward to intervene, but Susie puts one hand on his shoulder. "Whatever she does now is on her."

"Shoot 'em," Josh whispers from his own vantage point. "Shoot those fuckers." Pete throws an angry glance Josh's way, but it goes unnoticed.

Rose concentrates her aim; her targets are 35 meters away but dead in her sights. If anyone can make this shot, it's her. She steadies herself, then mock-pulls the trigger twice and makes a *"FFFP"* sound each time. The men return to the truck and make the same U-turn as the driver of the tractor. They will never know how close they came to death.

Rose turns around and continues her climb out from the hillside leading to the Pit. She stares at the ground as she walks and pays little notice to the others watching her. They resume their onward journey to the cave. Dixon waits behind and offers to put an arm around her shoulder. She motions for him to leave her alone. Dixon loves Rose like a sister, and this sad sack loner act of hers breaks his heart.


16


Dixon and Rose grew up without a lot of friends. With the former the youngest of five resentful, much older siblings and the latter a survivor of sexual abuse, it makes sense when you think about it. Born Albert Ignacio Dixon, *he* was the unexpected "surprise" baby, ten years younger than the next-youngest child in the family and born long after his mother (who was also named Rose) figured she could no longer bear children. His close-knit older siblings, who had to share a single bedroom so "Li'l Albert" could have his own room, rejected their younger brother. His cash-poor parents, meanwhile, had long since donated any hand-me-down clothes from his brothers to charity. As such, they resented him for costing so much money in new clothes. Frankly, dad should have gotten a vasectomy and mom a tubal ligation after three children.

Born Rosalina Aurea Martínez y Guadalupe, *she* was the second child of Mexican American parents, conceived out of love. Her father, a roly poly man who worked two jobs, one as a tool and die maker in the suburb of River Grove and another as a balloonist at the local park, died of massive heart attack when Rose was just 13 months old. Her mother, a homemaker who occasionally earned extra money cleaning houses, was overcome with grief and drowned her sorrows in the bottle. She would go on benders that lasted for days, her children left alone and unfed. It was only after a nosy neighbor reported her to the police that action was taken. Social Services arrived at the home to find Rose and her older brother "dangerously malnourished." They became wards of the state and were circulated through the abusive foster care system, only to become separated and lose permanent contact with one another not long afterwards. Some people survive a loveless childhood to become passively dependent adults. Others, like Rose, become hardened and independent to a fault.

. . .

Dixon was only too happy to move out of the crowded house he shared with his parents and siblings as soon as he turned 18. Although his oldest sister, Gina, moved in with her boyfriend three years prior, his other sister, Fiona, had a child out of wedlock, which meant that *she* got the private bedroom and that the net number of occupants in the house remained an even eight. He hated the city, though he could never articulate why. He was squat, not tall, and had a golden opportunity to make a name for himself in high school as a varsity standout on the wrestling team, but was kicked off the team for his temper after chin-checking a referee for making a bad call during a conference match. He studied hard and missed a 3.50 GPA due in part to an undeserved bad grade after his advanced algebra teacher docked his final mark by two letters following accusations—unfounded, of course—of cheating. For Dixon, this was a bridge too far. He moved to the west suburb of Bensenville the day after graduation with the wind at his back.

He wasn't through with Chicago, however, and his high school experience wasn't as bad as he sometimes claimed it to be. His school was the first in the city to offer CAD (Computer-Aided Drawing), and a recommendation from the instructor earned him his first full-time job—office assistant at a small architecture firm in the Lincoln Square neighborhood. He stole money from a church collection plate and used it to purchase a pair of suits from a second-hand shop. The pay was terrible, but he bided his time as an errand boy for over three years, having designs on being an architect and trying to remember that patience is a virtue. He finally received his own account to nurture after almost four years of loyal service, and at long last, it seemed his ship had finally come in.

He was abducted four weeks later.

. . .

Rose lost her virginity at age 11. Her foster parents, Billy and Patty, were like something out of a bad dream. Rose's first language was Spanish, and Patty yelled at Rose whenever she would break into Spanish mid-sentence—just her process of breaking down her line of thought from *español* into *inglés* aloud as she searched for the correct words. The rest of the time, her foster mother was little more than a wet blanket, sitting in front of the TV and smoking two packs of cigarettes a day, often with rollers still in her hair from the night before. Her foster father was an abusive drunk. Most days, he wouldn't say more than "What the fuck are you looking at?" to Rose, but the way the bed in the next room would squeak three nights each week suggested that eventually, once Billy got tired of banging Patty, he'd turn his attention to Rose. She was braver than any girl should have to be in that situation, biting her lip so as not to cry and uttering nary a word. The fourth time Billy came at her, he told her he wanted it "doggy style." Rose got on her hands and knees and waited until he was just about to enter her. She reached behind, grabbed his nuts in one hand, and squeezed. Billy screamed so loud every light in the surrounding homes turned on as neighbors wondered if someone had surprised a burglar. "I'm sorry," he rasped, and ran out of the house. He didn't call or come home for six weeks, but his paychecks were still deposited every Friday, so Rose and Patty knew he wasn't dead.

Billy returned a changed man. He gave Rose a wide berth and left the living room whenever she would enter it. One afternoon, Patty pulled Rose aside and gave her the address to her aunt's duplex in the Galewood neighborhood. "She's a spinster," Patty explained, "but you'll be safe there. All we ask is you keep quiet about what happened here so we don't lose that money from the state." Rose agreed, and her sexual abuse struggles became a thing of the past . . . except for the nightmares. She celebrated her 18th birthday by getting an apartment elsewhere in the city with a female classmate, and it wasn't until she got a job as a ticket agent at the Western Avenue Metra Station that she started feeling better about herself, and began attending a support group for battered women every Tuesday night.

She was abducted eight weeks later.

. . .

Dixon and Rose were not friends in Chicago, but they were acquainted with each other. Each weekday morning, Dixon exited the MetraRail at Western Avenue and caught a bus to his job from there, renewing his pass every 30 days at the counter where Rose worked. They never said much to each other beyond simple pleasantries, but one day he commented on her nametag. "Rose," he said. "That's my mother's name." With that, he took his newly stamped rail pass and left before she could ask for his name in return.

Dixon, by now completely estranged from his family, wanted to learn more about where he came from. His firm closed early on Fridays, and he made an appointment at CGC-Hancock one Friday afternoon for a genetics consultation. The visit included a blood test and heart monitor, which he found odd until the account representative explained, "Since we don't know much about the general life expectancy of your ancestors —not yet, anyway—we want to gauge a general bill of health from the person standing here today." Thinking the rep's response sounded reasonable, he signed the consent form, thereby sealing his own fate. Being in good shape and having no close relatives was tantamount to checking all the right boxes, for he answered a knock on his door eight days later and received a conk on the head from someone of the Loyalist persuasion. He was revived 30 minutes later in a VFW rec room somewhere unfamiliar to him, and was sent by porta-pad from there to CGC-Meigs in preparation for his longer journey to Mars. When he arrived, he was unable to remember anything about his name except that "Dixon" was part of it.

Rose, who had no memory of her late father and only fleeting images of what her alcoholic mother looked like, missed her older brother dearly. The foster care system refused to give her any information, and with that, she knew nothing about her own genealogy. She paid a visit to CGC-Meigs for a genetics consultation. Her account representative suggested that the curvature of her nose resembled that of the Mesoamericans of Mexico and Central America, and that poor record-keeping following Spanish colonization of the New World might make it more difficult (*read: costly*) to find her roots. Intrigued, she plunked down her credit card and signed up for the "full package," even though she couldn't afford it, and was terrified to discover, after coming home from work several days later while her roommate was conveniently out of town visiting relatives, a black CGC van parked outside and two Loyalist goons waiting for her. The time chamber techs on Mars marveled at how she was one of the only Journeywomen *not* to vomit upon arrival. She opted not to tell them that compared to crushing your foster dad's balls in one hand as a pre-teen, a little time travel is a breeze.

17

Conversation is sparse during the one-hour walk from the Pit to the cave. Dixon, whose knee swells and throbs, offers to stay behind and set up camp while the others, after a quick break to ingest another protein pack, seek out the grove. Susie asks if Rose wants to help Dixon, but the ball-busting Latina declines.

"No way, José. I want to find this *pinche* fruit."

"I'll stay," Leonard volunteers. "I gave up one of my protein packs earlier. Setting up camp seems less taxing than doing any more walking today."

"Thank you, Leonard," Susie says. "Everyone, leave your sleeping mats for Dixon and Leonard to lay out. This map's not to scale, but something tells me we're close. We leave in five!"

Ever mindful of the rapidly dropping temperatures that come with nightfall, Susie allots 30 minutes to find the grove, 30 minutes to spend on site, and 30 minutes to return. Their timing is fortuitous, for they reach the rim of the canyon spotted by Pete, Josh, and Underwood after just five minutes of walking.

"That's one helluva view," García marvels.

"You should've seen it from atop that peak," Josh says.

"Nothing in the distance that resembles a grove, though," Hawkins says.

Without being prompted, Pete gets down on all fours and crawls to the edge of the rim. He peers over the side. "Careful, Pete," Samara cautions.

"Someone grab his feet," Rose says.

"No, I'm okay," Pete replies. "I need to step outside my comfort zone."

"We don't have time for this," Susie says.

"Whoa, check it out, it's right down there!" Pete exclaims.

"Where?!" Underwood asks.

"Under our feet! I mean, at the bottom. Like, literally right below us!"

The others carefully peer over the side. Sure enough, a riparian blanket of green appears at the bottom, some 300 meters down.

"Is that water I hear running?" Samara asks.

"Impossible," García says.

"No, I hear it too," Susie adds.

"We've gotta find a way down!" Pete says. He bounds excitedly along the edge like a frog, looking for access and having apparently overcome his vertigo. The canyon rim curves around a giant boulder, and Pete disappears behind it. "Over here!" he shouts from behind the boulder 20 seconds later.

The others join him and confirm that the rock strata, countless millions of years old, provides a natural stairway of sorts to the canyon bottom. The "steps" are big and uneven, some up to a meter in height.

"Are you coming?" Pete asks from two steps down, as giddy as a kid pestering mom and dad to hurry downstairs on Christmas morning.

"Yes. Don't go too far," Susie cautions.

"Cute kid," Samara says to Susie.

They begin their descent and step gingerly. At times, all four limbs are needed to find purchase. Pete is three-quarters of the way down by the time Rose, who is next in line, reaches him. "Slow down, *joven!*"

"No, you guys hurry up!"

"*¡Osh!*" Rose rolls her eyes and continues down while Pete waits for the others to get closer before heading the rest of the way down.

"Nice find," Hawkins says as he approaches.

"Thanks," Pete replies. He continues down. Some of the rock steps are precipitous and narrow, and Pete knocks the clay loose from one of them as he missteps. "Careful," he says to Hawkins and Underwood, who are directly behind him. The clumsy Underwood, with his size 12 clodhoppers, is unsure of his footing. He steps on the same section of loose clay as Pete. The clay erodes and Underwood falls over the side. The greenery of the grove, seven meters below, breaks his fall, but he lands badly and a horrific crack sound punctuates his leg breaking.

"*YEE-OWW!*" he cries out. Rose stands watch while Susie, Pete, and Hawkins rush to his aid.

"How's your pain threshold?" Hawkins asks. "Can you walk?"

"I-I think so." Underwood attempts to stand up. He takes Hawkins's outstretched hand. All is well until he takes a single step forward. He puts too much weight on his injured left leg and howls in pain. He leans against the cliff face on his good leg and motions for Hawkins to let go of his hand. "That didn't go so well."

"Well the good news is, you made it," Samara says. Underwood nods, his face red with exhaustion as he and the others gaze upon their surroundings. An enormous grove of stupendous beauty, not unlike what one may imagine the Garden of Eden to resemble, spreads before them in three directions. The late afternoon sun's rays shine on the grove, and dozens of grapefruit-sized orange domes—gourds—crown above the greenery.

"*Santa María,*" Rose says, softly.

"Amazing," García adds.

"Hey, there's a creek over here!" Josh runs off in one direction.

"Careful!" Susie yells after him.

"It's okay, check it out!"

"I'll go with him," Samara offers.

Susie gives a nod of thanks. *He's as excited as Pete is,* she thinks.

A bubbling brook makes its way through the center of the grove. With water so clear Josh and Samara can make out pebbles on the bottom, this makes for a delightful discovery.

"Where'd this come from?" Rose asks, joining them but still on alert.

"Underground spring?" Samara posits.

"*Increíble.*"

Josh squats and sticks a finger in the water. "Cold. Should we take a drink?"

"I will if you will," Samara proposes. Josh nods and they each cup their hands and sample the wares.

"How is it?" Rose asks.

"Mmmm. Jane and I went hiking in Colorado once," Samara answers. "Tried water from one of the mountain streams there. This tastes just like it."

"She's right," Josh adds. "Try some."

"Okay. Watch my back, Loverboy." Rose sets down her anti-matter rifle and takes a sip.

"Whadoya think?" Josh asks her. She answers by taking another sip . . . and another. She pours the remaining tap water from her canteen and submerges it in the creek. She takes an enormous gulp of cold, fresh water, then refills it again.

"Careful," Samara cautions. "It's delicious, but if there're parasites, you could shi—I mean, you can get an upset stomach."

"It'd be worth it," Rose replies.

Pete and Hawkins prop up the much taller Underwood so he, too, can limp to the water's edge. "Lemme fill your canteen, dude," Pete offers.

"Sure. I'll take a load off while you do that." Underwood struggles to remove his pack; Hawkins lends a hand while Pete fills their canteens. Underwood takes a good-sized sip, then pours some over his head. "Thanks man. Hitting coach told me once I've got one hell of an arm and two left feet. Guess it's true."

"Eh, it happens," Pete replies. "It's gonna suck getting you out of here, though."

"Where's Susie?" Samara asks. She decides to live dangerously after all, and tops off her canteen. "Where's García?"

The FCB's spiritual leader and the reformed ex-shuttle driver are further afield. They pluck gourds from their root structures and stuff them in their packs. "Shouldn't we try these first?" García asks.

"Good idea, García." Susie jams her sharpened pinky finger into the gourd's thick skin like a knife. She peels back the skin and takes a bite. "Mmmm, this is delicious." Juice pours down her chin.

García bangs his gourd against a jagged rock to break the skin. He peels it back and takes a juicy bite. "Oh my. I've never tasted anything so sweet." He takes another bite, and winces when pulp squirts in his eye. He tilts his head back to douse his eye with water from his canteen. "Would you say this redeems the day from what we saw earlier?" he asks.

"Nothing can redeem that, but we made good time even after getting lost, and still managed to salvage the afternoon."

"That we did."

"Hey García, if your eye's okay, can you pack up as many of these gourds as you can? I'd like to bring home one or two apiece for everyone at the barracks. It'll give 'em a taste of what we're fighting for."

"No pun intended, right?"

"I'm not following."

"You said, 'It'll give 'em a taste.' "

"Oh. Right."


The others have the same idea. Even Underwood insists his pack be filled with gourds. He explains that with one person in front of him and one person behind him, he should be able to climb out of the canyon backward via the tried-and-true, bump-up-on-your-butt method; those with him can act as spotters should he need to be dragged by the shoulders or have his broken foot lifted over any sizable rock steps.

Rose sits on a creekside boulder a few meters away, morose, her pack bursting with gourds. Susie startles her from thought. "You okay, Rose?"

"*Sí.* I'm packed and ready."

"No, I mean, are you okay with what we saw earlier?"

"The Pit? *Creo que no.*" *I don't think so.*

"You wanted to kill those men."

"They deserved to die."

"Perhaps. But I've learned something."

"*¿Sí?*"

"Yes. With the work we're doing, I learned we may be people of action, but we're not empowered to take the law into our own hands. We can—and should—defend ourselves, but it isn't our role to play judge, jury, and executioner."

"Who are you to say that, *mujer?* How many people have you killed? I don't take shit from anyone, but *osh,* your body count is much higher than mine!"

Susie turns away, then decides Rose deserves to be looked in the eye. "A lot of people here believe in God, or in some other deity that promises to guide us into the next world once we perish in this one. I've never put much stock in such things myself, which is why I fight so hard for this world now. But I've done a lot of things I'm not proud of. Remember the raid when the Old Man was taken?"

"You lost Diego that day, *verdad?*"

"Diego . . . and Schaeffer . . . Hardy . . . Boyd and Holloway . . . and . . . I shot one of Ross's men in cold blood. Right after you and Dixon arrived on the scene."

"*Sí,* I remember. You asked him his name, and then you shot him."

"Rose, the soldier I shot, Abramson, I see in my nightmares. He's in them along with everyone else. Diego . . . Jasmine . . . Sebastián . . . Spiros . . . Dr. Spellman . . . Verónica . . . Abigail." Rose, a tough fighter but not the warmest member of the FCB, says nothing.

It takes a lot to make Susie cry. Aside from a single sniffle, she keeps her tears at bay. "I'm sorry," she continues. "My point is, his face is in there, same as everyone else's. I don't know what'll come of these peace talks. I hope Reynolds is a man of his word. And if that means taking me prisoner to free the Old Man and set everything else in motion, it's a sacrifice I'm willing to make. Because I don't deserve to be happy. I don't know if this 'heaven' some people talk about really exists, but if it does I'll never make it there, because all the good I've tried to do can't undo all the bad I've done along the way."

"*Dios mío,* I can't believe you remember that soldier's name."

"I remember all their names."

Rose ponders this before speaking. "You and the Old Man are the big speakers around here, not me, so I'll say just one thing, then I'll be quiet: There's no room in my heart for forgiveness. *Pero,* I will trust Reynolds because *you* trust Reynolds. And I know you trust Reynolds because in your heart you have to, even if in your gut and your brain you know it's a bad idea."

Susie shrugs, and Rose continues. "*Mujer,* you are my hero. You are Dixon's hero. You are Josh's hero. You are everyone's hero. Don't be so hard on yourself. This is not like the world I grew up in, which was filled with, *cómo se dice,* shades of grey. Here, everything is black and white. I would kill every one of those *cabrones* if I could, and I would sleep just fine after."

They sit in silence after that exchange, the trickle of the stream and the sound of the wind through the greenery notwithstanding. The others watch from the bottom of the natural rock steps, rapt, until Samara breaks the silence. "You mind if we head back, Suze?" Samara points to the sky—the sun is considerably lower and the wind has picked up.

"Good idea," Susie replies. "Thank you, Sam. Everyone's packs full?" The others nod. "Who's helping Underwood?" Pete and Hawkins raise their hands.

"Hold up," Underwood says. He stands up and leans against the cliff face. "I have a feeling this is gonna take a while. I'd better piss first."

"Okay. Josh, why don't you take the lead since you're packing. Rose, you and I can bring up the rear."

Underwood hobbles toward the stream to urinate, with Pete and Hawkins propping him up. He raises an elbow to shoo them away. "You guys mind backing off? I don't need you to hold it for me." Underwood unzips his pants.

"Not by the stream," Susie chastises.

"Right." Underwood zips up and hobbles away from the stream and toward the cliff wall, his back facing the rock steps. Pete and Hawkins give him space. He stands on his unbroken leg and retrieves his member with his right hand, bracing himself against the wall with his left. He urinates with gusto onto a thicket of greenery that grows directly along the wall, much to the chagrin of the belly beater hiding beneath. It darts out of the greenery and takes a meaty bite of Underwood's good, right ankle. He howls in pain as his foot is swept out from under him. He crashes on his back, piss spraying everywhere and his right leg kicking in the air to eject its hideous stowaway.

The beater is having none of this. It holds on for dear life and bites into the flesh and bone with its oversized teeth. Underwood's kicks work against him as the voracious creature quickly gnaws through the bone. With his last kick, Underwood inadvertently amputates his own foot. It flies two meters in the air and lands on the ground, beater still attached and determined to do to the talus what a pack of hyenas can do to an elephant carcass.

Pete and Hawkins can only babble in horror as Underwood screams. Susie reaches for the pistol inside her coat, but the zipper snags. Rose runs toward the action, in the moment and oblivious to Underwood's presence. She discharges a rapid-fire spray of plasma that annihilates the foot, the beater, and several nearby gourds. The cliff wall absorbs the anti-matter spray but leaves a black discoloration behind.

Susie runs to Underwood while Rose fires additional, precautionary blasts into the other cliff-hugging patches of green. Underwood writhes in agony. Pete leans over him but is unsure of what to do. "How you feeling?" he asks.

"How am I feeling? A-are you kidding?"

"I'm here," Susie says. She removes a spare blanket from her pack. "Brought two of these for the cold. Let's tie this one around your leg. Need to disinfect it, first." She douses the bloody stump that is his shin with water from her canteen. He howls in pain.

"Christ, that's cold!"

"It was necessary. I'm going to lift the leg and we're going to wrap this towel around it. Pete, don't just stand there."

A shocked Pete comes out of his stupor. "I'm here. W-whadoya need me to do?"

"When I lift his leg, slide the blanket underneath it and wrap it around tight."

"Got it."

"Underwood, you're about to hate me." The maimed ballplayer nods.

"On three, Pete. One . . . two . . . three!" Susie raises his leg while Pete wraps the blanket around. It makes two circuits of his lower leg. "Now, hold those two ends in your left hand and grab the side by the wound with your right. Pull them tight—he'll probably scream but don't let that stop you—and double-knot everything."

Underwood screams, alright—a blood-curdling din his colleagues won't soon forget. "Sorry," Pete says. "It's done."

"What's going on down there?" someone shouts from above.

"Keep moving!" Susie yells back. "We're on our way."

Rose, who exhausted the plasma magazine on her anti-matter rifle, joins Susie and the others. "I only found the one. I heard others skittering though, and fired in their general direction."

"It's okay. We should've been more careful." Susie looks up at the fading light. "Pete, Hawkins, let's get him ready. One of you grab him by the shoulders and one of you grab his left leg. I'll grab the right. We don't have much time."

"We should just leave him," Rose recommends.

"I can hear you," Underwood says, and coughs.

"We're not leaving him," Susie says. The blanket should act as a tourniquet until we reach the cave and can properly dress the wound. In the morning we'll make a stretcher."

"Out of what?!"

"We'll find a way. Come on, let's go."

"You ready?" Pete asks Hawkins.

"Yeah. I'll grab his shoulders. Don't forget your pack."

"Right. Thanks."

"Head on up, Rose," Susie orders. "We're right behind you."

17

Rose ascends to the rim of the canyon in no time at all. It takes almost 30 minutes for the others to carry Underwood out. They stop frequently, huffing and puffing. Underwood starts to shiver, so Susie removes her jacket and lays it across Underwood's chest like a blanket. Pete stops three-quarters of the way up, winded, to vomit.

They reach the top to find Rose waiting for them. Susie asks her to take Pete's place for the remainder of their trek to the cave. It's near dark when they arrive and find the others waiting inside the cave, sheltered from the rising wind. Some have set their flashlights on end; by removing the base, three-inch retractable legs extend to turn them into free-standing lanterns. Leonard and Josh struggle to roll a giant boulder in front of the cave entrance. García hauls wood he has gathered. He drops it and rushes Underwood's aid; the rising wind quickly scatters the branches. "What happened?!"

"Beater," Pete replies. He follows Susie, Rose, and Hawkins as they carry Underwood into the cave. They set him down near the ashy remnants of a fire circle and hope for a miracle.

# Chapter 4

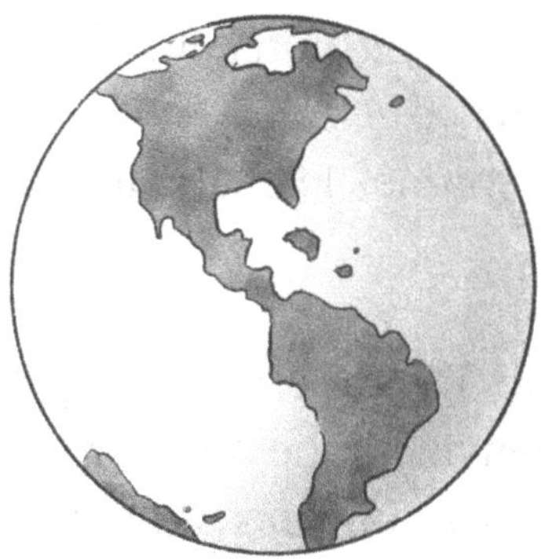

1

Bob returns to his motel room and takes a cleansing shower. He scrubs the bloodstains from his T-shirt in the sink, then dries it with the hairdryer. The shirt is still damp around the collar when he slips back into it. As he exits the bathroom, he is surprised to find the TV on and Lori sitting at the corner table. "You scared me," he says.

"Sorry." Despite not wearing any makeup, Lori looks like a million bucks after her shower. She bites into a Twinkie from the stash of wholly unhealthy vending machine foodstuffs spread across the table. "How were your phone calls? Did you get ahold of the detective?"

"I was gonna page him, but decided instead I'd just leave him a message saying you and I were okay but Dana and Pete were taken. Figured we oughta come up with a plan before talking to him for real. Oh, I tried calling my dad also."

"He works in Washington, right? How is he?"

"Dunno. His office phone rang like eight times and then went to his mailbox, which was full of course."

"I'm sorry." With food in her mouth, her apology sounds like a mush-mouthed mumble. She laughs, inadvertently spraying crumbs, and reaches for the remaining Hostess product. "Here, have this other Twinkie."

"Can you save it for me? I'm actually not very hungry right now."

"Totally."

Bob looks at the TV, which airs a spot for Victory Auto Wreckers of Bensenville. The omnipresent commercial, in which a bearded young man opens the door to his rust bucket car, only for it to come off its hinges, will run for three decades and become a bit of Chicagoland nostalgia. "You watching the news?" he asks Lori.

"Yeah. They went to commercial just as I turned it on."

Bob sits on the edge of the bed. The next commercial is a PSA from CGC. It opens with a video close-up of the American flag billowing. After the opening shot, the spot transitions to include epic establishing shots of Chicago—one taken from atop the John Hancock Center's observation deck, one of Oak Street Beach with the Hancock Center in the background, one of the city's Historic Water Tower, one of Buckingham Fountain in Grant Park, one looking up at Water Tower Place from ground level, one looking down on an Eisenhower Interstate Highway System cloverleaf from the Sears Tower's observation deck, and one—taken from the Goodyear Blimp, perhaps—of an "L" train speeding past Wrigley Field. All the while, the CGC logo appears at the bottom right of the screen. "What is this?" He leans forward and watches intently.

"I'm not sure." On the TV, the establishing shots fade to black and are replaced by a super that reads, THE WINDY CITY IS IN CRISIS. THOUSANDS ARE MISSING. The super fades and is replaced by a still of the Chicago Cultural Center's exterior, one of the Art Institute's Michigan Avenue lions, one of the Palmer House's ornate lobby, and one of Union Station's imposing Great Hall. Those images fade and another super appears that reads, DO NOT LOSE HOPE. IT IS ALWAYS DARKEST BEFORE THE DAWN. The super fades and is replaced by a time-lapse sequence of the sun rising above Lake Michigan. That clips dissolves into a repeat close-up of the American flag waving, which, in turn, fades to black and a pair of supers that read, STAY SAFE. THIS TOO SHALL PASS, and CHICAGO GENETICS CENTER—WE CARE.

"Give me a break," Bob remarks.

"Gag me with a spoon," Lori adds.

Disgusted, Bob grabs the remote and turns off the TV. "Now I'm *definitely* not hungry."

"You should still try to eat something."

"Later. Right now, uh, I think I'm gonna use the hot tub. It might do me some good."

"Okay." Lori gets up and grabs her purse.

"No no no, you don't have to leave. Hang out. Just . . . don't steal anything?"

"Ha ha, you got me." Lori jokingly raises her hands in surrender.

. . .

Bob tries the lobby payphone one last time. He deposits a quarter and dials his psychiatrist. After a few seconds of clicking, the call rings through to the therapist's answering machine: *"Hello, you've reached the office of Dr. Kirchner. If this is a life-threatening emergency, please hang up and dial 911. For all other issues, please contact me during my office hours, which are 8 a.m. to 3 p.m. Monday through Thursday and 9 a.m. to noon on Fridays, or leave a message after the beep."* BEEP!

Bob hangs up without leaving another message. "Damn," he says for the third time. He walks over to the pool room. He bypasses the pool itself and heads directly for the hot tub. He kicks off his shoes and strips to his tighty-whiteys. He returns to the pool and dips a single toe in the water. "Brrr!" He turns on the wall timer, starting the bubbles in the hot tub. He enters the tub and sits with his back to the wall. He exhales and closes his eyes in blissful relaxation.

2

Untold minutes pass and the bubbles have long since stopped when Lori enters. She sets a glass of water and a pair of towels on a chair beside the door. Bob perks up upon seeing her from afar. He perks up even more after she smiles and waves at him, and more still after she undresses to just a plain white bra and panties, surprisingly ordinary undergarments for someone so pretty. She glances in his direction and he quickly turns away, hoping she didn't catch him staring. She dives into the deep end and swims a single, back-and-forth lap before getting out. Bob can only manage a rear view, but likes what he sees. She wraps a towel around herself and carries the other towel and glass of water to Bob.

"Hey," he says.

"H-h-hey," she responds through chattery teeth. "I b-brought you some water."

"Thanks." He grabs the water and takes a sip. "Wouldn't wanna get light-headed. Cold, right?"

"F-f-freezing. Mind if I join you?"

"I'd like that. Um, can you get the timer first?"

"Uh, sure." Lori removes her towel and sets it down next to Bob's on the lounge chair closest to the hot tub. She makes her way to the timer, Bob once more enjoying the view as the bra and panties cling to her body and her nipples stand at attention through the thin, wet fabric. She realizes her nipples are hard and crosses her hands across her chest as she enters the hot tub and sits opposite Bob. "Much better."

"I'll bet." Bob takes another sip. They exchange smiles and sit in mutual silence.

Lori breaks the quietude after 30 long seconds. "I saved you the other Twinkie, some Slim Jims, a bag of popcorn, and a Mountain Dew. I know how much you love those."

"Hey, thanks."

"Oh, and there's a whole bag of powered donuts for the morning."

"I love those, too."

"How's your knee?"

"It's fine. I landed hard, but turns out it's just scraped." He flexes his leg so his knee emerges from the water, revealing little more than a superficial scratch.

"Good."

"Yeah." Behold, the uncomfortable silence. Finally, after a minute: "Hey Lori, I, um, I know should've said this earlier, but, um, I'm sorry about the thing at Vinnie's last week with Pete. That was so stupid."

"It's fine. I could tell you were as embarrassed as I was."

"Yeah, well your boyfriend almost kicked my ass the next day."

Lori sighs and shakes her head. "Josh is . . . Josh is Josh. One moment he can be really sweet, and the next he turns into this complete jerk. It's *sooo* infuriating."

Bob nods again. "It's sorta like that with Pete. I mean, he's not a jerk, but he's got this really strong personality, if you know what I mean. He and I have been friends since forever, but, uh, there've been days . . ."

"Do you think you'll see him again?"

"Well, if that Wesley guy goes back and forth from his office to the other location, maybe it's two-way for Mars travel, too. We still don't know much about the other side, but who knows? Maybe he'll escape. Maybe they'll *all* escape."

"I hope so."

"Anyway . . . I don't wanna talk about Pete, except to apologize for last Thursday. Tell me . . . tell me more about yourself. Not about you and Josh, or cheerleading, or stuff like that, but, you know, about *you*."

"Whadoya wanna know?"

"I dunno . . . just . . . stuff. Um . . . any other brothers or sisters besides the one in Michigan?"

"Minnesota."

"Minnesota. Sorry."

"It's fine. Just him."

"What's his name?"

"Charles, like his father. Everyone called him 'C.J.' growing up. It means . . ."

"Charles, Junior?"

"That's right."

"I'm a 'Junior' as well. What does he do?"

"He's a stockbroker. I don't know much about what that is."

"Didn't you take Econ with Mr. King?"

"Yeah, last semester, but it was my first class of the day and I was always so tired from cheer practice the night before. I totally didn't pay attention."

"In your defense, it *was* pretty boring."

"Totally."

"What does his wife do?"

"Mr. King's? How should I—"

"No, your brother's."

Lori playfully splashes Bob out of embarrassment. "She teaches kindergarten."

"Oh, fun!" He splashes her back.

"She's a great teacher, but she might take the fall semester off."

" 'Cause of the baby?"

"Yeah. I still think I'm too young to be an aunt, but I'm totally happy for her. She and C.J. just told everyone three weeks ago."

"I bet you'll make a great aunt."

"You're sweet."

"Do they know what they're having?"

"Not yet. They both want a boy, so we'll see."

"I dunno. Speaking as one, we can be trouble." Bob grits his teeth in jest.

"Don't I know it . . . What about you? Any brothers or sisters?

Bob shakes his head. "Only child."

Lori nods. "I knew that. Any pets?"

"No pets. I had a hamster once, but, uh, he got out of his cage one day and I never found him."

"Budweiser, right?"

"That's right. You remember!"

"Well, this isn't Mr. King's class."

"Much more interesting than Econ. How 'bout you? Any pets besides Molly?"

"Just her."

"She's awesome. I'll bet she misses you."

Lori smiles. "Daddy says she his other blond daughter."

"That's funny . . . What else . . . um . . . Whadoya like to do for fun?"

"What do I like to do for fun? Oh, I dunno . . . stuff . . . I like swimming, obviously. Um . . . Shopping, I guess . . .

cheerleading . . . choir . . . MTV . . . Vinnie's was always fun. What about you?"

Bob shrugs. "Yeah, I'm at Vinnie's a lot." He corrects himself. "*Was* at Vinnie's a lot. He was a good friend. Before . . ." He looks away. For the umpteenth time, what happened wasn't his fault, and although it seems like a thousand years in the past already, it still hurts.

"Yeah." Lori looks down. She dove in the water after Vinnie, but he died anyway. As such, she wants to carry some of Bob's burden.

"Pete and I went there all the time. I don't have a lot of other friends besides him and Vinnie. Or . . . didn't."

"Don't say that!"

"No no no, it's just . . . I-I don't fit in anywhere, really. I mean . . . I get good grades and all, but I'm not a brainiac so I don't hang out with that crowd, and I'm *definitely* not a jock or a stoner or a band geek. So where does that leave me?"

"That's okay. I don't have a lot of friends, either."

"Liar."

Lori looks at him with a coy smile that doth protest. "Bobby Wilkinson. You don't know me at all!"

Bob raises his arms above the water's surface as if to defend himself. "What?! You mean to tell me you're *not* the most popular girl in school?! Tiffany and Shauna and that other chick I see you with, uh, Amber What's-Her-Face? And the guys they go out with? Between them and Josh, you've got your whole Homecoming Court!"

"Well yeah, but, like, there's lots of students I *don't* hang out with, and a whole group of kids I hardly know at all. Like you."

Bob tilts his head. "Fair enough," he concedes. "But we're here now. Let's get to know each other." He immediately realizes how his words came across, and course corrects with, "Well, you know what I mean."

Lori smiles. "I know what you mean." After several seconds of silence: "Okay, so your mom died, right? Your real mom, I mean?"

Bob sighs. "Yeah, gosh, like, nine years ago."

"I'm so sorry. Can I ask what happened?"

"Yeah, she, um, she had leukemia."

"I think I had a cousin who had that. Not sure. I guess I don't know what leukemia is."

"So, it's cancer of the blood. Imagine, um . . . imagine being so tired you just lay on your back in bed, barely able to do more than lift your arms. *Then* imagine the chemo causes your hair to fall out and your teeth to turn black, and makes you so tired you basically wither away to nothing."

"That's awful. I had no idea."

Bob nods. "Well, some people do okay with it. I hope your cousin did. But, um, my mom was something of a hypochondriac, and she went quickly."

"I think my cousin beat it," Lori says. "Not sure. It was on mom's side of the family. I was young, and I don't know the whole story. I just remember growing up and mom saying, 'Well, let's have a prayer for Little Jessie.' So we would say the Lord's Prayer, which was sort of her remedy for everything, and from there I don't even know what happened. But we never got any phone calls saying Little Jessie had died."

"Wow, I didn't know you were so religious."

"I'm not. I mean, mom is—or can be—but she's not trying to convert anyone or anything. But yeah, that's the story of Little Jessie, who I guess beat blood cancer."

"It's a nasty disease. Is Little Jessie a boy or girl?"

"Well, that was years ago, so that would make him Grown Up Jessie now . . . and a boy . . . obviously."

"Grown Up Jessie doesn't live in Chicago, does he?"

"No. Michigan, I think. We used to go visit Mackinaw with some cousins when I was little. I *guess* it was the same cousins?

Not sure. But no relatives anywhere in Illinois, so I guess Grown Up Jessie is safe."

"I'm glad."

"Me too . . . Hey Bobby, I hope you're not upset that I asked about your mom. And again, I'm so sorry, even if it was a long time ago. Must be an awful way to die."

"Rain-Ra—I mean Lori—you have no idea. I remember once my dad was away in Washington, of course, and he had a neighbor drop me off at the hospital so I could visit my mom. I bought her flowers, her birthday was coming up and I thought she'd like 'em, but when I opened the door to her room, the nurses were helping her go to the bathroom. And not number one, either, if you know what I mean. I was horrified. I dropped the flowers on the floor and the petals went everywhere. I, um, I don't know who was more embarrassed, me or the nurses."

Lori puts a hand over her mouth, which is agape. "How awful!"

Bob smiles. "Yeah, but my mom was a good sport about it. Even though she was weak, she shooed away the nurses and asked me to give her a hug. That's just how she was." A single tear runs down his cheek despite the smile.

Lori scoots over beside him and offers him a hug. "Come here." He does as asked and buries his face in her chest, though not in a sexual way—and nor does she see it as such. She strokes his wet hair. "You were nine at the time?"

Bob looks up. "That's right." He composes himself, and scoots away from her so as not to send the wrong message or overstay his welcome.

"I'll bet it's hard to get over something like that at such a young age. Did they take you out of school?"

"Yeah, I was out of school for the rest of the year. Something like 2,000 people went to the funeral; even then my dad was connected. Some of my classmates went too, with their parents of course. So that was nice of them, I guess. My dad had already moved my grandma in to help around the house, and that first summer he hired a tutor to catch me up. I went back in the fall like nothing had happened. No one in school said anything at all or treated me any different, which was good. I can't help but think it's 'cause my dad was in politics and my mom was on the schoolboard, you know . . . before."

Lori nods, and Bob continues. "Eventually, though, it all changed. My dad met someone new—Gail—"

"Your stepmom?" Lori asks.

"Yep. They got married superfast . . . I don't even know where he found the time to date her . . . and they sent me off to therapy."

"What, like a shrink?"

"Like a shrink, exactly."

Lori is intrigued. "Did it help?"

"Not right away, but eventually. My first therapist, Dr. Remus, got me to see that yes, life can be unfair, and yes, it's okay to be upset about it, but it's how you bounce back that matters. Or something. Uh, she retired like four years ago, and I've been going to Dr. Kirchner ever since."

"Did you say 'Dr. *Kirchner?*' "

"That's right. His office is in Highland Park."

"Omigod, Bobby, I know him. He's in my parents' country club! He and daddy go golfing on Fridays sometimes!"

"Well, that explains his office hours," Bob surmises.

"He came to my Sweet 16."

"That's a bit creepy, isn't it?"

"Well, mom invited his daughter, Stacy, and he was her chaperone. Stacy's several years younger; I don't know her well. I didn't think much about it at the time, but now I'm pretty sure it was a sympathy invitation. I don't think she has many friends."

"Not many friends, just like you and me, right?"

Lori chuckles. "Not like me and you. She has, um, what's the term?"

"Down's syndrome?"

"Yeah, that."

"I could tell by the picture he has of her in his office."

"What's he like? I'm sure he's a good dad, but is he a good doctor, too?"

Bob shrugs. "He's a bit . . . Well, he picked up where Dr. Remus left, and now with him I, uh, just sort of talk about life as a teenager. He helped me get over my dad getting remarried so quickly, which I was mad about for *years*—even after all that time with Dr. Remus—and he helped me see that just because my dad and Gail travel so much and are gone more than they're here, that doesn't mean they hate me or anything. In fact, I started enjoying having the place to myself. So yeah, I guess he's a good doctor. And I only go every other week now."

"I'm glad it's helping. Mom asked if I wanted to go once I started getting my period, to talk about womanly things," Lori says, and adds a titter. "I was like, *mommm, ewww!* But . . . that's her way of dealing with those things."

"I'll bet she said a prayer," Bob jokes.

"Totally."

Bob smiles and stretches out in the hot tub. "Oh, this feels so good," he coos.

"And the company's good, too," Lori adds.

Bob turns red. "I think I've died and gone to heaven. What have I done to deserve such praises from the almighty Rain-Rain? Er, um, the almighty Lori?"

She smirks. "Why do you call me that?"

"Lor-*raine Rain*-smith. Hence . . . Rain-Rain."

Lori rolls her eyes. "You're silly."

"And good company, too," Bob points out, citing Lori's own words.

With an exasperated smile: "Don't push it." She splashes him again.

"I'll dial it back," Bob raises his arms again in surrender.

"But no, you're not bad company. No way Josh would be so level-headed over this whole thing. And Tiffany and those guys? Nuh-uh."

Bob makes it a point to maintain eye contact as he says, "For whatever it's worth, I hope your friends are okay. Including Josh. He's a lucky guy."

Lori's eyes glisten. "You're very sweet. And kinda cute, too."

Bob closes his mouth, puffs his cheeks in exaggeration, and submerges himself for a few seconds. He resurfaces to the sight and sound of Lori laughing. He opens his mouth as if to speak, but holds back. He tries again after a few beats. "So, um, I know I said I didn't wanna talk about Josh—and I really don't—but I *am* curious about one thing: Uh, you never said why you didn't go to prom with him. You obviously had second thoughts, 'cause you did show up in your dress that night, but, like . . . what happened?"

"We sort of broke up."

"What?!"

"He was trying to pressure me. I wasn't ready."

"Sorry, I didn't mean to pry. I just assumed . . . you know . . ."

"What, that he and I had *done it* before?"

Bob winces. "Sort of."

"Yeah, you and our whole senior class."

"Ouch."

"So . . . Josh is a great football player, but as for him and I and *that*, um, the moment just never felt right."

"Well, what's the right moment?" Lori smirks, so he elaborates, defensive: "No, I'm not trying to get you to go steady with me, but, like, we're just talking here. What would be the right moment?"

"Something special. Not fake romantic with tuxedoes and high heels like prom, but something . . . real. Seeing a person in the moment, for who they really are. I *liked* Josh, and thought for a minute maybe I loved him, you know, but . . . he's never struggled for anything in his life. I guess I haven't either, but with Josh, it wasn't the same. For example, he could talk for hours about football, but there wasn't much there otherwise."

Bob nods. "Makes sense."

"Does it?"

"Sure. This is good stuff. Wish I had a notepad to mark it all down."

"Oh, stop!" Lori blushes and splashes him again.

"I'm kidding! I'm kidding!" Bob splashes her back.

"What about you, Bobby? No one special in your life?"

"Just Pete." Pete's abduction is a delicate matter, but Bob is, mercifully, able to laugh. Lori joins him.

"I do think it's funny whenever he calls you 'Roberto.' "

"I hate it, but um, he's nothing if not persistent."

"Okay, so he calls you 'Roberto' and you call me 'Rain-Rain.' I've been calling you 'Bobby.' Is that okay?"

"Well, as my dad used to say when I was younger, 'You can call me anything you want, just don't call me late for dinner.' "

Lori giggles. "Omigod, daddy says the same thing."

"It's in the stars, Rain-Rain. We're fated to be together."

The timer ends and the bubbles stop.

"Perhaps," Lori compromises, "But the only thing we're fated for right now is to be without bubbles."

"Allow me, madam." Bob stands up and finds himself light-headed. "Oooh, need more water." He takes another sip before offering the glass to Lori. She shakes her head so he takes the final sip. He exits the hot tub on steadier feet and moseys to the timer. "Forgive the image of me Fruit of the Looms clinging so delicately to me virgin bottom, milady," he says, tongue firmly in cheek and with a piss-poor British accent.

"It's a lovely virgin bottom," Lori replies.

"Why thank you, mada—"

The power goes out.

"Uh-oh," Bob says from pitch black darkness. Five seconds later, emergency floodlights illuminate and there is once again light, though more subdued than before.

"I guess that's it." Lori gets up.

"Yeah, with no power this water'll turn cold quick." Bob grabs a towel for himself and hands the other one to Lori. Ever the gentlemen, he turns away as she emerges from the pool, nipples hard and pubis pronounced through near-sheer undergarments.

Lori wraps the towel around her midsection and kisses Bob on the side of his neck while he is looking away. His shoulders clench and goosebumps materialize. "Like I said Bobby, you're very sweet," Lori begins, "but don't think I'm unaware you could see every inch of me reflected in the window anyway."

"W-what?" Bob protests, but Lori is already headed for her room. He runs after her. They run into the desk clerk in the hall, who bears candles and matches.

"Hey, I brought you these in case the power doesn't come back on," he says.

"Thanks," Lori says. She takes two candles and a book of matches. Bob, whose head is in the stars, takes the other two candles and the remaining matchbook without saying a word.

"Have a good night." The clerk beats feet.

"You too." Lori keys into her room. Bob lingers in the hall-way, one hand to the nape of his neck, where Lori kissed him.

"Goodnight, Bobby." She closes her door behind her.

"What? Uh, yeah, goodnight," he responds, dreamlike, think-ing he may never wash his neck again.

# Chapter 5

1

It's almost fully dark as Susie and company finish shelter preparations against the nighttime cold from inside the cave. Josh, Rose, and Leonard struggle to roll a second boulder across the entrance to further block the wind. Susie helps as well; Rose tells her not to but as always, she insists. Once the boulder is in place, Leonard liberally squirts lighter fluid between the gap between it and the entrance while Josh and Rose look on. "What's that for?" Josh asks.

"Keeps the beaters out. They hate the scent," Leonard replies.

"Don't finish it, *pendejo,*" Rose interjects. "We still have to build a fire."

"*Por supuesto,*" Leonard replies, earning a raised eyebrow from Rose. *Of course.*

"*Español, muy bien.*"

"That's all I know."

Pete and Samara tend to Underwood. Dixon massages his knee; the cold stiffens the joint and leaves him feeling guilty he can't be of more use. García prepares the scraps he managed to recover, piling the driest pieces of kindling inside the fire ring. Someone has camped here before.

"I'm surprised you found natural wood," Hawkins observes. "Until this afternoon in the grove, I didn't think trees even grew here."

"Yeah, that canyon is a treasure trove," García says. "Aside from that, though, there aren't many trees. The ones that do exist tend to grow near the river. Most of the wood used for building is synthetic. These I plucked from the cliff face above us on our climb out earlier."

"I didn't even notice. I was . . . preoccupied." He glances over his shoulder at Underwood, whose profuse sweating through the nighttime chill puts him at risk of pneumonia.

Hawkins continues after a beat. "I have a question."

"What is it?"

"More of a curiosity than a question. Tell me about the resources we *do* have. On this planet, I mean."

"What would you like to know?"

"Well, for starters, did you bring all that stuff with you from Earth? Or rather, did your ancestors?"

"The latter. They were incredibly resourceful; We were taught in school that one out of every three settlers had a science background."

"I *hated* science class," Josh interrupts. Does his use of the past tense suggest he's resigned himself to never going back to finish his senior year? "Got to dissect a frog once. That was cool, I guess. But once they started talking about DNA molecules, I tuned out and started looking at my watch."

"What's a frog?" Susie asks as she checks on the wounded Underwood. He is asleep, his breath raspy and visible in the chilly air.

"A green amphibian, hops on all fours, lives in the woods."

"How do they taste?"

"I dunno, that's gross!"

"From all the stories I've heard, it sounds like there were a lot of wasted resources where you come from. I wonder if that's why Earth was destroyed?"

Josh runs his hands through his hair. "You're talking about stuff that hasn't happened yet, and you're using the past tense. It's so confusing!"

"I'm sorry," Susie replies. Never one to stop and rest, she goes from moving giant boulders one moment to tending to the wounded the next. She shoos Pete away and changes Underwood's dressing. "I forget sometimes that even though we're all humans, we're worlds apart."

"It's okay. It's different here, but not so horrible, I guess. Just cold." Josh rubs his hands together. He and his fellow abductees make nervous chit-chat, fighting the cold but never forgetting the elephant in the room (cave) that is Underwood.

"You ain't seen nothing yet, Loverboy," Dixon says. He squats by the fire ring and douses the wood García gathered with lighter fluid from a can Leonard tosses his way. He strikes a match along his boot and sets the kindling ablaze. The cave illuminates, the shadows of its inhabitants dancing on the walls to the rhythm of the flames. "Wait until 0400," he continues. "Your teeth'll chatter so hard you'll think they're gonna crack. It's like walking across the Michigan Avenue Bridge in January."

Pete, who has been mopping Underwood's brow, looks up at Dixon. "You're from Chicago, too?"

"Pretty much all of us are, kid. Didn't you know that?"

"No." Pete shakes his head. "I knew about Josh, obviously, and Underwood here and a few others back at the barracks. But everyone?!" He sighs, then continues. "I guess it makes sense."

"Chitown. What a shithole!"

"You think so? I love the—"

"Hey Dimkowski," Josh says, "do you remember sophomore year, when we had gym first period and Coach Bolzer made us run laps in the cold?"

A chill passes through Pete's body at the thought, and he shivers. "I'd forgotten that until you said something. P.E. Not my finest hour."

Josh smiles nostalgically, but the smile fades quickly. For one thing, he knows they are lucky to have left the grove alive, and supposes now is not the time to wax nostalgic. For another thing, Coach Bolzer is dead, having been crushed by a falling Sauron X. Leonard sifts through his pack for an oxygenator. The flames run low—the thin oxygen dissipates as the fire consumes it—and their gabbing uses more oxygen as well. He takes a hit of $O_2$, then toggles the directional switch on the oxygenator and aims it toward the dying fire. The flames instantly brighten, and everyone feels noticeably warmer. Josh warms his hands over the flames, and Pete joins him to do the same.

Leonard, always the practical one, addresses the group. "It's going to turn very cold as the hours go by. We may start coughing. With as many of us as there are, it's vital we ration our $O_2$. Underwood will need his own, and we'll need at least one canister to stoke the fire. Beyond that, we may have to buddy up and sleep in close quarters."

"Good call," Susie says. Leonard tosses her another oxygenator, which she carefully places in the crook of Underwood's arm, positioning his hand onto his chest so that when he wakes up, he'll merely have to raise his head for easy access. She motions for Samara to take over. Samara puts the oxygenator to Underwood's lips to test his wakefulness. His eyes remain closed but his chest rises and falls. His breathing sounds better; the natural instinct of his lungs is to grab whatever oxygen they can.

"Let's get some nutrients in us," Susie suggests. "There's jerky and . . . can someone pass out the gourds? One per person, we can use the vitamin C. After we eat, let's couple up. One canister per couple. You'll want to sleep close like Leonard said; use each other's body heat to keep warm. It's looking to be a long night."

"Who wants to stay with Underwood?" Samara asks.

"Excellent query, Sam. I recommend we move him closer to the fire, feet first. Keep his legs warm and dry. Whoever tends to Underwood gets to be closer as well. My ask is that this person also tends to the fire. That should keep you nice and warm. Any takers?"

"I can do it," Pete volunteers.

"You sure? I know you're tired of hearing this, but you haven't been with us long, and you don't weigh but 60 kilos."

Pete doesn't get the pounds-to-kilograms reference, but some of the others do, and there are a few titters. "I can do it. Just like I could climb that mountain earlier. Besides, I'm freezing. Closer to the fire sounds good if you ask me."

"Thank you, Pete."

2

It's full dark. The wind howls outside the cave as the rebels sleep . . . some better than others. Several of them cough, and almost all of them will develop sore throats over the coming days. The skinniest among them will wake up with pounding headaches as well.

Pete's sleep is broken—as it turns out, he isn't as acclimatized as he thought. He checks on Underwood several times, feeding him oxygen and stoking the fire with regularity. Underwood suffers from a debilitating coughing spell in the middle of the night, but Pete gives him an extra-generous hit of $O_2$ and the cough eventually stabilizes. Someone snores, and Pete is unsure who it is.

The coupling—Dixon and Rose, Susie and Josh, García and Hawkins, Leonard and Samara, Pete and Underwood—is practical, not romantic, but for Susie, a tough fighter whose only Achilles' heel is her longing for a meaningful connection, tonight represents a chance to get close to Josh. They spoon beneath a blanket, wearing hats and gloves as they sleep. Susie lays with her chest pressed into Josh's back and listens to him breathe. He, too, has a coughing fit, but it only lasts a few seconds. Susie responds by learning into him and kissing his cheek, now adorned with stubble. She can't believe she kissed him; it happened before she knew she was doing it.

Josh mumbles something incoherent, and the only thing she can whisper in return is, "Sorry."

He rolls onto his side. "What happened?" he whispers, sleepily. "What time is it?"

"Still dark. You okay?"

"Yeah. Had a nightmare, I think. Thirsty, too."

"Come here." She sits up and grabs his hand.

"What? Where?"

"Just come here." She removes a flashlight from her pack and slings the pack over one shoulder.

"Should I?" Josh motions for the blanket. She nods.

She leads him by hand to the back of the cave. The ceiling is lower and the natural sandstone wall contours to offer a bit of privacy away from the others. She retrieves a canteen from her pack and takes a small sip. She offers it Josh, who takes a much bigger swig. "Ahhh," he says, without thinking.

The sound echoes and he covers his mouth to stifle a snicker. Susie sets the flashlight lantern on the floor, its retractable legs extended and its light shining onto the roof of the cave. She lays the blanket beside her pack and invites Josh to do the same. Away from the fire, his hands shake even though he has gloves on. Susie rifles through a side pocket on her pack and removes palm warmers similar to Hot Hands. Without speaking, she inserts one warmer apiece into each glove. The warmers activate upon contact, heat beginning to course through them. She places a hand on Josh's cheek so he gets the idea, then gives him a pair of warmers to do the same. He nods and inserts one into each glove.

Josh helps himself to more water while Susie positions the standing flashlight lantern so it shines in his direction, the intensity set on low, the soft light flattering. He offers her the canteen, which she sets aside before taking his hand in hers again. Her fingertips rest against the warmth of his palm insert, and vice-versa. He doesn't recoil from the tenderness of the moment, and she takes that as a sign. She leans forward, head tilted sideways as she comes in for a kiss. He tilts his head and leans forward to receive her kiss, as well as the one that comes after. The initial kiss lasts for five seconds—a perfect first kiss, exploratory yet chaste. The second kiss lasts for twice as long, and is more probing in nature.

Their lips part and Josh looks at her. *Is this actually gonna happen?* his body language suggests. *Yes, if you live in the moment,* hers confirms. They scoot toward each other on the blanket and remove their pants with no small amount of difficulty, courtesy of fat fingers and cold hands. Josh, who has spent too much time around his fellow jocks and who has always assumed it's the guy who leads, is taken aback (but only for a moment) when Susie climbs on top of him. It's too cold for them to doff their tops, but not too cold for coitus. Josh clenches his jaw in concentration, hoping to make a good impression but fearing he won't fit. Susie guides him in with ease. There is some initial awkwardness as their movements are not quite in sync. Finally, Susie grabs his hands in hers, as if to seal the bond, and they mesh.

A few minutes pass. They have found their cadence and Susie is nearing climax when Josh gets cold feet. "I'm sorry," he whispers, and lets go of her hands. "I can't do this."

"No, Josh, don't . . . stop . . . Josh?"

"I'm sorry." He pulls back. "I just . . . I just can't."

"I . . . I understand." They quickly dress, shivers setting in within seconds. Susie offers him more water from her canteen, but he shakes his head. They return to their original spot near the fire, and she turns off the flashlight as soon as they leave the privacy curtain of the natural cave wall. Josh hurriedly throws down the blanket and snuggles beneath his half. Susie snuggles beneath hers.

"You should get in close to me like before," he whispers. "Nothing sexual; we need to keep each other warm."

"Okay." They spoon again, but when he coughs this time, she doesn't kiss his cheek.

Someone stirs. It's Pete. He knows what they did, and while he admits he'd probably do the same if the opportunity arose, he wonders what Lori would think. *Not that I'm likely to ever see her again,* he reminds himself.

Susie has had many partners, of both sexes. Looking back on this moment years from now, she'll remember that Josh wasn't her best lover, not because it was his first time but because it was dark and cold and because just a few hours before, they watched in horror as their dying colleague, Underwood, had his foot bitten off by a belly beater. Still and all—and knowing what will happen when they attack the time chamber—she has no regrets.

## 3

As was the case during her final morning with her previous lover, Diego, Susie find herself the last person to wake up. The boulders have been rolled away from the entrance. Several FCB rebels snack on gourds. Josh sits on the edge of the blanket, lacing his boots. "Morning," he says, curt and not wanting to talk about their midnight rendezvous.

"Good morning." She immediately picks up on his wavelength, and it's back to business as usual. "How's Underwood?"

"He's gone. Dimkowski said he started retching just before sunrise. Gave him some water. That just made it worse, and he was a goner by the time I woke up."

"This is the life we lead." Susie hangs her head and keeps an emotional distance.

Josh turns to Pete, who continues tending to the body. "You okay?"

Pete shakes his head. "No. I don't wanna go out the way he did."

Josh, in a failed attempt at empathy: "I saw Coach Bolzer get killed."

"Don't tell me that."

"Curtis Jackson, too."

"I said, 'Don't tell me that!' "

"Enough!" Everyone jumps at the sound of Dixon's voice. He lowers his voice before continuing. "Enough. We're all sorry about Underwood. Bad day yesterday, but we did find the grove, so the trip isn't a total loss."

"Dixon's right," Susie says, slipping back into her natural leadership role. "Now let's beat feet before the Saurons resume their patrols."

Pete points to the corpse. "Wait a minute. What do we do with his body? We can't carry it all the way back, can we?"

"We burn it."

Pete's blood runs cold at the thought. *First the bodies at the Pit, now Underwood,* he thinks. "Are you serious?"

"We burn it. Right where it lays. Then we go back."

"What about his family?"

Dixon puts a hand on Pete's shoulder and speaks. "He came from Chicago, kid, same as us. Who knows when he was snatched? Who knows if he has a family?"

"What are you asking me for?!" Pete barks. "All I knew is he played baseball!"

"It's not a question, it's a statement. Those of us here today, most of us have known each other for a while. Some people are newer. Like you. Like Hawkins. Like him." Dixon points to Underwood's corpse, then continues. "On New Earth, the one thing most of us have in common, at least among this group, is that courtesy of our Journeys, we're all orphans by default. With no one here to miss us when we're gone."

Pete looks down, resignedly. "Someone help me with his body." Hawkins steps forward and together they drag Underwood's body over the cooling ash of the fire pit.

Dixon is about to douse Underwood with lighter fluid when Leonard interrupts. "Let's get what we need off him, first."

Pete steps back, mortified, as Dixon, Rose, and Leonard remove the gloves, ammo belt, and hat from Underwood's corpse. Even Josh partakes—he removes the tactical knife and scabbard from the late ballplayer's person.

That unpleasantness over with, Dixon douses the corpse with lighter fluid. He removes a match and is about to strike it against his boot when Pete's humanity intervenes. "Can someone say a few words at least?" he pleads.

The others avoid eye contact with Pete until Susie steps forward to break the uncomfortable silence. "I'll say something, since you all turn to me for direction whenever the Old Man's not around." She clears her throat. "Underwood. We barely knew ye, but we salute ye. As it often is in war—or in this case, in the pursuit of forward progress—the sacrifices of some make the future possible for others. None of us here today know what exists in the world beyond this one, but if you had a family back home, I hope you can look down on them from above and shine your light upon them. If your family has passed on, as is the case for so many of us here today, I hope you are with them now, or will be soon. Underwood, we barely knew ye, but we salute ye. Godspeed."

"Godspeed," the others mumble. Dixon strikes a match that sets Underwood's corpse ablaze. The group watches for a minute, and some of them warm their hands over the fire. Not Pete, though.

One by one, they head out. "Let's make haste," Susie says. "No resting until we're past the turnoff for the Pit." She and Josh turn to leave. Pete lingers behind.

"Let's go, Dimkowski," Josh says.

Pete goes off on his high school nemesis. "Why are you such a dick, Josh?!"

"What're you talking about?"

"You know what I'm talking about. You were a dick in high school and you're a dick here today!"

"Hey, I wasn't the one air-humping Lori at Vinnie's."

"Are you still mad about that?! It was a joke! It was at Bob's expense more than anyone else's!"

Josh extends an olive branch ... sort of. "Look, forget it, okay? That thing in the shower, I overreacted. Besides, Coach Bolzer, who intervened? I told you he's dead, right?"

"Yeah, like not even five minutes ago."

"Seeing that changes a person."

"No shit. Did you know Vinnie—arcade Vinnie, where I embarrassed your girlfriend—did you know he's dead, too?"

Josh takes a step back. "No man, I didn't. That sucks. Vinnie was cool."

"Did you know I saw it happen?"

"No."

"Did you know your girlfriend tried to save his life?"

"Lori?!"

"Certainly not Susie. This happened in the city!"

"Hey man, Susie's *not* my girlfriend."

Susie hears this and leaves the cave. *I could be, though,* she reasons.

"It didn't look that way last night," Pete remarks.

"Alright you Polack, that was uncalled for!"

Pete nods and raises his hands in surrender. "Sorry, low blow. I shouldn't assume anything."

"Damn right you shouldn't! Besides, Lori dumped me."

"Believe it or not, I didn't jump to any conclusions about what happened between you two."

"Chill out, I believe it."

"Look, however things ended, you were a lucky guy. She's a stone fox. Well, obviously *I* feel that way. I mean, the thing at Vinnie's . . ."

"Do me a favor and stop mentioning it. But yeah, she's a righteous babe. Can't believe I messed that up. I put too much pressure on her."

Pete nods. "At least she didn't get sent here like the rest of us. As for you and me, I didn't mean to blow my top. It's just . . . you took shit off his dead body, and that was majorly uncool."

"We're at war, Dimkowski. We need all the supplies we can get. Besides, it was just his knife."

"I know. And when we put it that way, I suppose you're right. Can we go now?"

Josh turns around. Except for him, Pete, and a burning corpse, the cave is otherwise empty. "Shit, where'd everyone go?" Pete shrugs. They leave. After a few paces, Josh adds, "By the way, if we ever get out of here and make it home, not a word of this to Lori. Or I really will beat your ass."

"Such a dick," Pete says again, but does so in a wink-wink manner that suggests he and Josh are cool again. The group makes their return trek to Zone Omega without further incident. Susie walks alongside Josh for most of the trip, but says nothing.

4

Unlike Susie and Diego's close call the night of their two-person gourd hunt, plenty of daylight remains when the FCB rebels return to Zone Omega this time. They pass Gwendolyn's tailor shop. She waves as they pass and Susie returns the gesture, though no other pleasantries are exchanged. Gwendolyn is happy to see Susie alive and with friends. She was wary of Reynolds when he came by to have officer stripes sewn onto his uniform, but after hearing news of the upcoming peace talks, she decides her fears must've been for naught.

Susie and company enter the barracks. Pete stop to chit-chat with Johnny and Eric, who share sentry detail inside the main entrance. Pete offers them each a gourd while Josh shows off the contents of his pack to Mississippi-born Keith, whom he meets on the landing. The southerner carries coffee to the sentries, and has temporarily set his crutches aside so he can try his luck with the stairs. The cast over his broken leg is now fully adorned with signatures.

Downstairs, René teaches yoga in the commissary to the rebels who stayed behind, women and men both. Dana is one such student. She sits, cross-legged, each foot resting on the opposite thigh in the Lotus position. She sees the expedition members enter and throws a wave in Pete's direction.

Josh is the last person to enter the commissary. He is immediately taken aback when one of René's yoga students calls his name. That student, to his surprise, is Brandon Sayers, wide receiver on the Goodman High varsity football team. "Brewer!" Brandon exclaims.

"Sayers! How long have you been here?"

"As long as you have, I guess. But to this place? Got here yesterday. Kinda dumpy, isn't it?"

"Eh, it's not so bad."

"Yeah, but, like, where're all the chicks?"

"Hey!" Dana and René remark, simultaneously.

"No, I mean from school. Only one I saw was Shauna. Where're Tiffany and them?"

"No idea. I saw Curtis get killed—"

"Aw, man!"

"—but other than Dorkus Malorkus there"—he points to Joseph "Munch" Muenchen, a nerdy, taciturn Goodman High classmate, currently sitting in the back row of René's yoga class—"the only dude from our class I know is Dimkowski."

"Hey Brandon," Pete says. He sets his pack on a folding chair and sneaks a quick hit of supplemental, low-flow oxygen from the inch-thick tubing pumped into the room. "Want a gourd?"

"How 'bout your lunch money instead?"

"Seriously, don't." Pete's too tired for one of his usual wise-cracks. He hurls a gourd from his pack at Brandon.

Brandon catches the gourd one-handed. He blows on his fingers, which sting from the catch. "That was a joke, you little dipshit. Man, that hurt!"

"Stop it, you guys," Josh says. His classmates promptly fall in line. Not surprisingly, this doesn't escape Susie's notice. When Josh talks, people listen.

"Take five, everyone," René says to her yoga students. "Try to clear your heads of bad vibes." She turns to Leonard. "How'd it go?"

He motions her forward and whispers, "Let's go the galley."

Susie introduces herself to Brandon and asks how he first learned of the FCB's existence. He explains that he and five others from his dorm were custom-picked based on their rapid acclimatization to join an understaffed work crew laying a new road beyond the southern outskirts of Zone Omega, and that they were being bussed to the new jobsite when a fellow worker, perhaps unaware of the upcoming peace talks or perhaps with his own agenda, attacked the soldiers in their transport shuttle. The lone wolf's efforts were all for naught, as his solo rebellion ended with a hole being blasted into his chest by one of Ross's Loyalists. He fell overboard and his sweeping arm movements took Brandon with him. The squad leader radioed that the incident was under control and advised the shuttle driver not to stop.

Brandon was tended to by a local merchant, who offered gauze for Brandon's scraped elbow and suggested he consider joining the FCB if he doesn't fancy laboring at gunpoint. "Last I heard, they're two blocks down on the left. The building won't look like much, but just knock on the door—what's left of it, anyway—and someone should assist." As an afterthought, restauranteur Fred LaChance added, "Don't ask me how I know that, and don't tell anyone that I do."

"You look like you can take care of yourself," Susie says once Brandon finishes telling his story. "If you're willing to work hard and if Josh vouches for you, I'm happy to welcome you to the team."

"Uh, I vouch," Josh says.

Susie turns to Pete. "Pete, I saw you and Brandon arguing a moment ago. We're not going to have any problems, are we?"

"I'm cool if he's cool," Pete replies. "Besides, we can't exactly send him back, can we?"

"I suppose not. Brandon, you're in."

"Radical," Brandon says.

5

Once Leonard and René are in the relative privacy of the makeshift kitchen, he opens his pack to reveal his haul "Check this out."

"Those are the biggest gourds I've ever seen!" she remarks.

"Try one! We have more than we know what to do with."

René indulges. Juice runs down both sides of her chin after her first, vitamin-rich bite. "This is delicious." Dixon and Hawkins enter and load their gourds into bowls, which they then store in the cooler. René notices dried blood on Hawkins's clothing. "What happened? Did we lose someone?"

"Underwood. One of the new guys," Leonard says.

René closes her eyes. "What happened?"

"Beater. Got him by the ankle. He bled out."

"*Merde.*"

Leonard nods. "We also found Ross's crematorium. It was horrible."

"Awful," Samara adds as she enters the galley. She unloads gourds from her pack and pilfers one for herself.

"What are we going to do about it?" René asks.

Susie and Rose enter the galley in time to hear René's query. "I plan on adding it to the peace talks agenda," Susie says. "No one should spend eternity in that horrible place." She places a comforting hand on René's shoulder with one hand and unpacks gourds with the other. René nods and helps unpack the fruit. Susie once more uses her pinky nail to peel back the skin of a gourd before taking a juicy bite.

"If Reynolds tries anything on the bridge, don't say I didn't warn you, *mujer*," Rose cautions.

Alas, Rose's warning falls on deaf ears, and it is at everyone's peril.

## 6

Susie calls a meeting with FCB leadership the next afternoon. Before discussing the main topic, the plan for the following day's planned peace talks, she asks whether it's time to change barracks locations again, considering that a perfect stranger—Brandon—found it on his own. They agree to wait and see how the peace talks work out, but to be extra diligent when heading to the surface in the meantime. Leonard says he's happy to start moving basic provisions to the new location "just in case," and says he won't turn down anyone who wants to help.

The peace talks plan: Dixon and García will accompany Reynolds and his men, who will, in turn, escort Susie from the Century Bridge to the hall. Susie is to be unarmed at the chancellor's request, but according to the agreed-upon terms, so, too, is Reynolds. Dixon and García will be armed, and one of them will wait outside the meeting room alongside one of Reynolds's men from the bridge. The other escorts from each party will double as witnesses to the peace talks. Rose and Josh, meanwhile, will act as lookouts and snipers from afar, keeping an eye out for Saurons "and anything else." Josh's participation is heartily endorsed by Susie, who knows what a good shot he is, even though he has yet to prove himself in actual battle.

Leonard, René, Samara, Hawkins, and Pete all offer to tag along, but Susie insists they help the new arrivals acclimatize and otherwise stay behind in case something goes wrong.

"Do you think something will go wrong?" Josh asks her.

"Not sure. Reynolds's remorse seems genuine. And I know what a hold Ross's rhetoric can have on a person. But that's why I want you and Rose on lookout and two trained fighters with Reynolds and I." She turns to Dixon and García. "Dixon,

I've seen you in action. García, I know you can fight. If Barstow trained you, you'll be good under pressure. Besides . . ."

"I'm expendable," García concedes.

"Something like that." Making tough decisions is the least favorite part of Susie's job. "You've acquitted yourself nicely so far. I haven't always given as fair a shake to Ross's men in the past. I believed you when you said driving that shuttle was just a job. But yes, compared to everyone else at the table here, you are the most . . . *expendable*. An unfortunate word, but there you have it."

"I can see your point." Nevertheless, he is disheartened.

"As such, if you decide you don't want any part of this, I wouldn't think badly of you."

García sighs. "You're the bravest person I've ever met. It'll be an honor to escort you."

Susie kneels so as to look him in the eyes from where he sits. "Thank you. For what it's worth, I hope we *can* trust Reynolds. I hope the chancellor is a man of his word, and I hope he really is ready to work toward a common solution."

"I've never met him, Officer Walker, but I hope so, too."

"García, it's not 'Officer Walker.' I'm a fighter, sure, but I'm just a human being, same as you and everyone else here. It's 'Susie.' "

"Force of habit . . . Susie."

She rises and addresses the group. "Let's rest up before dinner. Tomorrow's an important day."

"What're we having?" Pete asks. "Headache's gone and I'm starving."

"That's a question for our culinarian. What do we have, René?"

René beams. "On tonight's menu, we have a choice between chicken and . . . chicken."

"I'll have the chicken," Pete replies, and everyone smiles . . . except Susie. As usual, she has the weight of the world on her shoulders.

The weight of New Earth, that is.

7

The nine resistance members who returned from the Great Gourd Expedition sleep better tonight than they did in the cave. No one makes mention of the Pit, nor of what befell poor Underwood. Those tenured rebels who stayed behind, René and Keith among them, helped the newer arrivals acclimate to the thinner air via hydration, yoga, and basic calisthenics. Of the newest members, Johnny and Eric had the easiest time settling in, and they cheered on Shauna, Barbara, and Dana, all three of whom finally overcame the illnesses or post-partum issues that plagued them after their Journeys.

Several FCB members—new and tenured alike—battle headaches and other maladies. A few suffer from nausea. Those who have been around longer—Earth-born Dixon and Rose and Mars-born Susie and García, to name just four—appreciate nesting environs warmer than what they experienced last night in the cave. The low-flow oxygen that circulates via tubing is like a breath of fresh air compared to what they endured in the rocky cavern that now serves as Underwood's ashy grave.

The cots creak as the rebels stir, or roll over, or cough—their sore throats have arrived. Susie sleeps unusually deep, but her dreams, as is often the case, are the stuff of nightmares.

*Little Abigail walks with Susie and Jasmine as they explore a crater. The three females hold hands, Susie in the middle, Jasmine on the right, Abigail on the left. The young girl, who seldom speaks, hugs her Benny the Beater stuffed animal, girl and toy equally dirty. They stop to tie Abigail's shoe, a challenge as Susie needs both hands for the task. She lets go of Abigail's hand, and the girl panics and clutches the cuff of Susie's pantleg. "Sweetheart, it's okay . . . There, see?" Abigail nods and immediately unclenches her tiny fingers from the pantleg in favor of Susie's hand.*

*Jasmine, Susie's lover before Diego, has hair as red as Martian cliffs in the setting sun, freckles that bring out the green in her eyes, and a smile to melt even the coldest heart. "C'mon, there's a great view of the river up ahead, just over that rise," Jasmine says. "I've wanted to kiss you there since we first met."*

*"Sounds nice," Susie replies. She looks at her inamorata with something that almost resembles a smile. Jasmine is the opposite of Susie. Feminine rather than tomboyish, fair-haired and pale instead of brunette and olive-skinned. Not much of a fighter, perhaps, but that's okay. Susie is only too happy to protect Jasmine, just as she is happy to protect young Abigail, who continues to hold her hand while they search for wildflowers. The purple flowers, which grow only on the sunniest of slopes, have an extract in their petals that cures myopia. For Abigail, picking flowers is a game. For Jasmine, it's a date. For Susie, it's a duty.*

*Susie heads in Jasmine's direction, but Abigail tugs on her arm. "Wait," the child says, her voice soft and inquisitive.*

*"I'll meet you over there," Susie tells Jasmine, who blows her a kiss and ambles toward the vista point.*

*The girl points to a small collection of flowers. "What is it?" Susie asks.*

*"Pretty," Abigail says. That's it—never more than one or two words at a time.*

*"Great find," Susie says. "So pretty indeed." She squats beside the flowers while Abigail sniffs them. She sets Benny on the ground and gathers flowers with her left hand, never letting go of Susie's left hand with her right. She hands Susie a few flowers*

*at a time. Susie grabs them with her right hand and makes a show of sniffing them. Abigail smiles.*

*"Look out!" Susie hears Jasmine shout from some distance away. She glances in the direction of Jasmine's voice and sees her lover cowering behind a boulder and pointing at something. Susie looks up and sees an enhanced Sauron X targeting her and Abigail.*

*"C'mon, let's go!" Susie yanks Abigail's arm in urgency. The girl's eyes grow wide; she looks first at her guardian and then at Benny. She runs toward the stuffed animal, dragging Susie with her. "No time, Abigail!" Susie yells.*

*It's too late. The Sauron fires, and—*

"Susie, are you okay?! Susie!"

Josh's voice. Susie opens her eyes. Josh, awakened from his own slumber two cots down from hers, stands overhead, flashlight in hand. She is as white as a ghost, her hair a tousled mess. "What happened?" she asks, awake but disoriented.

"You were screaming." Josh shines the light around the room. All eyes are on her.

"Must've had a nightmare," Susie responds. She reaches over the side of the cot and retrieves her canteen, from which she takes a healthy swig.

"What was it about?" Rose asks.

"It's already fading." Susie shrugs and preemptively wipes her face of any potential tears.

"You scared us, *mujer.*"

"Sorry. Go back to bed."

"Yeah right," Hawkins remarks through yawns. "That was scarier than Underwood screaming."

"Well, *try* to sleep at least. Tomorrow's an important day. I want all of us on our toes."

"And you?"

"I'll be fine."

A bold statement. Truth is, Susie will be anything but fine. Not from lack of sleep, though. From something—or someone—much, much worse.

His name is Donovan Barstow.

8

Unlike the self-made Ross or the opportunistic Reynolds, Barstow was born bad. Donovan Eugene Barstow was the only son of a buffet server at an upscale, all-you-can-eat cafeteria that catered to Loyalist officers and other Zone Alpha VIPs. His mother, Joyce, worked long hours and basically left her son to raise himself, so he became quite the juvenile delinquent. His voice broke when he was just 11; younger kids and numerous teachers cowered in his presence.

Barstow didn't meet his father until his late teens—one week before he killed the man. Joyce had a weakness for what she called "strong men" but who were little more than abusive louses. His father fell into that category, and when the man reentered Joyce's life 16 years after walking out on her while she was pregnant, Barstow told him in so many words he wasn't welcome. But some lessons are learned the hard way, and the prick refused to leave. Only a few days passed before he began using Joyce as a punching bag. Barstow returned the favor, beating him to death. Joyce's oblivious reply? "You got blood on the carpet!" Barstow enlisted in Ross's Loyalist Army the next day and rose quickly through the ranks.

He Journeyed to Chicago with Ross during the chancellor's first exploratory mission, where their contact, one Wesley Arendt, arranged a tour of the recently-completed CGC-Meigs operations center and of the Hancock administrative headquarters. (Wesley was sure to hold the meeting in mid-January, when the bitter temperatures would mislead his interstellar partners in terms of how lovely the city can be during warmer months.)

The chancellor, who seldom left the CCC complex, caught pneumonia and spent most of the trip in his hotel room. Barstow explored the city on his own; one of Wesley's security guards, Squiggy's cousin Rich, lent him a winter coat, but Barstow found the cold invigorating and preferred to wrap his cloak around himself for warmth. The concierge asked if he wanted tickets to a show at the Chicago Theatre, but Barstow's tastes were for something more primal. His manhood still intact at the time of his visit, he solicited a prostitute that evening and took her to a love motel. When she pulled a knife and tried to rob him, he snapped her neck and immediately ejaculated in his pants. Having no record of the perp's prints, Chicago homicide detectives under the command of Captain Marshall Bennett were stumped and the case was never solved.

Barstow deemed the visit a success. He encouraged Ross to push for a more aggressive recruitment quota, which ultimately forced Wesley Arendt and Gavin Berringer to come up with their ambitious Phase Two—the aforementioned Prom Night Massacre. In return for their efforts, Barstow shared engineering specs for voice-activated lights. The only item on Barstow's checklist to remain incomplete was to see what it looked like to spill crimson blood onto the city's snow-covered, ivory sidewalks.

9

Midday approaches as Susie, García, Josh, Dixon, and Rose emerge from the tunnels near a major crossroads. Shopkeepers hurry about outside, sweeping ever-present sand from their welcome mats, wheeling sundries via barrow or pushcart, and chatting with customers.

The FCB leaders take stock. Susie is unarmed, as per the rules, but García and Dixon visibly pack heat. Josh and Rose are armed as well. Josh unbuckles Underwood's tactical knife and scabbard from around one thigh and hands them to Dixon. "Here, you may need this."

"Only if it's up close and personal," Dixon replies. He belts the scabbard to his right thigh.

Susie addresses Josh and Rose. "You know what to do, right?"

They nod. "Get up on those rooftops, track and follow from afar. Take out Reynolds if anything bad goes down," Josh says.

"That's right. Be good. Stay safe."

"You too," Josh replies.

"*Con cuidado,*" Rose says.

"*Tú también,*" Dixon replies.

Rose sticks her tongue out at Dixon. Susie waves her and Josh on their way, then turns to García and Dixon. "Ready?"

"*Listo,*" Dixon replies.

Susie shrugs. "I don't know what that—"

"I'm ready," he explains.

"Thank you. García?"

"Ready." García takes a nervous swig of water from his canteen.

"Less than one klick to the bridge," Susie says. She clenches her fists in determination and walks onward toward the bridge.

She has never been this scared in her life.

· · ·

Josh and Rose scale a fire escape to the top of the three-story building and scamper onto the dusty roof. Its surface is warm to the touch, courtesy of the midday sun, but not as hot as a similar rooftop would be on a sunny Chicago afternoon during high summer. They scramble over a chimney and pass a collection of empty oxygen drums. *Who left those exposed to the elements?* Rose wonders. *Dangerous!* They leap across a gap between two buildings. Josh scales a precarious brick wall onto the higher rooftop of the neighboring building and offers Rose a helping hand. True to form, she waves him off.

. . .

Below, Susie, García, and Dixon proceed two blocks further north, then east. The buildings on their right fall away and a futuristic playground—not much different from a 1980s playground, as it happens—occupies the last half-block leading up to the Century Bridge. Two kids play on swings that squeak with each gyration, badly in need of oil. "Get outta here, kids," Dixon says. They stare at him with blank expressions and continue to swing. It takes him putting both hands on his rifle and entering the run-down playground for them to finally scatter.

The Century Bridge has been closed to traffic for the occasion. Reynolds stands in the middle and is flanked by a pair of Loyalists on each side—five people altogether instead of the agreed-upon three. Susie, Dixon, and García pause as they reach their end of the bridge. They look at each other, senses heightened, then step slowly, reluctantly forward.

. . .

Above, Josh and Rose stop at the highest rooftop on their side of the street. "They made it to the bridge," Rose says, binoculars in hand, as Josh gets into sniper mode, lying on his stomach and sighting his weapon. "They're starting across. I see Reynolds in the middle."

"I'm ready," Josh says. "You get ready, too. She's outnumbered."

The Century Bridge is a magnificent, one-kilometer (0.6-mile) span. The Red River, so named for the color of the natural rock walls on either side, rages below. Channeling the river, taming it, making it drinkable remains the foremost engineering feat in the planet's history.

The bridge and the canyon beneath serve as the dividing lines between gritty Zone Omega to the south and posh Zone Alpha to the north. A pedestrian walkway runs along the middle of the bridge, with two vehicle lanes on either side— the wider one for transport shuttles and hover-tanks and the narrower one for self-driving delivery cycles. Reynolds waits midway across the bridge, and the tension as Susie approaches is so great you can cut it with a knife.

Reynolds raises one hand in a wave once she is four meters away, and greets her with a smile that *seems* amiable enough. "Susie. Good to see you again."

"Where's Ross?"

"You know he rarely steps outside. He'll meet us in the audience hall; my instructions are for his men and I to escort you there."

"Four soldiers besides yourself? That's not what was agreed upon. Ross isn't *that* afraid of me, is he?"

"It's how the game is played." He states it matter-of-factly and extends his hand. She shakes it.

"I trust your Great Gourd Expedition was fruitful, if you'll forgive the pun?" he asks.

Her demeanor changes. "We'll talk about that."

. . .

Above, Rose looks through the binoculars, rifle at her side. "I don't trust Reynolds. We should've wasted him when he showed up 14 days ago."

Josh, who assumes firing position as if it's second nature, doesn't take his eye off the scope as he replies to Rose's insinuations. "I don't know the man, but I'll take your word for it. If you tell me to shoot, I'll shoot."

. . .

Susie and Reynolds begin negotiations. "I know your seconds are packing, but I assume you yourself are unarmed?" Reynolds asks.

"You assume correct." Susie unzips her jacket, raises her shirt above the beltline, and lifts her pantlegs above her boots. Once Reynolds nods in acknowledgment, Susie points to her escorts. "These two are here for my protection. Hopefully, I don't have anything to worry about."

"Hello again, Dixon," Reynolds says.

"Hi, asshole," Dixon replies.

Reynolds smiles and cocks his head. "That's fair." He turns to García. "You look familiar, but I'm afraid I don't know your name."

"I'm García García."

"He used to be one of Ross's drivers," Susie explains. "Guess he had a change of heart."

Reynolds nods. "That explains it. But like I said when last we met, I give you my word that what you want and what the chancellor wants are one in the same. An end to the fighting. A diplomatic solution." He coughs. It sounds fake, but Susie doesn't notice.

"We'll see. I'd like to believe you, but I've been told I need to stop trusting people. And you *did* abduct the Old Man."

"I did. Regrettably so. It earned me these officer stripes, sure, but it earned me a guilty conscience, too."

"Good," Dixon remarks. "Did you earn any stripes for the Pit?"

"Quiet, Dixon," Susie says.

Reynolds checks his watch. "My, it's almost half-past twelve already. The chancellor thought we could all meet for lunch. He's having food catered in for the occasion. Beater, I'm told."

"I can eat," Susie says. "But I want Dixon and García fed, too, and I request they remain armed."

"I acquiesce to your request. Now if you'll all follow me, the chancellor's waiting. And with that, a chance at peace."

"Very well." Susie follows Reynolds in the direction of Zone Alpha and the Ronald Reagan Audience Hall. The hall sits beyond the Century Bridge, perched above the lip of the canyon and across the boulevard from the CCC. It boasts impressive views, cathedral ceilings, and remarkable acoustics. Susie stepped foot inside the hall once as a child, when she attended a public safety lecture with her parents following a rise in beater attacks, and she never forgot how small it made her feel.

Reynolds marches two paces ahead of Susie as if he's her ranking military officer. Loyalist soldiers march ahead and on either side of him. Dixon and García bring up the rear.

. . .

Josh and Rose watch the action from above. "So far, so good," Josh says.

"Keep an eye on your girlfriend, Loverboy," Rose replies.

"She's not my girlfriend!"

"If you say so." Rose raises her binoculars for a closer look. "*Ay,* the suspense is killing me!"

. . .

Susie, Reynolds, and the others are three-quarters of the way across the bridge when the shit hits the fan. Reynolds fake-coughs again. The two soldiers to his immediate left and right turn to face him. He nods and fake-coughs a third time. This is the signal. The soldiers raise their weapons. Susie opens her mouth to warn her friends, but it's already too late. A plasma blast vaporizes García's chest cavity, and he dies with an expression of pure innocence on his face—he didn't see it coming.

"Get down!" Dixon yells. He returns fire at the soldier who blasted García. In the soldier's death spasm, he accidentally vaporizes his counterpart closest to him, and it's now three against two. Susie leaps forward and tackles Reynolds.

. . .

"*¡Cuidado!*" Rose yells to Josh. *Careful!*

"Not sure what you said, but I'm on it," Josh yells back as he squeezes off a few rounds. They go wild, but not by much. Rose takes aim but is forced to take cover before engaging as a series of rounds fired in her direction hit the rooftop she is sitting on.

"Rose!" Josh yells. He takes his aim off the action below as several rounds are fired at him as well. He ducks behind a cinder block wall and sees weapons fire coming from a building the same height as theirs and one street over. "Over there!" he yells, and lays a suppressing fire in that direction. More rounds are fired in return, but these come from the opposite direction. "I think they have us surrounded!"

"I'll cover you. Protect Susie!"

"Got it!" Josh re-sights his weapon as Rose fires haphazardly in both directions from which they appear to have been fired upon. She targets a pile of discarded oxygen drums on the rooftop behind them. The drums explode and take a pair of snipers with them.

. . .

The action on the bridge has attracted the attention of an enhanced Sauron X. It zooms in, seemingly out of nowhere, and sets its sights on Susie, whom its A.I. brain interprets as the aggressor.

A plasma blaster emerges from a door below the drone's surveillance eye and has our heroine in its crosshairs until the sound of an explosion from above and behind tells the drone's chip to change course.

. . .

"Whoa, where'd that come from?!" Josh blurts out.

"*No sé.* Get down and hold your fire!"

Josh and Rose duck below the cinder block wall along the edge of the roof. Their counterparts do the same, allowing the Sauron X the courtesy of taking out Josh and Rose once it flies high enough to spot them taking cover. Rose uses this pause in the action to change magazines. She tosses the empty magazine aside, and the clatter it makes as it lands on a pile of rubble is enough to draw the Sauron's attention. It races toward a distracted Rose at an alarming pace.

"Don't move, Rose!" Josh fires a steady blast at the fast-moving drone, which flies evasively. Rose looks up in wide-eyed terror as the drone's shadow falls upon her, and she's certain she can see its plasma blaster move into position when it drops out of the sky in an explosion of sparks.

"That was close!" Josh says. He loses his presence of mind for a moment and peers over the side at the drone's crash site below. The opposition snipers don't miss a moment. They open fire, and a steady plasma burst misses his head by just centimeters.

"*Ay,* Josh!" Rose says.

"I'm okay. What about you?" He retreats behind the cinder block and rubs his ear, which rings from the sonic discordance of the near-miss plasma blast. Rose fires blindly in the general direction of the remaining snipers.

"I'm okay! But Susie's not."

Sure enough, the stakes below have changed dramatically.

. . .

Susie drags Reynolds toward the edge of the bridge. She attempts to push him over the side, but he refuses to go quietly. One of the surviving Loyalists fires a plasma warning burst in her direction. It scorches the bridge. The soldier is reluctant to fire again, afraid of hitting Reynolds by mistake.

"Get away from her!" Dixon shouts. He fires at the soldier closest to him but is startled by the rooftop explosion and the anti-matter burst goes wild. Nguyen, the soldier who fired a warning burst, charges at Dixon. He returns fire, but Nguyen dodges the blasts. The fourth soldier, Brown, runs after Susie, who dangles Reynolds partway over the side of the bridge. Reynolds kicks Susie in the chest while pushing against the ground with one scraped hand and grabbing onto a bridge cable with the other. The cable cuts into his hand, but he doesn't notice in the heat of battle.

. . .

Josh fires at Brown from the rooftop. His hand spasms when a live plasma burst whizzes past. Rose cries out and Josh's blasts go wild. "You okay?" he yells out.

"Took one in the shoulder," she yells back. "I'm okay though. Got one of 'em. Maybe." She steps back behind a pile of cinderblocks to assess the flesh wound in her left arm. As if on cue, a tremendous barrage of weapons fire reigns down upon her and Josh from the rooftop one street over. "*¡Mierda,* maybe not!"

"I'm out!" Josh says. "Cover me!" He ducks below the cinderblock wall and changes magazines.

"*¡Claro!*" Rose stands up and fires again. She misses the sniper by a hair but drives him below their sightline. His partner returns fire, and the onslaught forces her backward. She attempts to engage, but her arm shakes from the shredded bicep and she can't get a steady aim. Not easily deterred, the sniper fires again, forcing her further back in self-defense until she falls backward over the side of the building.

Josh is unaware his comrade has fallen. "Rose, stay down!" He locks his replacement magazine into place and fires on the snipers in a display of weapons fire so excessive the whole top story of the building he fires upon will end up being razed.

• • •

Susie is determined to push Reynolds over the side over the bridge. She faces him and raises a foot to kick the charging Corporal Brown in the chest. He falls onto his ass and skids backward. He knows she's worth more alive than dead, but he doesn't want her killing Reynolds, technically his superior officer now that Reynolds finally has those sergeant stripes.

Nearby, Dixon and PFC Nguyen have exhausted their plasma magazines. Dixon withdraws the tactical knife from the scabbard on his thigh and plants it in the soldier's boot. It plunges all the way through and embeds itself in a crack in the deck of the bridge. Nguyen howls in pain, unable to flee. Dixon punches him in the face, driving him onto his back. He leaps onto Nguyen's lap and pummels him repeatedly in the face. Down but not out, Nguyen reaches inside his jacket and draws a back-up weapon, a plasma pistol similar in size to a 20$^{th}$-century Beretta. Dixon is on top of him, but as the former Chicagoan leans back to catch his breath before administering another punch, Nguyen seizes the moment. He plants the weapon's nose beneath Dixon's chin and pulls the trigger. Dixon is dead, his jawline vaporized before he has a chance to register what happened.

Susie sees this and screams his name. Her wannabe captor, Brown, charges at her again. She kicks him anew, this time connecting with his cheek and sending him backward. Hell hath no fury like a woman scorned . . . or like a Susie enraged. She turns toward Reynolds, who has regained his foothold. She shoves him over the side. He grabs the cables with his left hand and crooks his right elbow around them for critical support. His feet dangle, but he has purchase. Brown comes back for more, kicking Susie in the back of the knee and forcing her to the ground. She rolls onto her back and looks up to see the barrel of his plasma rifle in her face.

"It's over," he says. Susie nods in resigned acknowledgment. She rests her head on the ground and catches her breath. After binding Susie's wrists, Brown asks Sergeant Reynolds, still dangling precariously, if he needs a hand.

Reynolds shakes his head. "Take her and go. I'll meet you over there."

"Yessir!" Brown offers Reynolds a salute the sergeant is unable to return. Brown jerks Susie by the arm to an upright position and marches her toward the west end of the bridge, where two more Loyalist soldiers have gathered. Their colleague, Nguyen, has managed to unwedge the knife from his boot. He limps across the median toward Reynolds, leaving a trail of blood with each step. One of his eyes is swollen shut and his nose will never be the same, but he's alive.

"Nguyen," Reynolds says, one toehold on the bridge but the other leg swaying for purchase. "You look terrible. Help me up." Reynolds loses hold of the cable with his left hand after his nerve endings sense the pain of the cable ripping into his skin, and he struggles to regain the progress he made in climbing back onto the solid surface of the bridge itself. Nguyen attempts to speak, but when he opens his mouth, several teeth fall out.

· · ·

Josh's second magazine is empty. He lobs a pair of grenades with his quarterback's arm for good measure, and they explode a few seconds after landing on the opposite rooftop. His actions take out the opposing snipers, and the sudden silence as the smoke clears is downright eerie. He scurries on all fours to his original position. The rooftop is covered in rubble. He cuts his palm on a jagged piece of plaster but doesn't register the pain. He looks through the scope and sees Susie being rushed into an armored hover-tank at the northern end of the bridge. "Damn!" he utters at having missed his moment. He changes magazines one last time and focuses his attention on the bloody aftermath in the center on the bridge, where Dixon and García are dead and where Nguyen offers Reynolds a helping hand. "Like hell you will," Josh says, and takes aim.

· · ·

Nguyen lay on his side, his boots pressed against a trestle for stability. "Give me your arm, sir," he says to Reynolds, but with missing teeth and a mouthful of blood, it sounds like, "*Gib ne dur narm, dur.*" He reaches over the side for the sergeant's arm. The contact they make is short lived. A burst of plasma rounds rip through Nguyen's back. He releases his grip on Reynolds's hand and dies almost instantly.

"Shit!" Reynolds panics. He loses whatever upward progress he has made and tries not to look down. Hitting the river 250 meters below would break his back *at best,* and would almost certainly kill him.

. . .

The vantage point from the rooftop is less than ideal. The trestle blocks the headshot Josh *sooo* wants to take. He opts for the next best thing—a quick burst of plasma at Reynolds's right arm, which hugs the trestle for dear life. The single round annihilates his tricep. He falls from the bridge, screaming on the way down. Josh fires again. The burst hits Reynolds in the chest, killing him as he falls.

"That's better than you deserved, you prick," Josh says. He gets up and runs to the back of the building. He sees blood spatter where Rose presumably landed, but of Rose herself there is no sign.

She's gone.

# Chapter 6

1

An Air Force-owned Lockheed cargo plane, modified with hard seats to accommodate VIP passengers, flies above the Chicago skyline, which, for the first time since Thomas Edison gave the world electricity, is fully dark. Except for the tiny dot that is Northerly Island, the entire city appears to be without power.

Robert, Sr. peers out the porthole at the darkened skyline. "That's unsettling." He offers Gail a peek.

"I'm worried about Robbie," she says.

"That's our first stop. Forget the mayor's residence. Forget City Hall."

Gail grabs his hand. "What's going on down there?"

"I wish I knew." He checks his watch. "Dammit, it's hard being out of the loop!"

Gail pats his shoulder with her other hand. "It's okay, dear. You're a good man. If anyone can make sense of this, it's you. The people don't know how lucky they are to have you."

With a sigh: "How many people *are* there, though?" He shuts the window shade.

The overhead speaker crackles. The passengers and soldiers jump. "*Ladies and gentlemen, this is your captain speaking,*" a voice says. "*We have gotten reports that Midway is shuttered and that our plane will be shot down if we attempt to land. As such, we are circling back to O'Hare, where we have more options in the form of additional runways. Three armed motorcades will be greeting us immediately upon touchdown. Two of them are decoys, one headed downtown and the other toward McCormick Place. The third—and smallest, to draw the least attention—will take you to your homes. If you look out your portholes you may have noticed we are no longer alone. A pair of F14-A Tomcats joined us once we crossed into Chicago airspace. They will be our escorts until we drop below 500 feet. For everyone's safety, we are staying above 5,000 feet until we are 2,000 yards inside the outer marker. It's likely to get bumpy from here. At this time, please buckle up and remain seated. Godspeed.*"

"Would you look at that?" the senator remarks after spotting a Tomcat flying on the Lockheed's port side.

"Dear." Gail squeezes her husband's hand.

"Everything's okay, honey."

A scan of the VIPs and soldiers on board reveals everything is not, in fact, okay. A woman in a window seat secures her daughter's seatbelt. The daughter, hair tousled and no more than six years old, fusses from the adjacent seat with a Snoopy stuffed animal. A congressional representative ten years younger than Robert, Sr. occupies an aisle seat, tie loosened and top button of his shirt undone. He reaches for the vomit bag while an aide to his right crosses herself. A trio of soldiers sit next to one another along the fuselage, morose and silent. A reporter, busy scribbling shorthand notes recapping the pilot's announcement, drops his pen during a small lurch, and it rolls halfway down the aisle. He unfastens his seatbelt to fetch it, and the old woman to his left squeezes his right shoulder with all the strength she can muster. He'll notice a bruise in that spot the next morning. "What are you doing, son?" the woman asks. "You heard what the pilot said." The reporter purses his lips to chastise the woman, then looks at the pen, then back at the woman, then at the pen again. He decides she is right and refastens his seatbelt. A second lurch, this one much rougher, follows the first as the plane hits an air pocket. The young congressman christens the vomit bag. Someone screams.

. . .

In the cockpit, the pilot and co-pilot attempt to make sense of what's below them. "Sir, what happened to the skyline?" the co-pilot asks. His eyes are wide with fear. "I can see the city in the light of the moon, but where are the lights? This is crazy!"

"I concur, Captain Ramsey, but I don't have an answer for you. I made this same run twice on Sunday and everything looked normal both runs," the captain, whose metal nametag reads CAPT. HUNTER, answers. His uniform features one more bar than that of his co-pilot.

"Ain't nothing normal 'bout that, sir." The younger Captain Ramsey, whose accent confirms his Biloxi-born background, takes a cross from a chain draped around his neck, normally tucked out of sight inside his shirt, and kisses it.

"Keep it together, Captain," Captain Hunter says. "Watch your altitude. Let's get a vector. It's yours."

"Aye, sir," Captain Ramsey replies. He radios O'Hare. "O'Hare Tower, this is Captain Ramsey with Air Force flight number CZ257, carrying precious cargo, inbound headed north-northwest and awaiting runway and approach vector. I repeat, this is flight number Charlie-Zulu 2-5-7 with precious cargo, headed north-northwest at 5,100 feet and awaiting approach vector. Please advise, over."

No response. He lets go of the radio button and turns to his senior officer. "Sir, they're not responding. What do we do?"

"Radio again. And let's drop to 2,000. It's risky but necessary."

Captain Ramsey steels himself and tries again. "O'Hare Tower, do you read me? This is Captain Ramsey with USAF flight number Charlie-Zulu 2-5-7, dropping to 2,000 feet and heading north-northwest. We're inbound and in need of a runway, over."

Static.

"O'Hare Tower, do you read me? This is Air Force flight number Charlie-Zulu 2-5-7, awaiting further instructions, over!" Captain Ramsey, whose face is drenched with sweat, turns to Captain Hunter. "Sir?"

"Check your heading, Captain. You're doing good. Let's level out. Watch the altimeter."

On the ground below, a missile is fired from a Soviet-style mobile launcher, and soars toward the Lockheed C-130 above.

"Captain, we've got a bogie on our tail!" Ramsey cries out.

"Evasive maneuvers!" Hunter replies. He and Ramsey steer the wheels hard to the right, and the plane inverts 45 degrees as the missile cruises past them. The Tomcats turn to engage.

· · ·

Pandemonium ensues in the rear cabin. Luggage tears through the webbing designed to secure it, and a hardshell carry-on crushes one of the soldiers. An aide whose seatbelt wasn't tightly fastened flies out of her left side aisle seat. She elbows the civilian contractor across the aisle in the schnozz during her bungled attempt to reseat herself. More screams. Vomit and blood fly through the air; while the contractor takes credit for the blood, several passengers can lay claim to the vomit.

. . .

"That was close," Hunter says. Together, he and Ramsey level the plane. "Excellent flying, Captain."

The less-experienced Ramsey offers an uneasy smile. "Thank you, sir. Beg pardon, that was terrifying."

Hunter smiles, one hand on the radio mic. "I flew choppers during the war," he offers. "What a horror show. Had that Huey flying upside down once in a hot zone near Da Nang. Talk about terrifying, shew!"

He tries the tower a fourth time. "O'Hare Tower, this is Captain Hunter with USAF flight number CZ257, repeat, Charlie-Zulu 2-5-7. We are taking fire and are on rapid descent. We've circled around evasively and are coming in hot. We're carrying precious cargo and must land immediately, over."

Static . . . then a muffled response: *"Flight number CZ257, this is O'Hare Tower, we read you. We do have power and are illuminating east-west runway 32R, repeat, 32-Romeo. All commercial traffic has been suspended since 06:30 yesterday. Your glide path should be clear and we've got you on our radar, over."*

Hunter smiles. "Roger Tower, heading for runway 32-Romeo. This is Charlie-Zulu 2-5-7, we'll see you soon." He turns to Ramsey, who grips the throttle so tightly his hands turn red. "Captain, do your final approach check."

Ramsey nods as Hunter toggles the mic. "Ladies and gentlemen, this is your captain again. Apologies for that rough patch. We met some air pockets and another form of resistance as well, but are now on our final approach. Brace yourselves for landing. Possible hostiles. Assume crash positions . . . and Godspeed."

. . .

The two surviving soldiers, who dare not unbuckle their seatbelts, have managed to cover the smashed head and torso of the colleague between them as best they can with a blanket that flew their way during the 80-degree evasive maneuvers. That unfortunate task seen to, they lean forward and cover their heads with their hands, scared utterly shitless.

Gail clings to her husband, but Robert, Sr. gently removes her hand from his arm. "Crash positions, honey," he murmurs. She nods and crosses herself, something she hasn't done since before her senior viola recital at Boston's New England Conservatory of Music.

"I love you, Robert."

"I love you, too." He kisses her on the cheek, then tightens his seatbelt and leans forward in the crash position.

"Mommy, I'm scared," the young child says from two rows up. She hugs Snoopy tighter than ever.

"I'm scared too, sweetie," her mom says. She checks her daughter's seatbelt and helps her into the correct position. "Make sure you cover your head with your hands. Everything will be over soon."

"But who's gonna protect Snoopy?"

"I'll protect him, my little one." She wrests Snoopy from her daughter's hands and kisses the back of her head. *Is this how it ends?* she wonders. *Was it worth all this for the experience of working in our nation's capital?* She hopes that the plane lands safely and that the answer to her last question is "yes," but fears the affirmation only applies to her first question. The young woman, a first-term congresswoman for Chicago's fifth district, looks at Snoopy, kisses the back of his head as well, and assumes the crash position.

One row back and across the aisle, the young congressman, also new to D.C. politics, gives the vomit bag one last christening before leaning forward and covering his head with his hands. "Shit shit shit shit shit shit shit shit shit shit shit," his fellow passengers hear him utter until the roar of the engines becomes so loud it drowns him out.

. . .

Tensions ebb in the cockpit as Captains Hunter and Ramsey ease their bird the remaining distance. "Easy, Captain," Hunter says, "you're at 400 feet but not quite level. Remember to compensate for load."

"Aye, sir. Adjusting now." Ramsey grits his teeth as the cargo plane breaches the final yardage.

. . .

All over the suburb of Schiller Park below, people—those who neglected to leave town for safer horizons unlike many of their neighbors—emerge from their front doors after hearing the overhead roar. Some residents instinctively duck.

. . .

"300 . . ." Hunter says. ". . . 250 . . . 200 . . . 150 . . . 100 . . . 75 . . . 50 . . . steady on the throttle . . ."

The Lockheed C-130 Hercules touches down at 200 miles per hour, 50 mph faster than recommended but doable with a midsized plane such as this one.

"Success!" Hunter cheers as he and a shaken Captain Ramsey decelerate.

A Loyalist soldier, doing Chancellor Ross's bidding from behind a hillock near Irving Park Road, stands up and fires a rocket launcher at the plane as it speeds past. The projectile strikes the front wheels, which have already generated sparks from the too-fast landing. The plane goes into a spin as its nose droops. The landing gear is obliterated and the front of the plane catches fire.

The passengers scream. More luggage rips through the webbing.

"Hell was that?!" Ramsey panics from the cockpit.

"Steer into the spin," Hunter replies. Cool under pressure.

"I'm trying!" The men attempt to slow the plane's terrifying skid. It's now down to 125 mph—still dangerously fast but not their only problem; flames from the landing gear penetrate the cockpit's floorboards. "Shit!"

"Get the extinguisher, I've got control," Hunter says. Ramsey reaches behind him for the fire extinguisher and, struggling with the nozzle, douses foam in areas of the cockpit *not* on fire. "Here, by my legs!" Hunter shouts.

Ramsey manages a better hold of the nozzle and douses Hunter's feet and legs. Flames climb toward the instrument panel, and Ramsey is on it. Hunter, meanwhile, succeeds in slowing the plane to a stop. It skids off the runway and into a ditch, ending ass-up in the air.

"We did it, sir! We did it!" Ramsey cheers. He douses a renegade blaze, then checks on Captain Hunter. The senior captain isn't doing so well. Third-degree burns adorn his legs and the entire left side of his body. He may survive his burns, but the pain will be such that he won't want to.

With all the strength left in his body, Hunter nods at Ramsey with pride as he addresses the battered passengers. "Ladies and gentlemen, welcome to Chicago O'Hare." He drops the mic and passes out.

## 2

The cargo bay door at the rear of the Lockheed opens, hanging five feet in the air above the runway below. One of the surviving soldiers, weapon at the ready, is the first to gaze over the lip. He hears the 150-decibel roar of a low-flying Tomcat and looks up to see a missile launched from the Tomcat toward the hillock of activity. A fireball appears 100 yards away, and the soldier assumes the threat has been neutralized.

"It's okay, people, looks like we can climb over the side," he announces. "I'll go first to help you down from below." After scanning the horizon, the soldier carefully climbs down, rifle slung on the shoulder strap running across his chest. He reaches up to help the next person down. The Congresswoman hands her daughter to the soldier, Snoopy back in the kid's arms, before removing her heels and hopping off the side without assistance. The reporter and the old woman are next.

"Honey, why don't you go ahead," Robert, Sr. tells Gail. "I thought I'd thank our pilots."

"I'll wait for you," Gail insists.

The senator gives his wife of eight years a peck on the lips. "So *that* happened," he says, eliciting the faintest of smiles. The remaining passengers deboard as Robert, Sr. knocks on the cockpit door while Gail waits in her seat.

"It's jammed," Ramsey's muffled voice can be heard from the other side. Robert, Sr. sees the knob being jiggled from the other side.

"Captain, let's jimmy it together," he says. "I'll push and you pull. Gravity should be in our favor."

"Good idea, sir."

"I'm leaning in with my shoulder. Turning the knob and pushing it upward. On three, pull it upward toward you. One . . . two . . . three!" The door swings inward, and Robert, Sr. grabs the bulkhead with both hands to keep from flying forward.

He ducks into the cockpit once his footing stabilizes on the slanted floor. "Soldier, that was some good work on the landing. Guessing someone shot at us?"

"I believe so, sir," Ramsey turns to his co-pilot. "I'm worried about Captain Hunter here. He needs to be moved."

"Absolutely. Get his feet, I'll grab him by the shoulders."

"That's just it, sir. He's been badly burned. We'll need someone to cut through the fuselage and evac him that way."

Another rocket is launched. It strikes the right wing, which explodes inward, driving flame and debris through the side window and into the unfortunate Captain Ramsey's head.

"Robert!" Gail cries from the cabin. She is thrown against the seat in front of her. Blood pours from her nose. The blast sends Robert, Sr. backward into the bulkhead, which protects him from serious injury. The sound of automatic weapons can be heard, presumably from the two surviving soldiers firing into the direction of whoever is attacking them.

"I'm okay, Gail. Stay down!" More weapons fire, then another roar as the second Tomcat drops low for its targeted flyover. The explosion that follows represents a second missile hitting its target. The next sound is that of a whistle blowing, then silence. Robert, Sr. looks through the cockpit door toward the open hatch at the rear of the plane. Despite the angle, he can see the flashing red and blue lights of emergency responders heading their way.

"All clear, Senator!" a soldier's voice shouts from outside the plane. The senator takes one last look inside the cockpit. The heroic Captain Ramsey is now a headless corpse, and things looks dire for the seasoned Captain Hunter as well.

Robert, Sr. walks toward the hatch and grabs his wife's hand. She deboards as he pauses to assess the damage. His eyes settle on the soldier who was crushed by renegade luggage. The blanket shifted during landing to reveal the young man's face, and his final expression is one of agony. "Are you alright, sir?"

one of the surviving soldiers asks. (The other soldier scans the surroundings for additional Ross Army goons.)

"The co-pilot was just killed. The pilot's unconscious and badly burned. He'll need a medevac and Jaws of Life. Looks like you'll need a hand with your colleague there, too. I offer my condolences."

"Thank you, sir. Steinbeck and I can handle it. Right now, let's get you out of here. Looks like the motorcades are on their way." He points to the procession of flashing lights, closer now.

"Who shot at us? Was that a rocket launcher?"

"I believe so, Senator. An RPG-2, most likely."

"Do we know who the shooter was?"

"Intel says they're called 'Loyalists.' We were briefed about 'em yesterday. This is my third run, but my first actual encounter. If he somehow survived that Tomcat strike, I wouldn't mind finishing the job myself, if you beg my pardon, sir."

"If you take a shot, Soldier, take one for me, too."

"Yessir."

The motorcade is close. Robert, Sr. joins his wife, who congregates with the other VIPs and holds a wad of tissue to her bloody nose. She holds out her other hand and he takes it immediately, gently. "You okay?" he asks her.

"Yes. No. Not really."

He nods. "Let's go find Robert. Let's go find my son."

"*Our* son," Gail corrects him.

3

Still dark. The candles burn low in Bob's motel room. He tosses and turns, unable to sleep. His tighty-whiteys are hung out to dry on the back of a chair, and his jeans are crumpled in a pile in the corner. Not expecting company, he wears just his Bugle Boy tee, the blankets covering his naked bottom half. Following a knock on the door connecting his room to Lori's, she enters, clad in her pink T-shirt and a towel she's wrapped around her waist. "You awake?" she whispers.

"Yeah." He is unsurprised to see her. "Can't sleep."

"Me neither." She climbs in bed next to him. "Do you mind?"

"Uh, no, it's fine I guess." Bob cannot believe his good fortune.

"It's kinda spooky with just the candles, isn't it?"

"Yeah."

"Spooky but also romantic."

Bob turns to face her. "You think so?"

"Kind of. Like in those Depeche Mode videos."

"Good band."

"Totally. What's your favorite song of theirs?"

"Dunno. 'Blasphemous Rumours' is a good one, kind of appropriate, too. Mood-wise, I mean."

"I don't know that one. I really like 'Somebody.' " Bob furrows his brow, so she clarifies. "The song."

Bob nods. "Ah yes. That's from the same album, I think."

The song is a tender ballad about one person's yearning to find a true connection with "somebody" who truly gets them and who won't cut and run at the first sign of trouble.

Something compels Lori to sing. She changes the gender pronouns in the first verse accordingly. Bob is unsure of the lyrics but joins her as best he can for the second verse, which has no tricky pronouns. Lori feels Bob's foot slow tapping to the beat from under the covers.

She turns to him after their *a cappella* duet and smiles. "That was lovely. You have a nice voice. You should've joined choir."

"Tell that to my anxiety. But thanks. You have a good voice, too."

"Robert Wilkinson, this has been a strange week, but I'm so glad I got to know you."

"I thought you were gonna call me 'Bobby?' "

"I'm gonna call you late for dinner."

"Well played, Rain-Rain—I-I mean, Lori."

"Call me 'Rain-Rain.' I kinda like it."

"Goodnight, Rain-Rain." He turns to his side.

"Goodnight, Bobby." Lori respects his boundaries and turns to the opposite side, facing away from him. Perhaps Bob is a comforting presence, perhaps it's because the day has been so long, or perhaps she is falling in love, but for whatever reason, Lori falls asleep almost at once.

Nervous (and pants-less), Bob, on the other hand, has never felt less like sleeping. He lays motionless, waiting for the sandman to arrive. Sleep eventually comes, but not before Bob rips a loud fart—a real trombone blast, the dry kind in which you can practically hear the opposing butt cheeks vibrate against each other. Mortification! Sweaty palms! *Quelle horreur!*

# Chapter 7

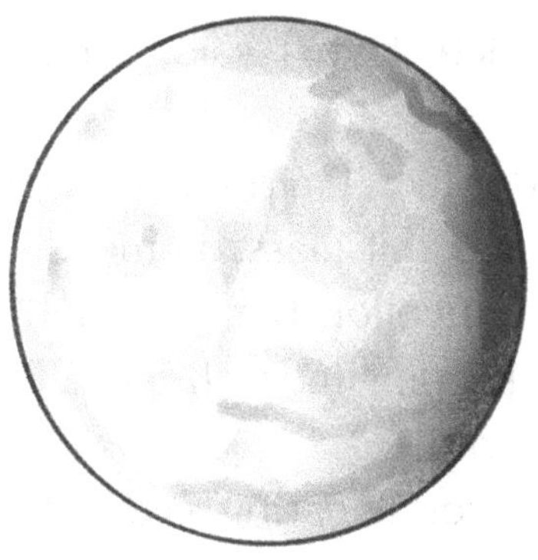

## 1

Susie awakens to darkness and a pounding headache. She's unsure what time it is, but based on the thinness of the mattress and the squeakiness of the bedsprings beneath, she is certain she's in a prison cell. Slowly, her eyes adjust and she makes out shapes that appear to be a washbasin and toilet. The thin, vertical columns that surround her on all sides are almost certainly iron bars. "Hello?" she calls out. "Is anyone here?"

"You're not alone," a male voice says from the darkness.

"Who is that? Your voice sounds familiar."

"Name's McCarthy. Most people just call me the 'Old Man.' "

"Sir!" She perks up at once. "It's Susie Walker."

"By Jove. Susie Walker, as I live and breathe."

"We—I—we were afraid you were dead." She proceeds toward the sound of his voice and puts her arms out until she feels the bars.

"Careful by those bars. The cell doors are laser-enforced. You'll get a nasty shock if you stick your arm through."

"Thank you, sir. I can hear electricity coursing through them. How have you been treated? I should've immediately recognized your voice. Like I said, for a while we thought maybe you were—"

"I'm not. Matter of fact, I'm doing well, aside from my back, which is as stiff as a tall glass of mead. Haven't made any inroads with the chancellor, but he's civil at least and I'll be damned if he's not keeping me well-fed. Of course it helps, like him, that I'm a tea drinker."

"I'm glad to hear you're eating well. I'd love to say this is a rescue mission, but . . . well . . . not exactly."

"I wouldn't imagine so. Rescuers usually come bearing arms."

Her eyes have fully adjusted to the dark. "Sir, we were betrayed. Twice. By Reynolds. Of course, I guess you knew that."

"He's a devious son-of-a-beater, isn't he? I watched in the tunnels as he shot Schaeffer in the back without the slightest hesitation or remorse."

"I don't remember who invited him to join our group in the first place, but this time it's on me. And it was costly."

"Who'd we lose?"

"A new recruit, García. Dixon. Maybe Josh, maybe Rose."

McCarthy groans at the mention of Dixon's name. "Josh is another new recruit?"

"He is. Or was . . . or . . . I dunno. You would've liked him."

"Well if you don't know his fate for sure, maybe there's still cause for hope."

"I hope so, sir. Still . . . I trusted Reynolds. I gave him a second chance. Like I said, this is on me."

"Nonsense. People have second thoughts. Except when they don't. And they can be good actors. Don't blame yourself."

Their palaver is interrupted by the sound of a breaker being flipped. The brig lights up with rows of overhead fluorescent tube bulbs, as non-flattering in the 24th century as they are in the twentieth. Once their eyes adjust to the light, Susie and McCarthy size each other up from their cells, across the corridor from one another.

Susie marvels at how good the Old Man looks. Has he gained weight? Aside from needing a beard trim, he looks better than Susie can recall. Whiling away the hours in the brig doesn't sound like anyone's idea of a good time, but it makes sense that resting, instead of leading a revolution, would be easier on a person's body.

The Old Man, on the other hand, is dismayed by Susie's disheveled appearance. With her left arm in a sling, a bandage across the bridge of her nose, and her shirt torn in several places, she is the worse for wear. While he knows she's tough and while he isn't surprised she continued recruiting for their cause while he was incarcerated, he can't imagine the toll this fight has taken. Revolutionaries have short life expectancies, and the Old Man knows both he and Susie have long exceeded their own.

"You look like hell, my friend," he remarks.

"I *feel* like hell," she replies, and promptly changes the subject. "I see they let you have books?"

"The ones that haven't been banned, anyway." He runs his thumb across the spines of several well-read classics on a shelf above his cot—*The Adventures of Huckleberry Finn, The Merchant of Venice, Moby Dick, One Hundred Years of Solitude,* and *Treasure Island.*

"I know what a voracious reader you are. I always felt bad you had to leave your books behind after our first relo. Charles De Gaulle Road, I think it was."

"Books are a nice luxury. They're like being with old friends."

"And a welcome distraction from worrying about me, I imagine."

The Old Man dismisses her sentiment with a flick of the wrist. "Nonsense. The Susie Walker I know can take care of herself just fine. Although . . . all evidence is to the contrary today, it appears."

"*Touché* . . . sir."

A magnetic card beep sounds and a pneumatic door opens. Corporal Brown, Susie's arresting officer and one of Ross's most trusted goons, enters the brig and stands in the corridor. Freshly re-armed, he sports a black eye from where Susie kicked him during their earlier struggle. "Chancellor wants to see you," he says.

"Oh, goodie." Susie raises her hands and backs away from her cell door.

Brown pulls out a magna-card from his utility belt. "You plan on behaving this time?"

"I behaved the last time. I only ever tried to defend myself."

"Don't make me use this." Brown caresses the muzzle of his plasma rifle.

*Men and their obsessions with all things phallic,* Susie thinks. It doesn't occur to her that were such a line said out loud, it would most likely be attributed to Rose.

Brown holds the magna-card against a reader. The translucent, electrified outer door slides open. He swipes the card through a second reader. The deadbolt retracts and the cell door swings outward. "Take three steps forward." Susie obeys and enters the corridor. "Take two steps to your right." She obeys, and he swipes the card again. The inner door swings closed. No need to close the outer door. "Let's go." He motions her forward with the muzzle and escorts her out of the room.

Old Man McCarthy's eyes follow her until she leaves the room. Their reunion was all too brief, and he wonders if he'll ever see her again. *If they're going to kill someone to send the people a message,* he thinks, *why can't it be me?*

2

Chancellor Ross is in the middle of a T'ai chi movement when his office door beeps and Corporal Brown enters with Susie in tow. "Here's the prisoner as requested, sir."

"Thank you, Corporal. You are dismissed."

"Sir, are you sure you don't want me to stick around?"

"I'm quite sure. You're dismissed, Corporal."

"Yessir."

Ross faces away from Susie as he continues his workout. He knows she won't kill him without first hearing what he has to say. "Miss Walker. Are you familiar with the lost art of T'ai chi?"

"By name only."

"It's an ancient form of meditation that fosters relaxation, boosts energy, and relieves tension. By centering your core through the art form's basic movements, you are alert and calm at the same time, and can handle the stresses of the day with the greatest of ease."

"Sounds like a useful art form to master."

"It is indeed. The movements I'm practicing now are two of the most basic—Flexible Waist and Beautiful Lady's Hand. Turn from the pelvis, not the navel. Keep your shoulders aligned with your pelvis as you turn. And as you outstretch your arms, keep them straight from the elbow all the way to the tip of your longest finger. Just . . . like . . . this."

"Ross . . . Chancellor . . . sir . . . I'm here under false pretenses. I was betrayed by a man I'd known for well over a year. After some time, he came back, bandied your name about, saying it was time to talk peace . . . and then he did it again. But to what end?"

"We'll get to that. Come. Join me. Try it out."

"I'd rather just talk."

"I have enormous respect for you, believe it or not, and I'd consider it an honor if you'd join me. No doubt your muscles are stiff. This will help. So please . . . watch my movements and join when you're ready. Afterwards, we'll talk over tea."

Susie gives a cursory sigh, but complies. She watches the chancellor pivot his pelvis and outstretch his arms, first one, then the other, then both at the same time. She eventually joins in, matching his pace. "Relax," Ross says. "Breathe, slow and deep. Hold it in . . . exhale on the pivot . . . That's right."

Wonder of wonders, it works! A weight lifts and Susie feels reenergized. Dixon . . . García . . . Rose . . . Josh . . . they fade into the background. Ross stops after a few movements and watches her. Her eyes appear to be closed, and if she can see him, she doesn't acknowledge his presence.

To Chancellor Ross, the Old Man—the resistance leader on paper—was a good catch, honorable mention in any contest. Susie Walker, however, is the grand prize. She's the person who commands the respect of the public. McCarthy is great with the big speeches, but he seldom gets his hands dirty. Susie, though, will cook, clean, play nursemaid, and get in the trenches with everyone else, and she'll do these things without being asked.

She finishes her T'ai chi. The chancellor stares at her in fascination and more than a little admiration. "Let's have tea at my desk," he says. As he turns on the warmer to his desktop insta-kettle, he finds he must stop himself from speaking his next thought aloud: *It's almost a shame I may have to kill you.*

"Chancellor Ross, I must ask again: Why have you abducted me, killed my men, and brought me here under false pretenses? I know I'm a wanted woman for the actions taken against your rule, but now you assuage me with compliments, mind-and-body exercises, and hot tea. Beg pardon, sir, but what gives?"

The chancellor takes out two tea cups and saucers, a sugar dish, a tin filled with tea leaves, and a pair of spoons from a cabinet beside his desk. He takes out a bowl of lemon slices from a mini-fridge inside an adjacent cabinet. Rather than answer Susie directly, he sprinkles tea leaves into each cup and returns the tin to the cabinet beneath. He activates his desktop insta-kettle. It steams quickly, and he pours hot water over the leaves in each cup. "Sugar? Lemon?" he asks.

"I'll take sugar. Lemon?! I haven't had lemon since I was a little girl."

"Ever have it with green tea? I recommend it." He squeezes a lemon slice over his tea, then drops the slice itself into the brew.

"I'll try it if you say it's good."

"It is. These lemons are harvested in a greenhouse two clicks from Memorial Landing." Ross refers to the park—little more than an ugly slab of concrete, really—that was erected over the crash site north of the CCC. Here, one of the first Mars shuttlecraft, Discovery X, missed its mark during touchdown in a ferocious sandstorm. 238 people perished.

Susie debates whether to tell Ross about the gourd grove she and her friends discovered, and decides to bites her tongue. She squeezes lemon into her tea and takes a sip. She closes her eyes as the hot tea soothes her throat, which has been sore since the night she and Josh made—

*Enough,* she thinks. *I need answers.* "Thank you for the tea. The lemon is a nice touch indeed. But you didn't answer my question. Why the chivalry now when earlier on the bridge you had the men on either side of me killed?"

"This from the woman who tried to push Lucien Reynolds over the side."

"He betrayed me *and* he betrayed the cause I fight for. Twice."

"This cause of yours has cost innumerable delays. Work on the canal extension, for one. Onboarding of new arrivals, for another. Countless drones destroyed. At least two transport shuttles rendered inoperable. And lest I even mention the body count?"

"Your men have killed far more people than my resistance fighters ever have. For my part, I'm sorry for every one of your men whose lives were lost, whether they died in self-defense or friendly fire or were merely killed in a fit of rage. Except for Reynolds. I don't know if he was able to climb back onto the bridge after I was taken, but for the record, I hope he wasn't. I hope he fell. And *if* he fell, I hope the impact of his body splashing into the river broke his back but didn't kill him outright. No, I hope he drowned in that river, unable to swim. I hope the water filling his lungs was ice cold, and I hope the sensation was one of agony."

"I see." Ross tops off his tea and squeezes another lemon slice over the steeping brew. "Lucien Reynolds was a remarkably competent soldier. I don't entrust just anyone to risk their life to return to your barracks and fib their way back into your good graces. But, with things being as they are, I suppose it's only fair you wish ill upon him. Too bad about your friends on the bridge. Albert Dixon, was it? He was one of the first to make the Journey here, almost 17 months ago. And García García, the other one? He was one of ours, I'm told. You're quite the recruiter, aren't you?"

"I recruited him at gunpoint. Seeing as he died in vain a month later, I wish I'd set him free instead."

"Yes, hindsight is 20/20, isn't it? My men are less sure what happened to your colleagues on the rooftop. A man and a woman, I'm told. Based on our intel, I might guess the woman to be Rosalina Martínez. She's been with you almost as long as Albert, and I'm told they were close. Knew each other from Earth Prime, I might guess."

*I never knew Dixon's first name was Albert,* Susie thinks. *He claimed he didn't remember it. Crazy.*

"Who was the man, I wonder?" Ross continues between sips of tea. "I know at one time there was a Sebastian Fournier. There was also a Spiros Apostolidis. What a name! More recently, there was a Diego Cantore. You've been intimate with a lot of men, haven't you, Miss Walker? A few women, too. Our missing persons roster shows what seems a probable match based on surveillance footage snapped by one of my drones on the rooftop: Joshua Brewer, recently arrived. Young. But then, you like them young, don't you? Could this be our mystery man?"

Susie gives the slightest wince at the sound of Josh's name. It's subtle, but the chancellor doesn't miss a thing. Susie puts on her best stone face. "Sounds like you don't have a body," she says. "That's a good sign."

"No body, but a nice blood trail, so I'm sure there's a corpse somewhere. Maybe two?" Ross finishes his tea and turns off the insta-kettle. "Best case scenario, I'd say they fled, Ms. Martínez and your mystery man, and almost certainly died of exposure by now. We'll find them, unless a beater finds them first. It'll be dark soon. And trust me: No one's going to give them shelter. My right-hand man, Mr. Barstow, drummed up a spectacular smear campaign, blaming them—and you as well, my dear—for the derailment of the peace talks. They won't live to see tomorrow."

Susie seethes. "You have no interest at all in peaceful diplomacy, do you?" She keeps her voice low and her cadence slow to hold back the rage she feels inside.

"Oh, I don't know that *that's* true. I *do* know that the FCB's idea of a peaceful, all-for-one-and-one-for-all utopia, with everyone working side by side voluntarily, is a fantasy. You honestly think everyone will pull their weight if they don't have weapons at their backs? I would've thought you less naïve than that."

"We'll never know if we don't try! Our settlers did it all without the threat of violence." It takes all the self-control she has not to throw what's left of her tea into Ross's face.

"Our settlers faced a different threat: extinction. Theirs was a one-way trip, with nowhere to go but the shelter of their shuttlecraft."

"Those people were fearless explorers. They learned to harvest the land, harness the sun's energy, and work *together*, not against one another. With time, they built a village, then a town, then a municipality, finally a proper city. It took 'em a couple centuries, but they did it."

"Yes. And then the Great Sandstorm of 2277 annihilated almost everything they worked so hard for."

"I wasn't around for that," Susie says.

"I was. And so were my mother and father. My mother lost both of her parents in the disaster. I was younger then than you are now, and whenever I would fuss, as the younger generation is wont to do, she would chastise me with the whole, *'Stop acting like it's the end of the world, at least you didn't have to live through a natural disaster,'* spiel. It wasn't until I was older and in the military that I knew what she meant about perspective. It took losing my whole unit for me to learn that lesson."

Susie can't help but be intrigued. "What happened?"

"So many people perished in the sandstorm that with production down, what seemed like basic infrastructure necessities—bridge maintenance, for example—went the way of the black rhinoceros . . . or of Earth Prime itself, if you will. The original span where the Century Bridge is today was once little more than a two-lane suspension bridge. It fell into disrepair, and one day when we were coming back from an exercise in Zone Omega, a tank in the lead was a bit too heavy and brought the whole bridge down. Down we went. Myself and another platoon mate managed to grab onto the cables to keep from falling, but the rest of the unit wasn't so lucky. Reynolds wasn't the first person to splash into the drink, oh no."

"For what it's worth, I'm sorry."

Ross nods. "For what it's worth, I believe you. That experience compelled me to enter politics. I knew I needed the top job because nothing less than a drastic plan would stave off further disaster. Thanks to Gavin Berringer's JourneyTech from, literally, another world, I was able to make my plan a reality. 'There is no great genius without some touch of madness,' as the old saying goes."

Susie bristles with anger over how casually Ross justifies his actions. "JourneyTech separates families! It takes parents away from children, husbands from wives, sisters from brothers, their loved ones left behind to forever wonder what happened. That's just one step shy of murder! And since the people taken never see their families again, to their loved ones it *might as well* be murder, because in the minds of those family members left behind, their missing relatives are as good as dead, anyway."

"If I could find a way to cable them and state that their loved ones are alive and working to ensure humankind's future —and do so in a manner that wouldn't bring down the entire house of cards from the Earth Prime side—I would. I doubt that'd offer much consolation, however, and I know in the months and years immediately following yours and my deaths that you'll be seen as the hero and I as the villain. With time though, the people will understand what I had to do, and whether my death is at the hands of someone like yourself, or of natural causes—and I doubt I have much time left either way, for I am already of advanced age—it is *I*, not you, who will be the martyr."

"So what's next, then? My life for the Old Man's?"

"What's next is an experiment. You're a far better prize than he is, but I think I'll keep you both around for now. When someone from your organization mounts a rescue mission—looks like it won't be Albert Dixon or Rosalina Martínez, although someone certainly will—it'll be interesting to see who they try to save first. You or the Old Man? I'd wager my chancellorship it's you."

"The movement is stronger than the Old Man and I put together. They know this."

"Methinks you overestimate them, my dear."

"I hope they kill you slow."

"Must it come to that? You asked why I was so cordial earlier. The T'ai chi, the tea, I dare say my good manners in general. You see, the simple truth is, I'm a good host. You are my guest, and I shall treat you with dignity. Sure, that cell you're in is a bit dank, and no doubt the mattress is lumpy, but I have every intention of serving you three squares a day, getting you whatever medical treatment you need, including opiates for your monthlies, and—whenever you're in my personal company—tea and other such refinements I very much doubt exist in your barracks. Not the ones near Karl Marx Avenue. Not the ones beneath Omega East Tenements. Not the ones you and your friends currently call home, under Haile Selassie Boulevard. And not the ones your advance team has been scouting behind the new primary school."

Susie's jaw drops at that revelation, but she is quick to close it, lest he notice. *How can Ross possibly know this?* she wonders.

The chancellor continues. "There's no future for your movement, Miss Walker. From time to time, we'll send a hover-tank to raid your barracks. Or we'll assign someone like Lucien Reynolds to infiltrate your ranks. Whatever we do and whoever we send, rest assured we know where you are and we know where you're going next.

"With that, seeing as you'd rather hurl threats upon me than finish your tea, I'll have you returned to your cell soon enough. But first, I thought you'd like to get acquainted with someone who'll take every ounce of that fight out of you."

"You son-of-a-bitch!" Susie gets out of her chair so quickly it falls backward. Ross holds up his left hand, and she knows it would be foolish to charge at him.

"Tsk, tsk." Ross presses an intercom button on his desk. "Corporal, send in Commander Barstow."

"*Perfect timing, sir. He just arrived,*" Corporal Brown's voice responds. With a beep, the door slides open and in strides Donovan Barstow, menacing as always, cloak billowing behind him.

"Commander," Ross says, "allow me to introduce you to the notorious Susie Walker."

"In my circles, you're the notorious one," Susie snarls.

"Apologies, Commander. She's a bit out of sorts. Doesn't know her place."

"I can help with that, Chancellor," Barstow replies. He ogles Susie. Repulsed, she curls her lips and looks away.

"I don't want her dead," Ross says, "just broken."

"Sir, I'm offended by the insinuation."

"Commander, everyone knows what you did to the McDonough sisters."

Barstow circles Susie as she talks. She is utterly skeeved out. "You don't have any proof of that. Of that . . . incredible bit of handiwork. One of my finest moments." He blows on his nails.

"Control yourself this time," Ross says. Even he is frightened of his enforcer. Barstow is a truly loathsome human being, one of the worst people in the history of mankind, both here and on Earth Prime.

"That's up to the young lady." Barstow's voice is both silky smooth and menacing at the same time.

"Don't you touch me." Barstow's reputation precedes him, and Susie finds herself trembling from head to toe.

"Hush," Barstow says. Lightning quick, he produces a rag dipped in chloroform from his pocket and puts it over Susie's nose and mouth. She slips into unconsciousness.

## 3

Nightfall approaches as Josh staggers through the streets of Zone Omega. He lost Rose's original blood trail in a zigzagging alley that finally dead-ended at a graffiti-tagged wall too high to scale. A family of beaters owned the enormous trash pile in front of the wall, but their ferret-like hissing barely masked how malnourished they were. Josh raised his weapon to put them out of their misery, but couldn't bring himself to squeeze the trigger.

He has since combed what feels like all of Zone Omega in search of Rose, but the two puddles of blood he spots turn out to be delivery cycle engine fluid. There is no further sign of the fiery resistance member. Josh fears she will die of exposure. He remembers being told by his dormitory guard, the late Corporal Henderson, how dangerous it is to be outside after dark, and he is already fighting a cold from his night in the cave. Josh coughs and leans against the side of a building to keep from falling over. He removes his pack with shaky hands and withdraws his oxygenator. He knows he should conserve it, but in his delirium he decides a long, deep snort will help replenish his strength. Fumbling, he drops the device on the dusty ground. The wind, picking up in intensity as it does most nights, blows it across the street. He runs after it and stumbles in the process. His pack is still unzipped, and its contents spill onto the ground. Rolling over onto his back, he takes a deep drag on the oxygenator and inhales until he breaks into a coughing fit. His temperature drops almost as rapidly as that of the air outside, but he pays it little mind. He needs to rest and refocus.

. . .

Voted Homecoming king after throwing a 47-yard touchdown pass during the big game against rival New Trier High School just two Saturdays before Homecoming itself, Josh was the definition of BMOC at Benjamin Goodman High School. A B-student on his report card but an A-student in the eyes of his peers, he was practically worshipped by everyone he knew. Sure, the band geeks and drama nerds avoided him, but for the most part he avoided them, too. Occasionally, when in the company of boors like Todd Boehner and trying too hard for their approval (he already had it, but needed occasional reinforcement), he might trip a freshman in the halls or snap someone with a towel in the locker room if that person screwed up a play in a game of flag football. (*Football is never just a game; football is life,* Josh was raised to believe by his father and grandfather.) If especially bored during class, he might shoot spitballs at someone; doing so was always good for a laugh from his peers. As the school's star footballer, he rightly figured he'd never receive punishment greater than a slap on the wrist.

Getting dumped by Lori so close to prom was a gut punch. Having had time to reflect upon his actions, he knows now he was too handsy for her liking. (He figured then that the time was right. He had taken her back to Lover's Leap, the site of their first date, and his rationale was that if a person's first sexual experience is awkward, why not just get it over with? That way, the next time they "do it," in the Palmer House Hilton after prom, say, it will be better. Sounds logical, except she was on a different timetable.)

*Spending time with Susie is different,* he thinks. *She's older and experienced, which is cool, but her body is different also. Harder? No, that's not the right word. More toned? Getting warmer.* It hits him: Susie is more into him than he is into her. With Lori, it was the other way around. This time, he's the one in the driver's seat. But he needs to obey the posted speed limit. He knows Lori wasn't among those taken on prom night, yet he worries about her all the same. Drunk or not, his apology phone call to her during prom came from the heart. He's glad, for her sake, that she arrived too late to become one of the abductees, but he wonders how she's weathering the loss all the same. Pete filled in enough of the blanks for Josh to be concerned about how much time Lori is spending with that Wilkinson nerd. Then again, there's no way she'd fall for *that guy,* is there? She's *wayyyy* out of his league.

Josh doubts he'll ever make it back to Earth regardless. He hopes Lori safe and Bob isn't trying to charm her with his car, which Josh admits is a cool set of wheels. Still, with things being what they are, perhaps Susie is his future? Taking out Reynolds was tremendously satisfying, but Josh was a few seconds too late and she was taken. He's certain she's still alive, but suspects that while she may currently be too valuable to kill, her "worth" will decrease with time until she is of little use to Ross and his goons.

*I have to rescue her,* he decides. *But I can't do it alone.* He gets to his feet, stows his oxygenator, and walks to the nearest corner. Bone-chilling shivers notwithstanding, he has regained his composure. He looks around and recognizes a familiar landmark: Gwendolyn's tailor shop. He steels himself and staggers against the wind the rest of the way to the barracks.

4

Hawkins is acting sentry this evening. He dozes, the front legs of his chair suspended in thin air as it reclines against the wall. He awakens at the sound of rapping on the door and rights himself seconds before the chair's rear legs slip out from under him. He runs to the door and opens it a crack, plasma muzzle sticking out to deliver a deadly surprise to anyone having ill intentions. "Josh!" he exclaims.

Josh barrels past him and all but collapses against an inside wall. Hawkins hurriedly closes the door, chilled to the bone from just a few seconds' exposure to the outside wind. "C-c-c-cold!" Josh blurts out through chattery teeth. He rubs his hands together and takes in a whale-sized breath of oxygenated air, courtesy of what flows through the intake tubing.

"Where's everyone else?" Hawkins asks.

Josh's shortness of breath indicates that he needs a moment. He drops to his knees in a coughing fit and retches in the corner—little more than dry heaves. He reaches into his pack, which is still unzipped, and realizes he lost his canteen along the way. "Do you"—cough—"have any water?" he asks, throat scratchy.

"Sure." Hawkins tosses him his canteen. Josh reaches to catch it, but his cold hand trembles and the canteen bounces off one of his fingers and falls to the ground. Josh howls in pain as Hawkins rushes to pick up the canteen and hand it to Josh. "Sorry. Here."

Josh takes too big of a gulp and has another coughing fit. He attempts a second, smaller sip, and manages to keep it down. He waits for his rapidly beating heart to slow, then takes one more sip. "Th-thanks." He offers Hawkins his canteen back.

"Keep it. You okay?"

Josh nods. "Th-they weren't kidding when they said to g-get indoors before sundown. M-man that was cold."

"Worse than the cave?"

"S-s-so much worse."

Hawkins allows him time to fully catch his breath, then continues his inquiry. "Why are you back so late? Where are Susie and the others?"

"They're gone. It was an ambush."

## 5

"We were set up. They even knew we'd have people on the roof."

Josh sits in the commissary and explains what happened to everyone in attendance: Pete, Leonard, Samara, René, Keith, Hawkins (who asked Munch to replace him as sentry), Brandon, Pete's friends Johnny and Eric, and the recently liberated women: Dana, Shauna, and Barbara. Samara, who once had a crush on Susie, dabs tears from her eyes.

"I should've known Reynolds was a snake," Leonard remarks. "Even before the Old Man went missing, there was just something about him." René sighs and puts her hand on his shoulder.

"Susie was taken and you said there's no sign of Rose?" Samara asks.

"Just a blood trail to a dead end," Josh says. "She's tough, but if she's injured and can't find warm shelter . . ."

"That may be hard," Pete says. "Listen to this." He looks up from the radio he's been tinkering with; it's tuned to a station broadcasting propaganda on a loop.

"Let's hear it," Samara's face bears a "brace yourselves" expression.

Pete turns up the volume. The reception is staticky from inside their concrete-walled, subterranean barracks, but they can still make out the words: "*Attention citizens, this is an All-Points Bulletin. The traitor Susie Walker has been arrested after taking out a security battalion on the Century Bridge. Authorities believe her intended targets were Chancellor Ross and the day's much-anticipated peace talks, believed by many to be a beacon of hope for a better future. Please be aware that anyone with known ties to the Freedom Contingent Brigade, recently under the leadership of Miss Walker following the mysterious disappearance of the group's founder, one Atwood J. McCarthy, is considered an enemy of the state. Report any sightings at your assigned municipal checkpoint, and do not attempt a citizen's arrest. Repeat, do not attempt a citizen's arrest, as Miss Walker's terrorist group is considered armed and dangerous."*

As if that isn't bad enough, the propaganda identifies several FCB leaders by name: *"Chief among those wanted for crimes against the state are Rosalina Martínez, female, 160 centimeters, of Latin ancestry; Samara Jones, 167 centimeters, brown skin; Leonard Debussy, 180 centimeters, spectacles and dark complexion; René de Rooij, 173 centimeters, mixed ancestry; Keith Sargent, 179 centimeters, Caucasian; Joshua Brewer, 186 centimeters, Caucasian. Capturing these individuals has been designated a Highest Priority Event. Harboring these fugitives is considered an act of treason, punishable by death. Please keep your moral compass facing north and remain watchful and vigilant, for your own safety and for that of others. Repeat, please stay alert and report any sightings at your assigned municipal checkpoint."*

. . .

People react differently throughout Zones Alpha and Omega. Fred LaChance, who scours pots and pans over the sink of his modest restaurant (on the menu: chicken, chicken, and more chicken), listens as the names are read off—nope, no names he recognizes—and continues with the task at hand. Gwendolyn Pierce, who sorts receipts in her tailor shop across the street and one block down before retiring to her modest upstairs apartment, where her children and soldier husband have already sat down for dinner, shakes her head in disbelief—she knows it's a crock of shit. Old Man McCarthy sits in his darkened cell, head against the cold, hard prison wall, and sighs—Susie never returned to her cell, and he is certain she's a goner. Chancellor Ross, on the other hand, sits at his desk, hands folded and tea steeping, and listens with a satisfied grin.

## 6

Emotions are high inside the barracks.

Samara: "They mentioned Rose's name. That means she's alive!"

Pete: "Don't count on it."

Leonard: "It could be another trap."

Dana: "Poor Susie."

Brandon: "Hey Josh, did you hear that?!"

Josh: "How'd they get *my* name? I haven't been here long at all!"

Keith: "I hardly even participate in y'all's raids; why's my name on their list?"

Eric: "What do the centimeters mean? Is that how tall everyone is? I don't know the conversion!"

Johnny: "I didn't hear my name, but this is bad."

Hawkins: "What does this mean?"

Shauna: "We're as good as dead."

Barbara: "Don't say that, honey."

Pete: "What about Susie?"

Pete's comment drives Josh to action. He claps twice to get everyone's attention. All eyes on him, he assumes the role of leader, just as he did as captain of the Goodman High varsity football team. "We're gonna go get her. We're gonna get her, we're gonna get this Old Man you keep telling me about, and we're gonna bring that whole place down. Ross, the Journey room or whatever you call it, everything."

With that, a few people glance uneasily at one another. Others, like the broken-legged Keith, whose tenure made him a lieutenant despite cowardice to the contrary; like Pete and Josh's meek classmate, Munch, who thinks of himself as too stocky to be a hero; and like the weak-willed Steve Myerson, who thus far has failed to accept that he's not in Kansas anymore, stare at the floor. Most FCB recruits in attendance simply look around the room, waiting for guidance. Hawkins coughs, and someone's chair squeaks when they shift their weight.

"Is no one with me?" Josh asks after a few beats.

"Josh, you can't destroy the time chamber," Pete reasons. "How would we get everyone home?"

"This was a one-way trip, Dimkowski."

"Not for me it wasn't." Pete looks over to Dana, Hawkins, Eric, Johnny, and the other new arrivals for support. "You wanna stay or you wanna go?"

"I wanna go," Johnny says. "It sucks here."

"Like a Boys Town Hoover," Eric adds.

"I agree, it sucks here," Josh says. "I've got a life back home! But what are we gonna do? They'll just keep grabbing people from back there and sending 'em here! Maybe if the cops get too close down there they'll leave town, but I imagine they'd just set up shop somewhere else and try again six months later."

"I hear you," Pete replies. "You're not wrong and I'm no coward, but . . ."

"But what? You're the one who told me what happened the two times you stuck your nose in. You got Vinnie killed!"

"Hey, that's not fair!"

"Forget fair! How are we possibly gonna track down everyone from our school and mass-evac them back to the time chamber thingy? You're only like the sixth person from my school I've seen here, and I'm telling you, they took *everyone!*"

"I know! Well, I *don't* know, but like I said, I hear you. And yes, we need to rescue Susie. And yes, I'll help. But I don't wanna stay here! If you plan on blowing up the time chamber, can I ask you to at least give those of us who wanna go back a chance to actually do so *before* you blow it up?"

Josh sighs, frustrated but sympathetic. "Personally, I don't think my mind can handle going back and seeing that stuff happen in reverse. How do you go back and convince everyone on Earth the planet they live on is gonna consume itself, and that it's all their fault anyway for destroying the environment?"

"I wasn't thinking that far ahead. But I know what I want and I know what the stakes are. I *also* know we're up against the clock." Pete looks around to gauge the pulse of the room. "Hey, I'm not trying to steal Josh's thunder you guys, but, like, what does everyone else think?"

Those in attendance look around at each other, and a few newbies are brave enough to speak.

"I've got a little girl at home," someone says.

"My mom needs me to take care of her," someone else volunteers.

"Can the IRS find me out here?" a third person inquires.

"I'm staying. No way I can go through that again. My stomach's still in knots from the first time," a fourth person comments.

Josh takes over for Pete. "What about those of you who've been here longer? Leonard? Sam? René?"

"First month I was here, I wanted nothing more than to go back," Leonard says. "But to what? My wife left me a few months before this whole thing happened. I miss Gino's East, but otherwise, there's nothing there for me anymore."

"My parents were deported," René reveals. "I haven't heard from them in over a year. Don't think there's much for me there, either."

"I'm so sorry," Dana says.

René gives Dana an obligatory nod and continues. "It's depressing here sometimes, but there are just too many sad memories back home. Believe it or not, I'm in a better space here than I was back there."

"I'm with ya, René." Leonard puts an arm around her, and she rests her head on his shoulder.

"Sam?" she asks.

"I can't believe we're having this conversation," Samara says. "I s'pose I always imagined there'd be a time I'd have to choose. But how can I? My partner and I opened a coffee shop in Old Town not long before I was taken. I need to get back there and do my part, but then again, what if the business failed after everyone went missing? What if she's moved on?"

"Old Town, huh?" Johnny asks. "What was the name?"

"Ernie's Coffee & Bagels. 1510 North Wells."

"I know that place. They got good coffee."

"So it's still around?" Exasperated.

"It's thriving. Is your friend named Ernie?"

"No, it's a chain. Ernie's the founder. My friend's name is Jane."

"Redhead, right?"

"That's right."

"She's waited on me before. My nephew's daycare is just down the street. I pick him up from there sometimes if his mom's gotta work late. If I'm early, I usually grab a coffee."

Tears of joy well up in Samara's face. "I can't tell you how happy I am to hear that."

"When were you taken?"

"I was one of the first ones. Went for a run in Lincoln Park, van pulled up and two guys in uniform got out. Back then they never sent more than three people through at once. I was so scared."

"Just three, huh? There were at least 15 when I went through."

"It was still dark. I shouldn't have been at the park at that hour. Jane was always telling me not to jog alone. So stupid of me."

"Nah, you were just going about your business."

"They got Leonard that way, too." Samara hangs her head.

"They got a lot of us."

"So what should we do?"

"Good question." Johnny addresses the room. "Sorry for the sidebar, but, um, is there a best-of-both-worlds scenario where we can send ourselves through and then blow it up behind us?"

All eyes pivot to Josh, the apparent ringleader of this rescue and sabotage mission. "How do I know?! Why am I the one with all the answers?!"

Leonard leans in close. Homecoming king and school bully Josh's first instinct would have been to flinch, but football captain and resistance fighter Josh's senses tell him Leonard's about to whisper in his ear. Sure enough: "Josh, they trust you because Susie trusts you."

"That's it?" Low and incredulous.

"That's it. Wherever she goes, they follow. Even the newest among them. That's the sway she has."

"Unbelievable."

"Maybe, but it also means that wherever *you* go, they follow, too. If you wanna rescue Susie and the Old Man, your wish'll be their command. If you feel like marching in there and destroying the whole works, they'll march right on in there with you, even if it means marching to certain death."

Josh rubs his eyes. "I'm just a football player. A-alright, maybe I'm good with guns. But what do I know about doing the right thing?!"

"You're not just a football player or a sharpshooter. You're a natural born leader. Susie saw that in you, even if you didn't see it in yourself. I see it, too. And so do they."

"This is crazy. I-I thought we were rescuing newcomers and searching for fruit and helping people settle in, not doing hardcore, Luke Skywalker-type shit. I know a minute ago I said let's bring the whole place down, but I was just going with the moment!"

"Then go with it. They'll go with you! And if you wanna destroy the time chamber so no one else can be sent here, I'm pretty sure they'll go with you to do that, too."

"What about you? Will you go with me? Leonard, w-whadoya say?"

Leonard gathers his thoughts before responding. "I said before there's nothing for me back home. I probably shouldn't call Chicago 'home' anymore, anyway. This is home now. My hope—and I know this was the Old Man's hope, too, and probably Susie's as well—is that those of us who are here now can make peace with being all that remains of the human race. For we really *are* the future of humankind. We're all that's left."

Pete, who knows the stakes both in Chicago and on Mars, sidles over to offer his own take. "I don't mean to eavesdrop, but maybe it doesn't have to be that way. Maybe, knowing what we know now, maybe we can do better?"

René joins the conversation circle and offers her $0.02. "That's a tall order, Peter."

"I meant, as a species, back on Earth. Maybe with this foresight, maybe the nukes won't fly. Maybe the people back home will litter less, conserve energy more, stop electing war-mongers."

"Wish in one hand, shit in the other . . ." Leonard begins.

". . . and see which one fills up first, yeah yeah. I've heard that one before."

"Pardon my *français,* but we're screwed," René opines. Then, after a moment: "The hell with it. If you want to go back, knowing what ultimately happens, that's on you."

"I wanna go back, yes," Pete says. "But I wanna go back and change things. I know I'm just one man, and not much of one at that, as Josh'll tell you."

"Hey Dimkowski, you and me are cool, alright?" Josh sounds testy.

It's Leonard turn. "No one's invalidating your opinion, Pete. If you wanna go back but everyone else wants to blow the time chamber to smithereens, then let's find a way to send you back *before* we blow it up. Or before we try to, I should say."

"Whadoya mean, 'before we try to?' " Pete and Josh ask, simultaneously.

"We may be able to rescue Susie and the Old Man. I have little doubt Ross's goons'll be waiting for us, but if we go as a group, we can at least make a stand. However, if we go there to bring down the time chamber as well, then you must know, like I said before, that doing so will be over our dead bodies. Ross's Army *vastly* outnumbers us, and attacking the time chamber will almost certainly be the last thing any of us ever do. Know that, accept it, and make sure everyone else knows and accepts it as well."

Pete and Josh feel gut-punched. "Well, shit," Pete says.

"I see," Josh adds. He scans the room, taking in the contributions of everyone in it, and ponders whether he can lead these people to their doom.

There is the level-headed Leonard, the group's moral compass, who removes his glasses and habitually cleans them on his shirt hem. There is the high-energy Hawkins, who leans against the wall, hands in his pockets, uncharacteristically quiet and still. There is Keith, who wordlessly peels a loose plaster thread from his cast. There is René, who approaches Dana to ask, for the umpteenth time, how she's doing. There is

Dana, who tells René she feels exhausted and says she wants little more than to see Savannah again. There is Brandon, who is historically at his best when he channels energy normally spent snapping bras and stealing lunch money into playing football with letterman accuracy, having never missed a single QB pass from Josh himself. There are Samara and Johnny, who distract themselves with a side conversation about the merits of Ernie's Coffee & Bagels and who debate whether the Cubs will *ever* win the World Series, a feat that, at the time of their abductions, hadn't been repeated since 1908. There is Eric, who is *clearly* gay in a way that no longer bothers Josh the way it would have before his world was turned on end. There is the self-proclaimed military brat Barbara, who held her own during the raid on the women's medical dorm. There is Pete, who twirls his usual lock of hair and who, wonder of wonders, is not the obnoxious waste of space Josh dismissed him as all through high school. Finally, there is Josh's classmate Shauna, who would jump off a bridge if he told her to do so, and who is not a leader but a follower. Will she follow him into battle? A shootout with soldiers wielding anti-matter plasma weapons is a far cry from the adolescent gossip and petty drama that regularly unfolds in the hallways of Goodman High.

"Can I have everyone's attention for a minute?" he asks. His voice squeaks on the first two words, but no one laughs. With all eyes on him, he clenches his fists, takes a deep breath, and begins to speak.

7

For the second time in 12 hours, Susie awakens in darkness. The room is warmer than the prison cell she found herself in earlier, and she can tell right away she's laying on something more luxurious than a lumpy cot. She looks around and sees a sliver of light shining under what must be a bathroom door, for she hears the unmistakable sound of water running from a faucet on the other side. Her stomach itches, and when she goes to scratch it, she realizes she isn't wearing a shirt. For one terrifying instant she is certain she was raped, but when she feels down below, she's relieved to find that not only is she wearing panties, she is dry and unmolested. She feels up top, and her sports bra remains securely fastened. "Lights," she says, and sure enough, two recessed ceiling bulbs illuminate the room at low wattage.

She finds herself in the middle of an enormous bed—what we know as a California king pales in comparison. The sheets are of the softest linen. Silk? She is not sure. She is naked except for her bra and panties, but folded neatly at the foot of the bed is a fresh change of clothes. The sling has been removed from her arm, and she marvels at a sizable bruise above her elbow. Her sharpened pinky nail has been filed down to the lamina. The room is big enough to feel sparsely furnished, even with such a large bed. The only other furnishings are identical dressers, three drawers apiece, that line either side of the bed. A giant mirror, wide enough to span the width of the bed and both dressers, lines the wall. She studies her body in the mirror, checking for other injuries but finding none except for the shiner above her elbow and a cut across the bridge of her nose. As she reaches for the change of clothes, she hears the water stop in the adjacent bathroom. She turns toward the sliver of light. A door without a handle, pressed into the wood such that a person wouldn't know it existed without being shown otherwise, opens outward, and a billow of condensation escapes.

Donovan Barstow emerges from the steam. Freshly showered, he is bare-chested and oily, dressed in what looks like shin-length spandex and moccasins. His ridiculous cloak is folded over one arm. *I'll bet he has a closet filled with identical cloaks,* is Susie's second thought. *I'm about to die,* is her first.

She retreats to the edge of the bed. "Don't touch me."

Barstow raises a hand to dismiss the notion. "Miss Walker, please. I won't hurt you. In fact, I'm happy to see you awake and looking refreshed."

"What's the meaning of how I'm dressed? Where are my clothes?"

Barstow shakes his head. "In the incinerator. They stank, you see. Well, that's putting it mildly. No sense sugarcoating things, warrior to warrior. They. Reeked. Shoes, too. Your undergarments also reek, but I wouldn't presume to strip you of those myself. I see you've found the fresh wardrobe at the foot of the bed there. It includes undergarments. They *should* fit; I had someone get your measurements." Susie glares in disgust, to which he adds, "It wasn't me, don't worry. I like to look, but I rarely touch."

"Yeah, I heard about what happened to you." She sifts through the change of clothes.

Barstow offers a dismissive shrug. "It wouldn't submit to my will. It's the only guest of mine that never submitted to my will."

"What's that supposed to mean?"

"You'll see. Go on now, change. In fact, I'm going to do the same." He walks over to the dresser nearest the bathroom, opens the top drawer, and selects a collarless white shirt—a futuristic Henley, if not for buttoning all the way up the front. Once the shirt is buttoned, he positions the cloak around his neck and shoulders to complete the bizarre ensemble.

"I'd like some privacy, please," Susie says.

"No, I think not."

"I think yes. You wouldn't want me to think you're some kind of pervert, would you?"

"I already told you: I like to watch. I won't touch."

"Learned your lesson the last time, did you?"

"A low blow, Miss Walker."

"I've heard the horror stores. We rescued a woman during one of our early raids. She said you handpicked her from a batch of Journeywomen and made her your prisoner for two weeks."

"I'm afraid that doesn't narrow it down much. See, I make it a point to greet every group of new arrivals. Sometimes I'll find someone—of the female persuasion, of course—having a hard time acclimating, and I'll give her the comfort of a warm bed and a perfect $O_2$ blend so getting used to the air level becomes a breeze."

"Well, this one said you did more than give her comfort. She was such a nervous wreck she ended up slashing her wrists."

"In your company, Miss Walker, not in mine. Let's be clear about that."

Susie fishes a new bra from the pile of clothes and wraps Barstow's silk sheet around her torso while changing. "She never stood a chance, thanks to you!"

"You've got some bite on you, I see—just like your reputation suggests. Now c'mon, play fair." He yanks one end of the bed sheet, and it becomes unfurled from Susie's body. She folds her arms across her chest, then changes her mind and flaunts her wares instead. She decides she won't give this man any power over her body.

"See something you like?"

"Most definitely." Barstow gives his crotch a single pat. The half-inch stump, all that remains of his manhood, throbs.

"You're a real gentleman. Get a good enough look?" She allows him a few more seconds to stare, then changes into the new bra and slips on a grey pullover. The clothes are warm and clean.

Barstow pats his crotch again. "If things were different, Miss Walker, you and I . . ."

"Never in a million years." Susie slips into fresh underwear and makes little effort at being discreet.

"Hush." Barstow climbs onto the bed. He makes his way toward Susie, walking on his knees like a penitent person might walk the final meters to a holy site such as Lourdes or the Basilica of Guadalupe. She extends one leg so she can slip into her new pants with ease. He places a hand on her leg, as if to protect himself from getting kicked in the face. "Careful."

"Don't touch me," she says again. "If you're going to kill me, let me get fully dressed first, so I don't die in my underwear."

"Whether you die is up to you. But you will submit to me."

"You don't scare me." Her poise and demeanor tell a different story. She backs as close to the edge of the bed as possible. Now fully clothed except for footwear, she reaches for the last article of clothing—wool socks. She is unable to reach them without crawling toward Barstow.

He balls up the socks. "Believe it not, Miss Walker, my favorite part of a woman isn't what you may think. It's the foot. There's something sexy about the foot. I had a woman wrap her toes around my dearly departed joystick once, and the sensation was something I'll remember forever. She took her time, and I was able to redirect the orgasm inward. It was . . . tantric.

"Ross is the one who's supposed to be into stuff from the Orient; this would just about blow his top. I never told him; figured his old ass would drop dead of a heart attack if he tried such a thing himself."

"Can I have my socks?" Susie's had her fill of Barstow's unsettling small talk.

Barstow waggles his eyebrows to acknowledge her request for the socks. He doesn't hand them to her outright, though; he tosses them from hand to hand, as if juggling. "The thing is, once you find someone willing to go outside her comfort zone, only to find herself enjoying it, that woman deserves to have her likeness printed on the local currency. And you better believe, what she did is added to the menu for every woman going forward."

"What if they refuse?"

"Some do. At first. But they always submit to my will in the end."

"And so shall I?" Barstow nods and Susie sneers. "What am I supposed to do? You didn't leave me much to work with."

"Alas, my greedy sexual appetite got the better of me. But as I said, I like to watch. I'm going to bring you items to play with. And you will play with them. With your toes."

"You're sick."

"We've already established that."

"I'm not doing anything with my toes or my feet except walking with them. And maybe, when you're not looking, kicking you in the chest."

Barstow shakes his head from left to right, then back to center. "Hush," he says again, and puts a finger to his lips. "Hush, and submit to my will."

"No."

"Submit to my will."

"Never."

"Submit to my will, Miss Walker."

"Not a chance."

"Submit to my will."

"I'd rather die."

"*SUBMIT TO MY WILL!*" Barstow hurls the balled-up socks at Susie. The impact is painless, but she is caught unawares and falls backward off the bed. An enraged Barstow leaps, wolf-like, to the edge of the bed. He plants both hands on the edge of the mattress, prepared to pounce on Susie. "*SUBMIT TO ME, YOU BITCH!*"

"No, you submit to me." With the speed of a cheetah, Susie leans forward, grabs the stays of his cloak with each hand, and pulls them taut, choking him. His immediate reaction is to grab at the collar with both hands, and he falls off the bed and lands on top of Susie. She still has the upper hand, however, and yanks the stays again. His face turns red, then purple. His eyes bulge out of their sockets and spittle flies from his mouth. Any attempts by Barstow to speak come out as little more than phlegmatic grunts.

Barstow's neck is seconds away from being broken when he has the good sense to let go of the collar with one hand. This sends the smallest burst of air from his lungs to his brain, and it's enough. He grabs Susie's hair with his free hand and slams the back of her head into the floor. Barstow backs away and loosens the stays on his cloak to take in some air. He makes a run for the door but she grabs the end of his cloak with both hands. He is yanked backward and falls to the floor.

Desperate, he reaches around for something, anything. The best he can manage is one of his own boots, foolishly left on the floor beside the foot of the bed. He hurls it at Susie. It misses her and hits the mirror above the dresser behind her. The mirror shatters, and the sound of breaking glass startles Susie. She lets go of the cloak in panic, and Barstow falls forward this time. He wriggles toward the door. Instinctively, Susie reaches for a shard of broken glass from the mirror with her three-fingered left hand, then races after Barstow. His attempt to stand up is interrupted by a dizzy spell, and he falls forward again.

"Come back here," Susie hisses. She grabs the end of his cloak and pulls it toward her. He flies backward. He kicks his legs in protest and cuts one of them on the shard of glass she wields. She winces as the piece of mirror digs into her palm, but holds it tight. To Susie, the wound—a deep cut in her palm that will later become infected—seems a small price to pay.

"You'll never leave this place alive!" he says.

Susie is beyond warnings at this point. "Hush," she says, and falls on him. She jams the shard into his throat. Barstow, stubborn to the end, takes a long time to die. His screams sound like gurgles as blood first gushes, then sprays, then flows, and finally oozes out of the hole in his neck from around the protruding shard. His cloak catches most of the spray. When at last his body stills, Susie takes a long look at her tormentor. His mouth is agape and his eyes are open wide. She feels little remorse as she wonders how many people—women, especially—were tortured and killed at his hands. "You sick fuck." She rolls onto her back to catch her breath.

After several minutes, she gets to her feet and limps to the far wall. She pushes a panel on the wall that looks like any other, and the panel—a handle-less door to the bathroom—pops open. "Lights," she says again, and lights on the mirror and ceiling illuminate the bathroom, as spacious as any in a $20^{th}$-century McMansion. She runs her wounded hand under the cold water of the tap, its contents custom-filtered for the elite of Zone Alpha (the late Donovan Barstow certainly qualified). She rinses out a water glass on the counter and takes a long, sweet gulp of water. "Shower." A spray of water starts from the oversized shower behind her. Gingerly, she undresses, careful not to get blood on her clothes—a parting gift from Barstow but also soft and clean, blood on the sleeve notwithstanding. She enters the shower and stands beneath the water. She adjusts the temperature via a waterproof, push button thermostat.

The temperature as hot as she can physically tolerate it, she soaps up every inch of her body, which feels filthy after her humiliating encounter with Barstow. Scrubbing herself clean is like cleansing the deepest recesses of her soul, and she lingers under the hot water long after the last suds have been washed down the drain. She turns down the thermostat a few degrees and drops to her knees. As the water pours over her and washes away her sins from the past two years, she begins to cry.

# Chapter 8

1

"Wakey wakey, eggs and bakey!"

Bob, who finally fell asleep around the time the rooster sounded its morning alarm, rolls onto his side. Lori leans in the doorway between rooms. Though dressed in yesterday's clothes, she appears well-rested otherwise. "Morning," Bob says through a yawn.

"Morning, stinky."

He jolts awake at once. "Oh, God!"

"I'm sorry Bobby, I'm trying not to laugh, but it was funny."

"Oh, God!"

"Nice underwear, by the way."

Bob sees his tighty-whiteys draped over the chair from the night before. "Oh, God!"

Lori gets her laughter under control. "Um, I'm gonna check out. I saved you some donuts. Power's still out, but there was some hot water when I took a shower. I may have used it all up, though."

"That's okay, pretty sure I'm still pruney from the hot tub."

"See you in the lobby, Bobby?"

"Keep those jokes up and you'll be sorry, Lori." He emphasizes the rhyming words at the end. Although his smile indicates he isn't mad, his red face suggests he'll be embarrassed about last night's fart for the rest of his life.

"Just for that, I'm taking one more donut." Lori says, and curtsies.

2

Refreshed after an invigorating cold shower, Bob enters the lobby, Mountain Dew in one hand and donut powder on his lips. Lori studies a map taken from a display case of tourist brochures along the opposite wall. Bob sets his key on the counter. "No desk clerk?"

"No sign of him, Bobby. But check this out."

He walks over to see what she is studying. "What's up?"

"Well, I was thinking: If they took Pete just a few blocks from here, they must be offloading him—is that a word?"

"That's a word."

"So they must be offloading him and Dana not far from here. Those trucks are easy to spot and the police are on high alert, so they may wanna go somewhere else."

"You're right! Where were you thinking?"

"Um, according to this map, there's a high school that's kinda close. Let's see . . . Casimir Pulaski High. If the scale's right, it's about three miles from here, maybe less. I bet they offloaded 'em from the gym. I can't think of any other place around here big enough. Schools are always getting deliveries, so, um, the vans wouldn't seem out of place. And they could always park 'em in the gym if they looked funny."

"Or the football field."

"Or there, if it's behind a wooden fence. They wouldn't want anyone to see what they were doing."

Bob's mouth is agape. "Vinnie said something similar; I bet you're right! And hey, if you are, I bet the same thing happened at prom. I'm thinkin' they used the Cultural Center to offload everyone. It's as big as a gym, makes perfect sense, right?!"

"Yeah, I found that pad there, remember? That must be it! Let's drive to that school and see what we can find."

"You're forgetting we ran out of gas."

"Kinda far, but could we walk?"

"Nah, I'll think of something. Let's get outta here."

They hear a noise and jump. The baby-faced desk clerk returns from down the hall. He is green, and covers his mouth with one hand. "You scared us!" Lori remarks.

The clerk holds up a finger as if to say, *"One moment, please."* "Sorry," he finally says, after swallowing and gathering his wits.

"What happened?"

"You don't wanna know."

"Is it the other guest?" Bob asks.

The clerk nods. "I finally checked on him. His brains are on the wall. There's blood everywhere. It's horrible."

Lori's eyes widen. "Omigod!"

Bob sighs. "Jesus."

The clerk dabs at the corners of his eyes. "He left a note on our stationery along with a picture of what must be his son. Kid was wearing a frat boy sweatshirt and a fez. Note said: 'I LOST MY BOY. RIP DAVID. GOODBYE CRUEL WORLD.' "

"How awful!" Lori sobs into Bob's arms, as he did into hers in the hot tub ten hours before. "It's only been a couple days, why would he do that?!"

"I dunno." Bob's hand trembles, but the shakes only last a moment.

"I should've knocked on his door yesterday," the clerk says. "Guess I was scared of what I'd find."

"Would it have made a difference?" Bob asks.

"I suppose not. Time to call the police, I guess." The clerk picks up the phone on the front counter and toggles the switchhook. No dial tone. "Or not."

Bob eases Lori out of her embrace and tries the lobby payphone. "This one's fully dead, too. Yesterday there was at least a clicking sound. Now . . . nothing."

Lori looks up. "Bobby, if the police are coming, with everything that happened, shouldn't we . . ."

"You're right." Bob turns to the clerk. "So, I know you probably want us to stick around as witnesses for the cops, but, um, if it's all the same, we need to get going."

"It's fine. You never signed the register anyway."

"Thanks. Put it this way: This isn't transmission fluid on my collar."

"I didn't think it was."

Lori is first to the door. She extends her hand and Bob takes it, tenderly. They stop, half-in and half-out of the door, and gaze, morose, into each other's eyes. Neither utters a word. Tragedy has brought them closer together, but the cruel hand of fate is only just getting warmed up.

By the time the Blockade and Occupation concludes and relatives of the missing learn what really happened, over four dozen grieving people will have taken their own lives . . . including someone Bob and Lori both know.

*RETCH!*

Bob gags as the initial rush of gasoline flows through the hose and into his mouth. He coughs, gags, and coughs again. He takes a big swig of Mountain Dew, swishing it around to rinse out his mouth. He downs the rest of the contents in a single gulp and fills the empty bottle with gasoline siphoned using a garden hose he and Lori swiped from a shuttered brownstone. Bob feeds the hose into the tank of a station wagon, forgotten on a side street not far from the motel. He caps the bottle and motions for Lori's half-finished Coca-Cola. She hands it over. He finishes its contents and fills it with gasoline as well. "That's enough, you can remove the hose," he tells Lori.

"Where'd you learn to do that?" she asks.

"*MacGyver.*"

"What'd it taste like?"

"Like Gorbachev's butthole."

"*Ewww!*"

"Following up Mountain Dew with Coca-Cola is also . . . not good . . . but I thought I was gonna gag."

"*Ewwwwwww!*"

"Yeah. I'm sure my breath is awful now, so no kissing me."

"You wish."

"I *do* wish." His reply, said before he can take it back, goes over her head.

"What now?"

"Now, we pour as much of this as we can into the Trans and head to that school to see what's going on." They walk one more block and turn the corner. Bob's car sits where it stalled yesterday.

"How do we keep it from spilling?" Lori asks.

"With this." Bob pops the trunk and removes a funnel.

4

Casimir Pulaski High School is a 70-year-old, three-story brick fortress on the city's northwest side. The U.S. flag on the front lawn flies at half-staff, and lettering on an announcement board outside reads, BRING BACK OUR MISSING on one side and PRAY FOR OUR CHILDREN on the other. Inevitably, an overreaching parent complained to the superintendent about how the board's message of prayer violated separation of church and state, but the superintendent, who counted his lucky stars it was the students of suburban Benjamin Goodman High School that had gone missing and not those from his own district, told the buttinsky she was being counterproductive and called her "something that rhymes with witch." He terminated the call and decided he would deal with blowback if and when it happened. (So far, so good.)

All city schools were ordered closed by Mayor Washington as a show of solidarity. As such, Loyalists were able to break into the school without issue; the lone security guard on duty didn't put up much of a fight. They parked their vans inside the fenced-in football field and set up porta-pads in the school's gymnasium. As with the Chicago Cultural Center's Preston Bradley Hall, the Palmer House's massive lobby, Union Station's Great Hall, and the Art Institute's Chicago Stock Exchange Trading Room during what will forever be known as the "Prom Night Massacre" thanks to the *Sun-Times*, the gymnasium makes the perfect staging point for moving abductees from this region of the city to the CGC-Meigs time chamber via quick, localized Journeys.

Mark-Lin Chang is the lone Loyalist on site when Bob and Lori make their surprise visit. Chang and Dawson returned here as instructed after the previous afternoon's botched offloading assignment. Dawson has since been recruited to help reinforce the nearest West Side border crossing, but Chang's been waiting here, alone, ever since. He thinks Wesley and Miles have forgotten about him, and supposes he deserves it.

Like his late colleagues, who didn't survive their run-in with Bob, Pete, Lori, and Dana, he's been sleeping on cots set up on a stage built into one end of the gym. Although some of the men on abduction duty here and elsewhere originally hail from Chicago, Chang is not one of them. Had he been a lifelong Chitown resident, he might've considered abandoning his post after yesterday's blunder. As it stands, however, he doesn't believe he's familiar enough with the city to make it on his own.

*What a glorious culture shock,* he thinks. He appreciates the heavier air and the warmer weather, and would find himself unable to fathom how cold Chicago gets during the winter months. More than anything, he has a soft spot for this planet's junk food. He has sampled almost everything in the school's vending machines. His favorite items are Coca-Cola and that crunchy Frito-Lay product, Cheetos. He particularly loves the three-step act of licking the cheese from his fingers, cleansing his mouth with an enormous swig of soda, and belching at prize-worthy decibels.

He exhausted the vending machine's stock of Cheetos in just two days, and has moved on to Doritos, which in his opinion offer a similar, cheesy crunch. He is sitting on the edge of his cot, polishing off a bag when Bob and Lori enter and fire a few AK-47 rounds at the ceiling to get his attention.

He panics, spilling tortilla chips onto the floor. He lunges for his Magnum plasma rifle, which rests on a nearby cot. Bob fires a few more rounds in the direction of the stage. The rounds shred one of the cots and Chang immediately raises his arms in surrender. "You got me!" he cries out. "Please don't shoot!"

"Get up." Bob motions for Chang to leave the stage. "Let's talk."

Chang jumps off the stage and onto the floor of the gymnasium. "Wh-what—"

"I recognize you from yesterday. You took our friends."

"A-and you killed mine."

"They had it coming. Lori, grab his weapon." Lori fetches the plasma rifle from the stage while Bob continues his interrogation. "Where's your co-pilot?"

"Y-you mean my map reader?"

"I guess. He's not hiding in the restroom, is he?"

"No, h-he's not here. I think he was sent to the line this morning. They told us to come here and wait for another delivery. He left, but I-I'm still waiting."

"Are you sure you're alone?"

"I'm sure."

Bob redirects to Lori. "Check the restrooms."

"I wanna hear what he says," Lori replies. "I'll stay alert, though."

"What happened to our friends?" Bob asks Chang.

"I-I don't know for sure, b-but I assume they were sent on their Journeys."

"By that do you mean killed, or by that do you mean sent forward in time?"

"Th-the second one."

"And the people we rescued yesterday? Did you just randomly snatch them, or was there some rhyme or reason behind who was taken?"

"I-I'm not the right person to ask, but when we were briefed, they told us these people had a history with us. That's all I know."

Bob directs his next question to Rain-Rain, and calls her by her actual name for the second time in a row. "Lori, whadoya think he means?"

"Not sure, Bobby. Maybe they applied for genetic research there, not knowing what the place really was, and a file was opened with their information?" Lori stands next to Bob. She has strapped the plasma rifle across her chest.

"Like, a record of their age and where they live?"

"Maybe?"

Bob redirects to Chang. "You can sit." He continues once the soldier parks himself on the gymnasium floor. "Does any of what she's saying ring a bell?"

"N-not sure. They gave us a clipboard with names and addresses. Said to pick these people up and silence any witnesses. That's it, really."

"How many witnesses did you silence?"

"Me? None. I was just the driver. My colleagues? Uh, six, according to the radio. I think most of the people we took lived alone."

"Your friends killed six people?" Lori asks.

"I-I think so. Someone's wife or husband . . . a maid . . . couple nosy neighbors . . ."

"Any children?"

"Absolutely not! Well . . . I don't think so, anyway."

"You people are monsters!" Lori is outraged, but she refuses to let this asshole see her cry.

"We were just doing our jobs, I swear!"

"Tell me how it works," Bob says.

"Wh-what would you like to know?"

"Help us fill in the blanks. Uh, for starters, um, how many of you are from Mars and—"

"You mean 'New Earth?' "

"Whatever it's called. How many of you are from there and how many of you are from here?"

"I'm not sure. I saw a few familiar faces from back home a-after I made my Journey here. You can usually tell the difference."

"How can you tell?"

"By the ID tags."

"I'm not following."

"Well, we all have ID tags on our fatigues, but those who were hired here on Earth in your time, their tags are sewn over the breast pocket. Those of us who came from New Earth, we have pin-on tags. It's . . . it's like they didn't have time to have them properly sewn on."

"Any other indicators? Weapons, maybe? I see you have one of those phasers, but your friend I got this from"—he waves his AK-47—"had something different."

"It's not a phaser, it's called a Winchester Magnum Anti-Matter Plasma Discharger, Rifle Series. There's a smaller pistol series as well."

Bob repeats the name, but gives up halfway through. "That's quite a mouthful," he concedes, "but you didn't answer my question."

"We're running low on the concentrated energy charges that power the plasma weapons. Soldiers who deplete theirs and neglected to bring spare magazines have to switch to your Earth weapons. I still have mine because as the driver, I don't engage as much."

"These don't blow up when you go through?"

"No. You have to break them down so they fit on the telepads, but there's no issue otherwise."

"What does it feel like?"

"To . . . to make the Journey?"

"Yes. Is my friend gonna be alright? Is her boyfriend"—he points to Lori—"gonna be alright?"

"Don't forget Dana, Bobby," Lori adds.

"Yes, what about the pregnant woman you took?" Bob clarifies.

"I'm not sure about the pregnant lady," Chang replies. "But a-as long as your friends don't have heart conditions, they should be okay. Th-that's why we don't take the elderly."

"Does it hurt?" Lori asks.

"I-I only went through once, but it's hard to describe. It doesn't hurt. Actually, you don't feel anything in your body —at least I didn't, except for some nausea afterwards. The sensation in your head, though . . . one of my colleagues described it as 'surreal,' which is as good a word for it as any."

"Give us a moment," Bob says. He and Lori step away and confer, voices lowered and one eye always on their prisoner. "This guy's obviously just a peon. I doubt we'll get much more out of him."

"I think you're right," Lori says. "Whadoya wanna do?"

They quickly rule out killing Chang; the shooting done at CGC-Meigs on Sunday and the two lives Bob took outside Dana's on Monday were done in self-defense. Killing an unarmed man is something else altogether. Bob and Lori debate whether to tie Chang up, and figure he would eventually break free or, if discovered by Wesley's men, end up back in Loyalist rotation. As such, they check the rest of the school to make sure Chang is indeed alone, then drive him to the nearest police precinct instead. They order him to turn himself in and have him request to be interrogated by Detective Lieutenant Mayotte "and no one else." They check the van for any remaining weapons or JourneyTech; finding a few more porta-pads, they take those, as well as the 24 pads already laid out on the gymnasium floor, and add them to the growing collection inside Bob's trunk, which is now so full Bob must sit on it before it will close.

They pull to the curb in front of the neighborhood precinct and wait as Chang surrenders to the police. He enters the building, arms up in surrender. Bob parks along the opposite curb, three car lengths down so as to be inconspicuous. He and Lori watch in the rearview mirror to see if Chang flees or if any deputies exit in search of them. Finally, after 20 long minutes —spent in anxious silence this time—they pull away from the curb and make their way to the Chicago/Evanston checkpoint.

5

"Are you sure this'll work?" Lori asks.

"Not at all," Bob replies. They idle in his Trans Am, parked along the curb just one block from the roadblock where Clark Street becomes Chicago Avenue and Chicago becomes Evanston.

"I'm ready, anyhow," Lori says. Bob's blanket is draped across her lap, the AK-47 hidden beneath it. The anti-matter rifle they confiscated from Chang is in the trunk; neither of them feel comfortable enough to attempt wielding it.

"Good, me too."

"Hopefully we won't need to use this. I've seen enough death these past few days."

"You and me both, Rain-Rain."

Bob nods, takes a deep breath, and shifts into gear. He pulls away from the curb and approaches the blockade, where he is waved to a stop. Four officers, dressed not in Loyalist garb but in CPD uniforms, guard the crossing. One of them approaches and motions for Bob to roll down his window, which was only open a crack.

"What's going on, Officer?" Bob asks. "Road closed?"

"Yeah, where've you been, in the twilight zone?" the officer, whose nameplate reads HOLOWITZ, says with sarcasm. He nudges his partner, Cherry, in the ribs.

"Any chance you can let us through? We don't live in the city. We just—my girlfriend and I just—uh, we were on vacation and got stuck in our motel for a few days. The manager said something weird happened . . . bunch of people missing . . . but there's no electricity to watch the news, so I don't know much more than that."

"Your girlfriend, huh?" Holowitz leers at a skeeved out Lori. "Hey Cherry, check out this babe. No way she's this guy's girlfriend."

"Oh yeah? Let's see," Cherry replies. He peeks inside. "Nice. Hey Sanchez, Brooker, get a look at this chick." Lori looks away. Suffice to say, she's mortified.

The third and fourth officers walk over. Brooker, the bookish one of the four, is less interested in babe-watching than his colleagues. He runs the Trans Am's tags from a list on his clipboard. Sanchez, on the other hand, is the lewdest of the bunch. He makes a wolf whistle. "Yo, she's with you?" he asks Bob.

"Yes, because he's got a huge dick!" Lori blurts out. Her forehead vein pulses.

"*Daaaamn!*" Sanchez says.

"Why should we let you through?" Holowitz asks. "The city's quarantined. We're not supposed to let just anyone in or out."

"Hey guys, they're on the green list," Brooker says. He points to the tag numbers on the clipboard.

"I'll be damned," Holowitz says. He motions for Cherry to move the gate aside, then turns to Bob. "You lucky son-of-a-bitch. Not only do you get that fine piece of ass, but you get to go through."

"It's because of my big dick, like she said." Bob glares at the chauvinistic officer and shifts into Drive. "Have a nice day." He crosses into Evanston without further incident, but the encounter has triggered his anxiety. He pulls over after a single block. Lori grabs one of his trembling hands in hers, and it stops shaking almost immediately. A few deep breaths and he's good.

Lori points to the AK beneath the blanket. "Those guys were jerks. Made me almost wanna use this."

"Nah, lemme just bash 'em in the head with my big dick."

"*Huge* dick."

"I was trying to be modest." They burst into nervous laughter. He clenches and unclenches his fists to relieve stress and keep the blood flowing, then pulls away from the curb.

6

Bob pulls into his driveway and is shocked to see Gail watering the rose bushes. She is delighted to see her stepson. He shuts off the engine and exits the car. "Oh, Robbie!" Gail lets go of the nozzle and half-jogs to Bob.

"Hi mom, you're home!"

"And now you are, too. Can I have a hug?"

"Uh, sure." He opens his arms so Gail can walk into his embrace—never the other way around—and she hugs him tighter than she has in months.

"It's so good to see you, Robbie, with all that's been happening."

"Yeah, good to see you, too. Although . . ." His voice trails off as he points to the bandage across the bridge of her nose. "What happened? Also, I thought you and dad weren't coming until the 1st?"

"We caught an emergency flight last night. The landing was a bit rough."

"Ouch. Does it hurt?"

"Looks worse than it is."

"It's not broken, is it?"

She shakes her head. "I just bumped it on the armrest, is all."

"What about dad?"

"Your father's fine. He went to get a few groceries. I offered to go, but you know how he is. Never stops to rest."

"Don't I know it."

Lori awkwardly exits from the passenger side. "Oh my, Robbie, who's this?"

"Uh, mom, this is Lori."

"Lorraine Rainsmith," Lori says, offering a hand. Gail shakes it, smiling.

"So nice to meet you, Lorraine."

" 'Lori's' fine."

" 'Lori' it is, then." *Does my stepson have a girlfriend?* Gail wonders. *What else has he been up to since Robert and I have been away?*

"Bobby, you didn't tell me your stepmom was gonna be home," Lori says.

"I-I-I didn't know."

"That's okay, Lori," Gail says. She nudges her stepson in the ribs. "He didn't tell me he was bringing a young lady home, either." Lori thinks Bob's stepmom disapproves until Gail continues. "It's okay, dear. It's fine. But when I saw the door open, I just assumed it was Pete getting out."

"Oh, Pete," Bob says, with a sigh.

"What's the matter? You two have a falling out?"

"No, he left for Florida yesterday with his parents. By the way, his mom told me to tell you 'Hi.' "

"That's nice of her. It's Deedee, right?"

"Dolores, but uh, yeah. Everyone calls her 'Deedee.' "

"Oh hey mom, uh, Lori doesn't have anywhere to stay. Her house got broken into, and her parents have been staying with relatives. She's kinda traumatized. She was gonna stay with her friend Shauna, but Shauna's, you know . . ."

Gail, to Lori: "Oh, you poor thing. I'm so glad you and Pete and my Robbie weren't involved with those awful abductions. They're calling it the Blockade and Occupation, the first letters capitalized like it's the Holocaust. Isn't that a terrible name?"

"It's horrible," Lori replies.

"Anyway, can she crash on our couch for a day or two?"

"She can stay as long as she wants. But don't put her on that awful couch. Put her up in Grandma Ruth's old room."

"It smells like formaldehyde," Bob whines.

"It does not. Your grandmother's been gone for five years now. I change the sheets twice a year just to keep things from getting musty. Besides, it's nice out. Open the window. Let the breeze in!"

"Yeah, I guess. Thanks, mom. I'll help her get settled."

"You do that."

"Thanks, Mrs. Wilkinson," Lori says. "It was nice to meet you."

"It was very nice meeting you, Lori," Gail replies. "Oh, and Robbie?"

"Yeah, mom?"

"It's good to see you."

7

Bob and Lori are upstairs in the guest bedroom where Robert, Sr.'s mother, Grandma Ruth, lived for almost five years. She moved in to help around the house when Bob's birth mother, Marie, got sick, and stayed after Marie passed for another four years until her own death, in 1982, at age 79. Cause of death: slipping in the bathtub.

Bob opens the window to a view of the large, fenced-in backyard. A trampoline sits in the far corner of the yard where a swing set once resided during his younger years. "Nice view," Lori says. "Trampoline yours?"

"Yeah, I rarely use it anymore. It was fun when I was little."

"I *adore* the trampoline." Her stomach lets out a loud growl, and she turns red from embarrassment. "Omigod."

"It's okay. I'm hungry, too. My dad should be back soon, but I think we've got pizza rolls in the freezer."

"That totally works. Thanks for letting me stay over again."

"Thank Gail, not me. I just hope the room doesn't still smell like my grandma."

Lori giggles. "It smells fine. Race you to the kitchen."

"Okay."

They run downstairs, Lori with a slight lead, into the kitchen. Gail startles them; she is sitting at the table, looking none too pleased. Sternly: "Sit down you two."

Their faces turn serious. "Uh, we were just about to heat up some pizza rolls," Bob says. "Want some?"

"Pizza rolls can wait. Tell me: Where were you last night?"

"Whadoya mean? We were here."

"No, Robbie, you weren't. Your father and I got back late. It was after midnight by the time the motorcade dropped us off, but the house was empty. I read in the paper about the curfew, and your father's been on the phone ever since this whole thing happened. His going to the store today was an excuse for him to get some alone time to think, without reporters and Mayor Washington and Governor Thompson and everyone else pulling on his ear. You're not mixed up in all this, are you?"

"What?! No! We—they, um, there was a candlelight vigil outside Vinnie's last night. Some church came by with blankets and hot chocolate, so we all headed to the beach afterwards and kinda turned it into a giant slumber party. It was fun, actually."

"And you expect me to believe that?"

"Uh, why wouldn't you?"

"What is this then?" Gail pulls out the AK-47, which she was hiding on her lap under the table.

"Where'd you find that?"

Gail sets the rifle on the floor with care. She knows nothing about guns and is uninterested in learning. "Robbie, after you two went inside and I finished watering my rosebushes, I thought I'd surprise you by hosing off your car—it was unusually dirty for someone who prides himself on keeping it clean. Except it wasn't dirt on the bumper, it was blood. At first, I figured you two went necking by the country club late last night. There're a lot of deer there as you know, and I thought maybe you backed into one with your car. Lord knows your father almost hit one there last summer. But then I looked inside. I don't know what possessed me, and I saw something sticking out from under the blanket in the back seat. This. Now what's going on? And don't give me some fish story about a candle-light vigil at Vinnie's, either. I wasn't born yesterday."

"We went into the city."

"*What?!*"

"Yesterday and the day before, too."

"Robert Dean, are you out of your mind?"

"Well, of course *you'd* think that, sending me to Dr. Remus and Dr. Kirchner all these years!"

Gail reaches across the table and slaps her stepson. Hearing the smack and watching Bob recoil, Gail immediately regrets her action.

Bob puts a shaky hand to his cheek and stands up abruptly. His chair falls onto its back. "Oh that's real nice! Just hit me while I'm down, why don't you?!"

"Robbie, I'm sorry!"

"You don't know what it's like being the only kid in school who sees a shrink! I try so hard to keep that a secret! I study hard. I-I take my meds. I get decent grades. You and dad m-mostly leave me alone, w-w-which I've grown to appreciate. But I'm a freak! Pete's like my only friend and maybe Lori now too. Well, there was also Vinnie, but . . . . I'm a *freak!* I've been doing good, but this week was really hard, and now you're giving me shit, too?! Y-you shouldn't even have the nerve! Y-y-y-you made the moves on my dad when my mom was barely cold in her grave, and now you have the nerve to question me?! You don't even know what I did! I saved 12 people yesterday! She . . . I . . . we saved 12 people! But not Pete, and not Dana. She's gonna have her baby soon, a-and they'll probably take it away, a-and . . ."

Bob's voice softens. His face is wet with tears, and a massive snot rocket dangles like a stalactite. Lori gestures to his nose, and he grabs a napkin to dab away the mucus.

"Robbie, please don't raise your voice." He nods in acknowledgment, and Gail continues. "Now . . . son . . . you are not a freak. There's no shame in seeing a psychiatrist. I guarantee you're not the only student at your school who sees one. You are not a freak. But you *are* scaring me. Why don't you tell me what's going on, and from the beginning?" She turns to Lori, who watches this interplay with wide eyes. "Lori, can you turn on the oven and make us those pizza rolls?"

"Um, okay, Mrs. Wilkinson," Lori replies.

Bob composes himself and wipes his eyes. "I'm sorry I blew up at you, mom."

"And I'm sorry I hit you." Gail reaches across the table and takes his hand in hers. "But when you fly home to see your son and your plane is damn near shot out of the sky, and you survive the landing only to come home and find blood on his car and a gun in his back seat, you start to wonder if this is somehow your fault. And I don't mean that as a slight on you. You're Robert's boy, and I love you with all my heart. But what on Earth is going on here? What did you mean when you said you couldn't save Pete? Did he go missing, too?"

Bob nods and clenches his fist. "All Pete and I wanted to do was crash prom. The weapon belonged to the people who did this. There's another one in the trunk, and some other stuff as well. I was gonna turn it all in to Detective Mayotte, honest I was."

"Who's this Detective Mayotte? And who's Dana?"

"I'll tell you everything. But it's a long story and I don't wanna tell it twice. I know dad's gonna wanna hear this, too. I *will* say that Detective Mayotte, who tried to help us, is a decent guy, and maybe the only one who believes me."

"*I* believe you."

"I mean, besides you and dad." Softly.

"It hasn't always been good between us, has it?"

"No, I guess not."

"I'd like to change that. I thought I *had* changed that. But you're not ten years old anymore, are you?"

"Is that how you think of me?"

"I think every mother thinks of their children as forever young." Bob nods, and Gail continues. "Of course, when I met you, you were already in fourth grade."

"Mrs. McFadden. She was a good teacher." Wistful now.

Lori gives Bob and Gail the privacy they need for their tough conversation. She waits for the oven to heat up and paces the foyer, looking at family photos. Bob as an infant, and again at age three. Bob in his Cub Scout uniform, missing his bottom front baby teeth. Bob and his father in front of the garage, picture taken perhaps three years ago. Robert, Sr. and Gail on their wedding day, smiling gloriously, Bob by his father's side, looking miserable. Bob in front of the Christmas tree alongside a white-haired woman who could only have been Grandma Ruth. Finally, Bob's senior picture—white collared shirt, grey wool tie, medium smile—suggests that while he may not be doing great, he's getting by.

# Chapter 9

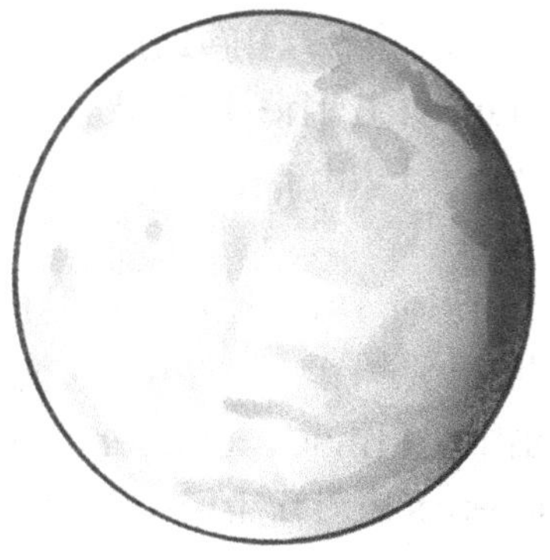

1

The enormous Central Command Complex in Zone Alpha that overlooks the Century Bridge occupies the equivalent of several city blocks. Inside are the offices of both Chancellor Ross and the dearly departed Donovan Barstow. Also inside is the brig in which Old Man McCarthy is currently the only inmate. Elsewhere inside the CCC, luxe digs serve as housing for senior staff, including Ross and Barstow. Finally, the control room, time chamber, and intake rooms comprise the middle of the complex.

A series of explosions rock the CCC at midday—exactly 48 hours after the disastrous clusterfuck on the Century Bridge. The Freedom Contingent Brigade, now led by Josh, mounts a siege that, while smaller in scale, will go down in history as perhaps the greatest battle against overwhelming odds since the Battle of Thermopylae on Earth Prime, when 300 Spartans faced down countless Xerxian hordes in 480 B.C. Josh is not alone in his belief that Susie and the Old Man's worth will decrease with each passing day. Leonard and the other senior lieutenants Josh has gotten to know during his sojourn on Mars want to act sooner, but realize they needed a plan. For one thing, with García dead, killed on the bridge, they don't have anyone familiar with the lay of land once inside. For another thing, they need guns, grenades, and magazines—and a lot of each.

Although a raid under the cover of darkness seems ideal, the weather doesn't allow for it. Josh and company figure their best shot at success is to hijack a hover-tank, as it's sure to be stocked with armaments and a driver who—at gunpoint, most likely—will have an access pass to the main CCC complex. The driver in question, Ashe, survived a previous assault on the old FCB barracks during the attack that took Diego's life. His squad leader at the time, Jacobs, has since been demoted to private, and when he and Jacobs are among those taken prisoner by Josh's team, he suspects their luck has, at long last, run out.

. . .

Josh, Pete, Samara, Hawkins, and Eric take Ashe and company by surprise while their hover-tank is parked for lunch along what they thought was a quiet, unassuming residential street in Zone Omega. With other FCB members lying in wait around the corner, Josh and his team tell Ashe, Jacobs, and their new squad leader, Youngren, that their options are simple: surrender or die. Jacobs, who walked away with his life once before, immediately surrenders. (*I can't believe you were once a squad leader,* the arrogant Youngren thinks, and puts up enough of a fight later to come within an inch of dying at Josh's hands.) For

Ashe, it's simpler—his picture is on the access badge, which gives him something to bargain with.

Leonard, René, Dana, and Johnny are among those waiting around the corner. Anti-matter rifles in hand, they march Youngren's eight-person team to an abandoned building and lock most of them inside. "You can thank us later," Josh says, implying that the men locked inside will live to see another sunrise. Samara suggests stealing their fatigues so those on Team Josh can at least *partially* blend in during the raid itself.

"Might I also suggest a helmet?" René says, pointing out hers and Samara's long hair.

"Good idea," Samara replies. She grabs a pair of flak helmets from the soldiers nearest her and hands one to René. The women tuck their hair inside the helmets to disguise their gender as best they can.

"You three get to keep your clothes on," Josh says to Ashe, Jacobs, and Youngren. "They might be expecting a familiar face or three." Jacobs opens his mouth to protest, but a glare from Youngren, who replaced him as squad leader, convinces him to keep his mouth shut.

The rebels search the compartments beneath the hover-tank's floorboards and take inventory. While there are only a few spare plasma magazines, there are plenty of grenades. A larger compartment in the rear of the tank houses flak vests that don't offer much protection from close-range plasma bursts but are able to repel knife attacks and withstand shrapnel. "Each of you grab a vest, then climb on board," Josh orders. "Once this thing is moving, there's no going back."

Dana is the last person to board the hover-tank. She's ready to atone for her association with Wesley Arendt. She struggled to master the plasma rifle when given a demonstration by Josh in the makeshift barracks firing range. He finally lost patience with her, so Pete gave her a smaller pistol instead once Josh left the room, and showed her how to at least wield it in a convincing manner. *My captors don't need to know I'm untrained,* she thinks, Caressing the handle of a butcher knife, stolen from the galley and sheathed in an inside pocket sewn into the waistband of her pants, she adds, *Besides, I've got this, too.*

Pete tries to talk her out of boarding. "Don't do this, Dana. Think about your little girl."

"I *am* thinking about her. I'm thinking of the horrible world she'll be raised in if we don't do something."

"It could cost you your life."

"I'd die for Savannah." And that's it. Conversation over.

Although the hover-tank is filled with 20 FCB fighters (and three prisoners, including one terrified driver), no one utters a word during the ride through Zone Omega. The time has come to take stock. Everyone on board believes they are heading into certain death . . . but some causes are worth fighting and dying for. Pete remembers a conversation he had with Bob and Lori on the afternoon following Vinnie's tragic death. They discussed whether they could actually take a life. They all agreed at the time that they could, but even then, Pete wasn't sure.

Now, though—after seeing Dana forcibly separated from her newborn, after hearing of the Century Bridge ambush, after waking up to the sound of Underwood taking his last breath—Pete is sure. *Let's kill 'em all,* he thinks. For Dana, who is incredibly brave. For Josh, who is a better dude than Pete ever gave the guy credit for. For his parents and sister, who remain blissfully ignorant in Tennessee or Florida or wherever. For Bob and Lori, whom he knows will continue the fight on Earth. And for Susie, whom he is certain is already dead.

Josh breaks the silence. "Thirty seconds." Pete looks around and sees they have reached the Century Bridge. He and five others are about to deboard. The massive Central Command Complex looms ominously from the hillside on the other side. He glances at Dana to gauge her level of nervousness. She squeezes his hand and forces a smile, but it doesn't disguise the look of ashen-faced dread that washes across her face.

The war is over after less than an hour of heavy fighting. Chancellor Ross is arrested, Susie and Old Man McCarthy are freed, and the time chamber is destroyed. But there are always casualties during battle, and the cost is dear.

So, so dear.

2

Susie sleeps for 12 hours—a record. Her hand hurts like hell, and she has never been so hungry in her life. She downs a few pain pills from the medicine cabinet of the late Donovan Barstow. (The pills have expired, but no bother; the FDA doesn't exist in the 24$^{th}$ century.) They work quickly, and the pain in her hand recedes to a dull throb.

Barstow's penthouse is a funhouse of horrors. Similar to the bathroom door, the door leading out of the bedroom is disguised as a hidden panel in the wall, and Susie shudders to think of how many women he may have "locked" in here in the past. The kitchen appears normal at first glance—a sterile, narrow sliver of gleaming white countertops with nary a single item that may be considered junk food—just protein packs, single-serve juice boxes, eggs, and vegetables, including tomatoes the size of softballs, the biggest she has ever seen. A rack on the far wall displays knives of every size imaginable. *What would such an apparent health food nut as Barstow use these knives for?* she wonders, and instantly grows queasy at the thought. Deep breathing *à la* Ross's T'ai chi settles Susie's stomach, and she cuts a seedless tomato into bite-sized slices. She pays little attention to the juice that squirts on her shirt, never before worn but already stained with blood spatter and tomato drippings. A protein pack and juice box provide additional nourishment, and she continues her exploration of this decidedly strange residence.

She eventually returns to Barstow's bedroom to take inventory of its contents. No effort has been made to hide his body, nor to cover it with a blanket (or cloak). The closet, behind another hidden panel, contains another half-dozen cloaks, just as she suspected, along with several pairs of moccasins, two sizes too big for her to slip into, and at least 15 more Henley shirts, all of them white. The drawers in the identical dressers house the suspected undergarments, and something cylindrical than can only be a butt plug. She peers under the bed and fishes out a box made of faux mahogany. Inside the box: used women's panties—whose she can only speculate. She is mortified when, sifting through the box's contents like a lecher, she discovers dried blood on one of the pairs.

The front parlor boasts a full-wall window overlooking the canyon and Zone Omega beyond. The room is sparsely furnished and decorated. A sofa and easy chair in garish, orange faux-leather resemble something we might find in an Ikea catalog curated by Stanley Kubrick, while a cocktail table is devoid of its glass pane; Susie speculates that Barstow tussled with a previous guest, probably female, and that the glass was shattered during the struggle.

Susie searches for a way out. The parlor window is a nonstarter, as it opens above a sheer drop to the lip of the canyon. The main door opens to a guard station, and the few times she dares to peek out, there are never less than two armed sentries posted. Finally, she tries her luck with the overhead ventilation system. The penthouse features high ceilings, and even after standing on tiptoe atop a bar stool she moved into place in the parlor, she must stretch to reach the ceiling panel. She grabs a butcher knife from the kitchen and uses it as a screwdriver, but the four screws holding the panel in place are secured so tightly she needs both hands for leverage. This activity reopens the wound in her hand, and as she crawls barefoot through the ventilation system on her hands and knees, several years' worth of dust seep through the hand towel she's fashioned into a bandage and infect the wound beyond the point of no return.

She spends what seems like hours crawling through the ventilation system, and even naps for a spell before finding the brig where Old Man McCarthy is now the lone inmate. The lights are on and McCarthy sits on his cot, back to the wall, rereading a dog-eared copy of *One Hundred Years of Solitude,* Gabriel García Marquez's remarkable novel about a South American utopia, which, just as remarkably, was written almost 350 years ago. *There's a fitting title for my autobiography,* Susie thinks.

It's critical everything goes well during the next few minutes. Corporal Brown sits on a chair in the corridor outside McCarthy's cell. He dozes but keeps one hand on his plasma rifle. The ceiling panel is half-above the cell next to McCarthy's and half-above the corridor itself. Like the other panels, it is secured by four screws, but Susie is on the wrong side of the panel. How will she ever manage to not only loosen four screws, but also catch them from noisily falling to the floor below? At least the panel itself opens upward, toward her. With a deep breath and after a few false starts, she uses the knife as a screwdriver to loosen the first two, then awkwardly removes them the rest of the way by hand. There is a moment of panic as the third screw falls to the floor with a clang. The corporal jumps to attention. "What was that?!" The Old Man shrugs, then looks up to see someone peering down at him through the slats of the ventilation panel overhead. He says nothing, and Brown, sated, sits back down and nods off again in less than a minute.

McCarthy watches as Susie carefully works the knife to loosen the fourth and final screw. He is certain he notices a few drops of blood drip onto the floor, and he grows worried for his lieutenant. He knows he would be nothing without Susie recruiting and working tirelessly to spread his message, and he's not a bit surprised she escaped and came back for him.

Susie removes the fourth screw and catches it before it falls. She opens the panel and carefully lowers herself to the floor. She takes pains not to make a sound and has to bite her tongue when her bare feet touch the cold floor. She holds the knife between her teeth by its spine, blade facing outward. McCarthy sets down his book and leans forward in anticipation as Susie takes the knife from between her teeth and sneaks up behind the slumbering Corporal Brown. She recognizes him as her captor from the bridge and slashes his throat—no mercy for this son-of-a-bitch. Brown's garbled cries for help are little more than gurgles, and he doesn't suffer long. Susie sheathes the knife in the waistband of her pants and checks her feet against his. It's a match. She tears the magna-card from his belt, aggravating her wound even more. She swipes the card on the inner and outer cell doors and enters McCarthy's cell like it's the most natural thing in the world. She eyes his tray of half-eaten food. "You plan on eating that?"

"It's yours," McCarthy replies. "Suffice to say, I haven't had much of an appetite."

Susie tears into the meal without another word. She wolfs down a roll and attacks what remains of a piece of giant mutant chicken breast. Never mind that the meat's gone cold. She takes a drink of water and leaves a bloody palm print on the plastic cup when she sets it on the tray.

"Your hand is bleeding."

"Couldn't be avoided." She devours what is left on McCarthy's plate, then slips into Brown's boots and tucks her pants into the footwear.

The Old Man sees her struggling to lace the boots. "Let me help you with those. Why don't you tell me what happened with Ross?"

"He passed me off to Barstow."

"And what happened with Barstow?"

"He died."

McCarthy thinks on this for a spell, and leaves it. He's heard the same horror stories about the man as Susie, and he doesn't doubt that her time spent with the depraved commander was wholly unpleasant. He watches as she takes the plasma rifle from Brown's corpse and wipes the blood off the stock and onto the late corporal's uniform sleeve. Same old Susie. "Let's get out of here," she says.

A pair of explosions rock the complex. Plaster crumbles from the ceiling and all hell breaks loose.

3

Chancellor Ross pours himself a fresh cup of tea as he sits at his desk. A logbook cataloging the names and blood types of the latest arrivals is open for review. He jumps at the sound of explosions and spills his tea onto the open logbook. With a beep and a whoosh, the pneumatic door to his office slides open and a tenured sentry, Lieutenant Pierce, enters, rifle at the ready. Soldiers race back and forth in the corridor behind him. "Sir, we're being attacked."

"I can hear, Lieutenant. Get Barstow. And bring me the Old Man and the Walker woman."

"Yessir. Let me get someone posted with you first."

"Never mind that. Just do as I asked. And be careful."

"Yessir."

Lieutenant William Pierce, husband of Gwendolyn, disappears down the hall in a hurry as the door slides closed. He curses, under his breath, at the sight of Barstow's dead body, and again at the discovery of an empty prison cell. Miraculous timing has him missing Susie and the Old Man by mere seconds. After 18 years of service in Ross's Loyalist Army, he decides the time has come to retire; his magna-card is coded for officer clearance, and he uses it to key into the tunnels and make his way to safety.

Ross removes a pistol series plasma gun from a desk drawer. He phones the control room. "Talk to me."

"Sir, we're getting reports of explosions on level two and on sublevel one," Greene replies. His voice sounds a million miles away because of the commotion. "Two of the monitors aren't broadcasting. Should we recall the enhanced Sauron X's to guard the exits?"

"Anything outside? Check Zone Omega."

"There's nothing out of the ordinary, sir. On the main monitor I see a dozen or so people near the bridge looking this way, but that's to be expected."

"Indeed. Protect the time chamber. That is your top priority. Over the exits and the tunnels and the Saurons and everything else. Understood?"

"10-4. Long live New Earth."

"Yeah yeah Corporal, may her bounty provide."

Ross ends the call and walks over to the window, which offers a view of Zone Alpha's high-rise district, Angeles Heights. He sees a plume of smoke rising from the south, and fidgets with the plasma pistol. He flips the safety to the "Off" position and waits for Barstow . . . who never arrives.

4

The four wings of the Central Command Complex that comprise its X shape intersect around a circular arrivals and departures center—the JourneyTech base of operations. The top-left wing is administrative—Ross's office and server rooms. The bottom-left is residential—penthouse suites for Ross, Barstow, and a few other VIPs. The top-right wing is military—weapons, uniforms, and brig. The bottom-right wing is still under construction. When completed, it will feature two more holding pens for new arrivals, as well as a medical bay to provide more convenient and secure access to treatment than the current option of escorting the injured through the tunnels to Clara Barton General Hospital. An enclosed, glass-roofed pedestrian concourse circles the control room and time chamber, with magna-card access required to pass from wing to wing. A two-story commissary with seating for several hundred is positioned on the left side of the X, between the top and bottom wings and accessible via the concourse. A visitor center of similar size occupies the right side of the X. Here, citizens can apply for jobs and housing permits, attend committee meetings, and air grievances (not that anyone dares to do such a thing).

Not counting this section of tunnels, which only Ross, Barstow, the control room operators, and a few Loyalist squad leaders and officers have access to, there are just two ways in and out of the CCC—the sidewalk passage to the visitor center and the vehicle entrance to the transport bay. The FCB members who signed up for this suicide mission divide into two groups. One (Team Josh) travels by hijacked hover-tank to the vehicle entrance. From there, the plan is to simply blast their way with rifles and grenades as far inside as they can get. The second, smaller group (Team Pete) is dropped off at the far end of the Century Bridge. From there, members will travel the remaining 0.3 klicks by foot to the visitor center entrance, armed not with rifles slung over their shoulders but with plasma pistols and tactical knives tucked inside their jacket pockets. No one has a blueprint of the layout, but as a group they are "fairly certain"—Leonard's words, based on his accountant's logic—that the time chamber is "somewhere in the middle."

All told, 20 brave souls sign up for the raid on central command —14 on Team Josh and six on Team Pete. When Josh asked for volunteers, he requested that others speak about what's at stake. Leonard and Samara spoke on behalf of those who'd been on Mars the longest, while Pete spoke of what he'd seen on Earth: namely, the events leading to Vinnie's death and to his and Dana's abductions. "If you're unwilling to kill anyone when we head out tomorrow," Pete cautioned, "I'd suggest you not raise your hand. And if you *do* come along and find yourself having to kill someone, just remember it's them or you." No fart jokes or lewd gestures this time.

He and Josh are joined on the raid by Leonard, René, Samara, Hawkins, Brandon, Eric, Johnny, former Marine Rico, athlete Joanna, ad exec Dustin, ex-cop Gonzales, high school math teacher Brad, DePaul grad student Arthur, pastry chef Amanda, mechanic Bert, and the three escapees from the women's medical dorm—Dana, Barbara, and Shauna, each of whom admits to finally feeling better. (Brandon volunteered for the mission after learning he might be allowed to fire a weapon. Pete's been keeping an uneasy peace with Brandon, who bullied Pete through middle school and freshman year. When Brandon asks if he has any idea where his girlfriend, Tiffany, may be since the Prom Night Massacre, Pete shrugs and says the last time he saw her was at Vinnie's. A lump immediately forms in his throat.)

Pete leads the pedestrian team, most of whom have limited weapons experience, through the visitor center entrance. The two Loyalist security guards outside the entrance never stand a chance; Pete shoots one in the chest at close range while Dana stabs the other in the neck. "That felt good," Dana confesses, and the unexpected adrenaline rush ensures her survival. Inside, the U-shaped information desk is staffed by a Loyalist soldier and a civilian receptionist. Although the receptionist is clueless, the soldier knows something is afoot. He reaches for his plasma rifle, but Team Pete is quicker on the draw. Five plasma pistols are drawn, barrels pointed at his head, with a sixth pistol pointed at the receptionist.

"Whatever happens next is up to you," Pete, who passes his gun between his left and right hands, says to the soldier.

"G-got it," the soldier, whose tag reads TRUJILLO, replies. It takes all the strength he has not to piss himself. He raises his hands in surrender and gets up from his chair with shaky legs. His knees, stiff from sitting, crack as he rises. A few members of Team Pete jump and he assumes he's a goner.

Pete waves his hands in a "relax" motion. He returns his pistol to his jacket pocket in favor of Trujillo's rifle. "Safety off on this thing?"

"It's always disengaged," Trujillo replies. "I know how to handle a rifle. Do you?"

"We'll soon find out."

"The chancellor's not in, i-if that's who you came for."

"I think you know who we're here for." Trujillo gives a resigned nod. "Take us there. Both of you." Pete waves the plasma rifle at the receptionist, then at Trujillo, then back at the receptionist again.

She wheels her chair backward from her desk. Calm and at a whisper: "Please don't kill us."

"Then stand up. Slowly. And come forward. No triggering silent alarms."

"I wasn't—"

Pete ignores her turns and turns to Dana. "Check behind the desk to be sure."

Dana looks perplexed. "I'm not sure what I'm looking for."

"Push buttons under the desk, flashing red lights maybe. You didn't have anything like that under your desk at the Hancock?"

"No." She feels along the underside of the desk by the receptionist's chair and the soldier's post, then squats, grimacing in post-delivery stomach pain, for an eye-level look. "We didn't get many visitors."

"Okay." To Trujillo: "Take us to our friends."

"They'll be in the brig. It's guarded."

"How many men?"

"Usually one guard for every four inmates. I don't know how many we have. B-brig's not part of my rotation."

"I hope for your sake you're right."

5

Trujillo is right—the brig has just one guard, the late Corporal Brown. His corpse sits slouched in its chair, throat slit and plasma rifle missing. Dana is also right—there aren't any hidden alarms built into the receptionist station. Nor do there need to be; hidden cameras mounted into the ceiling broadcast the lobby's feed into the control room from three different angles. Each angle broadcasts on a single monitor for seven seconds before the feed switches to the next vantage point. (And frankly, there was no need for push-button alarms until today, for no one would *dare* launch a raid on the CCC.)

"Oh, son-of-a-beater," bemoans Greene, who views the lobby action from a monitor in a left column—one of nine recording the happenings inside the CCC. He has just begun his shift, and isn't sufficiently caffeinated for what is about to go down.

"Should we get Barstow?" the younger Banks, who has also just clocked in, asks. His concern can't hide his beginning-of-shift yawn.

"Let's clean this up first." He leans into a radio mic. "Attention brigade, we have a 10-22 in the visitor center lobby. Six suspects, all armed. Desk staff compromised. Repeat, desk staff compromised."

"*Five-by-five,*" the radio crackles in acknowledgment.

"Suspects appear to be headed northeast, possibly toward the brig. Use caution."

"*Acknowledged.*"

Colm O'Malley, who is between Greene and Banks in age and whose red hair confirms the Irish ancestry his last name suggests, finished his shift just moments ago. He is second in line behind Greene in terms of tenure, and holds the same rank and title. He and his younger shift buddy, Andrés López Peña, work identical 12-hour schedules, although O'Malley regularly clocks more hours, as his last task each day is to review Peña's previous entries in the Daily Logbook. He hears the commotion as he checks the entries and asks, "Do you need Peña and I to stay?"

"Yeah, O'Malley. Keep an eye on the doors, why don't you?"

"On it." He uses his magna-card to open a corner door to a small ammunitions cache. He grabs the anti-matter rifle he stowed just minutes before, and selects a radio from the top shelf. He ensures it's tuned to a control room-only frequency, then radios his shift buddy. "Peña, you still here?"

"*Birthing a beater, sir,*" Peña's voice crackles from the radio. *Taking a shit,* in other words.

"You still armed? We may have a situation."

"*Still armed, affirmative.*"

"Stay where you are in case they try to break in. Safety disengaged. Remain alert."

"*Am I allowed to flush, sir?*"

. . .

As Team Pete is led to the brig and as Greene and Banks monitor the goings-on from the control room while O'Malley and Penn lie in wait, Team Josh enters the transport garage after swiping the magna-card from the driver and checking in with the gate guard. The driver, Ashe, has a rifle in his back and knows that if he signals to the guard that something is amiss, both he and the guard will be vaporized. As such, he says nothing and is waved in. He pulls into the garage bay, and armed attendants every ten meters motion the hover-tank onward. "Go all the way," Josh instructs. "Don't stop."

Ashe nods. He knows now that he's about to die, but reasons that if he simply looks forward, he won't actually see when the trigger is pulled and the rifle blast will therefore be less painful. He approaches the far end of the bay, where the foreman, Jenkins, motions for him to stop. "Keep going," Josh says. "If he raises his weapon, mow his ass down."

That's exactly what happens. Jenkins raises his plasma rifle at the last second but the tank never slows. Jenkins is crushed in the four-inch gap between the tank and the ground. *Payback for Curtis,* Josh thinks. The tank crashes through the wall and comes to a stop on a corridor ramp that slopes upward and narrows for use by pedestrians and motorized carts only. Ashe bangs his head on the steering wheel. Weapons fire discharges behind the tank, and those resistance fighters seated in the rear—Leonard, Rico, and Joanna—lob grenades and make mincemeat out of their pursuers.

"Gonzales, help me cuff these guys." Josh and the ex-cop cuff Ashe, Jacobs, and Youngren to the steering wheel and seat frames. "We'll take these, too," Josh adds. He hands one of the anti-matter rifles he confiscated to Gonzales. To Youngren and Jacobs: "You won't be needing these anymore."

Josh motions Gonzales and the 12 other volunteers forward, up the sloping corridor ramp. "You'll never get away with this," Youngren hisses. Josh turns back. He raises his rifle and places the muzzle against Youngren's forehead. The defense-less Loyalist squad leader puffs up his chest in bullshit, tough guy posturing.

"Waste him!" Brandon yells.

Josh musters up the nerve to pull the trigger. Youngren keeps his chest inflated, but sweat pours down his face in anticipation of death. After a minute's tension, with others watching so silently you could hear a pin drop, Josh lowers his gun. *If Rose found the humanity to not kill the men at the Pit, then so can I,* he thinks. "Do better," he tells Youngren before walking away to rejoin his friends.

"Why didn't you waste him, Brewer?!" Brandon asks.

"Shut up." Josh turns to the group. "There's no going back now." Heads collectively nod, and when Josh proceeds up the ramp, the others follow.

Most of them won't leave the complex alive.

6

The transport bay, always a hive of activity, had its walls and ceiling soundproofed six months ago following noise complaints. Chancellor Ross was thus unaware when Team Josh hurled grenades at their pursuers in the bay. The dual explosions he hears come a few minutes later, when Josh's team detonates an ammunition closet between the northeast and southeast wings—this one much larger than the one in the control room. Bert suggests pulling the pin on a grenade, tossing it into the air three seconds later, then firing a plasma burst at it. He goes first. Sure enough, this doubles the explosion and blows a hole in the back wall of the closet. The oxygen-scarce outside firmament greedily sucks out the thicker air from within the CCC—a veritable backdraft. "Beginner's luck," Bert marvels.

"Nice!" Brandon says, and offers high fives to both Bert and Josh. "Lemme try." He takes a few steps to an adjacent ammo closet, pulls the pin, and counts. "One . . . two . . . thr—" He counts too slowly and the grenade blows up in his hand.

"*SAYERS!*" Josh cries out. He and Bert, both thrown from the force of the blast, are covered in ash and blood. The explosions send soldiers in their direction, and a shootout commences in the corridor.

· · ·

Team Pete, meanwhile, has reached the brig. Trujillo swipes his magna-card for entry and is taken aback at the sight of Corporal Brown's slumped body.

"They're gone!" Pete marvels.

"That's good though, right?" Dana asks. She averts her eyes from Brown's corpse.

Pete no sooner notices the open ceiling panel when the sound of weapons fire erupts from elsewhere in the CCC. "As long as they're not where that rifle fire is." *Or where that blood is,* he thinks, noticing a trail of blood droplets leading out of the brig.

He rams his gun into Trujillo's back. "Get in there."

Trujillo and the receptionist, Aurora, enter the open cell that was previously occupied by Old Man McCarthy. Pete yanks the magna-card from Trujillo's belt. He scans it on the reader to lock the laser-enforced cell door. Instead of the beep he expected, he hears weapons fire from elsewhere in the CCC.

"I'm guessing that's the others," Johnny says.

"I'm guessing we should find out," Pete remarks.

Off they go.

· · ·

Susie and Old Man McCarthy make their way toward the north-west corridor in search of Ross. Susie wastes a trio of soldiers they encounter coming around a corner. Two of them die instantly, but Susie depletes her plasma magazine and the last burst merely blows the third soldier's right leg off, just above the knee. In agony, he begs her to end his life. "Where's Ross?" she barks.

"Kill me," the soldier replies. The name KITTRIDGE is emblazoned on the tag pinned to his uniform, and he can't be any older than 20.

"First things first, Kittridge," she repeats, "where's Ross?"

"T-that way. L-last suite at the end of the c-corridor. P-please kill me, I-I can't bear the pain."

The Old Man, who hasn't logged the battlefield hours Susie has, is mortified by what he sees. He looks at Susie, and his eyes show compassion whereas hers show weary exhaustion. "Susie, put him out of his misery."

Susie doesn't have to think on this for long. "Okay." She grabs the butcher knife from the waistband of her pants. She covers Kittridge's mouth with her left hand and forces the knife through his ribcage and into his heart with her right. Kittridge silently coughs up a single spurt of blood, which further infects the wound on Susie's palm. He dies, eyes wide open in terror despite her mercy kill.

She abandons her empty plasma rifle and grabs Kittridge's. "You did a good thing," McCarthy says. "Compassion during battle is rare, but it separates us from them."

She gives a single nod. "Let's find Ross." She heads in the direction Kittridge referenced, Ross at her heels. The trail of blood droplets she leaves behind is easy to follow; she is not in the right mindset to comprehend possibly losing her hand. Later, in hospital triage, she will find herself not even a little surprised.

As Susie and the Old Man seek out Chancellor Ross, Pete's B-squad rescues Josh's A-team during the corridor shoot-out. Unbeknownst to either team, the control room and time chamber are directly on the other side of the corridor's curved walls. Although everyone was given a crash course in the barracks by Josh and Leonard on how to best wield and fire the plasma rifles, by and large, those rebels with previous firearms handling experience—Pete, Samara, René, Bert, Rico, and Gonzalez—fare better than the others. Pete insists Dana and Barbara stay behind him, and Samara encourages Joanna, Shauna, and Amanda to do the same. Shauna, who watched as her classmate Brandon was blown to bits by a grenade, is happy to oblige, but Dana, Barbara, and the athletic Joanna insist on carrying their weight. "Don't orphan your little girl," Pete says to Dana. With that, the gender roles stand . . . for now.

Joanna, a software player-turned-coach for the Chicago Park District, has never fired or even *held* a gun in her life, but she finally gets her chance after the 38-year-old Bert, who owns a body shop on North Avenue in his other life, gets his arm blown off. He bleeds out knowing he "at least took a few of them with me." Five, to be precise. Joanna avenges him and, after a few plasma bursts go wild the first time she squeezes the trigger, manages to mow down three of her own. Rico, who fought in Grenada in 1983 and who was stationed at Guantanamo Bay for three years afterwards, covers her back. Joanna coached her players to watch their backs when stealing home, but neglects to watch her own. A Loyalist soldier whose plasma rifle has run dry unsheathes his tactical knife and runs, knife raised and in what seems like slow motion, toward the coach's back. Rico, who was on leave, visiting his parents in Avondale when he was abducted, blasts the soldier in the chest. He, in turn, is shot from behind.

*"RICOOOO!"* is the last thing he hears, yelled out by Joanna, and that's it. She takes out his assailant—her fourth kill—and makes it as far as the CCC control room before the watchful O'Malley blows a hole in her stomach. O'Malley's strategy is to fire at anyone coming through the reinforced doors; it succeeds until his weapon runs dry and Leonard makes Mrs. O'Malley a widow.

7

Susie and the Old Man make their way to Ross's office. He sits at his desk, pistol in his lap, and awaits whatever comes next. Susie swipes the magna-card. It beeps, but the door does not open; an avatar of a digital keypad materializes. PLEASE ENTER PASSCODE blinks repeatedly in yellow digital letters on a screen above. She turns to McCarthy. "I don't suppose he'll just tell us what it is, do you?"

"You can always ask."

*"ROSS!"* she shouts. *"OPEN UP! WE'RE PUTTING A STOP TO ALL OF THIS! GIVE US THE PASSCODE OR OPEN UP!"*

No response. "I didn't think it would be that easy," McCarthy remarks.

"In that case, let's try another way." Susie raises her plasma rifle. McCarthy steps out of the way as she shoots the door. The blast ricochets off the force field and almost hits McCarthy. Susie shoves him further out of the way and tries again, shooting the passcode reader instead. The unlock sensor is triggered and the door slides open. They enter as Chancellor Ross aims his plasma pistol in their direction. He is a few seconds too slow, and they dodge the single burst that discharges with little effort.

"Not so fast, Dorian!" McCarthy orders. "Drop the weapon!"

Ross motions as if he is about to set the pistol on the desk. Instead, he raises it to his right temple. "No!" Susie cries out. She and McCarthy sprint to him. Ross would have beaten them by a full second this time and blown his brains out, if not for dropping the gun onto the desk when his hand shook in an unexpected display of nerves. Susie gets to him first and grabs his arms to restrain him.

"I'll take that," McCarthy says. He grabs the pistol. Ross reaches for it in vain; his fingers, their knuckles gnarled with age, literally grab at thin air and come together in a pathetic clawing motion.

Susie marches him to the other side of the desk. She tears a strip from her sleeve and binds his wrists together behind his back. McCarthy again notices the blood from Susie's hand as it stains through the material, but says nothing.

"It's over, Chancellor," Susie remarks. "Or just about, any-way," she adds as a chorus of weapons fire punctuates her words from another corridor.

"We should go, Susie," McCarthy says.

"Absolutely. We have a bargaining chip now."

They exit Ross's office and make their way toward the cir-cular corridor and the source of the weapons fire. They emerge from the northwest wing into the corridor at the same time as a pair of Loyalist soldiers. Susie takes them both out while McCarthy, who has one hand placed on Ross's shoulder, mar-vels at Susie's fearlessness. "C'mon," she says. They continue toward the action, which has now moved to the control room.

. . .

Greene and Banks cower beneath their desks during Leonard's takedown of O'Malley. They raise their hands in surrender as soon as that burst of plasma fire ceases. From their vantage point, they notice a change in the shadows on the floor near the restroom. The door, which is built into a recess to their left, opens manually. The recess is not immediately noticeable by guests, and this gives Peña the advantage. He sticks his head outside the door and nods. He slinks behind a protective girder, raises a finger to his lips in a shushing motion, and awaits his opportunity. Leonard is an easy target, but Peña assumes other FCB rebels are on their way as well.

The death toll is high by the time Leonard and our remaining heroes reach the control room. In addition to Brandon, Bert, Rico, and Joanna, you can add Hawkins, Barbara, and Dustin to the list of the departed. Hawkins, who helped carry Underwood out of the canyon following the belly beater attack during their gourd expedition, fights valiantly. He takes down six Loyalist soldiers before falling at the hands of a seventh. Barbara, the young Army widow whose father was killed during the Tet Offensive in Vietnam and whose husband perished in a chopper crash in Germany, ultimately has no business joining such a high-stakes fight, and neither does Dustin, a media buying supervisor with Leo Burnett who, at 25, is one of the youngest supervisors in the ad agency's Chicago headquarters. Still, as the granddaughter, daughter, sister, and wife of an extended family of Army men, Barbara, who fails to heed Pete's warning to get down, has been instilled since childhood with a fierce sense of patriotism. She figures it's her responsibility to join the fight for freedom. Her heart is in the right place . . . until a plasma blast disintegrates it. As for Dustin, he has stubbornly believed since his abduction that he will eventually return safely to Earth, where he will pen a bestseller about his experience. *Accidental Martian,* he has decided to call it . . . until a plasma round blows his head off and brings those best-laid plans to an abrupt end.

Peña's sneak attack on the remaining rebels is only partially successful. He takes out Amanda, whose Lincoln Park *patisserie* was in the red at the time of her abduction, as well as an unsuspecting Eric, who thinks the coast is clear after Leonard blasts a hole through the torso of the unfortunate O'Malley, and whose bravery inside the CCC is his way of making up for being too scared to come out as gay to his evangelical parents. Leonard himself escapes harm. He turns left precisely when Peña pulls the trigger, and Eric's midsection is vaporized by the blast meant for him. Peña, the Mars-born ancestor of Salvadorian immigrants to the United States via refugee visas 300 years earlier, should have stayed hidden in the restroom, for Leonard and Gonzalez, the latter of whom follows the ill-fated Amanda and Eric into the control room, fire simultaneous plasma streams at the Loyalist and blast holes into both him and the wall behind him.

Josh enters the control room with purpose. "Anyone not wanting to get killed better step forward now," he exclaims. Sure enough, Greene and Banks step out from hiding. The crotch of Banks's pants is wet from urine. "Where's the time travel shit?"

"The what?" Banks tugs on his shirtfront to cover the wet spot.

"The platform. The portal. The whatever you call it. The way out of here."

"The time chamber?"

"Yes. That."

Banks points to a pair of reinforced blast doors along a concrete wall at the far side of the room. Greene glares as Banks as if to say, "*How dare you?*" Banks merely shrugs.

Josh turns to Pete. "What do you think, Dimkowski?"

Pete shrugs. "What's waiting for us on the other side?" he asks Greene and Banks.

"N-n-not much," Banks answers. "A-a few lab techs, maybe a doctor. Th-think they're getting ready for the next batch o-of Journeymen."

"Any weapons in there?"

"N-no. It's not safe, and new arrivals a-a-are usually too disoriented t-to fight."

"No shit. I puked my guts out after I came through."

"M-me too."

Pete and Josh turn to each other, and can't believe what they're hearing. "You're from Chicago?" Pete asks Banks.

"H-Hanson Park, born and raised."

"How long have you been here?"

" 'Bout a year."

And to Greene: "What about you?"

"Born here. Fifth generation, something like that."

To Greene again: "Did you recruit him or something?"

"I trained him, but I've only worked here for about four of your Earth Prime years myself."

"How'd you get this job?"

"My parents died in the Great Sandstorm. I was just a baby. My grandparents adopted me, but they died not long after. The chancellor took pity on me. He's a good man in his own way."

"I've only been here a few weeks, but that doesn't sound like the chancellor I heard of."

"It's complicated. Are you going to kill us?"

"Not if you're straight with me. Now, are you and your friend here *sure* there's no one lying in wait for us on the other side of that door?"

Greene looks at Banks, then back at Pete. "I don't control who comes and goes, like him"—he points to Peña's corpse—"but I think you'll be okay. Are you going back?"

"We're gonna destroy it," Josh answers.

"Why don't you just go back?"

"Come with us. Make a better future," Pete says. And to Banks: "You too."

"No chance," Greene replies. "Your world is doomed," Banks says nothing, but a look of introspection suggests he may be mulling over Pete's offer.

"Maybe we can save it?" Pete posits.

Greene stalls for time. "That's what we're trying here, with this one."

"By breaking up families? By forcing people to work? That's slavery."

"You say 'potato,' I say *potato.*' " He elongates the "a" sound on the second utterance of 'potato' to illustrate the difference.

Loyalist forces close in while Pete and Greene debate. Josh acts at the first sound of approaching enemy footsteps. "There's no time for this, Dimkowski. Move!" He motions for Greene to approach the blast doors and swipe his magna-card. This door, too, is passcode protected. Greene types five numbers with shaky fingers. In his haste, he mis-types. INVALID blinks repeatedly in alternating red and yellow.

"Shit," Greene mumbles, all traces of his usual cockiness having vanished. He keys in the password correctly on his second attempt. The doors, steel reinforced and not translucent like those in the brig or in the intake room, slide open pneumatically. Josh rushes everyone inside the time chamber as the doors close to the sound of weapons fire outside. A runaway plasma blast makes it through the doors at the last possible second and Brad, unmarried teacher of high school algebra and assistant varsity wrestling coach, is toast. No last words, just alive one moment and dead the next. The private high school at which he taught, West Side Preparatory Academy, will hold ten seconds of silence for him at their first match in December 1987, but that won't bring him back.

"Dammit!" Josh yells. The three time chamber technicians jump, startled. They cease their calibration and put their hands up in easy surrender.

"It's okay," Pete replies, and puts a hand on Josh's shoulder. "Let's just go home."

Josh brushes him off. "No. We need to destroy this thing." He turns to Leonard, Samara, and René, who each defer to him even though they've been lieutenants for longer. "Cover the doors."

Leonard nods. He, Samara, and René stand watch on this side of the double doors, weapons raised at the sound of plasma fire from the other side of the wall. He looks at the others. "What's . . ." They shrug, confused but ready for whatever happens next.

"Forget it," Pete de-escalates a vengeful Josh. "We'll destroy it from the other side. There can't be many of these things, can there?" He is nose-to-nose with Greene. "Can there?!"

"This is the only one on New Earth."

"How do we destroy it?" Josh asks.

"There isn't exactly a manual on how to blow up the chamber."

"Is there a computer we need to deprogram?" He turns to Pete. "Dimkowski, you're into nerd shit. What do you think?"

"I have no idea, but I'm guessing they do." Pete points to the unarmed technicians.

"Well?" Josh asks them. "How do we deprogram it?"

"We can't," Marquez answers. "There's a fail-safe built into each workstation. But I'm sure you could vaporize the machine with the, you know . . ." She points to the plasma rifle Josh is wielding.

"You want us to just shoot it and lob a bunch of grenades at the platform itself?"

"I-I guess so?" She turns to her male colleagues for confirmation. One nods and the other waves his hand in a *maybe sí, maybe no* gesture.

"It can't be as easy as all that, can it?"

They shrug.

. . .

Susie can rightfully lay claim to most of the weapons fire on the other side of the doors. Although done defensively, she racks up an impressive body count, much to the horror of McCarthy, who has long believed in peaceful diplomacy as the first course of action. He does his part, backing her up by providing cover fire with the plasma pistol that was confiscated from Ross, but he is not weapons-trained, however, and his shots go wild. Ross, hands tied, pathetic, watches Susie in action and is simultaneously impressed and dismayed. *She's going to succeed me,* he thinks.

Susie corners the last soldier after his rifle runs dry. She orders him to open the passcode-protected double doors to the time chamber. "Passcode!" she yells. The soldier sees Ross but hasn't otherwise gotten word that the chancellor's been deposed. Foolishly brave or simply not knowing the code, he refuses Susie's order. *"PASSCODE!"* she shouts again, louder this time, rifle raised and finger on the trigger, temporarily losing sight of her humanity and ready to blow the unfortunate young man away.

"Susie, stop," McCarthy yells.

*"PASSCODE!"* she bellows a third time, at the top of her lungs.

*"SUSIE!"* McCarthy yells again, matching her volume. She flashes back, like in the nightmares she once told Rose about, to when she executed Abramson. She knows that while she can kill in self-defense, she can no longer shoot someone in cold blood. Still, she is at her wit's end. She's tired of waiting.

Today's soldier, whose tag reads SMITHSON, cowers in fear as he looks, one by one, at her, McCarthy, and Ross, who offers a sympathetic nod and turns around to show his hands are bound. The Old Man puts a hand on Susie's shoulder to ease her down. "There has to be another way," he says, stern but reassuring. Finally, Susie lowers her gun and Smithson utters a single wail.

Susie backpedals. "It's not my wish to kill you," she tells Smithson. She lowers her weapon partway and takes a single step backward. "But I need you to open the door."

He gulps, a bucket of nerves. "D-d-d-don't have the p-p-passcode."

"It's okay, Soldier," McCarthy says. To Ross: "I don't suppose you can lend a hand?"

"I never come down here, sorry." Ross says. McCarthy nods, dejected but unsurprised.

The deposed chancellor looks at Susie, whose face is drenched with sweat. "That gash on your hand isn't getting any better, Miss Walker."

"I'm trying not to notice." She looks around and sees a first aid kit, denoted by a red cross, on the back wall. She walks over to the kit and jumps as the double doors beep, then open from the other side.

With a weapon pointed at her back by Leonard, Marquez has entered the passcode into the digital keypad from inside the time chamber.

"Anyone wanna time travel?" Samara asks. Her expression changes when she sees the bloody mess that is Susie's hand.

Susie recognizes her concern. "I know. Working on it." She uses her teeth to tear the lid off a can of disinfectant spray. She douses her palm and howls in pain.

"Miss Jones," McCarthy says in response to Samara's smiling visage.

"So good to see you, sir." Samara motions in Susie's direction. "Is she okay?"

"So she says." McCarthy and Samara watch as Susie secures one end of a gauze roll in her mouth and unspools the roll around her hand.

"You're just in time. We're about to destroy the chamber."

McCarthy nods. "Miss Walker, let's make haste. There're sure to be more of them."

"Don't I know it." Susie tucks the excess gauze inside a fold in the bandage, grabs her plasma rifle, and follows McCarthy into the time chamber. On the way, she grabs two pairs of futuristic handcuffs (the same as 20th-century handcuffs, really) from the supply closet O'Malley opened. She unknots the fabric binding from Ross's wrists and shackles one cuff to his right wrist and the second cuff to a piece of floor-to-ceiling intake pipework in the corner of the time chamber nearest the entry doors. She tosses the other pair of cuffs to Smithson, who knows what to do. He handcuffs himself to the same piece of pipework and can barely glance at Ross without hanging his head in shame.

Josh, Pete, Dana, Leonard, Samara, René, Gonzales, Shauna, Arthur, and Johnny stand idly by while Greene, Banks, and the technicians await instructions. Leonard and René, who have served faithfully in the FCB since not long after its inception, smile at the sight of their esteemed leaders. Josh and Susie exchange nods. Their reunion can wait; there is work to be done.

"We need to figure out who's going and who's staying," Leonard says.

Josh gestures to Marquez. "She says there isn't a way to shut it down from the computer."

"There's a fail-safe," she explains.

"Yes, but we can just cross the circuits and overload it," time chamber technician Maxwell clarifies. Marquez pays him a surprised look.

"Whoa whoa whoa," their colleague, Singh, remarks.

"It's dangerous, but it's more of a sure thing than just tossing grenades at it," Maxwell reasons. "Besides, do you want 'em to shoot us?"

"Explain," Josh says. Susie looks not at the technicians but at Josh. *I'm glad he didn't die on that rooftop,* she thinks. *Leadership suits him.*

"Not much to it. We activate inbound and outbound at the same time. All telepads. Switch the red and blue inputs from the control panel when we get full greens across the board. Engage the auxiliary, and every pad should fry and each workstation here should short circuit. If you do that, though, I hope you like the smell of burning metal."

"You'll need to be ready to run," Marquez adds.

"What the hell, you two?" Singh remarks.

Josh turn to Susie. "Whadoya think?"

She defers to Old Man McCarthy. "Sir?"

"If we do this, we as a planet are on our own," McCarthy says. "No more lifelines from the past." The clomping of Loyalist boots from outside the chamber cut his speechifying short.

"We've got company," Pete says.

McCarthy turns toward the door. Radios crackle from the other side. He looks at Susie, then at Leonard, Samara, and René, and finally at Josh, Pete and the other fighters he is meeting for the first time. "It's time we make our stand," he says. "Anyone not from here who wants to go back, now's your only chance."

"Start it up!" Josh motions to the techs. "Return trip first, we cross the circuits after."

"We'll cover you," René says. She, Leonard, Samara, Josh, Susie, and Gonzales face the doors, armed and ready. McCarthy joins them in solidarity, but René shakes her head. "Take cover, sir."

"No can do, Miss de Rooij. I've decided to fight."

"We're not losing you again." Then, after a pause: "That's an order."

"Well then, I see how it is." He retreats with Pete, Dana, Johnny, Shauna, and Arthur.

Arthur steps forward and extends his hand to the Old Man. "I'm Arthur, sir."

"Atwood McCarthy, Arthur. Most people just call me the 'Old Man.' " He shakes Arthur's hand.

"I haven't been here long, but I've already heard so much about you. I'm outta ammo, but if you wanna offer up your gun, I'd be honored to stand for you."

"That's not necessary, Arthur."

"Sir, I insist."

"Your bravery is to be commended." He hands over the plasma pistol. "Be careful. She's small, but she's powerful. Safety's off, all you have to do is . . ."

". . . pull the trigger. I've got it, sir." Arthur joins the line next to Gonzales.

Gonzales, who was abducted at the same time as Pete, Dana, Johnny, and Eric, retired from the Joliet Police Department at 38 after refusing to testify against a colleague in an officer-involved shooting. He moved to Chicago with a buddy from high school; the two men, proud bachelors both, opened a bar in Little Italy that caused a rift in the neighborhood until they added Peroni to the list of on-tap options. He gives the slightest of nods to the 24-year-old graduate student. "Not going back either?" he asks Arthur.

"I'm failing my classes and have 30 grand in student loan debt. I'd go back if that thing would let us stop off to check Super Bowl winners for the next five years so I can make a few wagers, but somehow I don't think that's an option."

"That doesn't mean dying in a shootout on another planet should be, either."

"And yet you're standing here with me."

"We all have our reasons, kid."

"Anyone gonna get the door?" Josh asks.

"On it," Banks says. Pete grabs him by the arm as he passes.

"Careful," he whispers. "Stay low when the shooting starts. And come back with us. You don't belong here any more than I do."

"We'll see." Banks types the passcode into the digital key-pad and ducks low behind the wall.

Susie grabs Josh's left hand with her right and gives it the briefest of squeezes. She lets go and aims her rifle as best she can with one bum hand.

The double doors open and both sides engage.

8

Marquez motions for Pete and the other return travelers to get out of the line of fire and hide in the orientation bay. "C'mon, Dana!" Pete yells.

"I'm not going back, Pete. I have a daughter now."

"I was afraid you'd say that. Now get in here so you don't get shot!"

She retreats into the bay as stray weapons fire whizzes past. Screams suggest the shootout isn't going well, but which side is faring better?

Second-year MBA student Arthur is the first to get obliter-ated; his meager pistol doesn't stand a chance, and the only plasma burst he manages to fire goes wild. Gonzales avenges him by taking out three Loyalist soldiers before a fourth blows his head off. Susie, who makes her stand directly next to him, finds her face covered in his blood. She takes down his assail-ant and yells for Josh to take cover.

"I'm not leaving the line!" Josh replies. He blasts an ap-proaching soldier in the cheek, blowing off one side of the man's face and sending him flying backward.

"Go back with the others!" Susie yells.

"Let's finish this first!"

They continue fighting and bag two more soldiers apiece.

The chamber technicians take cover behind a padded, anti-radiation wall as the departures platform powers up. Greene cowers beside them. "Any weapons here?" he asks.

"What?!" Marquez yells over the noise of weapons fire and of the chamber powering up for a Journey of 55 million kilometers (34 million miles) when the two planets' orbits most closely align.

"Are there any weapons here?" he repeats, louder.

"Just theirs." She points toward Susie's line.

"We have to do something!"

Marquez shrugs. "They're holding all the cards."

"Damn!" Greene looks around, determined—somehow—to salvage this disastrous day.

The shootout is over less than 30 seconds after it began. Leonard, René, Samara, Josh, and Susie remain standing once the smoke clears. Banks steps out of hiding from behind a support column and joins them. His jaw drops at the sight of the bloodbath in front of him.

The gauze wrapped around Susie's hand is soaked through with blood. "We have to get you to the hospital," Josh says.

"I'm okay." Susie's speech is slurred as she subsides on her last reserves of adrenaline. "L-let's s-see this through."

"Welcome back, Susie," René says. "I'm sorry about Dixon and Rose." She offers Susie a one-armed hug and is careful not to lean against her wounded limb.

To René: "G-good to be back." To the technicians: "H-how are we doing?"

Marquez steps out from behind the anti-radiation wall and checks the monitors. "We're fully charged for up to six."

"You cockteasing bitch," Greene hisses. "You're just going to send them through?! They know too much!"

"I don't like it any more than you do," she replies, "but in case you haven't noticed, there are more of them than there are of us, and they're the ones giving orders."

"This is a death sentence! New Earth needs all the laborers we can find!"

"Not like this, son, not like this." McCarthy addresses Greene as he and the others step out of hiding from the orientation bay.

Greene sneers. "Stifle it, Old Man."

Shauna emerges from the bay and screams at the sight of so many dead bodies. "It's okay," Dana says. She opens her arms to embrace the traumatized cheerleader, who once shared a rented limo for the ride to prom with her friends Curtis, Brandon, and Tiffany, two of whom are now dead.

McCarthy turns to Pete and the others. "You ready to go home?"

Pete, normally the incessant chatterbox, finds himself at a loss for words. He turns to Dana, who continues to comfort a clingy Shauna. "You sure you're not going back?"

"You know I can't." Dana eyes well up with tears.

"Anyone else?" McCarthy asks. "Don't be shy. We're up against the clock. There are sure to be more of them."

"I hate to sound selfish, but I'm going back," Johnny says. "I'll take Chicago winters over this any day." He is sure he hears Samara chuckle, and he turns to her. "Come with. Ernie's Bagels misses you."

Samara looks at Susie, then stares at the ground, torn. She made peace several months ago with the likelihood that she would never return home, and found a second family with the Freedom Contingent Brigade. *Will I actually get to see Jane again?* she wonders.

"I wanna go, too," Banks is surprised to find himself saying.

"C'mon then," Pete motions him toward the platform.

Banks steps forward. "W-what do I do?"

"You've seen what we do in here before, Operator, I'm sure of it!" Marquez says.

"Actually, no. Always just the aftermath."

"In that case, step on one of the individual telepads," Marquez says. "Make sure your entire body is inside the circle—it's 1.5 meters in circumference, so there should be enough room. Try to remain still, but breathe normally."

"W-when are you sending me back to?"

"It has to be later than when you took your first Journey, otherwise there could be a paradox."

"W-what's a paradox?"

"That's when you run into your former, pre-Journey self," Singh chimes in.

"Like in *Back to the Future?*" Pete asks.

"I-I don't know what that is," Singh, who was born on Mars, says.

"I know that movie!" Banks says with excited recognition, His voice deflates after he realizes that, yeah, running into your former self would be trippy at best and catastrophic at worst. "Okay, yeah . . . definitely wouldn't wanna do that." To Pete: "You were taken after I was, right?"

"Yeah, I remember the date. It was May 25th, 1987. Three days after prom. It was in the afternoon. So I guess for me, send me back 12 hours later? Say . . . three o'clock the next morning?"

"Th-the 26th? That date works for me too," Banks decides.

"Me three," Johnny says.

"And me," Shauna squeaks. Her face is wet from crying. "Josh, you coming?"

"I . . ." Josh, who tears off a fresh strip of gauze for Susie, doesn't complete his sentence. *What does Susie want?* he asks himself.

"There's no time, dude," Pete interrupts. "Yes or no?"

"I'll go," Samara declares. She sets her plasma rifle on its end against a support wall. This will prove to be a mistake. She turns to Susie and Old Man McCarthy. "Sorry. I think I have to."

Susie applies a fresh gauze strip to the open wound on her palm. She pulls the end of the strip as tight as she can tolerate, then turns to Samara. "I don't know your world, Sam, but I can't blame you."

"Do what you have to do, Miss Jones," McCarthy adds. With the slightest of nods: "And thank you for joining our cause."

Samara looks at the ground, sad and happy at the same time. "Good luck. And congrats on today." She makes her way to the departures telepad.

"Glad you're coming," Johnny says. "I'll have to stop by Ernie's for coffee."

"You get free coffee for life." She bursts into a joyous smile as she thinks, *I can't believe this moment has actually come!*

"You should get going," Susie says. "In case there's more of them, like he said." She motions to the Old Man.

"Go home," McCarthy adds. "And Godspeed."

"Long live New Earth." Samara cries happy tears.

"May her bounty provide," Susie, McCarthy, Leonard, and René reply, in unison.

"Josh?" Pete again.

Sad about Samara's imminent departure, Susie turns her attention back to Josh. He toys with what remains of the gauze roll. "Go," she whispers.

"You sure?" he asks. She shakes her head, then nods.

"Everyone ready?" Marquez asks.

"Wait, can we go back and get Tiffany?" Shauna asks from out of the blue.

Pete shakes his head. "It's now or never."

Shauna scowls. She beckons her high school's star quarterback. "C'mon, Josh, hurry!"

"Be right there."

"You're coming, right?"

"You go first. Curtis would want you home safe." Josh remains torn. "*You go first*" is not a definitive answer. Shauna doesn't pick up on that, however. She wipes back tears at the mention of her late boyfriend's name. Josh could never bring himself to tell Shauna he saw Curtis die, so she thinks he's still alive and believes she's being a coward for leaving her man behind. Even so, it's better than staying.

Banks steps forward. "I-I think they need a minute to say goodbye, b-but I'm ready. Well, scared I'm gonna have a heart attack."

"If you didn't have one on the way over here, you won't have one going back," Pete reasons. "Now go home and find your folks. And be good."

Banks nods and steps onto the center-most pad. He takes three deep breaths and clenches his fists.

"I'm right behind you," Pete adds, "but don't wait for me."

"Ready on my mark," Singh says. "Three . . . two . . . one . . . mark!" He and his colleagues watch as the dual columns of light turn from gold to green and stabilize. Banks's molecules disassemble into a spinning, human-shaped mass. The shape holds for several seconds, then disappears.

"Who's next?" Marquez asks.

Samara steps forward. "I guess it's time to bid you all *adieu*. My brave Susie . . . Len . . . René . . . sir . . . bye everyone."

"*Adieu,* Sam." René is crying heavily. Leonard whispers something in her ear. She nods, wipes away her tears, and addresses Susie. "Len and I will check the corridor. Make sure the coast is clear and buy you some time."

With a nod of approval, Leonard and René exit the time chamber and the control room, sidestepping bodies as they go. He remains stoic as ever while she wipes away tears, ready for anything except saying goodbye. Leonard pats the younger, braver Josh on the back as he passes.

Susie maintains a straight face as Samara steps onto the departures telepad. Old Man McCarthy, with 60 years of life experience behind him, offers Samara a simple wave.

"Go find your Jane," Johnny instructs Samara. "And be happy."

"Remember, free coffee for life," she replies. The dual rows of spinning lights surrounding her turn from gold to green and slow down. She knows to remain still. She manages the quickest of waves, however—just a flick of the wrist.

Singh: "Three . . . two . . . one . . . mark!"

Samara closes her eyes as the columns of light extend to encase her body and her molecules disassemble. It is just as well she has shut her eyes, for she would hate to see what happens next.

"Good for her," Johnny says with a smile.

Pete motions him forward into the chamber. "Well go on, dude."

"Here's hoping I don't shit myself." Johnny chooses an illuminated pad. As he turns around to wave goodbye to his new friends, an unexpected plasma blast rips a hole through his chest. While everyone else was distracted by the action on the departures telepad, Greene grabbed Samara's discarded rifle!

Johnny flies backward from the impact and into the wall behind him. The hole in his chest drips red with plasma residue and blood. He doesn't have a chance to register what happened. If he suffers, it's for a second or two at most.

"Shit!" Pete grabs Dana by the hand and yanks her out of the line of fire. They duck behind an anti-radiation column. A stray plasma blast takes out a chunk of the column but misses them both.

"You dick!" Josh returns a blast in Greene's direction. The shot is rushed and wild. It hits the computer array behind them, sending sparks flying in all directions and sounding an alarm in the chamber. Greene fires back, but Maxwell, the technician who had a change of heart and suggested they simply cross the wires, charges him. His act of heroism backfires when Greene's weapon discharges while he is shoved.

This blast goes wild as well; it passes clean through Maxwell's midsection, killing the technician instantly and losing impact on its way to Josh. The plasma blast strikes Josh just left of his stomach and ruptures a kidney. Josh falls to the ground and fires a stray blast into the ceiling upon impact.

"Josh!" Susie fires back at Greene, but the shot misses as he skids across the concrete floor after being charged by Maxwell. Marquez screams, her white lab coat once again splattered with blood—Maxwell's this time. Greene skids to a halt when his body reaches the outside wall of the chamber. He pivots into a forward-facing position and lunges for his scattered plasma rifle. He grabs it and whirls around to fire at Susie, who is already tending to the gut-shot Josh.

Three pistol blasts sound and a trio of small, but fatal, holes appear in Greene's chest, stomach, and shoulder. His assassin: Old Man McCarthy, who calmly steps forward to take the CCC control room operator's life. This is McCarthy's first kill, and he will never speak of it.

Leonard and René rush back into the room, weapons at the ready. "What happened?" René asks.

"Someone decided to play hero," Pete replies as he steps out from behind the column. He turns to Dana and Shauna. "You two okay?"

Dana nods, and Pete lets go of her hand. Shauna, on the other hand, shakes her head as she cowers in the corner. "I can't do this."

"Yes you can," Pete says. "It's time to go home. Now c'mon."

Shauna steps forward, her trembles having evolved into full-body quavers. Seeing Josh wounded doesn't help matters. "Oh no!" She rushes to where he lays.

"Don't touch him!" An overprotective Susie shoos her away.

"I-is he okay?"

"I don't know." Susie looks down at Josh, the stalwart jock who refuses to die. "Josh, can you hear me?"

Growing weak, he barely manages a nod. "Yes. L-let's see this through." He fails in his attempt to crawl toward the chamber, where Pete and Dana look on. Shauna shakes her head in disbelief at the sight of Josh's pained grimace—this is more than she signed on for when she agreed to join the rescue party.

"Josh, buddy, you're one tough son-of-a-bitch," Pete says through a forced smile. As wisecracks go, this is not one of his better ones.

"C-come here, Dim-k-kowski." Weaker now.

As Pete kneels next to Josh, Susie turns to Leonard. "Get the first aid kit! He's bleeding out! Stat!"

"On it."

Susie applies pressure to the considerable wound on Josh's left side. If not for Maxwell taking the brunt of the impact and slowing down the plasma burst, it would have gone straight through. "I know this hurts, but we have to compress the bleeding," she says.

"It's fine." Josh fails to hold back a wince. His teeth chatter when he turns to face Pete directly. "Sorry I s-s-snapped your ass in gym. I-I-I may have been wrong ab-ab-about you."

"I was *definitely* wrong about you," Pete replies. His lip quivers as it did at the Pit. He reaches over to help Susie compress the wound, but Josh pushes his hand away.

"I-I knew going in today th-this would be a-a-all she wrote. I-I don't know w-what that alarm means, but i-if it's still p-possible to go, I w-w-w-want you to."

"I'm not gonna lie, Josh, that looks bad. But maybe you can still make it. Isn't it worth trying?"

Josh shakes his head, which sends a shiver of agony through his body. "Y-your face doesn't match your words." He coughs.

"We're losing him!" Susie cries out.

Leonard and René rush to Josh's side with morphine and a fresh can of disinfectant spray. "They didn't have much we could use," Leonard says. He shoves a morphine tablet into

Josh's mouth. "Here, this'll help with the pain. I think you're supposed to swallow it whole. Susie, we need to expose the wound so I can apply this."

Susie removes her two-handed compress. Her bandage is soaked through with a combination of her blood and his. Leonard shakes the can of disinfectant spray and tosses the lid aside.

"Is he gonna die?" Shauna asks.

Pete waves her back. "I dunno. If you're going back, why don't you get ready? Guessing that alarm means there isn't much time."

Shauna nods, but doesn't move. Josh howls as Leonard applies the disinfectant. "Sorry Josh," Leonard says. "Just cleaning the wound."

"We can dress it with this," René suggests. She holds out the dropped roll of gauze Josh was holding earlier. She discards the surface layer and unfurls what is left.

Dana taps Pete on the shoulder. She points out that Singh is beckoning. "What is it?"

"That weapons blast depleted the charge," the stern-faced tech replies. "If you're going back, you've got less than five minutes." Unlike Marquez's lab coat, his was spared most of Maxwell's blood spatter.

"Can you still cross the wires or whatever afterwards?" Pete asks.

"I-I think so."

Pete points to Marquez, who removes her coat and covers Maxwell's body with it. "She didn't sound so sure. Something about a fail-safe?"

"We can never fully shut it down. Pulling the plug, so to speak, sends a fatal charge up the arm of anyone who tries. We *can* put it in standby mode, however. From there, if we cross the circuits we essentially fry its brains."

He turns to Marquez. "Is he right? Is that fatal charge what he meant by 'pulling the plug?' "

"Yes." She regrets her role in everything that has transpired, and can't quite look Pete or Dana in the eye.

"What happens to whoever crosses the circuits?"

"I'd give 'em about 90 seconds to run like hell."

"Okay. How much time do I have to get outta here? That whooshing noise doesn't sound very encouraging."

"That's the turbine fan for the particle accelerator," Singh explains. "It's running overdrive to keep the chamber charged, so you're down to maybe four minutes tops."

"Are you sure it's safe?"

"More or less." Lacking in confidence.

Pete shrugs. "Great. Three to beam down, Scotty."

"Who's Scotty?"

"Never mind. Just—" To Marquez: "Be right back."

"I'd advise you to hurry," she replies.

Pete joins Shauna and the others as they pay their respects to Josh. His leg spasms and his eyes are red with hyphema.

René puts an arm on Pete's shoulder. "You went to school with him?"

Pete nods. "Me and Shauna there."

"I'm sorry."

"Honor his memory and go back," McCarthy says. "Don't wait for him to die, or it will have been in vain. Go now. Both of you."

Pete nods again. "C'mon, Shauna. We are all out of time."

Shauna trembles. "I'm scared."

"Me too. We'll go together."

" 'K. By the way, this is embarrassing, but, um, I remember you from Vinnie's and, like, school and stuff . . . but I don't actually know your name."

"Yeah, we didn't exactly hang out in the same clique, did we? I'm Pete."

"I'd shake your hand, Pete, but it's all gross from wiping my nose."

"It's okay. Let's just go." He leads her to the platform, and stops for the quickest of goodbyes with Dana.

"What a mess," she says.

Pete nods. "Last chance. You *sure* you're not going? Your testimony to the fuzz will help us nail your boss."

"Yeah, and put me in prison, too, as an accessory. While my daughter grows up without a mother. On Mars."

"You wouldn't go to prison. You didn't know what was going on."

"No, but they'll never believe me."

"I'll convince 'em. So will Bob and Lori."

"I'm staying. But you need to go." She motions toward a random outburst of sparks from the arrivals side of the chamber.

"Take care of yourself and your little girl."

"I'm gonna find her. That's the real reason I came today."

"I knew it was."

"Someone here must know where she is. But first, I'll make sure we destroy this thing as soon as you're gone."

"Good." Pete fights back tears.

A shrill, hair-raising WAIL, like nails on a chalkboard, is heard from across the room. Pete and Dana don't have to look in that direction to know Josh has died and Susie has become overtaken with grief.

"Don't ever get on her bad side," Pete says, hoping this joke will hold his tears at bay.

"That's not funny," Dana says.

"Yeah, I'm *sooo* going to hell for that one."

"Time's up!" Singh yells.

Dana holds out her arms. "Give me a hug before you go."

Pete steps into her embrace. Leaving it is one of the hardest things he will ever do. There is no romantic charge between them, but in their brief acquaintance, Pete has come to think of Dana as a sister—a better one than the unfairly maligned Pizza Face. Finally, they part. He steps onto the departure platform of the time chamber and drags Johnny's corpse out of the way with haste and grace. "So sorry, man," he whispers.

He motions Shauna forward. "Come on. I guess try to find a pad that doesn't have blood on it? We'll go at the same time." He gives a defeated wave to Susie and the others.

René returns the wave and McCarthy gives a nod, but Susie and Leonard are preoccupied with Josh—Leonard performs fruitless CPR and Susie holds one of Josh's cold hands in hers.

"I'm scared," Shauna says.

"I know. You heard what they said though. Get your whole body inside the circle. Breathe normal and try to be still. Just like when you came here."

"I have no memory of that."

"Do the best you can."

"You're so brave."

"So are you." He gives the technicians a thumb's up. Marquez returns the gesture.

The coils beneath Pete's and Shauna's pads rotate and flash gold, then stop rotating and turn green. Singh waits for the optimal readout on his single functioning monitor. "Three . . . two . . . one . . . mark!"

The chamber malfunctions. A similar array of sparks to those Dana observed in the arrivals section ignite on the outbound side—under Shauna's pad in particular. She screams. "Abort!" Marquez yells.

It's too late. A larger burst of sparks ignites and Shauna catches on fire. Her screams are agonizing.

Pete panics and steps forward. "*STAND STILL!*" Marquez bellows. Pete steps back onto his pad at the last second, clutching his chest as Shauna's burning body flails.

"Fu—" he yells, and is overtaken by a column of light as his molecules disassemble. He disappears. His time and location displacement *appears* to have worked, but those left behind in the CCC will never know for sure.

## 9

Marquez and Singh struggle to put the chamber into standby mode. René grabs a futuristic fire extinguisher—still red in the $24^{th}$ century, but with a retracting hose and a white instead of black nozzle—and hoses down Shauna's body along with a fresh array of sparks that ignite on a nearby telepad.

Dana covers her mouth in horror. McCarthy approaches the two surviving techs. "Is it safe?"

"Yessir, we've got it on standby now," Singh says. He turns a final knob to silence the alarm. "I suppose you'll be having us killed, but you should know that was an accident. And I had nothing to do with *his* actions." He points to Greene's corpse.

"I believe you. But there's one more thing to do, isn't there?" McCarthy turns to Dana.

She nods. "You know there is. And you know *what* it is."

Singh looks at Marquez, then at Dana, then at the Old Man. "I will do as you ask. But just know this will seal our fate, like Greene said."

"Morally, our fate was sealed when your chancellor began abducting people from a different world and bringing them here for indentured servitude," McCarthy replies. Ross hears this from across the room and hangs his head. Now is not the time to make a point.

Marquez takes the metaphorical gavel. "The chamber's already damaged. I'd say we have 30 seconds, max, once the wires are crossed before it implodes. Whoever's in the room will never get clear in time. Everyone else'll want a head start on getting out of here."

"Understood," McCarthy says. "Is this a two-person job?"

"Just one, but I assume you want someone to stay behind and oversee?"

"In light of the day's events, I'm not sure we can go on the honor system."

"I can stay," a voice, hoarse from crying and weak from blood loss, says from behind them.

"Susie," Dana whispers.

"I can stay," Susie says again.

"You fought harder in this battle than I ever did, Miss Walker," McCarthy replies. "Don't throw that away now. I'm a dinosaur compared to everyone else here. This task should fall on me."

"No way, sir. I know you've always considered yourself more of a political leader than a frontlines leader, but the people revere you. Your picture is on posters all over Zone Omega. Sure, people know my name, too, but few of them even know what I look like."

"You don't exactly leave a lot of survivors behind to live and tell the tale."

"I'm working on that, sir. Or I was. Let me do this. Let me die with dignity. I've lost everyone I've ever loved."

"It just hit me," Marquez interrupts. "You're *her!*"

"Who?" Singh asks. The question is no sooner out of his mouth before recognition spreads across his face. "*Ohhh.*"

Susie neither confirms nor denies this accusation. McCarthy addresses everyone in the room—Susie, Dana, Leonard, René, Marquez, Singh, Ross, and Smithson, the last two still hand-cuffed to the intake pipe. "Everyone, we've accomplished our mission but for the destruction of the time chamber, which it seems will be quite catastrophic. As such, it's time for us to make haste. Let us go as one, for there is safety in numbers. Leonard and René, I ask that you take point. Stay alert. Susie, I ask that you help me escort the chancellor if you're up to it. Does anyone know the way out?

"I think I can find it," Leonard says.

"Sir—" Susie begins.

"For the last time, Miss Walker, forget it. I cannot lose my top lieutenant."

## 10

Singh stays behind in the end. He insists he can handle his task without supervision, lest anyone else perish. Marquez volunteers first, but Singh intervenes. "You have a child. He needs his mother. I, on the other hand . . . it's just me."

"Why the change of heart?" Marquez asks. "You were furious when Maxwell spoke of crossing the wires."

"Yes, but after that woman burned up on the platform, I realized this thing may never work right again, anyway. And when I saw the chancellor in the corner, cuffed and looking pathetic, I, um, I knew we'd lost. I don't want to rot away in prison. This seems more . . . noble?"

Marquez nods, dismayed. She supposes that if a bigwig like Chancellor Ross is going to prison, then surely a small fry such as herself will also serve time. "Are you sure you've got this, Abe?"

"I'm sure. Take care of your little boy." And, after another array of sparks, larger this time, ignites inside the chamber: "Please hurry."

"Long live New Earth," Marquez says.

"May her bounty provide." Singh smiles, but it isn't particularly convincing. He mouths the word "*Go*" and returns to the mainframe for some impromptu rewiring.

Marquez is the last one out of the time chamber. She trails the others as they leave the CCC and turn left. McCarthy assumes the position of rear guard and motions for Marquez to go ahead of him. As she rounds the corner, the chamber alarm sounds anew.

Up ahead, the corridor splits in two. A quartet of Loyalist stragglers open fire on them from the right fork. "Get down!" Leonard shouts. The incoming plasma blasts miss everyone, and he and René take out two soldiers apiece. Leonard considers the right fork for a moment, then reorients himself and decides left is better – away from Ross's executive apartment, not toward it.

Marquez, urgent: "We need to hurry."

. . .

Inside the time chamber, Singh bites his lip and sweats bullets as he crosses the circuits. A workstation short circuits prematurely as he finishes connecting the second input. He is electrocuted. He falls to his knees, drool on his chin, and is dead before the chamber itself implodes a few seconds later.

The glass on every window in the X-shaped CCC complex explodes outward, and the blast bursts the eardrums of our heroes as they run for cover. They reach the lower-level visitors desk as the building shakes around them and plaster falls from the ceiling.

"C'mon!" René cries. They exit the building and pass the guards taken out by Team Pete not even one hour ago. They don't stop running until they reach the road, where a crowd has already gathered.

"What happened?!" someone asks.

"Tremor?" someone else posits.

"Meltdown?" another person wonders.

"Hope no one was killed," a fourth person says.

"Hope they went quick," a fifth person remarks.

"¡Chingado¡" a sixth person exclaims, *en español*.

Dana gasps for breath. She rests her hands on her knees as she dry heaves. René comes to her aid. "Don't breathe so quickly. Remember, slow and deep. Hold it in here." She points to her diaphragm. Dana nods and slowly gets her wind back.

Marquez walks over to Susie and Old Man McCarthy. She holds out her hands, wrists upward in a signal of arrest and surrender. "What's this for, then?" McCarthy asks.

"I imagine you'll be arresting me as well?" she asks. The now-deposed Chancellor Ross looks at her curiously.

"Come again?" McCarthy puts one hand to his ringing ear. His fingers are wet with blood.

"Am I under arrest?"

"We'll get to all that," McCarthy replies.

Marquez looks at the ground and folds her arms across her chest, shivering. She retreats to the back of the group, next to Dana, whose gasping has morphed into a coughing fit. The two women share the briefest of smiles on this strangest of days. "You're on your 18th day here, right?" Marquez asks.

"S-something like that. H-how'd you know?"

"I helped process you after your Journey. A real miracle, your delivery."

"My little fighter."

"I'm not a bad person."

"Trust me, I'm in no position to judge."

"I have a son. He's 14 months. Do you think maybe one day our kids might play together?"

"I bet they'd like that."

After a moment, Marquez extends her hand. "I'm Vanessa."

Dana shakes it with the hand opposite of the one she used to cover her mouth during her coughing spell. "Dana."

Leonard and René stand watch, weapons ready, but with more spectators gathering and a non-weaponized Sauron hovering overhead, it appears they have survived the day. Susie motions for Leonard to watch Ross and Smithson, then walks over to René, feeling lightheaded. René, whose eardrums also bleed, turns her head so she can hear. "J-just the five of us?" Susie asks. "I-is that all that's left?"

"I'm afraid so."

"How many people were able to go back while I was with Josh? B-besides Sam, I mean."

"One of the techs went back. And Peter."

"That's it?" René nods. Susie defends herself unnecessarily. "I-I was so p-p-preoccupied, I didn't even get to pass on Josh's m-message for Pete to bring back."

"What was the message?"

"What?!"

"What was the message?" Louder.

" *'T-tell Lori I love her.'* "

"I'm sorry."

"M-me too." She slurs these two words.

"Susie, you okay?"

"D-don't f-feel so g-good."

She passes out on the pavement.

# Chapter 10

1

Lori wears an oven mitt as she dumps piping hot pizza rolls from the baking sheet into a Corelle serving bowl. Bob passes her, AK-47 in hand. "Where you going?" she asks.

"Hiding this in the garage. Those smell great, by the way!"

"Hurry up or your stepmom and I'll eat 'em all!"

Bob's playful warning, *"You'd better not,"* echoes down the hall.

Lori sets the serving dish on the table in the dinette. "Here you go, Mrs. Wilkinson."

"Thank you, Lori. I'm sorry for what you witnessed earlier. Robbie's a good boy, but for years things have been a bit cold between us. I thought we were finally getting somewhere."

"I'm sure it's everything that's been going on. People missing and stuff."

"Could be. Won't you take a seat, dear? Tell me about Robbie and what he's been up to. I never see him. Tell me about my son."

"He'll be back in a moment."

"I know. And so will his father. Then, the two of you can tell Mr. Wilkinson and I everything. Right now, I just want to hear from you about something unrelated to this craziness. How is that beautiful boy?"

"I really don't know him well, Mrs. Wilkinson. Honest. We happened to be in the same place at the same time. That's it."

"You're not dating?"

"Gosh, no!" Lori turns red.

"Is it so outrageous?"

"No, but . . . just, like . . . it's totally complicated."

"It always is."

. . .

Bob stows the AK-47 inside a workbench cabinet in the garage, away from prying eyes. He pushes a button on the garage door opener and the overhead chain grinds in noisy efficiency. The driveway is wet from where Gail was watering. He pops the trunk and removes the anti-matter rifle and the 28 porta-pads. As he closes the trunk, he notices Gail missed a spot of blood when she hosed off the bumper. He unspools the garden hose and hoses off the remaining splotch. After stowing the plasma rifle and JourneyTech inside the workbench alongside the AK, he takes a slow look around the garage at personal belongings that feel as if they belong to a much younger and more innocent kid than his current, 18-year-old self. His ten-speed Schwinn bike, a gift on his ninth birthday, when he was still too short to ride it. A Goodman High Spartans pennant, thumbtacked to the wall above the workbench. A T-ball stand and bat, both forgotten in a corner. Father-and-son fishing poles, gifts for him and Robert, Sr. from Gail three Christmases ago, ironically never used.

Over the past 48 hours, he has viewed horrifying videos of failed time travel experiments that would turn even the strongest stomach. He has watched his older friend Vinnie perish in a tragic boating accident, with himself at the helm of the boat in question. He has stabbed a bad guy in the neck and run over another with his car, yet neither act prevented his best friend Pete from being abducted. How can he look forward to the simpler things, like riding a bike, attending a pep rally, playing wiffle ball, or going fishing, ever again? *I'm losing it,* he thinks. *But I have to do something . . . because I don't think anyone else can.*

*"Bobby?"* He hears his name being called from inside and heads back to the dinette.

"Smells good!" he says.

"They're hot, so be careful," Lori cautions.

"Robbie, Lori was just telling us how you two met," Gail remarks.

"Uh-oh," Bob replies.

"I'll bet she was stunning in her prom dress."

"She looked great. *Looks.* Great."

"And he's smooth!" Gail observes. This earns a hearty laugh from Lori and an eye roll from Bob.

"Oh, God!"

"Awww, you embarrassed him, Mrs. Wilkinson."

"I'll bet if you went there as a couple, all eyes would've been on you both," Gail says.

"Yeah, wondering how the heck I got her." Self-deprecating.

"Robbie, don't say that."

"Why not? Everyone else has been saying it."

"Now, now. You two are cute together."

"Mom, we barely know each other."

A door slams in the foyer to announce Robert, Sr.'s arrival, saving his son from further embarrassment.

"Something smells good," Robert, Sr. says.

"We're in here, darling." Gail turns to Lori. "My dear, the best way to a man's heart is through his stomach."

Robert, Sr. enters the room, a Dominick's grocery bag under each arm. "Robert my boy! I can't tell you how pleased I was to see your car in the driveway. Your stepmother and I missed you last night."

"I know, dad. I'm pleased to see you, too."

"Pizza rolls?" Robert, Sr. sets the bags on the counter. "Don't spoil your appetites, I bought a roast."

"I'm surprised they had any meat at all," Gail says. "We heard from the governor about the mad dash on Sunday."

"Butcher said I got there at the right time, that the shelves were all but stripped bare Sunday like you said. They were restocking when I arrived, but there still wasn't much. Funny enough, place was a ghost town today."

"Everyone got scared and left town by now," Bob explains.

"The pizza rolls are just a quick snack for the kids," Gail answers her husband's original question.

"Kids, huh? Robert, who's your special friend?"

"Not a special friend, dad, just a friend."

"Hi, I'm Lori. Can I help you with the groceries?"

"Nice to meet you, Lori. I'm Robert's father."

"Meetcha." A timid reply after Robert, Sr. practically crushes her hand with his strong handshake, the grip solidified by over 20 years of schmoozing in elected office.

"And no help necessary, Lori. Stay seated. You're our guest."

"Sit down, Robert," Gail says. "The groceries can wait. The kids have something to tell us."

"Lemme throw this in the fridge. Be right there." He places the perishables inside the refrigerator, then takes his rightful place at the head of the table.

"It's so good to see you, son."

"Dad, I called your offices yesterday but no one answered. It said the mailbox was full."

"Sorry about that. It's been . . . busy, as I'm sure you can imagine."

"I'm sure. Did you ever call the mayor? I left a message with mom on Sunday morning for you to call him."

"I was already on that. Let me reassure you, the mayor, the governor, and everyone in between is extremely concerned about what happened to your classmates."

Bob chooses his next words carefully. "You don't have to make a stump speech; I'm not some undecided voter. But I *do* have one question: You're about as connected as it gets. What do you know about what's been happening?"

"Well son, I know countless Chicagoans and nearby residents such as your classmates have gone missing. I know it's happened over a few waves, with Saturday night's being the biggest, and I know all passage in and out of the city has been effectively halted. Trains, planes, expressways, you name it."

"Have there been any attempts to enter the city? You know, by the Army or whatever?"

"Well, all the military bases around here—Great Lakes and such—are on high alert. All leave's been cancelled. We had military choppers with searchlights Saturday night and police choppers on Sunday, 'til one of them was shot out of the sky. We also attempted a ground breach near Oak Park, but it didn't end well. And I'm sure your stepmother told you what happened when our plane attempted to land last night."

Bob looks down. He has been too busy to keep up with the news, and was unaware of the chopper crash and failed breach. "And what do you know about who's responsible?" he asks.

"Government's chasing a few leads, but you know I can't speak to what those are, not even to my own son."

"No, of course not. National security."

"That's right. I know you're worried about your friends, but like I said—"

"What about the president? What does he know?"

"Son, between you and me, the president doesn't know his ass from a hole in the ground. His focus is on the Soviet Union. That and trying to remember whether he put his underpants on inside out or not." Although Robert, Sr. thinks what he said was quite funny—and it *will* be publicly revealed in 1994 that Ronald Reagan suffers from Alzheimer's disease—no one laughs.

"But like I said before, Mayor Washington is very concerned. Governor Thompson, too. You'll be pleased to learn I'm meeting personally with the mayor and the chief of police tomorrow evening. Now, I know you have a vested interest considering what happened to your classmates, but this is something more. Why the 20 questions?"

Bob looks up at Gail, whose face is pallid with worry, and then at Lori, who gives an encouraging nod. With that, he turns to his father. "Dad, I've heard so many different versions of the truth it makes my head spin. I've even told a few versions myself, and so has she." He points to Lori, who fights her first instinct, which is to look away. "But here goes."

Bob brings his dad and stepmom up to speed. He begins by telling how he and Pete decided to crash prom on a lark, and explains how they ran into Lori and met the mayor and his entourage shortly afterwards. He summarizes Rich's confession of strange goings-on at CGC-Meigs (as relayed through Squiggy and Vinnie), and pauses while Lori summarizes her father's similar theory. Bob struggles to say what happened after he and his friends forced their way into the Meigs complex, and how they finally broke down and called in Detective

Lieutenant Mayotte for help. He concludes by stating that if not for uncertainly over whether Pete and Dana will return, he wants to destroy the time chamber. Lori grabs his hand when he reveals Vinnie's fate, and her gesture doesn't escape Gail's notice. *These two have grown close,* she thinks.

Robert, Sr. studies the room and sees nothing but pensive faces. "My little boy is all grown up." He turns to Gail. "I don't think he needs us anymore."

She grabs her husband's hand and folds her fingers over his. "That's quite a story, Robbie. How do your father and I know it's true?"

Robert, Sr. surprises himself and everyone else by answering in place of his son. "It's true." Bob and Lori look up, mouths agape. "Everything Robert told us is true."

Bob, forgetting his father chairs the U.S. Senate Committee on Commerce, Science, and Transportation, is stunned by the man's easy acceptance of the facts. "Dad?"

"What I'm telling you stays in this room. Washington's been investigating CGC for almost 36 months now. Gathering intel, little-by-little. Their front as a genetics research firm, with an omnipresent media campaign and generous philanthropy to lend it an air of legitimacy, has been well-established. After Meigs Airport was shut down almost overnight five years ago and a modern operations facility built in its place that CGC said was, and I quote, 'largely for research,' the FBI started getting curious. They found Wesley Arendt to be both cooperative and elusive. I met with him once myself maybe seven, eight months ago. He donated generously to both my re-election campaign the previous year and to the sciences in general, so on the surface, that was the purpose of our meeting. On a deeper level, I wanted to get a read on him."

"Dad, I asked you a few months ago if you could use your connections to arrange a tour for Mr. Hunt's class. You said you'd keep trying, and of course I never got an answer, but you never told me you'd actually met Mr. Arendt."

"Why would I, son? It wasn't until nine months or so ago—couple months before he and I met, anyway—when we finally figured out some version of what was going on, but to tell you the truth, no I didn't ask him if he would arrange a tour, because I already knew he was messing with stuff that could shape the very fabric of time and space. Frankly, I didn't want you or your friends anywhere near that place."

"That was last fall when I asked! You knew even then?!"

"Some stuff, yes."

"How'd you find out?"

"We sent two undercover agents in with tie clip cameras and guns. They sent us footage of what they saw—ghastly, sci-fi stuff that mirrors what you described—but when we sent them in a second time for more footage . . . well, they never came out."

"They died?"

Robert, Sr. shrugs. "We never saw them again."

Gail scolds her husband. "How could you have let this happen?"

"We didn't fully understand what they were creating. We knew it had a name—time and location displacement technology—or TLDT for short. Once we knew what it was called, little-by-little we built a case. I guess we didn't build it quickly enough."

"And two men died. And Robbie's friend Vinnie. And Vinnie's friend Rich. And now Pete's been taken. And thousands of others. *Shame on you.*" Gail gets up to leave, but Robert, Sr. grabs her arm in the same delicate manner he might grab the arm of a campaign donor with cold feet.

"Gail, honey, the wheels of government grind slowly but exceedingly fine. You know this. It takes time to build a case and get the facts straight. This isn't Al Capone running numbers and pouring illegal liquor. This is people disappearing from here and reappearing somewhere else, hundreds of years from now and millions of miles away, *if* they even survive the trip!"

"Yes, and now Robbie's involved. You told your staff we were coming home to provide real leadership and you told *me* we were coming home to check on him"—she points to Bob—"once all this started happening. Which is it?"

"Both. As I said earlier, I'm meeting with Mayor Washington and Chief Barnes tomorrow evening, and consulting with Governor Thompson over the phone tomorrow afternoon as well. Today though, is to be spent with you and Robert and his new girlfr—"

"Dad, Lori's not my girlfriend."

Robert, Sr. looks his son in the eye. "I went to the store today and it was the first quiet moment I've had since this whole thing started," he confesses. "But it was tainted in sadness. When we got here last night and found you not at home, my heart sank. Gail said she spoke with you the morning after prom so there was some initial relief, but I figured the abductions would continue. I wanted to . . . I wanted to do something about it, yes, but more than anything, I wanted to see you again. I know I've been a terrible father."

"Dad, you've not been a—"

"No, son, I have. I'm gone more than I'm here. I give you the run of the place and let you do pretty much whatever you want. Your stepmother and I bought you a car to make up for it—"

"I wasn't exactly complaining."

"—you get decent grades, you apply for Northwestern to appease me, you visit Dr. Kirchner regular as rain . . . but you're left alone here all the time. That's deplorable! Now, you're headed off to college in a few months and I hardly know you. I hardly know my own son! I'd like to work on that."

Lori finds herself moved by the senator's words. Her eyes glisten; she blinks rapidly to avert incoming tears. Bob, on the other hand, merely stares at the table. This is the most his father has said to him in years. When he finally opens his mouth to speak, a rap on the front door and the *DING-DONG-DING* of the doorbell cut him off. No one moves; they study one another from across the table until Robert, Sr. gets up—this is *his* house, after all.

He opens the front door while the others hover in the foyer behind him. A squad car is parked in their driveway. Three males stand on the front porch—two state troopers and in between them, hair tousled and looking worse for wear, Pete!

"Peter!" Robert, Sr. exclaims.

Pete, raspy-voiced: "Hi, Mr. W."

Ecstatic, Bob and Lori are without words.

"Does this belong to you?" one of the troopers asks.

2

The state troopers lock arms to prop up Pete, whose eyelids are heavy and whose elbow is bleeding.

Robert, Sr. immediately takes charge. "We know this boy, Officers. Bring him inside. Parlor's this way." They half-escort, half-drag Pete into the next room and set him down on the middle cushion of the sofa. Pete immediately closes his eyes. "No no no Peter, don't fall asleep."

"We checked the boy's vitals, sir. They look good. He should be okay. He appears to be exhausted more than anything. Says he woke up in his bed a half-hour ago with no memory of how he got there." The trooper saying this wears a brass nametag that reads CONNORS.

"Thank you, Trooper Connors. Can we offer you and your partner something to drink? Coffee or water, perhaps?"

"That's not necessary, sir," the second trooper, Novak, replies.

"As you wish. Thanks for bringing him here. Where'd you find him?"

"Just down the street. We've been assigned to watch you."

Gail motions for Lori to help her with Pete. They take off Pete's shoes and lay him on his side across the three sofa cushions. He is already snoring. Bob, meanwhile, is engrossed in the conversation with his father and the two state troopers. *Are they the same ones that escorted Lori's parents to the state line?* he wonders.

"Ah yes, the motorcade leader said they'd try to arrange a security detail," Robert, Sr. remarks.

"Motorcade, sir?"

"I'm sorry, who sent you? Sergeant Maguire, I think, was our motorcade leader. Was it him?"

"Captain Bennett, CPD. Said he was calling in another favor for one of his men. Don't remember his name, I'm afraid."

"Was it Mayotte, by any chance?" Bob interrupts.

"Mayotte, that's it, yes."

"Dad, that's the guy I was telling you about." Bob turns to the state troopers. "Did he say anything else?"

"Uh, he mostly asked us to keep an eye on the place. He said not to go out of our way, but if we see you, to tell you 'Message received but lost in transmission.' Make sense to you?"

Bob sighs. "Yeah, I've got an idea what that means."

Robert, Sr. takes over. "Thank you again, Officers. And for the lookout as well. I just got home a moment ago myself. Not sure how I didn't see you out front."

"We're parked a few doors down to keep a low profile," Connors explains.

"Ah. Grey Bonneville?"

"That's the one, sir."

"Good to know. Why is the boy banged up?"

"He was pedaling his bike like a man possessed. Went around the corner down the block and wiped out something fierce. Saw the whole thing happen in my sideview mirror. Kid was running on empty."

"Again, Officers, thank you. If you need anything—food, water, clean bathroom, commendation letter, what have you—just name it."

"That's not necessary, sir. We're just doing our jobs."

The troopers take their leave. Gail returns to her husband and stepson and leaves Lori to tend to Pete in the next room. "How is he?" Robert, Sr. asks.

"Snoring," Gail answers. "His elbow's pretty banged up, but it doesn't look like anything's broken. Everything okay outside?"

"Yes, just a lookout unit. I'm glad they're here."

"I'm glad they found him. And if you and Robbie insist on standing by this bizarre story you've both concocted, which is stranger than anything I ever learned in school, it's at least good to know people can come back from . . . there."

"It's no concoction, Gail, now can I speak with Robert alone?"

"I'll check on Pete again."

Bob follows his dad into the ground floor study. It isn't a man cave but, rather, a proper 1980s home office—dark wood paneling, olive green curtains, free-standing globe, oak desk and credenza, Northwestern pennant and framed Bachelor's degree on the wall, model frigate ship, Nefertiti bust, and auto-graphed Harold Baines baseball on a bookcase.

"Have a seat." Bob parks himself across from his dad in a chair with a rattan wicker back. Robert, Sr. takes the executive chair—Bordeaux leather, nail head trim, brass casters—behind the desk. "Tell me about this Detective Mayotte."

"What do you wanna know, dad?"

"Can he be trusted?"

"Uh, I think so. I hope so. He was the lead investigator on the prom night disappearances, so I *wanna* trust him, if that makes sense."

"It does. I'm asking because I need someone in the city we can rely on. And not Chief Barnes."

"The detective and his captain talked about him when were questioned that night, too."

"Who? Barnes?"

"Yeah. They didn't seem to like him."

"Barnes is a political appointee left over from the last administration. He'll play ball and say what we want him to say, but he's not someone you want as your only ally when the shit hits the fan. Guy like that, if you were in a foxhole with him in 'Nam, he'd throw you in front of Charlie as a distraction, and still sleep like a baby at night."

Bob nods. "Yeah. Like I said, they didn't have many good things to say about him."

Robert, Sr. redirects. "Mayotte, though. Could you trust him in a foxhole?"

"I-I think so."

"Good. We may need his help on Thursday."

"What happens Thursday?"

"Possible action plan. I want you home, safe, but . . ."

"No way, dad. I need to be a part of this. Lori and I, we need to be part of this. Pete, too, I imagine, if he's feeling up to it."

"I had a feeling you'd say that."

"Dad, we still have those pads Lori and I found. Um, I'm a little scared to show you how they work from here 'cause I'm pretty sure they have geo-trackers in 'em that go live whenever they're turned on. I *certainly* don't wanna try one on myself, but you can borrow one for your meeting tomorrow if you think it'll help. It's at City Hall, right?"

"That's right, why?"

"If you wanted to demonstrate it there, I can't imagine they'd attack City Hall. Probably the best place to show it off. Just don't use it on yourself. Use something inanimate instead."

"Did you show what it could do to that detective of yours?"

"No. He said he saw some other crazy stuff that matched up with what Pete and Lori and I saw. By the context, I think he was referring to the phaser or plasma gun or whatever."

"So he didn't need much convincing?"

"No."

"Good. Barnes and some of the others, though . . . they'll be tougher nuts to crack. That pad may help sway 'em."

"Take it! Weapons, too. Take 'em off my hands completely."

"You said they're in the workbench?"

"Uh, that's right. Pads, too."

"Terrific. I'll make sure they get disposed of."

"Whatever you do, *don't* bring 'em back to Washington with you. They have to be destroyed."

"Understood."

"Good . . . So about the raid or special op or whatever the technical term is . . . I can't come with?"

"You know you can't."

Bob raises his voice. "Why?! I'm a part of this, don't you see?!"

"Robert, if we send in a team to rescue your friends, there's no telling what kind of resistance they'll be up against. You already lost your friend from the arcade. Peter's back, which is terrific. Count that as a wash and celebrate. I thank you for what you've shared, but I don't want you having any further involvement."

"That's not fair!"

"My word on this is final. Now go check on Peter and see what time your stepmom wants to have supper."

"Fine." Bob's hand twitches; he is certain it escapes his father's notice.

"And son?"

"Yeah?"

"Go easy on her. Gail really does love you."

"I know. I yelled at her earlier, and she didn't deserve it."

"Well, apologize if you haven't done so already, then check on Peter like I asked. Let's salvage the rest of this day, okay? We have a good meal to look forward to. I'll be done in here soon enough. Just need to make a few phone calls."

"About what happens Thursday?"

Robert, Sr. shakes his head. "One of the pilots from last night didn't make it, and the other one isn't doing so hot, either. I owe each of their families a courtesy phone call."

3

Detective Lieutenant Mayotte hasn't eaten anything all day. His stomach rumbles with the frequency of a rush hour "L" train, but he ignores its pangs. Sitting on the carpet in Wesley Arendt's office and avoiding the crime scene-taped blood trail that marks the death-and-drag of the late Gavin Berringer, the detective attempts to literally piece together with masking tape the two-millimeter-thick strips of paper fed into Wesley's document shredder. A man haunted, Mayotte has worked through the night, and subsides only on coffee and adrenaline.

. . .

John David Mayotte—J.D. to his friends—rose quickly through the ranks at police headquarters. With the tireless work ethic of a man possessed, Mayotte earned the respect of his colleagues and superiors, none moreso than his commanding officer, Marshall Bennett. Water cooler rumors occasionally circulate that Mayotte is the logical choice to one day succeed Bennett, if Mayotte doesn't end up getting a command of his own elsewhere in the city. The detective is always quick to quash such rumors. "I'm perfectly happy at this desk right here," he says, pointing to a cluttered metal *escritoire* in Missing Persons. His partner, Reginald Boretti, took early retirement two years ago and hastily relocated to Florida. Mayotte has had his work cut out for himself ever since. Stacks of paperwork weigh down his inbox and spill over onto Boretti's former desk as well, but Mayotte works them efficiently and with nary a complaint filed against him. He learned whilst whetting his teeth in narcotics and watching those around him get busted by Internal Affairs that falsifying evidence and beating confessions out of perps is no way to get a conviction, as the truth always comes to light.

Mayotte is 37, and skinny as a rail. His diet is atrocious, however, and his hair is greying at the temples. Missing Persons is a depressing, thankless job, and except for teenage runaways, the Missing are rarely found—or rarely found *alive.* Younger officers often wonder what drives the detective, whose only pastime (aside from bending the ear of the Superdawg manager, Dave) is White Sox baseball. Tenured officers usually tell rookies to mind their own business, but the framed picture on Mayotte's desk of a young boy tells a thousand words.

Jonathan Saunders, age eight when he went missing, was Detective Lieutenant Mayotte's godson, born to his cousin, Trish, and her husband, Carl. The boy was snatched from a playground near the family's Garfield Park home while Trish turned her back for what she said was the briefest of moments to chat with a friend. Mayotte had just turned 30 when it happened, and he tore the city upside down in search of the boy. Alas, every suspect had an iron-clad alibi, and the darkest mark any of them had on their records was little more than a few unpaid parking tickets. The trail turned cold and the police eventually declared the boy, who had been working on his second merit badge in Cub Scouts at the time of his disappearance, presumed dead.

Little Jonathan's empty-casket funeral was a heartrending affair. Carl was told in confidence by Detective Lieutenant Mayotte that the "friend" Trish was talking to when Jonathan was taken was in fact an amorous single father from the same after-school volunteer reading program Trish participated in three times a week. As such, Carl called his wife a "slut" at the top of his lungs during an argument at the wake, and things spiraled out of control from there. Trish slapped her husband, he punched her in the arm, and Mayotte had to restrain him from doing something he would *really* regret. Trish filed for divorce the next morning and got everything in the settlement —her black-and-blue, upper-arm souvenir went a long way in earning sympathy with the judge. Mayotte was furious. Yes, Trish was his blood relative, not Carl, but she was also the unfaithful one, and her open-air canoodling at the worst possible time resulted in her son being taken. The detective had little doubt his godson was dead. He hoped the boy didn't suffer, but his gut told him otherwise. He requested a transfer to Missing Persons the next afternoon, and badgered his C.O. every week until his request was granted.

. . .

When first called to the prom night crime scene at the Chicago Cultural Center, Detective Lieutenant Mayotte didn't know what to think. Who would kidnap an entire graduating class of horny teenagers in formal wear? He immediately ordered background checks on the families of each student, checking for ties to the Mob and to the cartels. These checks drew blanks, as did those run on the guest list of VIP RSVPs at the Art Institute benefit and of the fraternity convention attendees at the Palmer House. As for the creative industry types abducted during the commercial shoot inside Union Station's Great Hall, aside from a few pieces of recording equipment discarded during the melee, there was simply no way of knowing who was taken. For one thing, the cameras used for the shoot weren't rolling at the time of the abductions. For another thing, the ad agency's thirty-something creative director was among the missing.

Mayotte believed Bob, Pete, and Lori when they said they arrived late to prom and found their friends missing. If nothing else, he believed them because Lori, who looked like a million bucks in her purple dress and lavender heels, *surely* wouldn't willingly attend such an affair with the likes of T-shirt-and-jeans-wearing Bob and Pete. The blockade of the city the following morning made the case even more bizarre. Additionally, arriving at the aftermath of the Skyway school bus "incident" and discovering that the Skyway tragedy and the Prom Night Massacre were linked reminded him that he needed to consider any scenario, no matter how random or strange. What kind of ghastly human being would shoot up a bus filled with special needs children? What kind of sick son-of-a-bitch would murder a man and dispose of the corpse by sending it—or the half of it that would fit, anyway—through a portal? Whoever did such things or ordered such things to be done is not someone to underestimate.

Captain Bennett, busy with a paperwork nightmare of his own at the State Street HQ, has left Detective Lieutenant Mayotte to his own devices. After all, Mayotte always produces results, and his two requests—to have Staties escort Charles and Helen Rainsmith to the state line and to keep a watchful eye on the Wilkinson home—seem reasonable enough. The other outsourced tasks—to track down the former geneticists who worked in the Hancock HQ but have since vanished; to interview the escapees of the CGC van outside Dana Golding's house; and to run prints on the Loyalist corpses found there (no matches found)—are standard operating procedures anyway.

The detective begins to tire at long last. His pager beeps as he fights a yawn. He picks up Wesley's office phone and calls HQ to return his commanding officer's page. "Hey Captain," he says after the never-enthusiastic operator connects him.

"Wanted to let you know the Dimkowski boy has been reunited with his friends," Captain Bennett says from the other end.

"In the city or up north?"

"Just outside the Wilkinson home."

"Terrific. How's the northern blockade façade holding up?"

"So far so good. We're turning people back, same as everywhere else. Different uniforms, but no pushback otherwise. Good work on that one. We're about to try it on the southside as well."

"Don't push your luck, sir. We don't want them knowing we're onto 'em."

"Understood."

"Anything from forensics on those prints?"

"Yeah, I put Heinbrenner on it. Let me follow up, one sec." Bennett puts Mayotte on hold, and the detective is subjected to that annoying Nancy Reagan PSA. Finally: "No match domestically. None from our border collars and none from the Kilbourn incident, either. Reaching out to Interpol."

"Don't bother. We won't find anything there. Arendt's smart."

"Listen J.D., I've always given you enough rope to hang yourself with, but are you sure about this one? We could get an emergency warrant and be at Meigs by nightfall."

"Sir, I have no doubt we'll end up there at some point, but it's not time yet. It's going slower than molasses over here, and I want something substantial so we can really nail this guy."

"Get some sleep. I'll send over some men."

"All due respect sir, no. There's an 'a-ha' moment here, and I'd like to find it myself."

"As you wish. Barnes and Hizzoner are meeting with the Wilkinson kid's old man tomorrow. The chief asked me to come along. I'd like you to be there, too."

"I'll be there if I've found my moment. That's a promise, sir."

"Fair enough. Take a break."

"You know I won't." Mayotte hangs up the receiver. He stands up and stretches. His back cracks. He proceeds to re-fill the coffee mug, emblazoned with a CGC logo, that he borrowed from a cabinet above the coffee maker in the hall. The pot is empty. He looks around as he prepares a fresh pot. *I need something on paper,* he thinks. *Give me something I can bring to the press. I'm going to get you regardless, Wesley. But I need something to show the press. Because people won't believe otherwise.*

*And they need to know. When this is done, they'll need to know so the healing can begin.*

4

Untold hours have elapsed since Wesley Arendt passed out after being hauled off the arrivals telepad at CGC-Meigs. Miles acquitted himself admirably during Wesley's "rest." He ordered the power cut, grid-by-grid, through each of the city's residential areas, and orientated nauseous new Loyalist reinforcements from Ross's New Earth. He made sure they were fed and hydrated, then sent them by van and boat to double up border checkpoints and secure the city's Lake Michigan shoreline. His one mistake—one that will ultimately cost him his life—was when he assumed the western border was the most vulnerable, when in fact CPD officers had already taken over the *northern* crossings at Sheridan Road, Clark/Chicago, Ridge, Asbury, and Dodge Avenues.

The front half of CGC-Meigs is divided in two. On one side: a state-of-the-art infirmary, including a blood work chem lab that puts most major hospitals to shame. Beyond the infirmary, a formidable weapons depot sure to make any doomsday prophet salivate. The depot—the ultimate walk-in closet—is stocked with AK-47 guns and .62 x 39mm rounds, RPG-2 rocket launchers, Kevlar vests, and a handful of Winchester Magnum anti-matter rifles.

On the other side: a holding area for passengers recently arrived from Mars or awaiting their outbound trip. Eight cells, sex-segregated and of varying size, that can hold a combined 500 people in close quarters. The cells closest to the time chamber are singles, perfect for an employee in need of a catnap . . . or for an injured CEO, perhaps.

Wesley comes to from a lumpy cot in one of these singles. Twenty-five hungry, confused abductees occupy the adjacent cell and sit in quiet contemplation until they hear Wesley's mattress squeak. He sits up, a simple task that takes considerable effort and sends a lightning bolt of pain up his spine. As things come into focus, he sees 50 beady eyes staring at him through the bars.

"Why are you in there by yourself?" an abductee asks.

"Do you know what this is all about?" another one asks.

"Hell happened to you?" a third one asks.

"*MILES!*" Wesley yells, bleary-eyed. He squints as pain much worse than any migraine shoots through his head.

A young Loyalist soldier approaches, apprehensive, plasma rifle at the ready. He motions for the other holding cell prisoners to be quiet.

"Who are you, Soldier?" Wesley asks.

"Name's Gilman. I'm new here."

"How was your Journey?"

"It was unreal. After I got here I couldn't stop throwing up."

"That happens a lot. I've spent a small fortune in ammonia and Pepto-Bismol."

"I don't know what that is, sir."

"How long have I been here?"

"At least a day. I arrived here maybe 36 hours ago, and you were in that cell then, too."

"Well can you let me out, Soldier?"

"Of course. We're glad to see you awake." As he inserts a key into the cell's lock, an abductee from the next cell lashes through the bars for the keyring. Gilman thwaps the man's hands with a baton. He retreats into the cell and howls in pain.

Wesley exits his cell. He limps into the next room on unsteady feet as Miles sends six abductees forward in time. They disappear into pixels before his eyes.

"Miles, didn't you hear me shouting?" he asks.

Miles holds up a finger that says, *"one moment, please,"* as he calibrates the settings for another load while trainee Balthazar watches and learns the ropes.

"So as you see, once they're gone it takes about 40 seconds for the telepad to cool down. The portable ones cool down in a third that time. Why do you think that is?" Miles asks.

"Because they don't generate as much energy?" the eager beaver Balthazar posits. Although he's been monitoring the time chamber for transmissions over the past two weeks, he spent most of prom night helping abductees stagger to and from their cells, and is still green in many regards. Miles gave him the Sunday after prom off, as the young men had worked 12 days without a break. *It's exciting to finally learn what all this stuff really means,* Balthazar thinks.

"That's right, B," Miles says. "And in just under seven minutes, those six passengers will have finished their Journeys and arrived safely on the other side." Miles sets his clipboard down and turns to greet Wesley. "Hey boss," he says. "So glad you're awake."

"My my, you've been busy," Wesley observes. "I am impressed, Miles."

"Just dotting the I's and crossing the T's like you requested, and bringing B here fully up to speed like we discussed."

"And?"

"And I was just quizzing him. He did great."

"How you feeling, sir?" Balthazar pipes in.

Wesley ignores him. "What about my MIT buddy?"

"Taken care of, sir. And might I say, that was quite a mess."

Wesley stares down at his shirt and slacks, both of which are caked with dried blood. "It was unfortunate. Of course, the onus is on me for that one. I should've kept a spare Magnum in my office. Would've made for cleaner disposal."

"We're running low on those. Mags, too. I blitzed a request for more."

"Excellent."

"Also, we left a change of clothes for you in your cell."

"I didn't notice. My vision was blurry."

"Yeah, I think maybe you did some real damage when you hit your head, sir."

"Here or in my office?"

"In your office, I presume. You had a massive bump on the back of your head when you came through, and your shoes were covered in blood."

"Ah yes, I slipped."

"Figured as much. And sir, I hate to be a noodge, but are you *sure* I can't call you a doctor? You get sick every time you go through, and . . . shouldn't your system have gotten used to that by now?"

"No doctors."

"But this last time . . . your head . . . For the right price I'm sure we can find someone who makes house calls."

"No doctors."

"Whatever you say, sir."

Wesley's stomach growls savagely. He puts one hand to his stomach and moans. "That can't be good," he says.

"Boss, we can get you some food if you're hungry. I'll get on it right away. Why don't you get changed?"

"That's not a hunger pang, Miles, that's something else."

"Sir—"

"No doctors. Once Phase Three is complete and we've made our big Journey, then I can get checked out. Up there, not down here."

"I'd feel better if you got a clean bill of health first, but it's as you wish."

"Damn right it's as I wish. Any doctor down here saw what's going on with my innards would send me straight to the CDC, or to some military base in the desert where I'd be sharing a room with E.T."

"I was thinking we could pay someone private."

"Never mind all that. What's been happening since I arrived here with Gavin-What's-His-Fuck in my arms? How's building security?"

"The police have 875 North off limits."

"That's to be expected, I suppose."

"As for here, sir, check this out." Miles walks over to his workstation and turns on two smaller, seldom-used monitors. Cameras mounted on either end of the CGC-Meigs roof show a pair of armed Loyalist sentries standing watch.

"Perfect. What about the woman?"

"Your secretary? She's now in the 24th century, either very pregnant or very miscarried. Either way, she's not our problem anymore."

# Chapter 11

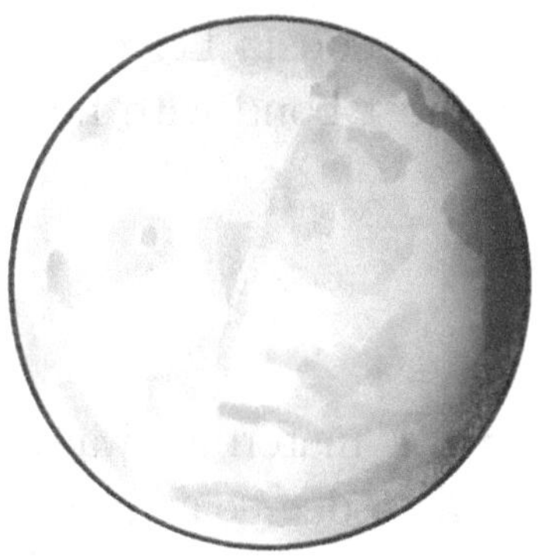

1

Dana looks in on her premie daughter, Savannah, who slumbers in an oxygen-enriched incubator with the carefree sleep of the innocent. *What a precious angel,* Dana thinks. Born five weeks premature and under the most horrifying of circumstances, Savannah is lucky to have survived at all. Though less than a month old, she has already shown signs of being a fighter.

The surviving FCB lieutenants are nice enough to give Dana a bed and a privacy curtain in their officer quarters, and they even offer to bunk with the enlisted fighters once Savannah is cleared by pediatricians to stay with her mother. Dana never sleeps there, however. She spends her time in the waiting room outside the ground level maternity ward of Clara Barton

Memorial Hospital, and discovers that if she pushes three chairs together, they form a makeshift bed. Nurses know her as the mother of Savannah, the Miracle Baby, and refuse any orders from doctors to chase her away.

There are lots of unanswered questions, and Dana isn't the one to answer them. As it is, she has barely processed the reality that she will never see her mother again, nor her best friend Kimberly, nor her cousin Lexie. There will be time to grieve. But first, she must bond with her newborn daughter. And sleep.

2

Down the hall from the maternity ward and waiting room, Susie lays reclined at a 75-degree angle on an operating table. Her left arm is secured in a sling as a nurse preps an IV while the attending surgeon looks on. A second nurse attaches a heart monitor to Susie's chest and waits for the pulse to register on the monitor. It does, beating steadily, just a bit faster than normal. A third nurse, with KITTS embroidered over the breast of her smock, prepares the anesthetic sedative that will render Susie unconscious for the procedure.

"You're in good hands with Nurse Kitts, Miss Walker," the surgeon says. Susie nods, straight-faced, as Nurse Kitts feels for the vein.

"This'll only hurt for a moment," Nurse Kitts says. She swabs the entry point, then injects the needle and pushes through the IV. Susie gnashes her teeth, but the pain—which moves from her hand to the injection site further up her arm—is brief. "Now, count backward from 100. When you wake up, it'll all be over."

Susie nods, already feeling light-headed. "One-hundred . . . 99 . . . 98 . . . 97 . . . 96 . . ." Out cold.

"Thank you, Nurse Kitts," the surgeon says. "Nurse Wilkes, hand me the scalpel. Nurse Rutherford, how are we looking on the monitor?"

"Down from 95 BPM and now steady at 60."

"Thank you, Nurse Rutherford. Keep me updated. Nurse Kitts, be ready to cauterize."

"Yes doctor," Nurse Kitts replies.

The surgeon powers up the oscillating saw and amputates below the elbow. The sound of crunching bone and the geyser-like spray of blood would turn even the strongest of stomachs, so let's give credit to those present for maintaining their nerve. Nurse Rutherford, whose gag reflex is the most pronounced, vomits into her mouth and swallows it back down. She immediately looks back at the heart monitor as if nothing is the matter.

3

Three days pass before Susie and Old Man McCarthy officially address the surviving members of the FCB, who gather alongside a collection of concerned citizens, the majority from Zone Omega. A lectern has been set up in the middle of the Century Bridge. It's windy and overcast, but the victory speech represents a good occasion for a public gathering regardless. People dress accordingly, and most of them pay little attention to the cold.

McCarthy's original suggestion of holding the speech at Memorial Landing, which isn't buffeted by crosswinds blowing through the canyon, is vetoed by Susie and company, who fear civilians from Zone Omega would be reluctant to attend an event held in Zone Alpha. While there has never been any regulation prohibiting residents of one zone from traveling to the other zone, the class divide has always kept the haves on one side of the Red River and the have-nots on the other.

A few minutes before beginning his address, McCarthy has Leonard and René low-key ask for volunteers from the Zone Omega side of the crowd to intermingle with the thinner, Zone Alpha side. "We're not enemies, we're neighbors," he reminds them. "If everything we fought for is to work, we must remember that."

Dana, Fred LaChance, and Gwendolyn and her husband, former (AWOL) Ross Army Lieutenant William Pierce, are among the resistance members and concerned citizens in attendance. They accept the Old Man's challenge and move to the Zone Alpha side. Gwendolyn's pleasant manner, combined with Dana's introduction of herself as the mother of the famous Miracle Baby, go a long way toward thawing cross-river relations.

. . .

Susie scratches at her phantom limb. She is so lost in thought she fails to realize she's scratching at thin air. *The cost of the double cross on this very bridge, and of the subsequent rescue mission, was dear,* she thinks. Susie never got the chance to know García well, but he behaved with honor once he changed alliances following the canal extension jobsite raid, and she shudders upon remembering that he literally died at her side. She *did* know Dixon and Rose, and fought alongside them for more than a year. She misses them. Rose, who was buddy-buddy with Dixon, is still missing in action, and Susie knows that if Rose is alive—and she *hopes* she is—Rose will have her own period of mourning.

And then there's Josh. Susie still doesn't know what football is, but Josh boasted about being an accomplished steward of the sport. He certainly proved his mettle as a resistance fighter. Susie thinks back to the night they made love. It only lasted a few minutes, and she has mixed feelings at having wanted it more than he did. Was she dishonoring Diego's memory during the act? Was he dishonoring Lori's? Does it matter? She and Josh *connected.* She decides he would have sacrificed his life for the cause even if it wasn't in so undignified a manner as bleeding out from an errant plasma burst. With that, she makes peace with their act of lovemaking. After all, moments of comfort are few and far between when you are at war.

. . .

"Miss Walker? Whenever you're ready."

The Old Man's words call Susie back to reality. "Thank you, sir. I was just taking inventory of all we lost."

"There are always casualties in war," McCarthy says. "I'd like to think they've made peace with their passing into the world beyond this one, but the truth is, the ghosts are everywhere."

Risers have been erected on the center of the bridge. Susie and the Old Man stand on the middle riser, at the head of the assembly. Keith, who is down to one crutch, his cast replaced with a thick bandage wrapping, joins Leonard and René on the top riser. They are VIPs, *sort of,* but not quite the top dogs. A microphone is centered on the bottom riser and extended so the Old Man can speak without having to stoop. His back hurts like the dickens as it is.

Susie turns to the Old Man. "You asked me once, not long after we met, why I work so hard. You told me I didn't have to answer right away, and I never did."

"I remember. That conversation seems like a thousand years ago."

"Indeed, sir. But to finally answer you, the reason I work so hard is to keep the ghosts at bay. Because you're right: they're everywhere." Old Man McCarthy puts a hand on her shoulder. A single tear betrays her steely façade. She wipes it away quickly with her right hand, lest anyone notice (which everyone does).

What remains of her left arm is covered in a plaster cast that ends just below the elbow. Suffice to say, people can't help but stare. Is *this* the Susie of such notoriety she was classified as an enemy of the state not even one week prior?

"Aren't you going to introduce me?" the Old Man asks her.

"Of course, sir." Susie turns on the mic, which gives the requisite squeal of feedback. The wind blows her hair in her face as she begins to speak:

"Humans have lived here for almost three centuries. Over those centuries we built something remarkable, and did so with the sparsest of resources. But with there being more work to do than bodies to do it, time forced us to turn to more extreme measures. The Freedom Contingent Brigade has fought for a change in working conditions, for a cessation in off-world immigration, and for the prioritization of a work-life balance, based on the sharing of resources; on the importance of safe working conditions; and on a platform of gender equality.

"The fight has been long and trying, with losses greater than we ever hoped they would be. But finally, by hard work, by God, or by the stars being in alignment, we have emerged victorious. To celebrate, reflect, and talk about what's next, I'd like to turn things over to my nominee for the position of interim chancellor, a good man and a great leader, Atwood J. McCarthy."

The audience roars in applause. Susie retreats to the top riser alongside Leonard, René, and Keith. Although there are just 200 people in attendance on this nippy day—most of whom have never actually met the FCB's leader—it takes two minutes for the applause to die down. Old Man McCarthy motions for everyone to cease their applause. Instead, it crescendos. Leonard activates a recorder as McCarthy starts his victory speech, and those in attendance learn why he is so revered as a leader, or have their previous faith in him confirmed.

"Settle down, everyone . . . Settle down . . . Thank you for the applause . . . Thank you . . . As my friend and colleague, Susie Walker, said, we are victorious." More applause, subsiding quicker. "Thank you again. Friends, this has been a historic couple of days indeed. Much blood was spilt, but for a good cause, in the name of safer working conditions for all and no more forced labor for anyone. A few of you attending today—reluctantly, I'm sure—joined Susie Walker, Leonard Debussy, René de Rooij, and others in raiding Chancellor Ross's base of operations, built into the cliffside over my shoulder. When Susie herself was taken prisoner, joining me in captivity, you fought harder still, and we owe you our lives. Many of you were taken from your homes on Earth Prime over an extended period of time, first a few at a time and then in larger and larger groups. I myself was born here, and I won't pretend to have any idea of what your individual Journeys were like, nor of what you were forced to leave behind. For those of you brought to this place against your will, I hope you are making or have made peace with the fact that you have loved ones back home you will never see again. The newest arrivals among you will struggle with this for some time, I suspect.

"The question foremost on everyone's mind is: What comes next? Well, that's an important question indeed. Will there be a trial? Yes. Chancellor Ross surrendered, and we thank him for his cooperation. But justice must be served in accordance with the bylaws of our constitution, and we must not rush the verdict. As for those of you here today, and for everyone on New Earth, imprisoned or free, we have work to do. Most of the forced labor projects begun under Chancellor Ross—the tunnels, dams, roads, and canals—have infrastructure merit that make them worth continuing. But with added safety precautions, with reduced working hours per person, and without the unwelcome pressure of knowing there is a weapon aimed at your back while you toil away.

"The Saurons, those omnipresent drones, some of which merely watch and others of which have the capacity to kill, must be reprogrammed as well. I hope much of this can be done at whatever remains of central command, because I do not envy anyone who may have to swap out a drone chip in the field."

4

Old Man McCarthy's speech, patriotic and inspirational but also sobering in its honesty, is rebroadcast hourly over the next few weeks. He becomes something of a legend, even among the three million citizens who have never met him. The speech plays throughout Zones Alpha and Omega from loudspeakers mounted on the corners of buildings, and in the Outlands by the handful of Saurons to have thus far been reprogrammed.

The server room inside the CCC was far enough from the time chamber that despite damage elsewhere in the complex, surveillance-only Saurons can still be reprogrammed from here. But due to a network update that failed—another system issue like the one Gustav Greene complained about at the beginning of our story—the enhanced-to-kill Sauron X drones can only be reprogrammed manually. The task is as unenviable as the Old Man predicted, and is seldom successful unless tackled in pairs or in threes—with some poor sap always acting as bait.

One such scenario follows three citizens—no longer FCB fighters but just regular New Earthlings (or Martians, if you prefer)—as they track an enhanced Sauron X, the model identical to the one Diego took out so many moons ago.

*"The days and weeks and months that follow will not be easy, and we are not yet free from the vicious cycle of death. The Sauron X's will fight back, the bridges will collapse, the tunnels will cave in, the dams will fail, the roads will crumble, and the levees will break."*

· · ·

Keith, the long-time FCB lieutenant who survived the rebellion by acting as a follower, not a leader, plays the role of guinea pig in one of the final Sauron X disarmings. His crutches discarded, his broken leg fully healed, and his conscience filled with guilt over having not participated in the raid that led to the time chamber's destruction, he decides it's high time to fully step up. He emerges from behind a pile of boulders and fires his plasma rifle in the air to draw the armed drone's attention. The second volunteer in this scouting party, Lori and Shauna's displaced friend Tiffany, fires her rifle at the drone's nozzle. She misses, and ducks safely behind the rusty ruins of a bombed-out hover-tank as the drone spins in the direction of the blast. The bombed-out tank is a remnant from the months-earlier skirmish at Quinn's Gully. It offers cover not only for Tiffany but also for fellow Goodman High alumnus Munch, the third volunteer on this particular fool's errand. Munch carries netting in his hands. The drone circles around and targets Keith in its sights. The former truck driver, whose leg only regained 75% range of motion, fails to duck low enough behind the boulder pile. The mistake costs him his life. Tiffany, who joined the clean-up crew to honor her boyfriend, Brandon, after learning how he died, fires a second round at the drone's nozzle. Direct hit! The firing nozzle falls off in an array of sparks. Munch, who sat quietly in the background at the FCB barracks while his classmates Pete, Josh, Brandon, and Shauna volunteered, none of them to be heard from again, runs forward and releases the netting. It expands like Malawian fishing tackle and wraps around the drone. He gives the netting a tug and the drone is pulled to the ground. It lands with a thud. Munch hurriedly replaces the arming chip with a surveillance-only chip. Tiffany smashes the arming chip with the heel of her boot. Deed done, she and Munch remove their caps and bow their heads for Keith, whom they hope didn't suffer.

*"Those who will inevitably fall during our best efforts to finish —with dignity—what Chancellor Ross began, will join those who perished in our recent victory campaign as being gone but not forgotten. It is our hope that with whatever goes wrong from here—for things* will *go wrong—those who are destined to perish do not suffer."*

...

Another scenario, this one with a higher body count, is at the site of a tunnel being built to ferry construction traffic to Canal Extension Alpha Lambda. When completed, the tunnel will offer a more direct route to the water source than the notorious 27 switchbacks, a hazardous incline of zigzags that have taken out more than one vehicle, usually during a sandstorm or early in the morning, when the rising sun temporarily blinds whoever is behind the wheel.

Workers digging the tunnel begin by hosing down the natural wall, then inserting blasting caps, then detonating them. The explosion is ear-shattering; Old Man McCarthy's insistence on earplugs for the workers is just one of many welcome safety concessions. The initial explosion serves two functions —to loosen the clay around the intended path and to frighten any belly beaters dozing nearby.

The cave-in—not the first, not the last, but the deadliest— occurs despite extra attention being paid to ensure safe passage through the chamber for all workers. One of the support posts was not inserted at a precise 90-degree angle, and when a transport shuttle outside makes its way along the switchbacks some 35 meters overhead, the ground shifts just enough to bring all 35 meters worth of earthworks down on the men (and a few women) beneath.

*"EVERYONE OUTTA THERE!"* the foreman shouts after sensing the first vibration. The four workers closest to the entrance make it out safely, but in his haste, the fourth one knocks over a ladder on his way out. The few seconds of delay it causes for those behind him to move it out of the way are just a few seconds too many, and everyone remaining in the tunnel perishes as a result of the cave-in—26 in all.

. . .

Zones Alpha and Omega—Omega in particular—quickly become hives of activity, with pavers laying asphalt and the sound of hammers and chainsaws signifying new construction in the form of heated apartments and duplex-style homes. Dormitory living, temporary or otherwise, will soon be a thing of the past and there will likewise be no more need for subterranean barracks such as those used by the FCB, except perhaps as emergency shelters during the severest of sandstorms.

A group of citizens in hardhats tamp down with shovels the edges of asphalt left behind after a bulldozer makes its way down a main road through the garment district. An unarmed Sauron floats past and rebroadcasts the conclusion to Old Man McCarthy's speech for the umpteenth time:

*"Rest assured, it is not all doom and gloom. There will be civic enhancements too, with safer labor. Paved roads, above-ground housing for all. Yearly physicals for maternity-eligible women, physical therapy for miners and other hard laborers. End-of-life care centers for the elderly. It shames me these things were not already a reality, but with time, they will be. Immigration complications have stifled our population growth for the immediate future, but I believe there are enough of us to get the job done, if you are willing to work, side by side, each of you watching your neighbor's back, for the common good. Remember, we do this not just for our futures, but for our children's futures."*

As the Old Man's speech runs on a loop, two young children play on an unpaved side street. They kick around a baseball-sized stone, unearthed when the main road was combed prior to paving. The older child, a boy of about five, kicks the stone toward the freshly poured asphalt. The younger child, a girl of around four, runs after the stone, but her attentive mother is faster and yanks her out of harm's way at the last second. One of the workers observes this and reaches across the lip of asphalt to pick up the stone. He holds it out, palm up, and the girl's mother nods for her to retrieve the stone, which she does with a smile and a curtsy. The worker smiles, tips his hardhat, and continues about his day.

5

Old Man McCarthy, the interim chancellor of New Earth, surveys the crowd at the end of his speech. Marquez, who had trouble finding a sitter for her son and who carries the bundled toddler in a baby carrier on her chest, arrives late to McCarthy's address and sidles over to Dana. The women exchange smiles, already on the fast track to friendship.

Someone coughs, a baby cries, and several people dab tears from their eyes. A gust of wind carries someone's hat over the side of the bridge.

"Long live New Earth," the Old Man concludes.

"*May her bounty provide,*" 200 people reply, in unison.

# Chapter 12

1

Having phoned the spouses of Air Force pilots Ramsey and Hunter to let them know their husbands served their country with honor but will not be coming home, Robert Wilkinson, Sr. needs the distraction of grilling to clear his head. He prepares a roast on the backyard Weber grill and browns asparagus while Gail steams rice in the kitchen.

The senator is hard-pressed to recall the last time he, Gail, and Bob ate dinner around the dining room table as a family. Has it been *months*? Surely not. At any rate, the food is good (the beef a perfect, juicy pink), the company is amiable (Lori is polite and well-mannered), and the conversation is innocuous enough (college plans, the weather, the latest exhibit at Washington's National Gallery of Art).

Robert, Sr. gets his wife's blessing before offering wine to the kids, who choose not to imbibe. Lori says she's fine with milk and Bob says he prefers his Mountain Dew. "These kids need culture," Robert, Sr. says. He pours himself and Gail glasses full enough to make up for the tipple Bob and Lori declined.

They avoid all talk of anything related to the Blockade and Occupation and instead discuss the potential merits of the action-comedy *Beverly Hills Cop II,* which opened the day before prom and which Bob and Lori look forward to seeing. Robert, Sr. impresses them by revealing he met star Eddie Murphy at the White House two years prior. Bob, who *can't believe* he never heard this story before, is about to ask his old man what the actor is really like when Pete enters. "Pete!" Lori remarks. The room grows silent.

Gail escorts Pete to the table. He looks out of sorts, so she gets an extra place setting from the kitchen and offers to serve him. "Thanks, Mrs. W. This smells great."

"How're you feeling, Peter?" Robert, Sr. asks.

"Starving."

"Well, there's plenty," Gail says. She holds the plate while Robert, Sr. slices off an especially large piece of meat for him.

The others wait with baited breath for Pete to start eating. Once he swallows his first big bite and follows up an especially large swig of Tab, his beverage of choice, with an enormous belch, the tension dissipates and the casual conversation resumes. "Pete, dad was just telling us about the time he met Eddie Murphy," Bob says.

"A-heh-heh-heh-heh," Pete replies. It's a weak imitation of the movie star's famous laugh, but then, he just slept the afternoon away.

"Eddie's handlers kept him on his best behavior," Robert, Sr. explains. "It was all rather strained, if I remember correctly. I don't think the president was much of a fan."

"Did you get your picture taken with him?" Bob asks.

"Of course. It's in my office."

"How cool!"

Robert, Sr. addresses Bob's best friend since childhood. "So, Peter, Gail says your folks are in Florida?"

"They might still be in Tennessee. I should call 'em after dinner and check in."

"I'm sure they'd love to hear from you. How are you feeling?"

"Better, now that I'm getting some food in me."

"And how's the elbow?"

"Hurts." Pete turns to Gail. "This is really good, Mrs. W."

"Thank you, Pete, but I'm only responsible for the rice."

"Best rice I've ever had."

"My, aren't you the gentleman?" Pete shrugs, and Gail continues. "It's good to see you up and at it. Are you *sure* you're feeling alright?"

"I guess I'm a little out of it still."

"The trooper told us you took a nasty spill on your bike," Robert, Sr. says.

"I came here on my bike?"

Lori leans forward. "You don't remember?"

"Nothing."

"He remembers our names though," Bob remarks. "And where he is. Hey Pete, how many fingers am I holding up?" He flips Pete the bird.

"Robbie, that's not necessary," Gail scolds.

"A-heh-heh-heh-heh," Pete's Eddie Murphy impression is better this time.

"Eat up, Peter," Robert, Sr. says. "Mind that elbow and get yourself plenty of rest."

"Sounds like a plan, Mr. W."

Dinner, with Neapolitan ice cream for dessert, is a hit. A subdued Pete is on his best behavior; his Eddie Murphy laugh is all he can manage in terms of humor. *I hope he's okay,* Gail thinks. She and Lori unload the dishwasher in preparation for a fresh load while Pete phones his parents from the next room. He may not remember what happened on Mars, but he still remembers his uncle's phone number in East Tennessee.

"Where do the glasses go?" Lori asks.

"Upper cabinet, just left of the sink, dear." Gail only half-listens to Lori—she *really* wants to hear the conversation between Pete and his parents, whom she's always viewed as being somewhat aloof.

Pete has stretched the kitchen phone cord as far as it will go. His parents and sister are on their final night in Tennessee, and all four parties are running out of things to say. "What time are you leaving for Florida tomorrow?"

Stan has positioned the receiver in his lap, face up, in speaker mode. This keeps his hands free to peel the price tag from the souvenir PIGEON FORGE coffee mug his wife bought him. "Right after breakfast," he says. "Long way to go still."

"Where's breakfast?"

"Do you remember that pancake cabin, just outside the national park?" Dolores asks. She wets a wad of bathroom tissue and wipes away her makeup at the mirror.

"The one with the Mickey Mouse pancakes?"

"That's the one."

"Your sister loved those pancakes. Grinning from ear to ear!" Stan adds.

"*Daaad!*" Becky bemoans. As if to punctuate her embarrassment, a glob of chocolate from the ice cream bar she purchased from the motel vending machine dribbles onto her new Dollywood T-shirt. "Awww, dang it!"

"Becky Sue!" her mother chastises.

"Didn't she pee her pants on the drive down the first time?" Pete asks.

"Shut up, Booger Head!"

"You shut up, Pizza Face!"

"Both of you shut up," Stan barks.

"Sorry," Pete and Becky reply, simultaneously.

"No news on your friends yet?" Dolores asks. "They barely gave it a mention on the news down here."

"No news," Pete replies after a moment's hesitation.

"Are you okay? You don't sound like your usual self."

"Like your usual Booger Head self," Becky clarifies.

"I'm okay. Wiped out on my bike earlier. Messed up my elbow. It's not broken though."

"You need to be more careful."

"I know, pop."

"Well, if it doesn't feel better in the morning, go see Dr. Chakrabarti."

"Pretty sure he's left town, ma, but I'll live. It's just a bad scrape."

"Well, if you're sure . . ."

"I'm sure, ma. How's Uncle Bill?"

"He's fine. Took me gem mining yesterday after dropping your father and your sister off at Dollywood for the day. Still drives that same rusty pickup. He jokes that the rust is the only thing holding it together."

"Hey Blechy, how was Dollywood?"

"Radical like always. There's this one little dip on the Blazing Fury. Gets me every time."

"No thanks."

"You're such a lame-o. You could've at least rode the train."

"Rebecca, don't tease your brother," Stan interjects.

"*Daaad!* He started it. He called me 'Blechy!' "

"See? Aren't you happy I didn't come with?"

"Of course not, son," Dolores replies.

"We respect your feelings," Stan adds. "We just hope you and Robert are enjoying the early start to your summer vacation." Pete's dad sighs before he says Bob's name, still half-convinced Bob is turning his son gay.

This irks Pete into ending the call as soon as possible. "Thanks, pop. Drive safe tomorrow. Ma, say 'Hi' to Uncle Bill for me."

"Will do, son," Stan replies.

"What about me?!" Becky asks.

"Have fun in Florida, Blechy."

"That's it? No 'Pizza Face?' "

"No 'Pizza Face.' "

Elated: "Wow. It's a new day."

"Thanks for finally checking in," Dolores says. "We were starting to worry."

"I know, ma. Sorry I forgot. Bye for now."

"Bye, Peter."

Pete gets up from the sofa and returns to the kitchen. He can't help but notice Gail loitering about the kitchen as she wipes the same section of counter over and over again with a sponge. "Everything okay?" she asks.

"You don't have to keep asking, Mrs. W. Everything's good."

"You look like you're still out of it, is why I asked."

"Think I ate too much."

"Robbie's father and I will take that as a compliment. You're too skinny—you and Robbie both."

"Uh, my headache's back, so I think I'll lie down."

"There should be some Tylenol in the medicine cabinet upstairs. Check the expiration date."

"I will, thanks."

"Well . . . goodnight, Pete."

" 'Night." Pete leaves the room as an unsettled Gail, who is sure Pete saw something that will forever traumatize him, continues to wipe the same section of counter. She hopes her stepson isn't similarly traumatized.

Pete heads upstairs and stops outside the guest room Lori has claimed. The door is ajar. He knocks and it swings open wider, to the sight of Lori changing into an oversized Northwestern University sweatshirt she borrowed from Gail.

The old Pete would have filed this away for mental masturbation. The new Pete, who has no memory of what happened to him once he was abducted but knows it couldn't have been good considering his current fugue state, has a newfound respect for boundaries. "Oh, I'm sorry," he says. His face is beet red.

Lori, too, is a changed person. She ducks behind the closet door but isn't mortified the way she was when he humiliated her at Vinnie's—a day not so long ago. "What is it, Pete?"

"I, um, just wanted to say I'm done on the phone if you wanna call your folks."

"Okay, thanks."

Pete crosses the hall to Bob's room, where his friend is on his hands and knees, ass in the air, on his bed, tossing contents from inside his headboard onto the mattress for no apparent reason. "What are you doing?"

"Hey. Looking for lorazepam."

"Your pills?"

"Yeah. Thought I might have a bottle stashed away in here somewhere."

"It's bad, huh?"

"It's creepin' up."

"I haven't seen 'em, but can I help you look?"

"Eh, it's a lost cause. I already went through my backpack and tore the dresser apart. Just wanted something to take the edge off."

"Bummer. Never got a hold of Dr. Kirchner?"

Bob shakes his head. "He must still be out of town. I'll be alright."

"Absolutely you will," Pete replies. He helps Bob tidy up. Handing him a stack of comic books Bob uprooted from their hiding place, he adds, "This won't help your nerves any, but you should know I just walked in on Rain-Rain undressing."

"I'll bet you enjoyed that."

"No, it was by accident. I felt embarrassed."

"I already apologized to her for what happened at Vinnie's. I think she's moved past it."

"I hope so. I was a dumbass that day."

"Yeah you were." Bob goes through the stack of comic books. He stops at a real gem—a first edition from 1984 of *Marvel Super Heroes Secret Wars #8: First Encounter between Symbiote and Spider-Man*. Though he doesn't know it, a first edition of this rarity will eventually fetch $32,250. "I forgot I had this one."

"Sweet! Careful not to bend the corners."

"I know." Bob sandwiches the rare edition between other comics for protection and returns it to the storage drawer built into his headboard. And out of nowhere, the words said before he can take them back: "I saw her in her undies."

"Dude! And you didn't die of a heart attack?!"

"Just a small one."

"Sounds like you two are getting close. What happened?"

Bob shakes his head. "I don't kiss and tell. But, um, we had a moment."

"High five!" Pete, finally showing signs of his old, jovial self, raises his right hand. Bob humors him with a high five but wishes he kept his mouth shut.

"I'm almost sorry I missed it," Pete continues. "Of course if I was there, I probably would've said something stupid and ruined it."

"Don't be so down on yourself, dude. *I'm* supposed to be the anxious one here, remember?"

"I'm just saying."

"I know." Bob gives up his search for lorazepam and re-folds the shorts strewn across his bed. "Elbow any better?"

"Still hurts."

"Too much for an *Astro Warrior* rematch?"

"Nah, no shooting games for me. You can play if you want. I'm kinda tired."

"You slept all afternoon!"

"Sorry, Roberto. I'm just not feeling it. Like I told your mom, I think I ate too much."

"All good. I'll just play *Alex Kidd* then. I can use the distraction. Lemme know if the volume's too loud."

"You rich kids with your multiple game systems."

"Still bummed your ColecoVision wasn't the more popular console?"

"Damn skippy."

3

*Roughly six minutes and 39 seconds into each person's Journey, the hollow and unsettling silence that drives some people insane is replaced in an instant with an intense roar that could best be described as the sound of a Shop-Vac being amplified into a megaphone. The noise gets progressively louder for the final 16 seconds, and has ruptured more than a few eardrums. Just as trippy, the visual sensation of time slowing, similar to the Millennium Falcon coming out of hyperdrive, is nothing less than completely disorienting. Partner those sensations with a tingling in one's extremities as their molecules reassemble, and it's a wonder each person's hair doesn't turn white during the Journey, like it did for the late Gavin Berringer. Time and location displacement doesn't hurt, but it doesn't tickle, either. Two out of every five passengers fall to their knees after emerging from either end of the time chamber.*

*Pete's return trip is well timed; he arrives at CGC-Meigs 12 hours after his original outbound Journey to find the place all but deserted. (Despite Wesley's insistence upon 24/7 staffing, there was nothing on the docket, so Miles sent Balthazar and Gilman home to get some much-overdue shuteye. Gilman, not of this world, bunked in a nondescript Streeterville hotel his fellow Loyalists had taken over, not by violence but by throwing money at the manager. Before leaving for the night himself, Miles set the time chamber to auto-calibrate and arranged for overnight patrols consisting of two soldiers on the roof and four on the water. His last order of business was to check on Wesley, who had drifted in and out of consciousness all evening and who was currently asleep, wheezing as if suffering from sleep apnea.)*

*A woozy Pete pauses in front of a workstation monitor, the only source of light in the room aside from the circles that represent the time chamber's telepad coils. He sees in the monitor's reflection that his vest is spattered with blood—Johnny's or Josh's. He removes the vest and folds it reverently, as if it's a piece of funeral garb. His ears are ringing. He feels the lobes for blood. Finding none, he cracks his jaw to clear the ringing.*

*He looks at the vest. "What am I doing?" he asks himself, and tosses it in the wastebasket near Miles's desk. He tiptoes on unsteady feet in near-darkness toward the new door that replaces the one he, Bob, Lori, and Vinnie entered during their first fact-finding mission. He reaches for the handle with dread, half-expecting an alarm to be tripped.*

*A voice calls out from the darkness.*

*"Who's there?" Wesley Arendt rasps.*

*"It's Chancellor Ross," Pete replies, saying the first name to spring to mind that he surmises Wesley may know.*

*"No it's not. But your voice does sound familiar. Come to the holding room, where I can see you. I'm alone."*

*"No surprises this time." Pete steps gingerly, ready for any-thing, toward the holding area beyond the mainframe room.*

*"No surprises. But wait . . . Lights." With that, overhead lights illuminate. The shadows of the holding area—all horizontal bars and dark corners—are replaced with a fluorescent glow that causes both men to squint. "Well well well," Wesley says from his cell. He lays on his side, near-death. His lips are severely chapped and a cold sore festers on one corner of his mouth. A pile of vomit laced with blood dries on the cement floor beneath his cot. "It's nice to see a familiar face."*

*"Neat trick with the lights," Pete replies. He keeps his distance and feels suitably woozy. "Only other place I've been with tech-nology like that won't even be colonized for another 40 years. So go figure."*

*"We gave them fresh recruits, they gave us voice-activated technology. I see you made it back. Might I surmise you're an even trickier little SOB than I pegged you for the other night?"*

*"You might indeed. And that Journey sucked." Pete touches his gut and winces, nauseous.*

*"As much as I'd love to disagree with you, in hindsight I'd say you're right. Might I appeal to your humanity and ask for some water? Cooler's on the opposite wall there."*

*Pete ambles to the water cooler and removes two paper cups from a sleeve on the side. He takes two full swigs but spits up the second. Post-Journey vomit races into his mouth. He hurls. The discharge lands half-in, half-out of the wastebasket beside the cooler. He takes a third swig of water to rinse out his mouth. "Yeah, I'm never doing that again." He carries the second cup to Wesley's cell. Wesley reaches for the water but Pete holds it at arm's length.*

*"Burns your throat, doesn't it?" Wesley rasps. "Stomach prob-lems are the unfortunate side effect of too many Journeys, and the one thing we could never truly solve."*

*Pete touches his gut again. There is still discomfort, but less than before. The fact that Wesley is in far worse shape does not escape his notice. "Is that what's wrong with you?" he asks.*

*"I suppose I should've driven here from my office more instead of Journeying."*

*"How many times have you gone through that thing?"*

*"To Mars? Three times. Locally? More times than I can count." He lunges for the water, still out of reach.*

*"Yeah, that's a hard pass, asshole."*

*"Sticks and stones. Can I have that water now?"*

*Pete extends his hand toward the cell, then retracts it at the last second. Wesley groans—a wholly unhealthy sound. A string of bile runs down his chin. "That's disgusting," Pete says.*

*"I overplayed my hand," Wesley concedes. He breaks into a coughing fit. Pete sets the cup of the water on the floor and slides it under the cell. A third of it spills, but he doesn't care. Wesley grabs the cup with shaky hands. Another third spills as he brings it to his lips. Best water he's ever tasted.*

*"Two others came through here right before me," Pete says. "Did you see 'em?"*

*Stiff-necked from the wafer-thin mattress, Wesley struggles to shake his head. "I was counting sheep 'til I heard some weapons fire outside. It came from the roof."*

*Pete scans the other cells to make sure no one is lying in wait. "The other alarms didn't wake you up?"*

*"I have slept the sleep of the dead, you meddlesome little turd. Bruce Springsteen could perform across the way and I wouldn't hear it." He breaks into another coughing fit. This one leaves him gasping. (Previous episodes were fixed by taking a painkiller or swallowing an antacid, but this time it's different. His head pounds, his ears ring, his vision is spotty, and his stomach is in literal knots. He knows he should've taken up Miles on his offer to bring in a doctor.)*

Pete continues once Wesley's coughing spell abates. "You lost. It's over. We destroyed that thing on the other side."

"I don't believe you." Wesley coughs again. "The chancellor wouldn't let that happen."

"The chancellor is not a chancellor anymore."

Pete thinks he hears Wesley gasp at the news, but the glottal stop could have just been the after-effects of his coughing spell. He doesn't care either way. As he turns to make his leave, with no idea how he's going to get home, Wesley calls out to him, his words pathetic and raspy: "A million dollars."

"What?" Pete stops in his tracks.

"A million dollars. If you get me out of here and drive me out of the city. As you can see, I can't quite manage on my own."

"Are you kidding me?"

"Two million dollars."

"I don't have a car."

"By boat, then. I have contacts that can guarantee safe passage. I just need help making the trip." Wesley speaks louder now, but his words are tinged with pain.

"No more boats."

"Another way, then. Just name your price."

"No." Pete replies in a whisper, his decision final.

He walks away. Wesley makes one last offer, yelling it out with the last of his energy. "Ten million dollars!" Pete stops for three seconds, but does not turn around. He exits the building without granting the founder and chief executive officer of Chicago Genetics Corporation, Inc. his final wish.

Outside, Pete scans his surroundings closely. As he passes the building's periphery and approaches the passageway cut into the chain-link fence by Bob not so long ago, his eyes are drawn to a ladder descending from the building's roof. A Loyalist soldier is slumped over the edge of the ladder, dead. His rifle—this one an AK-47—hangs suspended from his upside-down torso. A few *yards further on, a second Loyalist soldier is sprawled on the ground, a hole blasted in his midsection and his weapon missing. Pete has never given much thought to the idea of fate, but if he stopped to study this soldier's face, he would see it is that of Sergeant Burns, who led three other goons in an attack against Pete and his friends inside this facility 30 hours prior.*

*Samara, he thinks. This has to have been her work. As he makes his way to the steps between the Adler Planetarium and the Shedd Aquarium—the steps beside which his friend Vincent Modigliani met his Maker—he notices what appears to be a lump beneath a crab apple tree. A closer look reveals the lump to be Banks, the abductee-turned-control room operator second class who would have been given a second chance if not for the rounds in his back from the rooftop sniper hit. Pete removes Banks's lab coat and covers his body with it. He looks over his shoulder at the CGC operations center and at the dual Loyalist corpses. "Fuck," he whispers. After a sigh, he makes haste—first walking, then jogging, then all-out running.*

4

Pete awakens from his nightmare with a hard dose of memory recall. He sits up in his sleeping bag, laid out on the carpet next to Bob's bed, and damn near hyperventilates. Bob comes fully awake at the sound of his best friend's frantic breathing. He turns on the nightstand light to find Pete drenched in sweat. "You okay?"

Pete checks his pulse. His heart races. He breathes deep to slow his heart rate and compose himself. Wiping the sweat from his brow, he says, "I remember everything."

Although the stubborn, hard-charging Detective Lieutenant Mayotte would never admit it, he is running on empty. He's sure it's unhealthy to drink two pots of coffee in a single waking period, but he's likewise sure he's on the verge of finding evidence of wrongdoing by Wesley Arendt and CGC that will hold up in a court of law.

Captain Bennett phoned him two more times, offering assistance and urging him to get some rest. He turned his C.O. down both times, and is glad he did. Mayotte has reconstructed three shredded documents in full. His fingers are raw from the act of taping so many thin strips of paper together, but his efforts have paid off.

## CONTRACT OF GENETICS RESEARCH AND BLOOD GENOME PATHOLOGY

PARTY A: ______________________________

PARTY B: CHICAGO GENETICS CENTER, INC.

DATE: ____/____/_______ (MM/DD/YYYY)

The top page of each document features the header above, with the name(s) of party A and the date(s) written in ink. The second page of each document includes a rectangle for a passport photo-sized insert. In each case, the photo has been scanned onto the document, so the picture of the genetics research applicant is little more than a black-and-white, dot matrix image. Combine this with vertical shreds every two millimeters and the presence of masking tape, and the images aren't much to look at. Still, Mayotte is sure he's seen these faces before.

He phones the precinct and asks for Captain Bennett. Taken aback when told the captain is home asleep, he looks at his watch and sees it's 3:47 a.m. *How long have I been awake?* he wonders. The dispatcher patches him through to the only detective officially on duty in Missing Persons at this hour: a tall, blue-eyed immigrant named Martin Heinbrenner.

"Heinbrenner."

"It's Mayotte. I need you to pull three files for me."

"Mayotte! Haven't seen you around these parts in a minute."

"Yeah yeah. I've got a hot one."

"I'm listening."

"Check for files on Leonard Horatio Debussy, Rosalina Aurea Martínez y Guadalupe, and Lymott Joseph Banks."

"Writing it down. How do you spell Leonard's surname?"

"D-E-B-U-double-S-Y. Debussy. Need help with the others?"

"No. What are we looking for?"

"Facial descriptions to start. I'm looking for an African American with glasses, a young Latina, and a Caucasian with brown hair in his early 20s, I'd say. Also, dates they went missing."

"Anything else?"

"No. I need it yesterday."

"On it."

Mayotte ends the call. He stretches, cracks his neck, and rocks on the balls of his feet to get the blood flowing. Never one for petty office politics, he is impressed by the no-nonsense junior detective. He doesn't know much about Martin Heinbrenner except that he grew up behind the Iron Curtain, that he immigrated to the U.S. under mysterious circumstances, and that he is similarly hard-working. Mayotte wonders what drives him, but respects his colleague enough to let him tell his story in his own time.

He is on his way back from the coffee station when the phone rings. "Mayotte," he answers.

"Heinbrenner. Found 'em."

"That was fast."

"I saw your name on the Martínez and Banks cases. No one less than the captain's on the Debussy case."

"Yeah, the Martínez one in particular struck a chord. I remember her foster father getting on his knees like he had something to atone for and groveling at my feet to find his daughter. Was a complete dead end."

"Did you finally find something?"

"Looks that way. What were the dates for each of those?"

"Uh, let's see. Martínez was January 28th, '86, Banks was March 22nd of that year, and Debussy was February 3rd, also '86."

"Perfect. Those dates match up to around when this whole thing started."

"What are you thinking?"

"I'm gonna try and piece together more names. This is great. When the captain comes in, tell him, 'We've got him.' "

"You're still at 875 North? . . . Detective? . . . Hello?"

Mayotte resumes his reconstruction of shredded documents from Wesley's office without bothering to hang up his end of the line.

6

Lori sits at the dinette table with Bob by her side. Tears stream down her cheeks. She listens, flabbergasted, as Pete regales what happened, including the inane fate that befell Josh. Three soft drinks at various levels of consumption make moisture rings into the coasters upon which they rest. It's almost noon, and Bob and Pete were late to wake. It took Pete an hour to tell Bob what transpired on Mars, and almost as long for him to repeat the story to Robert, Sr., who, as always, was up at the crack of dawn. The two teens fell back asleep afterwards, but their sleep was broken as Pete came to terms with everything he saw and as Bob dreaded losing the inroads made with Lori once she learned of her on-again, off-again quarterback boy-friend's untimely death.

Bob's dad and stepmom observe as Pete gives Lori the bad news; Robert, Sr. sits at the head of the table, his turkey sandwich untouched save for a single bite. Gail leans against the counter, arms folded, still unsure what to make of all this.

"He was decent," Pete says. "He nearly beat me up in school last week—or whenever it was, time is so confusing now—and then go figure, next thing I know, he rescued me from the dorm. He was . . . decent. I can't think of a better word." He sips his soda—Tab, of course.

"And the girl? Tell me more about her." Lori fiddles with her flexi straw but doesn't actually take a drink.

"Susie? I-I dunno. She's a freedom fighter and something of a legend up there. A real tough bitch." Pete shrugs, feeling he is telling one of those you-had-to-be-there stories. "Sorry," he adds when Lori winces at his utterance of the B-word.

"He was sweet on her?" Accusatory in tone.

"They were sweet on each other, as far as I could tell."

"Unbelievable." Lori wipes away her tears and runs a hand through her hair.

"Lori, I'm not trying to defend the guy's honor. I mean, I've never really liked him, not down here at least, but it's just . . . you don't know how horrible it is up there. I was there for *maybe* three weeks and I doubt I'll *ever* stop having nightmares. The stuff I saw! These things that come out of nowhere and snap at your ankles. The cold. The wind. The Pit! Josh said he figured he'd been there a little over a month, yet he had this haunted look about him. Poor Susie, she was *born* there. I can't imagine spending 25 or however many years in that place."

"She was older than him?"

"I'm pretty sure, yeah. She was, like, high up in the Freedom Contingent Brigade or whatever; I keep wanting to call it the 'Rebel Alliance.'"

"And you're sure they were a couple, and he was into her?"

"I'm maybe 60 percent sure. Like I said, he looked haunted. And when we found that mass grave, he turned whiter than snow. In the few quiet moments we had, though, when he was with her, he . . . he looked happy."

"Tell me again how he died." Pete sighs, reluctant, but Lori squeezes his hand. "Don't spare my feelings."

Bob is silently furious toward Pete. He has enjoyed the last few days in the company of a young woman who, although she may be out of his league in terms of physical attributes and social circles, has warmed to him in promising ways. He knows it's selfish of him to feel this way and to be angry with his friend, who barely escaped with his life. Still and all, Josh may be out of the picture, but caught-in-the-crossfire death or not, he died a martyr. What can Bob offer compared to that?

"There isn't much to tell," Pete explains. "We all made a last stand at the time chamber, I guess is what it's called. The whole thing was his idea, actually. We went there, a few of us got picked off along the way, but, uh, we mostly held our own until we got to the chamber itself. That's when the shit really hit the fan. Some flunky tried to get the better of us and Josh got hit. Uh, your friend Shauna was killed, too. She burned to death, right on the telepad."

"Shauna was there?!" Lori cries out. "Why didn't you tell me?!"

"I'm telling you now; I didn't remember until late last night. I-I didn't see anyone else I recognized." After a moment: "No wait, Brandon was there, too!"

"This just gets worse and worse!"

Pete looks away as he concludes his tale with a lie. "For what it's worth, they didn't suffer."

Lori sobs uncontrollably. Her chest heaves as she all-out wails. Bob puts an arm on her shoulder to comfort her, but she rebuffs him. He motions for Pete to follow him into the next room. Gail pats Pete on the arm as he passes.

"Dude," Bob says, angrily, once he and Pete are in the family room and out of Lori's earshot, "what are you doing?!"

"I'm just telling her what happened," Pete answers.

"I know, but, it's just, you . . . y-y-you're cockblocking me!"

"Cockblocking you, what?! I'm *helping* you. Josh is dead. She's all yours!"

"Dammit, Pete, you just . . . you don't get it at all . . . Look, after you were taken, Lori and I grew close. We slept in the same bed the other night."

"You slept with her?!"

"Yes. Nothing happened . . . but yes."

"So what's the problem?"

"The problem is, what can I offer her in comparison to a guy who died in battle?! That's some real hero shit. Me, I can't even beat *Super Mario Bros!*"

Pete shakes his head. He can barely recognize his friend by how he is acting. "Unbelievable. I almost died up there and all you can think about is yourself. Why did I even come here?!"

"Because I'm your only friend." The words are harsh, almost guttural, and Bob immediately regrets saying them.

Pete shakes his head. "I'm outta here. Tell your dad and Gail thanks for the food."

"Where you going?"

"Not sure. Maybe home. Maybe for a walk. I gotta clear my head. You're being a dick."

Pete storms off in a huff. He slams the patio door behind him. Bob stares at the carpet, ashamed by his behavior. He plods back to the kitchen and is surprised to find Lori washing the handful of dishes in the sink. Robert, Sr. and Gail have made themselves scarce. Lori sees him enter and manages a half-smile. Her eyes are red from crying. "Hey," she said, setting the glasses in the strainer to air dry. "I sort of figured we were done with these."

"We have a dishwasher, you know."

"Such a waste for just a plate and three glasses," Lori says. "Mom never even uses ours. Says it doesn't get the dishes as clean."

"They're just soda glasses."

"I don't mind. Where'd Pete go?"

"Not sure. He's mad about something. You okay? Uh, about Josh, I mean?"

Lori gives an uncertain head tilt. "I'll be alright. I made a fool of myself there, acting all jealous."

"No you didn't."

"But I *did*. We were broken up. Sort of. I think right now I'm more angry than sad. Or maybe it hasn't sunk in yet."

"The five stages of grief." Bob rattles them off from memory —four years of treatment at the hands of his previous shrink, Dr. Remus. "Denial, anger, bargaining, depression, acceptance. I know 'em well."

"Well, if I'm already at the 'anger' stage, I guess I'm making good progress." Lori forces a smile and a chuckle.

"Again, I'm sorry. If you wanna talk about it . . ."

"Thank you . . . I think I'm just gonna lie down. I'm sure my makeup's running; I must look like a clown."

"You look beautiful."

"As I said before, Bobby, you're sweet. Tell your dad and your stepmom thanks for letting me stay here."

"I will. Have a good rest."

Lori suppresses a sniffle as she heads upstairs.

7

For Bob, Pete, Lori, and Gail, the afternoon is all about silent reflection. Only Robert, Sr., on the phone in his study with

Governor Thompson and other VIPs, is actively productive. In the basement, Gail busies herself with laundry. She irons blouses while the dryer tumbles, the occasional *clink* of a metal snap against the dryer door offering reassurance that some things are still right with the world. Upstairs, Lori cries into her pillow. The eye shadow she borrowed from Gail runs and stains the pillowcase. Outside, Pete stews in the passenger seat of Bob's Trans Am. He replays their last conversation in his head to convince himself he said nothing wrong. In the leafy backyard, Bob sits in the middle of his trampoline. He listens to "Somebody" on his Sony Walkman, his legs folded in what he and his friends call "Indian-style" but what, years later, will be referred to as "Criss Cross applesauce."

Robert, Sr. barks orders into his phone, something about "holding them accountable." A worn manila file older is open on his desk. Inside the folder, a thick document entitled TLDT EXPERIMENTATION AT CHICAGO GENETICS CENTER is secured by a binder clip and emblazoned with an FBI logo and a red CLASSIFIED stamp.

· · ·

Gail, upstairs in Bob's room 15 minutes later with a basket of fresh laundry, places clean, folded garments on the bed—pants in one pile, shirts in another, socks and underwear in a third. On her way out of the room, basket under one arm, she pauses to study a picture of Bob's birth mother, Marie, in a frame on his dresser. She long ago accepted she would never measure up in her stepson's eyes as an equal to that of his real mom, but she loves Bob just the same. Unable to bear children herself, Bob is the only child she will ever have, and she is grateful for his restrained love, which has thawed, slowly, over eight tough years.

Lori stands at the bathroom mirror and splashes water on her face. Having finally composed herself, she dries her face and proceeds to apply fresh makeup. She pauses, eye shadow brush halfway to her lid. What does she need makeup for, anyway? For one thing, she may start crying again. For another thing, Bob, who she never expected to find herself drawn to, doesn't seem especially picky. He lives in a gorgeous home, sure, but he acts remarkably down to earth.

Pete paces back and forth in the driveway and pieces his words together. The breeze blows a forgotten soda can to a stop at the curb. He kicks the can and makes his way toward the rear of the house. He and Bob have been friends since kindergarten, when the teacher busted them both for eating paste, and Bob cried into his shoulders upon getting the call from hospice during fourth grade that his mother had passed away. Sure, Bob has no way of knowing the horrors Pete witnessed on Mars, but—silver spoon or not—Bob's lived through horrors of his own. Mostly, Pete's just happy to see his friend again.

Bob's cassette skips, producing garbled audio. "Damn," he says. He ejects the cassette, a mix tape he made himself, and carefully removes the exposed tape that is snagged in the Walkman's rubber wheels. With gritted teeth, he rewinds the tape by using his pinky in place of a pencil. Pete startles him from thought.

"Uh oh," Pete says. "My boombox does that too sometimes."

"Yeah, I think I've got it," Bob replies. "This thing acts weird when the batteries run low."

"Yeah." Pete climbs onto the trampoline and sits next to his friend. "Hey, by the way."

"Hey."

"Roberto, I'm sorry if I mucked it up between you and Lori. I just thought she needed to hear what happened to Josh."

Bob gives a resigned nod. "Yeah. I know. And she *did* need to hear. I just . . . I . . ."

"You don't think you'll measure up."

"Something like that." Bob sets the Walkman to the side and lays on his back, hands folded behind his head. Pete follows suit. "Nice day out," Bob adds. Not much of an olive branch, but sometimes bygones are bygones.

"Yeah. Kinda eerie though, this whole neighborhood just, like, devoid of people, you know?"

"Big time. Except for my dad and Mr. Cavanaugh from Dominick's, pretty much everyone around here works downtown. I hope they were able to get out. I mean, I *guess* they were; I haven't seen any kids running around and I don't hear dogs barking like I usually do. Definitely eerie."

"You okay?"

"Wish I could get ahold of Dr. Kirchner. I left him like three messages."

"Why don't you just drive over there? I mean, I'm sure he left town like everyone else, but . . . you won't know if you don't go."

"I was trying to work through this without him, but yeah, I think maybe you're right." After a beat: "So it was bad up there, huh?"

"Dude. I wouldn't go back in a million years. Not even if it meant seeing Rain-Rain in a bra again . . . which I'm still sorry about, by the way."

"Don't tell her I told you this, but when I saw her in her undies, they were soaked through. I basically saw everything."

"Lucky bastard!" Pete being Pete, he can't stop there. "Bush?"

Bob shrugs, but a smile that forms on the corners of his mouth suggests the answer is in the affirmative.

"Radical!"

"Don't get too excited. Like I said before, nothing happened. It's just . . . I dunno, I can't describe it . . . W-we made a good connection. It was nice."

"While she was in her undies? I'll bet it was!"

"You must be feeling better. You seem like your same old, obnoxious self."

"Put it this way: I'm glad I'm back."

"I'm glad you're back, too."

"I'm rooting for the two of you. Don't hold out on me if you actually—"

"Yeah, don't hold out," Lori chimes in, startling them both.

"Hey Lori," Bob says, embarrassed at the idea that she may have heard them talking about her.

"Rain-Rain!" Pete says with overstated exuberance.

"Only Bobby can call me that, Pete."

"Bobby?" Pete teases. "*Bobby?* Awww. Wittle Bobby Wilkinson has a girlfwend!"

Bob blows a raspberry and flips dual birds at Pete. Lori laughs. "How are you boys doing?" she asks.

Bob answers for both of them. "I'm good, Pete's good, and he was just leaving."

"Yeah, I was just leaving. I gotta pinch a loaf anyway."

"*Ewww!*" Lori responds.

"Dude!" Bob adds.

Pete hops off the trampoline as Lori hops on. "Later, you crazy kids."

Bob makes a shooing motion. "Go!"

"Bye, Pete," Lori adds.

Pete heads in the direction of the house, but leaves them with a juvenile rhyme. "Bob and Lori sitting in a tree, F-U-C—"

"*Duuuuuude!*" Bob protests.

"I'm kidding, I'm kidding!" Pete teases, then continues on his way.

Bob, red-faced, shakes his head and turns to Lori. "He was doing so good."

"I see what you mean, how you described him the other night."

"I'll give him a free pass this time, all things considered."

Lori nods. "Mars sounds awful."

"Yeah. How are you doing with all that?"

"I'm okay. Had myself a good cry. Not sure if I was mad at Josh or just sad he's gone."

"It's a fair question. Like I said earlier, lemme know if you wanna talk."

Lori points to his Walkman. "What were you listening to?"

"Just a mix tape. Some songs I recorded on Z-95. Depeche Mode, Def Leppard, Run DMC, a good mix."

"That *is* a good mix."

"I have a bunch of mix tapes. All rap songs, all slow songs, all rock songs. And sometimes just stuff from the radio, like this one, whenever the deejay isn't talking over the intro."

"I hate that," Lori says. Then, after a pause: "Your stepmom's real nice. She did my laundry, which I didn't ask her to do."

Bob nods. "Gail's alright. We're not close, but we mostly get along. I was mad at my dad for a long time after he got remarried, and that complicated things. But what do I know? Maybe she helped him with his grief. He certainly didn't talk to *me* about it."

"It must be tough, losing somebody. I mean, I'm totally sad about Josh, but we didn't go out very long. No way it's the same as a husband or wife or anything like that."

"Yeah. That's why I don't think I'll ever get married. Too much sadness."

"Don't say that, Bobby. There's sadness, sure, but there's also, like, love and romance and growing old together."

"I guess. But look at that girl Susie Pete was telling us about. Just surrounded by tragedy."

"I don't wanna talk about Susie."

"You're right. I'm sorry."

"Hey, I've got an idea! Why don't we just go for a drive? No agenda this time, stay away from the city. Just . . . drive somewhere."

Bob nods. "We can do that. And actually, if you don't mind, I've got an errand I've been meaning to run while we're out. Lemme just run to the bathroom real quick."

"Of course. I'll grab my purse."

. . .

Moments later, Lori finds herself subconsciously fixing her hair as she waits in the shotgun seat of Bob's Trans Am. She makes a final, hurried adjustment once she hears Bob shutting the front door of *Casa de Wilkinson* behind him.

He gets in the car and starts the engine. "Pete's playing *Galaga*. He beat it once last fall and is determined to beat it again. Game's brutal, though."

Lori smiles and fastens her seatbelt. "Skee-Ball's more my thing."

Bob looks down for a minute, glad she neglected to mention the time, not so long ago, when Pete objectified her at Vinnie's Arcade Alley, in front of the Skee-Ball lanes of all places. He places his right hand on her chin, gently but unexpectedly, and turns her head so she faces him. "Lori—Rain-Rain—you look very pretty without makeup."

Lori opens her mouth as if to say something, an abashed *"Thank you,"* perhaps, but stays mute. The tiniest smile purses her lips. Bob shifts into Reverse and floors it. The car peels away, leaving tire tracks on the driveway that, he suspects, won't bother Gail the way they would've in the past.

8

Bob scans his presets during a commercial break and settles on a radio station playing "In the Air Tonight" by Phil Collins. He stops at a red light just in time for the song's epic drum riff; he and Lori play air drums and exchange giggles. The day is an emotional roller coaster, and Lori, who was bawling her eyes out just one hour earlier, is remarkably so at ease in Bob's company she fails to register this as the same song that played when Josh copped one feel too many at Lover's Leap not so long ago.

A honk from the car idling behind them—the first one they've seen since setting out—startles them back to reality. Bob extends his left hand out the window, gives a courtesy wave to the other driver, and continues through the intersection.

"Hey, turn right up ahead," Lori says. "Next street."

"Here?"

"Yeah."

Bob signals and turns onto a leafy North Shore residential street. "Where we going?"

"Fourth house on the right."

Bob turns into the driveway of a grey brick home—a sprawling, single-story ranch with considerable curb appeal. "Who lives here?"

Lori swallows before answering. "Josh . . . Or his folks, anyway."

"Ah. They didn't leave town?" Lori shakes her head, and Bob continues. "Of course they didn't, duh! You spoke with them Sunday about the boat. You gonna tell 'em what happened to Josh?"

"They deserve to hear it from someone who knew him, don't you think?"

"I-I guess. Need me to come with?"

"No, just wait here. I may need a hug after."

"O-of course."

"Thank you, Bobby." She gets out of the car, closes the door, and proceeds to the front door.

She's as white as a ghost.

## 9

Bob would no doubt be surprised how little time has elapsed before Lori returns to the car. He is examining his teeth in the rearview mirror and is startled out of thought when she opens the door.

"Sorry," Lori says.

"That was fast."

Lori looks down, ashamed. "I couldn't do it. I couldn't tell her."

"Just his mom?"

Lori nods. "She said his dad's at the tavern, and he's been there a lot since . . . you know."

"Is he not working?"

"No Bobby, nothing like that. He's just a big drinker."

"What does he do?"

"He works in construction. Foreman, I think. Mom's a realtor. I wasn't sure she'd even be home."

"Probably not a lot of people buying houses this week."

"Probably not."

"So what'd you end up telling her?"

"I just told her the boat ran out of gas and let her know where we tied down."

"What'd you say the other day when you asked to borrow it in the first place?"

"I said some of us wanted to go on the water for a moonlight vigil. She asked if it was safe and I said we'd take every precaution. She said she trusted me and said I could borrow it any time I wanted."

With that, Bob starts the car and backs out of the driveway. "I'm sorry you weren't able to tell her. You got your color back, though."

Lori nods and plays with the presets. Hearing nothing but commercials, she turns off the radio.

Bob breaks the uncomfortable silence after an interminable length of time. "Where to? Wanna head by your house and see how bad those van guys trashed the place?"

"No way."

"What about your other friends, uh, Shauna and Brandon? Should we see if their parents are home?"

"I'm not up for that. Just drive."

"O-kay."

This time, it's Lori who breaks the heavy silence after another awkward lull. "Why'd you ask that about Josh's dad?"

"Why'd I ask what?"

"Why'd you ask if Mr. Brewer was out of work?"

"Uh, no reason. You said he was at the tavern. It's daytime on a work day. It sounds like he goes there a lot, so I just figured . . ."

"You figured he was an out-of-work drunk. You hate Josh and you hate his dad."

"Wait . . . I . . . um . . . what?! What're you talking about?" He pulls to the curb.

"That was a shitty assumption to make."

"What assumption? I-I-I don't know Josh's parents. I don't really even know Josh. A-and until a few days ago, I didn't know you, either. I mean, I knew who Josh was and I *definitely* knew who you were, not gonna lie about that, but . . . what business is it of mine what Josh's parents do for a living? I asked, but it was just small talk. W-where is this coming from?"

The argument reaches fever pitch. Their next words are barbed. Lori goes first. "Yes, Bobby, Josh's dad drinks. He drinks *a lot.* He works in construction, makes good money from what I understand but it's still construction. He works in construction, he's obsessed with football, and he drinks a lot. And maybe he's been too tough on his son. Who is a good guy.

*Was* a good guy. Fuck. The complete opposite of you, but a good guy."

"I know, I heard Pete's story! I wasn't Josh's biggest fan—a-a-and neither was Pete for that matter—b-but I don't hate the guy. He died a hero, Lori! I-I'm sorry for your loss and yeah, maybe I have a crush on you myself, but I'm not trying to steal his girl or tramp on his grave or anything like that. I swear!" Bob's hand trembles anew. He breathes slow and deep as he dials back his emotions.

Calmer now: "Lori. I didn't mean anything by what I said. Not consciously, anyway. And if what Pete said is true, maybe when all this is over, they'll build a monument for Josh and Vinnie and all the others. If they do, I'll be sitting at the dedication with my usual anxiety, watching you cry for him and yearning for you from afar."

Lori watches as the tremors in Bob's hand slowly subside. She takes his hand in hers. "I'm sorry I blew up at you. I'm mad at myself. I couldn't tell Josh's mom the truth, and I took it out on you."

"I'm sorry too. And, um, this next part is kind of embarrassing, but let's head to Highland Park. I need something to take the edge off."

Lori looks at him funny. *Drugs?* she thinks. *No, that can't be.* She offers a nervous smile. Not her best effort, but it'll do.

Bob removes his hand from hers, places it on the wheel, and resumes driving.

10

"Oh cool, he's here."

Bob steers his car into an angled parking space on a deserted street in downtown Highland Park, He parks two slots down from a luxury sedan—Dr. Kirchner's Lincoln Town Car.

Aside from Bob's Trans Am and the doctor's Lincoln, the row of spaces is empty.

"Who's 'he?' " Lori asks.

"Doctor Kirchner."

"Oh. Is this the errand you mentioned earlier?"

"Yeah. I just need a refill."

"Refill?"

"This is embarrassing, but, um, I take meds for anxiety. Forgot to get a refill last time I was here."

"Oh."

"Do me a favor and don't tell anyone at school, okay?"

"It's fine, don't worry. Do you want me to wait in the car?"

"I shouldn't be long, but you can come in if you want. It'd totally blow Dr. Kirchner's mind to see us together. I don't know if he'd be happy for you, but he'd *definitely* be happy for me."

"No, I wouldn't feel comfortable prying on a therapy session. I'll wait in the car."

"It's not a session, just a quick visit. But, uh, suit yourself."

Bob exits the car and crosses the sidewalk to a suite of downtown offices. A sign listing the tenants, including GERALD J. KIRCHNER, PsyD * SUITE 201, is mounted to the right of the exterior doors. Bob enters a small building so quiet you can almost hear the mice living in the walls. He bounds the carpeted stairs, two at a time, to a pair of doors on the second floor. He tries the door to Suite 201. Unlocked. He enters a cream-colored waiting room with a receptionist desk in an alcove to the left of a frosted glass window. Four chairs are placed around the room, and a coffee table displays a spread of '80s magazines. A print from Monet's *"Nymphéas"* series hangs on one wall, and a Cézanne still life faces it from across the room. A children's play area is set up in the far corner, with an enormous teddy bear sitting atop a wooden toybox. A floor lamp is dimly lit and a half-full coffee pot rests on an illuminated burner near the reception station, suggesting someone brewed coffee earlier in the day but forgot about it. Was his therapist abducted? Has the Blockade and Occupation crossed into the North Shore? "Hello?" Bob asks the empty room. No answer.

He tries the internal door leading to Dr. Kirchner's office, a guest office, and a padded, windowless restraining room the doctor has only had to use twice. Silence. "Hello?" he asks again. He reluctantly enters and notices the doctor's door half-ajar. "Doctor Kirchner?" He raps on the door, which swings open another 30 degrees to reveal a hand, palm up, laying on the desk. "Jesus, Dr. Kirchner!" He barges into the office.

Bob's psychiatrist of the last four years, so helpful in adjusting his medication and getting him thinking with a clear head, sits in his chair, head tilted back and to the right, mouth open, dead from a self-inflicted gunshot wound. A maroon splatter of blood adorns the wall behind him, including his framed doctoral degree. The gun lies in his lap, half-in and half-out of the hand that gave the trigger a fatal squeeze. An answering machine sits on the credenza behind Dr. Kirchner's body, mes-sage light flashing. Stacy's picture has been returned to the credenza as well but is on its side, face down, as if the good doctor couldn't bear to look at it anymore.

Bob collapses against the wall. His anxiety reaches DEF-CON 1. He is too unnerved to form words. He staggers to the desk and opens the drawers, searching for prescription drugs. No luck. He checks the credenza. Nothing. He accidentally backs into Dr. Kirchner's body, and the doctor's head slumps forward. "Oh, God!" Bob shrieks. He backs out of the room, light-headed, and lurches, *Frankenstein* monster-like, to the waiting area and receptionist cubby. His hands trembling, he fumbles with a medicine cabinet behind the receptionist's desk. Locked. "Oh, c'mon!" Bob searches in vain for keys, then returns to the doctor's office. Mortified, he reaches into the doctor's pants pocket and removes a thick ring of keys. He returns to the cubby and tries each key, dropping the ring more than once. Finally, what seems like the last key unlocks the cabinet, half-stocked with pill bottles. Most of them are lorazepam. With one hand, he scoops everything into a sort of pocket he makes with his other arm, then stumbles out of the room, into the hall, and down the stairs, where he drops half of the contents. He trips on his way down and must grab the rail with both hands to stop from falling. He finally reaches the bottom, stuffs his pockets with as many pill bottles as he can, and stumbles out the door.

Lori sees his panicked state and stuffed pockets. She gets out of the car to help. "Bobby, what is it?"

"Dead," Bob mumbles, delirious.

"What? Did you say 'dead?' "

Bob nods and sets a hand on the hood of his car to keep from falling over. "H-h-h-he's dead."

"Doctor Kirchner?"

"Yes. God . . . oh, God!" He falls to the same knee that was scuffed after Pete was taken and yowls in pain.

Lori rushes to his side and kneels to comfort him. "Take it easy, it's okay. It's . . . it'll be okay."

"I-I-I . . . I can't do this," Bob says between through panicked breaths. He struggles to his feet and removes a pill bottle from his pants pocket. He tears the lid off the bottle, struggles with the cotton stuffed inside, and pours several pills into his other shaky hand. Most of them fall to the ground, and he dry swallows the five or six that managed not to fall.

"Bob . . . Bobby . . . take it easy with that stuff." Bob covers his mouth with a clenched fist. His whole arm shakes. He opens the driver's door and tosses the remaining bottles in the back with his other arm.

"I just . . . I-I . . . just . . . what the hell is happening?" Bob is barely coherent. The full spectrum of grief is on display in all its ugly ecstasy.

Lori attempts to comfort him. She places one hand on his shoulder and the other on his arm. "Here, it's okay. C'mon." Bob thinks she wants him to get in the driver's seat, but she redirects him around to the other side. "No no, I'm driving today."

"N-nobody drives my car but me," Bob insists.

Lori helps him into the front passenger seat. "I'm not nobody. I'm Rain-Rain, remember?"

"Yes." He nods, his head moving like a fishing bobber. The meds are already kicking in, courtesy of the high dosage. Softly: "L-l-l-love me some R-Rain-Rain."

"I'm glad." She returns to the driver's side and starts the engine.

"W-where are we going?"

"I know a place." Lori grabs his left hand in her right, as he did earlier, and backs out of the parking space.

"O-kay."

11

Lori pulls into Lover's Leap, where she and Josh had reached a relationship impasse the day before prom, not even seven days past but seemingly ages ago; she and Bob have done a lot of growing up since then. Fifteen minutes ago, however, Bob was barely holding on.

Lori parks haphazardly, straddling two spaces. The majestic, multi-trunk oak tree that provides shade is older than her parents, grandparents, and great-grandparents. She kills the engine and points out the panoramic view of Lake Michigan to their right, below the rocky bluff that gives this park its name. "Nice view, isn't it?"

The drive (not to mention the pills he ingested) has given Bob time to mellow. He cranes his neck to take in the view. "I can't believe I've never been here. It's so close." He opens his door and immediately notices her parking job. He can't help but comment, "Wow, you're a terrible driver."

"Shut up," she says, with a knowing smile.

After a moment: "This is sort of a 'couples only' place," she explains. "Josh and I, well . . . you know."

"It's none of my business."

"No, nothing like that. We came here for the view some-times, is all. He took me here for our first date . . . and I thought I'd take you here for ours." Lori takes his hand in hers. "Let's go for a walk."

He looks down at their entwined hands. If this is finally his moment, he doesn't want to blow it. "O-kay."

"Do you still have that blanket? It's nice out there on the rocks, but they can be cold."

"Uh, yeah, pop the trunk."

"Where's the, um, oh never mind, I see it." She pops the trunk and grabs the blanket. Twenty-four hours ago, the trunk was filled with JourneyTech. Now, its only contents are a funnel, lug wrench, flashlight, jack, and spare tire.

"Here, let me carry that," he offers.

"Always the gentleman." She hands over the blanket. They stroll, slowly, like a young couple in love, along a paved, wind-ing path, past benches that haven't been sat in, except perhaps by winos, since the Blockade and Occupation began. A small, grassy slope descends to a rocky outcropping, the Lover's Leap of horny teenager renown.

Bob unfolds the blanket. "Is this good?" Lori nods and he sets the blanket on the rocks. They sit, knees folded. There is a distance between them, both physical and spiritual, so Lori takes his hand again and squeezes it—she hopes he will take the hint. He does, and scoots closer. She rests her head on his shoulder. Bob looks down at Lori and strokes her wrist with his free hand. "So this is our first date, huh?" he asks.

"Our first *official* date, how 'bout that?"

"We'll pencil it in the history books. A teensy sliver of a footnote amidst this crazy Martian Occupation." Lucid words for someone who has far exceeded the recommended daily intake of lorazepam.

"Except the Martians look like us."

"Remember that old radio broadcast we listened to in Mrs. Edwards' class that one time? I think you were in that class. Uh, *War of the Worlds,* I think it was called?"

"Yeah, I remember!" Lori perks up.

"Well as it turns out, whoever came up with it wasn't too far off the mark, although the whole 'time traveling humans' thing would've thrown 'em for a loop, I guess."

"Totally!"

Silence again, but not for long. Even while medicated, Bob can't leave a quiet moment to its own devices. "Hey, I'm sorry I sort of freaked out back there."

"It's fine, Bobby, I swear."

"It's *not* fine. I was doing good, I was doing *sooo* good! D-Doctor Kirchner and I cut back my visits to just twice a month, but then he said he was going out of town and wouldn't answer his phone a-and I guess, w-with Vinnie dying a-a-and Pete being taken and all this craziness and—"

Bob speed-talks a mile a minute. Lori covers his mouth with her hand. "I'm hurting too, now would you stop talking?! You're almost as bad as Pete!"

Bob nods. "I guess I had that coming." His words are muffled as he speaks through her hand.

"Stop. Talking." She looks him in the eye. He finally takes the hint and shuts the fuck up. She kisses him, soft and brief. He retreats, caught off guard, then comes back to try again. He looks her in the eyes, tilts his head, and moves in for another kiss. Soft and brief . . . and tender. They part lips, then kiss again. A real one this time, lasting several seconds. And again.

Lori leans backward and they recline onto the blanket, their tongues exploring, cautious but curious.

Lori leads Bob into a standing position. Still kissing. She takes his hand and motions them toward a copse of trees, private and sheltered from the breeze. They take a few steps and the wind carries away the blanket almost instantly. Bob turns to chase after it, but Lori squeezes his hand. He lets the blanket go and follows her into the small grove. She kicks off her shoes and he follows suit with his. She unties the flannel from around her waist and he untucks his shirt. Time out for another kiss. She doffs her top and he removes his belt, and she, hers. Another kiss. She unhooks her bra and it falls to her elbows, exposing breasts Bob has dreamt of seeing since freshman year. She straightens her arms and the bra falls to the ground. Bob cups her breasts like a disbelieving schoolboy, then kisses them. He hits an erogenous zone and Lori shivers with unexpected delight. She gets on her knees, unbuttons his jeans, and lowers them. One leg at a time, she lifts his ankles to remove the pantlegs from around his feet, and Bob manages not to fall. Jeans tossed aside, she cups his penis, still inside his underwear but growing in size and searching for the escape hatch. Bob tenses up, folds his arms across his chest, and looks down. She looks up at him, gets back on her feet, and unzips her own jeans. She guides Bob's hands to the waistband of her jeans. He pulls them partway down while they tongue wrestle. Lori uses her big toe like a hook to pull her jeans down the rest of the way. She loses her balance and they fall to the ground, simultaneously wincing and giggling. He removes her jeans, bunched up around her ankles, the rest of the way, and turns her on her back. He puts a finger to his lips in a "hush" motion, then kisses her lips, her neck, her breasts, her stomach, her thighs, her calves, and back up to her stomach. He lowers her panties to reveal something wonderful. He gently removes them, and has to lift one of her legs above his own head acrobatically to do so. He pulls down his own underwear, with less regard for passion in this instance. He kisses her thighs again, then her labia, then her stomach. He looks up at her and mouths the words, *"Is this okay?"* She nods, innocent and sexy at the same time. He reaches for his wallet in the back pocket of his discarded jeans and removes a condom that has been stowed away for months. The wrapper gets the better of him until Lori grabs it from him and tosses it aside—she trusts him. Propped up with one hand, he grits his teeth, concentrates, and enters her. She cries out and he feels her entire body shiver, but the pain only lasts a moment. He thrusts, slowly, and she matches his rhythm.

Most people want their first time to be special and often tell themselves it was, when in fact it was little more than an awkward, fumbling affair, much ado about nothing and over way too quickly. Most people, however, don't know the love Bob and Lori know in this moment . . . and most of them never will.

As for Bob and Lori themselves, while they don't realize it yet, they will only ever make love this once. That being said, it is all they ever hoped it would be and more. Worth dying for, even? We shall see.

# Chapter 13

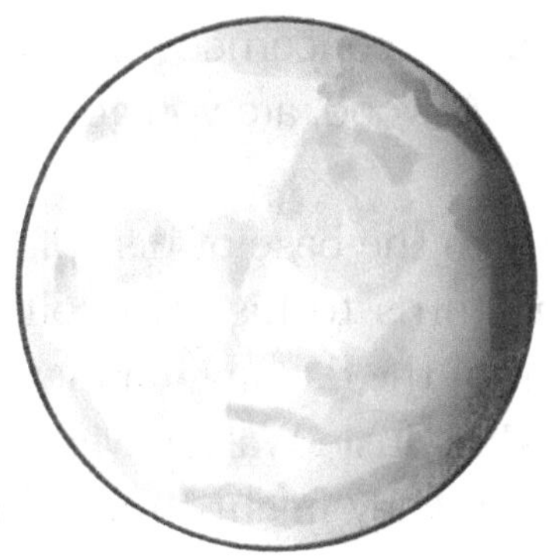

1

The attempt on Old Man McCarthy's life comes out of nowhere. He shoos Susie, Leonard, and René away when they instinctively crowd him as a man and woman approach on the Century Bridge following his victory speech; Dana and Marquez have already left for the hospital to look in on Savannah.

It turns out that the man and woman are McCarthy's brother and sister-in-law, longtime Zone Alpha residents who kept low profiles once it came to light that the Old Man was leading a resistance movement. Their estrangement was his idea, lest they become pawns in Ross's game of dirty politics.

"Atwood, you haven't lost your touch," his brother says. "You still have a way with words."

"My hope is they don't fall upon deaf ears," McCarthy replies. "How've you been, Braxton? Delia?"

Braxton and Delia McCarthy offer polite nods. "How long's it been since we last saw Atwood, Brax?" Delia asks. "A thousand days?"

"A beater's age for sure," Braxton answers.

"Too long," McCarthy adds. "Thank you both for coming."

Delia notices an antsy, concerned Susie chomping at the bit. Old habits die hard. "Atwood, are you going to introduce us to your friends?"

Putting one hand to the base of his spine, those old bones brittle with age, he turns to his FCB colleagues. "I'm afraid with the excitement of the day my manners have escaped me. I'd like to present Miss Susie Walker, Miss René de Rooij, and Mr. Leonard Debussy. They might think of themselves as my lieutenants, or my protectors perhaps, but I'll simply call them my friends."

Handshakes all around. Delia hesitates only once, when she has to switch to her less-dominant hand in order to shake Susie's only remaining paw. Delia is about to ask her brother-in-law if he has a place to stay, post-rebellion, when a pair of plasma pistol blasts disrupt the idyll. They miss the Old Man by mere centimeters and char the bridge's deck.

"Everyone get down!" Susie cries out. She instinctively throws her right arm around the Old Man and forces him to the deck. His back doth protest.

The remaining people on the bridge, who have already begun to amble to their homes on either bank of the Red River, scatter. A third shot is fired. René shrieks in pain and puts one hand to her ear. The lobe, which was seared by the blast, drips blood.

"What's going on?!" Delia asks.

"Len, I think René's been hit!" Susie cries out.

René waves with her free hand to indicate the wound isn't mortal. "She's okay," Leonard tells Susie. "Who's that over there?"

Susie cranes her neck and sees someone in a thick coat, hands in his pockets, speed-walking as he brings up the rear of the fleeing crowd. She shrugs and proceeds to get up, but Leonard motions for her to stay put.

"I'm on it," he says. "Stay with the Old Man."

He unzips his vest and draws a plasma pistol from a shoulder holster. "Excuse me, sir," he calls out to the mysterious straggler, "can I have a word?"

The man ignores him and quickens his pace. "Sir?" Leonard says again. The man bursts into a run, and Leonard aims his weapon. "Hold it right there!" he yells. The man stops dead in his tracks. "Hands up!" He raises one hand but pats his jacket with the other, as if searching for something.

*"DON'T DO THAT! PUT YOUR OTHER HAND UP!"*

The man complies, and as Leonard jogs to catch up, he sees the man's shoulders visibly sag. "Keep your hands up," Leonard says. He pats him down and collects the plasma pistol the man's stowed in an inside pocket. Its muzzle is still warm to the touch. "On your knees!" The man drops to his knees, lowers his head, and looks like he is about to cry. Leonard faces him. "Look at me." The man lifts his head and reveals his pathetic visage.

Leonard can't believe his eyes. "Jesus! Steve!"

2

During discussions of a rescue mission/raid on the CCC, Leonard and the other FCB lieutenants had all but forgotten about Steve Myerson, a displaced Chicagoan who was among those liberated during the canal extension jobsite raid that saw Josh and Hawkins stepping up as if was second nature. It was none other than Josh, Leonard, and Susie—of course—who calmed down Steve and fellow abductee Jacob Tremont during a commissary scuffle later that day, a silly tiff brought about when one of them (no one remembers which) commented that they'll likely never see loved ones back home again, triggering the baser emotions of the other.

"If you wanted to go home so bad, why didn't you join us when we raided the CCC?" Leonard asks Steve as he, Susie, and the Old Man interrogate him inside the director's office of the Ronald Reagan Audience Hall, the nearest building to the Century Bridge and a warm alternative to the windswept span. Keith, meanwhile, has taken up Delia, a nurse, on her offer to change his bandage in the hall's poorly-stocked first aid room. René, who thinks she might make a good caregiver herself now that the Freedom Contingent Brigade has disbanded, tags along to lend a hand and find disinfectant for her singed earlobe.

"I figured you were fools for trying," Steve explains. "I saw how many of you left that day on your mission, or whatever you call it, but only like five of you returned. To be honest, I didn't think the number would even be *that* high, and I knew if I volunteered, I'd be one of the ones who didn't make it back. But that's not why I did what I did today."

He swallows, then continues. "When you decided—well, I guess it wasn't *you* so much as it was that Josh guy—to destroy the time machine thingy, with it you destroyed the last shred of hope we had for getting home."

"I don't remember hearing your dissent when the decision was made," Leonard points out. "We presented our case to everyone in the barracks that day. It certainly wasn't an easy choice to make. And like you, I figured destroying the time chamber would be the last thing I'd ever do, if I even made it that far. But you know the old saying: It's better to die on your feet than live on your knees."

"Yeah, but . . . but . . ." Steve realizes that since he didn't volunteer to join the raid/rescue, which would have offered him a chance to go home before the chamber was destroyed, he isn't going to win this argument. His shoulders slump. ". . . I suppose you'll be having me killed, then?"

McCarthy fields this question. "That's not our way, young man, unless you leave us no other choice."

. . .

"What happened today won't be an isolated incident."

Leonard lays out the state of the state from inside the director's office. Susie, René, Keith, and the Old Man are also in attendance; Braxton and Delia have returned home to prepare a spare mattress for Braxton's brother. The mattress once belonged to their son, Tom, who broke his parents' hearts when he enlisted in Ross's Loyalist Army, and again when he perished in a training exercise gone awry. "You're gonna need a full time security detail."

"Thank you, Leonard," the Old Man says. "I suppose you're right. It's like I said in my speech: These next days will be uneasy ones."

"What do we do with Steve?" Susie asks. The subject in question is locked in the building's cloakroom, his wrists bound by an abandoned scarf.

"What do the bylaws say about anyone who attempts to assassinate a political leader?" Leonard asks.

"Execution by hanging," McCarthy answers, "but that doesn't apply here. Technically, Ross is still chancellor. To the public, he's been deposed, but we haven't had the changeover yet."

"He tried to kill you, sir," Keith, normally the quiet one, points out. With his Mississippi accent, *tried* comes out as *"trod."*

"Miss de Rooij, what do *you* think?" McCarthy asks. "He tried to kill you, too."

René caresses her bandaged earlobe, then shakes her head. "Pretty sure he was just shooting in our general direction. I don't think he was in his right mind."

"So . . . clemency, then?"

"From execution, sir? Yes."

"Very well then. Let's incarcerate him. We can still send a clear message. Who wants to make sure it goes out to the general public?"

"I can do it, sir," Susie says. She gives her phantom limb a good scratch.

"I knew you were going to say that, Miss Walker."

• • •

Ultimately, they decide to incarcerate Steve in a neighborhood lock-up at the municipal checkpoint closest to his address, which for the displaced such as himself, happens to be the District 12 FCB barracks. This keeps him as far as possible from the influential words of the CCC brig's charismatic, VIP inmate, ex-Chancellor Ross. Steve is the checkpoint's only prisoner, and the isolation offers endless hours for him to reflect upon his actions.

None of them are surprised when they learn, two days later, that Steve killed himself, although his method leaves them speechless. With no overhead bars in the cell for him to toss his blanket over and fashion a noose, he instead hurls himself repeatedly into the translucent laser force field that constitutes the cell's door. The startled checkpoint guard is still fumbling with his magna-card when Steve's heart gives way.

No loss there.

## 3

The deposed Dorian Ross practices T'ai chi in the same brig Susie and Old Man McCarthy found themselves incarcerated in. Ross has a cell all to himself, the largest in the facility. He is not the brig's only prisoner; a dozen unrepentant Loyalist soldiers are incarcerated as well, two per cell. A sizable crack—a side effect of the time chamber's destruction—runs across the ceiling.

Leonard is part of a rotating watch. He arrives with a tray of food, ready to relieve Marquez. "I'm guessing your debriefing went okay if they're letting you stand watch?" he asks her.

"It went well," Marquez says as she gets up from her chair, the same one Corporal Brown was dozing in when Susie slashed his throat. "Dana told me to say I had a lot to atone for. Also, I told 'em that except for my colleagues in the chamber and Lymott, who you met, and maybe Foreman Jenkins, I didn't have many friends at work. They're all dead now anyway, so maybe the Old Man took pity on me?"

"Maybe. Watch my six until I'm clear of the prisoner's cell."

"Okay. They've been pretty animated this morning."

Leonard carries the tray of food to Ross as Marquez stands watch. Sure enough, the inmates make their presence known.

"Hey, let us outta here," a prisoner complains.

"Yeah, c'mon, man!" another prisoner pleads.

"I want some of that," a third prisoner says.

These taunts don't phase Leonard. The electrified hum of the force field over the cell doors is harder to ignore, however, and turns his blood cold.

He stops outside Ross's cell. "Back against the wall." Ross steps back as ordered, but continues his mind and body exercises. Leonard enters the cell via magna-card and balances the tray on the edge of the washbasin. "Is that yoga?"

"T'ai chi, Mr. Debussy. It's good for the soul."

"Your soul can use some good."

"Hey man, don't talk to him like that!" a fourth prisoner barks.

Ross concludes his T'ai chi and waves dismissively at the taunting prisoner. Leonard backs out and locks the inner and outer doors behind him. Ross examines his meal. Mutant chicken, of course, bread, water, and greens—a rare treat. The only utensil is a spork, lest the ex-chancellor try to stab himself or slash his wrists. "I must confess, this looks good," he says.

"I'm afraid we don't have any tea," Leonard replies. "I'm told you're an enthusiast for the stuff, but we don't have your connections."

"I appreciate the thought, as I appreciate you treating me with humanity."

"We're not animals, sir. Even though you brainwashed them into believing we are." He points to the other jailbirds.

"A means to end, I'm afraid. Alas, the wrong side won. But for whatever it's worth, I hope your people know what they're doing."

"I hope so, too."

Leonard passes the others on his way out. He continues to ignore their taunts, which are along the lines of, "You won't get away with this," "Let us out of here," and that *bon mot* of Shakespearean finesse, "Come back here, asshole!"

He doesn't see Ross again until the trial.

<h2 style="text-align:center">4</h2>

The most recent FCB barracks is deserted. The group's newest members have returned to their dormitory lodgings for the short term—not great but at least airier. Its more tenured members, Leonard and René among them, have begun bunking with friends they trust on the surface.

Not *quite* deserted, as it turns out. Susie attempts T'ai chi in the commissary but is unable to make heads or tails of it—the pain from her phantom limb is still too much of a distraction. She parks herself at a dusty table and reflects once more on all she's gained and lost. She's come here a lot since the Old Man's victory speech; not only is this the most recent of several barracks over the past 24 months, but it also symbolizes the only type of home she has ever really known—one that's had her forever looking over her shoulder, with friends who would always have her back. People like Diego, Jasmine, Dixon, Samara, Dr. Spellman, Verónica, Sebastian, Spiros, her parents.

And Josh.

She sees a shadow flit across the wall and whirls around defensively, out of habit. She reaches for a weapon, but of course, there are none to be found. They have all been housed in a depot to which only the Old Man has access.

"Hi. Sorry to startle you." It's Dana.

"Good to see you. How's your daughter?"

"She's good. Sleeping a lot but gaining weight, and *sooo, sooo* beautiful."

"That's wonderful news. What are you doing here?"

"Not sure. I guess I needed a change of scenery from the nursery waiting room."

"Have you signed up for housing yet? I know we set aside a space here for you and your daughter, but I see the cot hasn't been slept in."

"Not yet. I'll probably do that tomorrow."

"Have you fully acclimatized?"

"I still get headaches once in a while, but not like before."

"Good."

"Yeah. Anyway, I just wanted to thank you."

"Whatever for?"

"Well, you gave us shelter when we needed it. Pete and I, that is."

"You two weren't together, were you?"

"No no no."

"Okay. Only asking because he looked awfully young. Of course, so was Josh."

"Can you believe they knew each other? From back home, I mean?"

"There's a saying I never understood, mostly because I think it didn't come from here. It goes, 'It's a small world.' "

"It really is."

"I think I know what it means now." Susie avoids eye contact as she says this. She slips back into her thoughts.

"Did you love him?" Dana asks after a few beats.

"Who?"

"Josh. Did you love him?"

Susie ponders this for a few beats. "I *could've* loved him," she answers. Dana nods, and it's Susie's turn for a question. "What about you? Were you in love with the father? Apologies if I'm prying or if it's a strange question."

"Not a strange question. And no, I wasn't in love with him."

"Will you miss him?"

"I'll miss some people, but not him. I'll miss Pete. Like I said, we weren't together, but . . . he was quite brave."

"So was Josh."

The women experience a few seconds of quiet bonding. The calm is cut short by another shadow on the wall. Susie turns, ready for anything, and sees Rose, limping but alive. "Rose!" Susie knocks over a chair in her haste to greet her FCB colleague.

"*Hola, mujer.*" Rose limps in Susie's direction, but Susie runs over and saves her the effort. They hug, gingerly. Rose's bruises are fading but her body still hurts.

"I thought you were . . ."

"Dead? No, *chinga,* no. I'm immortal. Looks like you are, too."

"Not immortal. Just lucky. More or less." She points to what remains of her left arm. "Where've you been?"

"Hiding in the tunnels. I thought we lost, so I was laying low. There's a chicken restaurant a few klicks from here that always throws away good scraps, so I came out this morning to see what I could scavenge when I heard the Old Man's announcement."

"It's what we've been fighting for. And it's what Dixon would've wanted."

Rose winces at the sound of name, and Susie apologizes.

"It's okay. And you're right. Did you know he hated Chicago?"

"I didn't."

"For me, Chicago was home. This place . . . *no mucho mejor.* Like the *barrio.* But him, he thought this world was a step up. Can you imagine?"

"I wouldn't know, but if he isn't the only one to feel that way, maybe resettlement will be easy."

"Maybe." To Dana: "How's your kid?"

"She's wonderful."

"*Bueno.* C'mon, it's a beautiful day. I'm hungry and I'm sure someone, somewhere, is serving beater."

"Beater?! The creature?!"

"*Sí.* I know you can't imagine something so ugly tasting so good. But it is. *Delicioso.*" She smacks her lips and turns to leave. Dana follows and Susie brings up the rear. She lingers for a minute, savoring the musty barracks smell that has come to symbolize home. To Susie, every underground hovel smells the same.

She sighs, turns out the lights via voice command, and follows Rose and Dana to the surface. They emerge to a bright afternoon, the sun high in the sky and the day surprisingly warm.

Susie, who sat in the barracks for so long she lost track of time, doesn't expect to find a newly paved road in front of her. A young woman wheels a crate of gourds, freshly harvested from the grove Susie's crew discovered, in the direction of the crewmen paving the road. She offers a gourd to Susie, Dana, and Rose, and the women oblige. Each juicy bite sends pulp dribbling down their chins, and the moment is glorious. For the first time in years—decades, even—everyone feels free.

# Chapter 14

1

It's nightfall by the time Bob and Lori make it back to *Casa de Wilkinson*. The foyer and parlor are dark when they enter, but a light shines from the back of the house. *"Robbie, is that you?"* Gail asks from the kitchen.

"Yeah, I'm back. Lori's still with me, if that's okay."

*"Fine, dear."*

"How's your nose?"

*"Still sore, but better than yesterday. Thanks for asking."*

"Of course."

*"A letter came for you."*

"Oh yeah?"

*"I'm not sure who it's from. I noticed it wasn't postmarked. Whoever sent it must've dropped it off directly. You know I'd never open it."*

"Huh."

*"It's in here on the table. There're some casserole leftovers, too. I just put 'em in the fridge."*

Bob enters the kitchen to find Gail loading the dishwasher. "Oh, there you are," she says.

"Hi mom," he replies. "What kind of casserole?"

"Baked ziti."

"Yum."

"Where'd you two go? You were gone for a good bit."

"Nowhere special, just out for a drive. Went for a walk along the lake."

"Sounds delightful."

Lori enters. "Mrs. Wilkinson, can I help you clean up?"

"No dear, I'm just finishing up." Gail starts the dishwater and dries her hands on a dishtowel. She studies Lori's face, then Bob's, then Lori's again. "My. You two are glowing."

Bob turns red. "We had a nice day. Well . . . it didn't start out that way."

"I know it didn't. Better now?"

"Yeah, now that I got a refill." He removes a pill bottle from his pants pocket and shakes it for effect. "Ran out earlier and had an episode. It was bad. You know I hate when that happens in public."

"Now now, Robbie, it's nothing to be embarrassed about. We talked about this yesterday, remember? You are not the only one. Besides, I'm glad you're still following Dr. Kirchner's prescription."

"Not every day," Bob confesses.

"As needed, then?"

Bob shrugs. "Something like that. Where's dad?"

"Late meeting with Mayor Washington. He's been gone since 5:30."

"How did he get into the city? Did he know which route to take?"

"He drove to the Northwestern campus and a helicopter picked him up."

"Oh, okay." And as an afterthought: "VIP."

"He called an hour ago. Said not to worry, and that the flight was better than our last one, which I suppose was meant to be funny, although I didn't laugh."

Bob thinks about it for a few seconds. "It's *kind of* funny," he decides. "Pete upstairs?"

"He went back to his place to get a change of clothes. The state troopers escorted him—he's going to drop off his bike and ride back with them. I guess the handlebars are bent."

"Cool. And yeah, their car wasn't parked out front, now that I think about it."

Gail changes the subject. "Well, I'll get out of your hair. Lori, will you be spending the night again? We're glad to have you."

"That would be lovely, Mrs. Wilkinson."

"Terrific. I'll leave you two alone. I already set some ziti aside in a Tupperware dish for Robert, Sr. Except for that, have all you want, son. Make sure you have a good-sized portion. You're too skinny!"

"Thanks, mom." Though embarrassed, Bob has grown used to the comment. And his stepmom, when she's around, is a good cook. He turns to Lori after Gail leaves the room. "Do you think she knows?"

"She knows."

"Oh, God!"

Lori smiles, and puts her hands on his shoulders. "Who's your letter from?"

Bob picks up the letter, which sits alone next to a thick pile of mail—bills and department store flyers. It seems commerce continues even during a blockade and occupation. There's no return address, but ROBERT WILKINSON, JR. is written on the envelope in what can only be a doctor's scrawl. He tears open the envelope and his eyes go first, to the letterhead at the top and second, to the signature at the bottom. "It's from Dr. Kirchner." He can hardly believe his eyes.

Lori takes the hint. "I'll give you some space."

He quickly scans the letter, practically devouring it, then reads it again, slower this time:

*"May 22, 1987*

*Dear Bob,*

*It is with a heavy heart that I announce my retirement, not from the profession of child and adolescent psychiatry, but from this world. Upon receiving news that my daughter Stacy has perished, a casualty of the events in the city, I learned my heart cannot take such sorrow. A famous saying goes, 'If life gives you lemons, you should make lemonade,' but as you yourself know better than most, life is cruel and lemons are sour.*

*I believe in the process of therapy; you may recall from our first meeting four years ago my stating that I, too, saw a therapist, and did so until he retired in 1983 . . . not long after I first started treating you, as it happens. There is comfort in the ritual, just as there is something to be said for having a non-friend and non-family member to reach out to for help and support. Of course, it can be argued that doctor-patient relationships often evolve into ones of friendship as well, and there is truth in the thought that doctors eventually begin to think of their long-time patients as family.*

*You are stronger than your anxieties make you believe, and you are capable of great things. I have seen you make peace with your father for remarrying so quickly, and I can hear it in your voice that you and your stepmother are finally in a relationship space such that the words 'friends' and 'family' can apply there, as well. It took several years, sure, but know that for many others who have found themselves in your situation, several lifetimes might not be sufficient time to make such amends. I imagine some of my more cynical colleagues may have shirked at my decision last autumn to cut back our sessions to just twice per month. Sure, it means a reduction in billing, but then, believe it or not, I was never in this for the money.*

*I have phoned in your refill to Walgreens as you requested, though I encourage you to continue self-medicating only as needed. I trust you'll show good judgment in that regard. I hesitate to name a replacement doctor so close to the end of your last year of high school. This is assuming, of course, that whatever craziness has plagued Chicagoland and taken my daughter from me passes, and that you are able to actually finish your senior year. In the meantime, savor these days away from school, and the summer afterwards, and do something that makes you proud. Not your father, not your stepmother, and not your friends. Do something for you. And do it big.*

*This is not the only letter I am writing, as you are not my only patient. But it is the hardest letter for me to write, because you have been my patient the longest. I take it as a final, personal victory when I say you will be okay. Not every moment and not even every day, but most moments, and most days. In life, that may just have to be good enough.*

*As for me, my own heart has a hole in it that I fear I cannot mend. Maybe, with my daughter gone, it is less that I cannot mend it than it is that I choose not to mend it. There is beauty in this world, as there was in my daughter's smile. I choose to follow her into the next world, and to grab onto that beauty while I still can.*

*Take care of yourself, Bob, and do not think I abandoned you. If you think it now, do not think it for long, for nothing can be further from the truth. I believe in you.*

*All the best,*
*Gerry Kirchner"*

Bob sets the letter down. "Jesus," he says, otherwise at a loss for words. He grabs a glass of water and takes the letter into the family room, where Lori waits at one end of an overstuffed loveseat.

"Everything okay?"

Bob shakes his head. His hand twitches and water spills from the glass. "I feel like a selfish fool." He hands her the letter, which she, too, reads twice to fully comprehend.

"How awful. Stacy was a sweet girl."

Bob sits beside Lori so they can reread the letter together. "He had her picture in his office. She had a real nice smile."

"I like what he says here," Lori says. " *'Do something for you . . .'* "

" *'. . . and do it big,'* yeah. I met you. Think that's what he's referring to?"

"No, don't be silly." And, as an afterthought: "Well . . . maybe."

Bob kisses her forehead. She rests her head on his shoulder and they enjoy a quiet moment, interrupted only by Bob's stomach rumbling.

"Uh oh, someone's hungry," Lori teases.

"Starving."

"Me too." Her stomach rumbles to match his, and they cannot help but laugh.

They make a beeline for the refrigerator and Gail's casserole dish.

2

Army barricades and razor wire fencing surround City Hall on all sides. Four U.S. Army soldiers are positioned on the roof, and additional soldiers guard each street-level entrance. The Pedway entrance, via a subterranean tunnel connecting City Hall with two "L" lines as well as the South Shore Metra Electric Line, is temporarily shuttered.

Movers and shakers inside the mayor's office in addition to Hizzoner include Robert, Sr., Deputy Mayor David Orr, Press Secretary Alton Miller, Captain Marshall Bennett, and Police Chief Leslie Barnes, that red-nosed political appointee left over from the previous administration. Two more soldiers stand guard just inside the door. A plate of cold cuts on a table has been picked over.

"So what exactly are you saying?" Mayor Washington asks. He helps himself to a rolled-up ham slice.

"I'm saying," Robert, Sr. explains, "those CGC swines have been separating families."

"Now wait a minute, Senator," Barnes interrupts. "CEO Wes Arendt is one of the most respected businessmen in the city. He's given to the Police Foundation twice a year for the past three years!"

"Yes. So you'd turn your head and look the other way, like you're doing right now."

"Now that's not fair!"

"He's done it on a national level as well. He gave money to Reagan and Mondale's campaigns both, and he donated to mine too, I'm ashamed to say."

"Your Honor," the deputy mayor points out, "political bribery or not, this is a lot to swallow."

"I can handle this, David," the mayor chastises his next-in-line, a man who, though he doesn't know it yet, will serve as acting mayor for a brief spell six months from now. Mayor Washington turns to Robert, Sr. "Senator, I appreciate your transparency. And I know you serve on the science committee. But just what proof do you have?"

Robert, Sr. opens his briefcase and removes one of the porta-pads previously stashed in his garage workbench. He depresses the power button on the bottom and places the pad on the floor, face-up. He grabs a piece of lunch meat and sets it on the tray, using a pen to push it through with care. "Stand back and watch closely." The outer ring of the mat begins to glow, and the two circles of dotted gold light rotate in opposite directions.

"What the hell?" the deputy mayor asks. The lunch meat is overtaken by green light and disappears. The others jump. Chief Barnes draws his gun and the soldiers warily take a half-step forward, each with one arm on their service weapons. The porta-pad powers down on its own.

"Still not convinced?" Robert, Sr. asks. He uses his pen to turn the pad upside down and push the power button a second time. Afraid to stick his hand within the circumference of the teleportation coil, he carefully flips it back, pad facing up. It powers up quicker this time, and he cautiously drops the pen onto the platform, where it lands, half-in and half-out of the halo. The half that's inside the halo disappears after seven seconds, and the half that's outside sprays ink every which way. The people watching instinctively jump back to avoid getting sprayed.

Robert, Sr. scans the silent faces surrounding him, making eye contact one by one. "Now I ask you, gentlemen, just what do you think that is?"

3

Phase Three is underway and it's another busy evening at CGC-Meigs. Balthazar naps in an empty cell, having working 12 hours straight. Miles shows 22-year-old Christopher Gilman, who arrived from the future as a Ross Army Loyalist but whose intellectual curiosity and pint-sized frame suggested he might be better suited for computer work, how to recalibrate the time chamber. Gilman watches as one of its stationary arrivals coils illuminates.

"Incoming, boss," he says. "Looks like two separate transmissions. I thought you said there was nothing scheduled until the drivers report in?"

"You're right, nothing's on the slate. This is local. Remember which color's local?"

"Uh, green?"

"Correct. Inbound packages from a different time can take up to 30 seconds to materialize on our end, though it's usually faster. Inanimate ones generally take less than ten. Outbounds take about seven seconds, regardless of their composition and destination."

"Thirty, ten, and seven . . . Got it. Uh, looks like the transmission's complete. Is that a piece of bologna? A-a-and a pen?"

"I'll be damned."

"Shouldn't we log this?"

Miles, who's seen these bizarre transmissions before, looks up at Lori's Lionel Richie tape before crafting his response. "Historically, I'd say no. But now . . . leave it to me. I'll be right back."

"Do what you have to do, boss."

"Keep alert." Miles heads over to the darkened holding area, where Wesley and Balthazar are currently the sole occupants. He stops in front of Wesley's cell. "Boss, we just got a package. Silly, inane stuff. We haven't tracked its origins yet, but it's not the first time, so I thought you'd like to know . . . Boss?"

No response. "Lights," Miles says aloud, and the room brightens. Then: "Oh, crap."

Wesley is dead. He lies in his cot, his expression one of agony. He died clutching his arm, which suggests his heart gave way—punishment for too many Journeys, local and interstellar, through the cosmos. Miles pulls the top sheet on the cot over Wesley's body. "So sorry, sir." He bows his head for a few seconds, pats his shirt pocket for his cigs, and locks the cell door behind him.

Balthazar stirs from his nearby cell when the lights come on, and becomes further awake at the sound of Wesley's cell door locking. "Wh-what's up?"

"Mr. Arendt's not feeling good. Go back to sleep, B. We'll need you in a couple hours when the drivers start radioing in."

" 'K, whatever." He falls back asleep within seconds.

Miles whispers his final goodbye to Wesley through the bars: "We'll see everything through for you."

"Everything okay, boss?" Gilman asks once Miles returns to his workstation. "How's Mr. Arendt?"

"He's resting." Miles watches as Gilman retrieves the lunch-meat and pen so delicately it's as if they're hot to the touch. "I'm grabbing a smoke. After you dispose of those items, Chris, I'll show you how to cable our counterparts for reinforcements."

"Is that necessary, do you think?"

"It's necessary."

The porta-pad in the mayor's office powers down a second time. One of the soldiers sidesteps the ink drying on the carpet as he cautiously approaches the pad. He pokes it with the barrel of his rifle. Nothing happens.

"That is the goddamned-est thing I've ever seen," Chief Barnes remarks.

"You're telling me," the mayor replies. Poor Mayor Washington has lost his appetite.

"We need the FBI. Hell, the CIA! I'll bet the Soviet Union's behind this." Barnes is foolish and rash, a dangerous combination.

"We need to do no such thing." Robert, Sr., puts Barnes in his place, then turns to Hizzoner. "Mr. Mayor, as you know, the city is, for all intents and purposes, quarantined. I'm sure a few brave souls have made it out via the side streets, but they're the exception. No one gets in or out unless they have a death wish. You all know what happened when Gail and I flew back from Washington. Right now, there are untold thousands of Chicagoans missing, and half my suburban constituents have split. You've done a bang-up job calming an anxious city; supermarket rationing has worked and generators have kept the freezers going where we haven't yet gotten the power turned back on. And even if the gennies fail, man can live on dry goods for a long time. Worst case scenario, we can do an airlift. Thankfully, we're not there yet."

"Who the hell put you in charge?" Barnes barks.

"Let's hear him out, Barnes," Hizzoner replies.

The senator continues. "At the risk of raining on your parade, however, people will start growing impatient. And when people grow impatient, other people lose elections."

"What are you proposing?" Hizzoner asks.

"Give us 24 hours for a plan of action and don't breathe a word of this to the press."

"Sir, you can't be serious," the press secretary objects. He turns to the mayor. "Your Honor, he can't be serious. The people have a right to know!"

"Take it easy, Alton," Hizzoner replies. "I get the senator's gist."

"But sir—"

The mayor raises a hand to silence his media-savvy lapdog. "Apologies, Senator. My press secretary appears to be chomping at the bit."

"I suppose I can't blame him," Robert, Sr. replies. "If we wait 24 hours, though, we can use this in our favor. Come forward tomorrow night or the morning after with good news and you'll have untold political capital to spend."

"Political capital is the last thing on my mind, Senator. Now what's your plan?"

"Thanks to intel from my son and his friends, half our job is already done. For the other half, we'll need to destroy the unit on our end and formerly press charges against Arendt and his co-conspirators."

"Be careful," Barnes cautions.

"If it's proof you're looking for, Chief Barnes—proof beyond the little science project I demonstrated for you—it's proof we have."

"Let's see it."

"It's actually from one of yours. Captain Bennett?"

"Thank you, Senator," Bennett replies. To the soldiers guarding the door: "You can show him in now."

They open the door to motion in Detective Lieutenant Mayotte. He enters, manila folder in one hand and Styrofoam coffee cup in the other. He makes eye contact with each individual VIP and, with a straight face, greets each of them by name.

"This is Detective Lieutenant J.D. Mayotte," Bennett explains. "He's one of our best men, and he's been taking point on this. Detective, tell us what you found in Arendt's office."

"Thank you, Captain," Mayotte says. "I'll make this quick; I still need to write this up and I have a few more strips to reconstruct. But let me begin by introducing you to Leonard Debussy, Rosalina Martínez, and Lymott Banks."

"And they are?" Barnes's patience is tried.

"They are the first victims we can definitively pin on Wesley Arendt and CGC."

"I'm not following, John."

"Sir, they were all missing persons we were charged with finding as far back as 15 months ago."

"And?"

"*And,* they were dead ends. Destined to become cold cases until about seven hours ago. Each of these MisPers showed up at CGC within ten days before they were reported missing. I was the lead DT on two of them, and had a helluva time getting anyone to tell me anything. None of them had a lot of friends and two of them lived alone. I went to the Hancock location Monday on a hunch. Found a trail of blood, a bunch of shredded documents including these applications, and one of those." He points to the porta-pad near the catering table. "Plus another one in Arendt's condo next door."

"What was the hunch that sent you there Monday?" Barnes asks.

"A phone call. A phone call from the senator's kid, of all people."

"How the hell would some kid know? Even if his old man is a Washington insider." He turns to Robert, Sr. "No offense."

"None taken. But you should listen to your detective."

With a grunt, Barnes addresses the over-caffeinated gumshoe. "Go on."

Mayotte walks the VIPs through the timeline of his investigation, beginning with the post-prom interrogation. He credits his captain with confirming that a shootout occurred near Dana's Belmont Gardens home. When he reveals the *pièce de résistance,* an invite list he had faxed to him at CGC-Hancock of potential honorees at the "40 under 40" gala, his audience groans as if gobsmacked. Alphabetically, honoree Wesley Arendt, age 32, is second from the top of the invite list. "The event sponsor said Arendt never RSVP'd, but receiving this invitation *has to* have been the catalyst that planted the seed in his mind to go big and target all these mass-gatherings at once. It was as if he'd hit the jackpot!" Despite his lack of sleep, Mayotte's as giddy as a schoolgirl when he makes this big reveal.

He asks the chief of police how many more names he will need to recreate from the shredded documents and cross-check against the MisPer archives before the chief will believe him. Chief Barnes, whose foot has been firmly inserted into his mouth, doesn't reply.

The senator goes next. "Thank you, Detective. My boy Robert's just a teenager, but I trust him. And everything you said corresponds with everything he and his friends told me. One of my science committee colleagues is on the defense committee as well. I spoke with her this afternoon and she tells me the Feds and the Joint Chiefs are chomping at the bit." He turns to the mayor. "Believe me, Your Honor, you don't want the FBI or the military running roughshod through your city."

"I believe you, Senator," Hizzoner replies. He turns to his chief of police. "Chief Barnes, what do you think?"

"Harry, I think Detective Lieutenant Mayotte should file those documents as evidence. And if the plan is to raid the facility at Meigs, give me a day and I'll get you all the air and SWAT support you need."

Mayotte, adamant: "I want in, sir."

"Negative. You don't have SWAT training. Best I can do is have you join us at the staging area."

"Chief, if I may, I don't want Mayotte there in *any* capacity," Bennett interjects. "He hasn't slept since . . . when was it, Friday, J.D?"

"I'll sleep when I'm dead."

"How 'bout the kid then?" Barnes suggests.

"My Robert?" the senator asks, stupefied.

"Not to go in, Senator, just to consult from the staging area."

"Out of the question."

"Captain . . . Chief . . . I'm good," Mayotte insists. "If that time gizmo really is destroyed on the other end, we won't be able to get back the people who've been taken. I for one wouldn't presume to know what dates they were sent to in the first place, and nor would I dare hypothesize on the ripple effects of sending a unit through on a rescue mission. It's like *The Terminator,* only going forward, not backward. That being said, if there's even a *chance* that cocksucker Arendt can snatch more people and change the date to send 'em back to an earlier time, then we absolutely need to destroy it on this end. And I need to be there. For Debussy, Martínez, and Banks. For my godson. For everyone we couldn't save."

"He's a stubborn son-of-a-bitch, isn't he, Marshall?" Barnes observes.

"He certainly is, Chief."

Barnes turns to Mayotte. "Alright John, since you seem to have all the answers, what about the ten or 15 or however many it is men you've got clogging my jails?"

"I can answer that, Chief," Bennett says.

"I'm listening."

"For starters, none of them are talking. I've got Detective Heinbrenner trying to break 'em, but so far mum's the word."

"That Kraut needs to try harder."

"He's one of my best, sir, along with J.D. here. He'll break 'em. Of greater concern—and this supports our theory—is the fact that 70 percent of these perps have no matching prints. Not from anywhere . . . at least not anywhere in this century."

"I see." Barnes eats crow for the second time this evening. "Keep at it, then."

Bennett nods. Mayor Washington collects his pinstriped jacket from the back of his chair. "It's late, gentlemen. I don't know that there's anything left to cover until we have a definitive action plan. Chief Barnes, looks like you have the next move. What an . . . enlightening . . . evening."

"Thank you, Harry," Barnes replies.

Robert, Sr. addresses Detective Lieutenant Mayotte. "I appreciate you being there for my son and his friends."

"It's what I do, Senator." He offers his hand.

Robert, Sr. shakes it, then offers his own hand to Mayor Washington. "Your Honor, thank you for your support. Sounds like we're in the home stretch. What do you need from me?"

"Just be available, Senator," the mayor replies. "Someone from Barnes's office will call you later with a time for tomorrow."

"I can be reached at home, no matter the hour." Robert, Sr. picks up the porta-pad and tucks it under one arm. He turns to Alton, who scribbles shorthand like mad. "And just to confirm, not a word of this to the press until after."

"You're still serious about that?" the press secretary asks again, quizzical. He pleads to the mayor. "Your Honor, he can't be serious."

Hizzoner nods. "I'm afraid he is." Alton looks dejected, so the mayor puts a hand on his shoulder. "Relax, Alton. After we save the city, you can write all about it!"

5

It's early in the Wilkinson house, before dawn, and Bob is the only creature stirring. Yesterday was a long day for everyone. Gail went to bed early; she's been "tired" since the traumatic plane ride from DC-National to O'Hare. She figured Robert, Sr. wouldn't get home until late, and knew he'd try not to wake her. Her senator spouse—this is her second marriage as well—has boundless energy most days, and is one of those *über*-Alpha sorts who gets by, even thrives, on less than four hours of sleep each night. It's not uncommon for him to arrive home past midnight, after an emergency session or a strategy meeting, and even then, to work for another hour before turning in.

Bob, Pete, and Lori went to bed early as well. (Before hitting the hay, Bob and Lori discussed whether to tell the others they had fallen in love, and agreed to let them figure it out for themselves.) Lori sleeps soundly, the sleep of the well-loved and well-fucked. Her dreams, which she will not remember upon waking, are those of a wealthy teenage girl from a good home, someone without a care in the world. Bob and Pete's slumbers, on the other hand, are restless. Pete cannot erase the horrifying image he saw during his Journey of Earth's continents being absorbed by rising sea levels after the melting of the ice caps. Bob, meanwhile, has a nightmare about Dr. Kirchner, and awakens in the middle of the night with the fleeting image on his retinas of being trapped in his car, driving upside down, a fireball left in his wake. What was *that* all about? He falls back asleep soon afterwards, but wakes up 40 minutes later with a cottonmouth taste that suggests he needs something to drink.

6

Bob stands in front of the refrigerator and chugs Mountain Dew straight from the bottle. His father's voice startles him out of his stupor. "Robert, you shouldn't drink that stuff at this hour. It'll keep you awake."

"Hey dad. Don't worry, the caffeine doesn't affect me."

"I didn't know that. But then, there are a lot of things about you I don't know. I suppose that's my fault."

"It's nobody's fault, dad. You have an important job. I know how it is."

"All the same, I can't help but think if I was home more, if I spent more time with you, somehow, everything'd be different. Maybe you and Peter wouldn't have gone hellraising on prom night and would've stayed home instead, safe and sound and ignorant and the better for it."

"Well, we can't exactly turn back time, can we?"

"We could at CGC though. Isn't that right, son?"

"Uh, yeah, I guess. But it would be the *me-from-here-and-now* doing it, not the *me-from-before-prom*."

"Ah yes, I didn't think about it that way." Robert, Sr. pours himself a glass of milk.

"How was your meeting?"

"Productive. Police Chief Barnes is stubborn, but Mayor Washington authorized all the support we need."

"When I met the mayor that night, he said he voted for you."

"He told me in person as well. Whether it's true or not, he's a good man. The city's lucky to have him."

"You didn't tell him about what happened to Vinnie, did you?"

"Heavens, no! I kept his name out of the conversation."

"Did you ever get ahold of Lori's FBI guy? The one who told her CGC is clean?"

"Bill Melchior?"

"Yeah, him."

"I actually know Melchior. Worked with him before for my work on the science committee. He has a special kind of hatred for CGC. Found all kinds of stuff on them."

"So he lied to Lori and her parents?"

"Melchior wants a piece of the action. Of course he lied."

"And what about that pad I gave you?"

"Pad's back in the workbench, alongside the firearms and the other ones just like it. Barnes'll probably want it all for the evidence locker, but I say no dice. We can't let these fall into the wrong hands."

"Toss 'em in the lake, dad. Or incinerate 'em. Do something. Whatever it is, don't turn those in to Barnes or the FBI or anyone."

"Never . . . Son, a lot of this is on me."

"Whadoya mean?"

"I knew even more than I let on yesterday. Melchior sent me a copy last summer of his file on CGC. Much of what's in there was redacted, but—"

"What, you mean blacked out?"

"I mean blacked out, yes. Much of what's in there was blacked out, but what you and your friends told me corresponds almost exactly with what was in Melchior's file. Like I said yesterday, the FBI said it was called 'time and location displacement.' The only discrepancy was the timeline—the report suggested CGC was still over two years away from making it viable. As such, we sat on it."

Bob sits down, afraid his legs will give way. "Jesus."

"Robert, I'm sorry. Truth is, we kinda wanted to see what would happen. We knew it couldn't possibly be good, but you know there's always a vested military interest."

"Wait, are you saying the Army knows about this, too?"

"Not yet. But Melchior's no fool. He'd sell what he knew to the Joint Chiefs if he thought the price was right."

Bob's hand twitches. His father notices this and is convinced his son has stopped taking his meds with regularity. His love for Bob is stronger now than ever before, and he staunchly that believes his belated confession about what he knew, while tough for his son to hear in the moment, was the right thing to do . . . albeit a bit too late in the game.

"Robert. Son. I offer no excuses for my secrecy. To say 'national security' seems pretty flimsy right about now."

"Stop. Just stop." Bob's voice wavers. He looks up at his father with a devasted expression on his face.

Robert, Sr. takes a seat opposite his son. He folds his hands across the tabletop and sits in silence. After several seconds: "What can I do to make this right?"

"You can tell me if there a plan."

"SWAT team hits CGC tomorrow night, with an arrest warrant for Wesley Arendt."

"What about his guards? I'm sure he won't be alone."

"Whether they surrender willingly or die fighting is entirely up to them."

"And you're gonna destroy that thing, right?"

"The SWAT commanders will be carrying plastic explosives, yes."

"What are you gonna tell the FBI guy?"

"We've arranged a total media blackout. Melchior won't know a thing until the following morning."

"What about local FBI? I'm assuming he's got friends here."

"We threw some bones their way about Springfield being the next target, so they all high-tailed it to the capital."

"And they bought it?"

"After the governor's urging, yes. He's pissed as hell at me, but he knows the importance of keeping this local, so he'll take one for the team. And who knows? Maybe they'll find some actual bad guys down there while they're at it. Unrelated bad guys, but bad guys all the same."

"Are we gonna bring those pads with us tomorrow night and destroy 'em along with everything else?"

"I will, yes. You, however, are staying right here."

Bob slowly processes everything, and he doesn't sound as dejected as he feels. "I figured you'd say that . . . But wait a minute; my brain's still three questions behind. You said we're gonna arrest the CEO. But if we destroy the time chamber, won't he get off for lack of evidence?"

"That's the kicker—your detective friend saved everyone's bacon."

"How?"

"He patched together shredded documents found in Arendt's office of CGC applicant files. Applicant names match those of several people reported missing over the last 15 or so months —before your classmates, even. One or two could be a coincidence, but he came up with three names, none of whom are anywhere to be found. He's hoping to piece together at least two more."

"That . . . that's great!"

Even after the sharing of promising news, father and son can't quite make eye contact with one another. They sit in silence at opposite ends of the table for several seconds. Robert, Sr. is the one to break the quiescence. "It's late, son. You should get some sleep."

"I know dad, I just came down to get something to drink." Bob returns the two liter of Mountain Dew to the fridge.

"Two things before you go. First, I realize you and your friends want in on the action tomorrow. I get that. However, you've had enough close calls, and I need to reiterate that I simply *cannot* have you on-site. The best I can offer is for your detective to call you with a play-by-play. He'll be there, and I have a feeling you trust him more than me right now anyway."

"I do trust him, but it's just—"

"Second, I hope you believe me when I say I played my cards poorly in terms of what I knew—or *thought* I knew—about what CGC was up to. At the very least, I thought we had more time. I was wrong, and your friends paid the price. This will haunt me for the rest of my life. I want you to know that when this is over, I plan to hold a press conference during which I'll announce I won't be seeking another term."

"W-what?! Dad, don't do that! You made a mistake, that's all! Just . . . I dunno, just keep the investigation local like you said, a-a-and whatever happens, make sure the FBI doesn't get any of those pads, or those guns, especially the plasma one. I know I keep bugging you about that, but I think that might be as important as everything else."

"Robert, I already told you I'm bringing those items with me tomorrow. I promise to personally supervise their destruction along with the operations center."

"How do we know there won't be more lying about?"

"That's a fair question. Your detective found one of those pads at Arendt's Hancock offices, and another in his condo in the same building. As for the weapons, I'm sure more of those will be seized when we take back the remaining border check-points. Beyond that, I suppose there's no way to be sure we got 'em all unless something like this happens again."

"It shouldn't. I mean, Pete said they blew up the time chamber on the other side as far as he knew."

"There are a lot of moving parts."

"Don't I know it."

"Robert, it's important for you to know we couldn't have gotten this far without you. But your involvement ends to-night." Bob looks at the linoleum. His father allows him a few beats to take in what he says before continuing. "Now . . . do you forgive me?"

"Do I . . . W-what I am supposed to say? I'm pissed you knew what those guys were up to all along. I'm glad you told me, though. I'm glad there's a plan. I . . . I'm glad you came home. I hope *you're* glad you came home."

"I am. And I should've come home more often. Seems like just yesterday you were singing '*Frère Jacques*' with your mother at the dinner table in the next room. Now she's gone, and you're 18 and off to college in the fall. I know you missed the cutoff for Northwestern, and I'm sure you didn't want to tell me, but in the bigger picture, it doesn't matter. It's all those moments in between that I wasn't around for. All those years, gone in the blink of an eye."

A single tear streams unexpectedly down Bob's cheek. "I miss her, dad. I miss her every day."

"I know you do. I miss her, too." Robert, Sr. gets up to give his son a hug, but they aren't there yet.

Bob sniffles as he composes himself. He leaves the room and walks past his father's waiting embrace. "I'm going back to bed. Goodnight."

Robert Dean Wilkinson, Sr. is one of the most respected members of Congress. He's always on time, he rarely misses a session, he's unafraid to reach across the aisle in bipartisan compromise, and he usually has the right answer. Right now, though, he is deeply troubled and deeply saddened. He knows he should've put his son's life ahead of his career these past nine years. "Goodnight, my son," he says, once Bob is out of earshot.

He turns off the kitchen light and shuffles upstairs. Light shines from the crack under Bob's bedroom door as Robert, Sr. passes it on the way to his and Gail's bedroom at the end of the hall. He quietly strips to a V-neck and boxers in the dark and manages to drape his tie and collared shirt over a hassock without stubbing a toe. He crawls into bed and kisses Gail on the cheek. She stirs. "Sorry to wake you," he whispers.

Groggily, with one eye open: "Good meeting?"

"Productive. We'll talk about it tomorrow."

Gail glances at the alarm clock and notices the ridiculous hour. "It *is* tomorrow."

"I'm going to dial it back," he states.

She turns on her bedside lamp. "What do you mean?"

"I've decided to be more available. Dial back the trips and the meetings. Spend more time with you. Spend more time with Robert. Lobbyists and committees be damned. What do you think?"

"You know I back you in every decision you make. Question is, will dialing it back make you happy?"

"It'll make me happy if it makes Robert happy."

"There's your answer, then."

"I think it's too late. I think I've lost him."

"Darling, no. He's a good boy. A bit troubled perhaps, but extremely bright. Not warm, exactly, but thoughtful in his own way. We had a terrible argument the other day, but did you know he apologized right after? It was just a little thing, but still, it was so thoughtful."

"I *told him* to apologize."

"No, this was while you were still at the store. I'm so glad we decided to come back, even if that was the worst landing ever."

Robert, Sr. kisses his index finger and places it, tenderly, on Gail's bandaged nose. With his thumb, he touches Gail's chin—a gesture identical to Bob's gesture toward Lori in the car that afternoon. "Tell me about the girl," he says.

"I'm hardly the right person to ask; I think she and Robbie are a relatively new thing."

"So they're courting? '*Going steady*,' to use the parlance of today's youth?"

"I made that assumption, but they were quick to deny it," Gail says. "And you know I try to respect Robbie's privacy. They got home late, though, long after you left for your meeting, and the two of them were positively glowing. If they aren't going steady, then I'm a monkey's uncle."

Robert, Sr. kisses his wife's shoulder. "Good for them. Is she a good influence?"

Gail takes her husband's hand in hers. "He's still cold sometimes, but he's starting to thaw. Could be Lori has something to do with it, but personally I think it's all those visits to Dr.

Kirchner over the years. They've worked wonders! Remember how he used to hate me?"

"He never hated you," Robert, Sr. says. "He hated *me.*"

7

Gail and Robert, Sr. sleep in—a rarity. Lori basks in a 30-minute shower, the hot water symbolically washing away the last of her tears for Josh. Bob and Pete throw in the towel on a good night's rest after their slumber is interrupted, multiple times, by nightmares. Daylight brings with it a fresh start, and the boys are ravenous. They gorge on breakfast in the dinette—orange juice and Honeycomb for Pete, Mountain Dew (always) and Wheaties for Bob. They consume several bowlfuls apiece as Pete regales Bob with humorous anecdotes from their 13 years of friendship. With the horror of the Pit, the trauma from the beater attack, and the tragedy surrounding the CCC raid, you would expect Pete to be taciturn and withdrawn. His memory recall came with a new lease on life, however, and Pete is elated to see his friend. But there will be more nightmares to come, and Pete has no idea what the next 24 hours will bring. It's said that whatever doesn't kill you makes you stronger, but as Pete will discover, that's a goddamn lie.

He pours himself the last of the Honeycomb. A toy tumbles out of the box along with the last few cereal crumbs—a plastic, clip-on, heart-shaped Bell Charm accessory. Wistful, he waxes nostalgic about happier times. "Hey Roberto, remember that time in Miss Benson's class when everyone made Valentine's Day cards?"

"I do. What was it Stephanie Marcum wrote inside yours again?"

"She wrote, '*HAPPY VALENTINE'S DAY. YOU ARE A TOTAL NURD.'* "

"Aw, how sweet."

"She spelled 'nerd' with a 'u.' Not traveling in the fast lane, that one."

"Even then, she knew. *Nerd.*"

"When was it, seventh grade, maybe, she came back from summer vacation and, like—" Pete illustrates what he is trying to say by making hand gestures that suggest the presence of a generous chest cavity.

"There they were."

"There they were."

"Remember Mrs. Mayer's class?"

"The paste thing?"

"Yeah, the paste thing. Did we actually do that?"

"According to Todd Boehner, we did. Freshman year he signed my yearbook, *'HOPE YOU DON'T STILL EAT PASTE. HAVE A GOOD SUMMER, TODD BOEHNER.'* What a dillhole!"

"Did you run into him on Mars?"

Pete shakes his head, unaware that the severed arm he, Pete, and Lori discovered at the Chicago Cultural Center belonged to Todd, whose shoulder was vaporized after he mouthed off to Loyalist goons while in a drunken stupor. The varsity football coach, Chad Bolzer, dragged Todd's body toward the men's room in search of a towel to wrap around the gaping wound, but forgot the arm. Todd died in his arms on the way, and Coach Bolzer was rounded up along with everyone else.

"What about Rain-Rain?" Pete asks. "When did you first notice her?"

"Rain-Rain? Gosh. Kindergarten, probably."

"Ah, during our paste-eating days!"

Bob snickers. "I always thought she was cute."

"She still is. Hence my behavior at Vinnie's." He rises from his chair to demonstrate the humping motions that led to Lori and her friends walking out in disgust, but Bob cuts him off after a single gyration.

"I was so pissed at you for doing that."

Pete shrugs. "I think my libido acted before my brain had a chance to say, 'Uh, wait a minute, ya Polack. Abort! Abort!' "

Bob rolls his eyes. "Fortunately, she seems to have gotten over it."

"See?! And all it cost was the 7 Up she threw in my face!"

"That, and Josh nearly beating your ass in the locker room."

"That too . . . but in light of what happened, I'll give him a free pass."

"Pete, do you remember when—I think it was freshman year—she and I were paired up in Biology on that science project? I couldn't believe it!"

"Of course! You bragged about that every day for like a month!"

"I was supposed to go to her house one day after school to work on it, but she said, 'Let's meet at McDonald's instead.' I was like, 'O-kay.' Her stupid friends came into the place and started teasing us. It was the same thing you said yesterday: 'Bob and Lori sitting in a tree, K-I-S-S-I-N-G.' "

"I changed the words slightly in my version."

Bob sighs. "Anyway, she decided to hang out with them instead, and I ended up doing the whole thing myself."

"Dang, dude. You never told me that part."

Bob nods. "That was the last time I spoke with her face to face until prom night."

"A lot's changed since then. Maybe she has, too."

"I'm not gonna lie, the last few days have been great. I mean, everything except for you and Dana getting taken . . . and Dr. Kirchner . . . a-and what happened in the boat, and . . ."

"Let's not talk about that."

"No no no. I'm trying to put things in perspective, is all."

"But other than finding your doctor—that must've sucked— what'd you two do yesterday? I know you said the other day you don't kiss and tell. Believe it or not, I respect that. It's just, when I saw you last night, you looked . . . *different.* Happy, even. And, uh, you're not exactly the happiest guy I know."

"We . . . um . . . we . . ."

"Spit it out!"

"We . . . we went to Lover's Leap."

"What?! Dude!"

Bob can feel his face turning red. He looks away, but the curl of a telltale smile doesn't escape his friend's notice. "Dude!" Pete says a second time. "Did you see her in her undies again?"

"I guess you can say I saw what's *inside* her undies."

"*DUUUDE!*" Pete looks up and raises his hands as if singing praises to the heavens. "He wakes up a boy, he goes to bed a man!"

"Don't say anything to her, okay?"

"Are you kidding me?! I'm taking out an ad in the *Tribune!*"

"I wouldn't put it past you."

"Nah. C'mon though. High five." They slap skin. "Other hand." They slap skin again. "Roberto, Roberto, Roberto, you absolute stud of a man. Now that you're officially cool—not just cool in my opinion, but, like, *officially* cool—I'll understand if you don't wanna hang out with me anymore, or if you shun me at reunions and such."

"Be gone, ye virgin simpleton," Bob replies, tongue firmly in cheek.

"Last question, I promise: What was it like?"

For the second time in two days, Lori catches them by surprise. "It was great," she says, smiling from ear to ear. She wears Gail's Northwestern University sweatshirt and a pair of tennis shorts, and her hair is up in a towel.

Bob coughs. His hand twitches and the cereal he was spooning into his mouth spills onto the table. Pete bursts into laughter and milk sprays out of his nostrils. "Ow, my nose!"

"He's got a huge dick," Lori adds, with a cheeky grin.

"Oh, God!" Bob's face turns red. He sops up his mess with a handful of napkins.

Lori pours herself a glass of orange juice. "Don't be modest, Bobby."

Bob turns to Pete. "Apparently, she's telling everyone. She told the cops at the Evanston border the same thing."

"We should call you 'John Holmes,' " Pete remarks.

"Yeah, not so much. She flatters me."

"Don't be modest!"

"She flatters me. Trust me."

Pete points accusingly at Bob and Lori. "So . . . you two, huh?" They look at each other before breaking into mile-wide smiles. "I knew it!"

"It just sort of happened," Bob admits with a shrug.

"Yeah it did," Lori takes a seat next to Bob and places his hand in hers. "And I'm glad."

The phone rings, but stops midway through the second ring. "*Robbie!*" Gail's voice yells out from upstairs.

"I've got it, mom!" Bob picks up the handset in the kitchen. "Uh, hello?"

"Bob, this is Detective Lieutenant Mayotte."

"Oh, hey Detective." He motions to Pete and Lori, who gather around the receiver alongside Bob. "I've got Pete and Rain-Ra—er, Lori—with me."

"Did your old man go over the plan with you for tonight?"

"Vaguely. I know it's going down and I know you're supposed to brief us after. But I don't know when or how."

"The SWAT team will arrive by boat. They'll probably alight directly on the beach near where you said you tied down. The mayor, the deputy mayor, the chief, Captain Bennett, myself, and your old man will coordinate and observe from the parking deck just south of Soldier Field."

"Bring those two pads you found. My dad wants to destroy 'em. He's gonna bring the stuff Lori and Pete and I found as well."

After a moment: "Good thinking. Don't want to leave those lying around for just anyone to find."

"They probably wouldn't work anymore anyway, but . . ."

Bob and Mayotte finish the sentence together: ". . . we shouldn't leave things to chance."

"So what time's this going down?" Bob asks.

"Late. 9:30. I gave your father my word I'd call you with a play-by-play. I know it isn't the same as being there in person, and you've certainly earned those front row seats. Trust me though: Things can get really bad, really quick. Your father couldn't live with himself if you fell in harm's way."

"I can take care of myself. Been doing it for the last nine years."

"That's between you and him. But until he tells me otherwise, I need you to stay away from the city tonight. Don't worry though, I'll keep you in the loop. For now, I want the three of you to relax. Have fun this afternoon. Play some videogames. Go to McDonald's. Tonight, have a nice dinner with your folks. We'll be setting up early. How 'bout I call you with a play-by-play? Let's say . . . 8:45?"

"Y-yessir," Lori replies.

"Works for me, Detective," Pete offers.

"Thank you," Bob adds, defeated.

"Terrific. Talk to you then." The call ends.

• • • •

Unbeknownst to Bob and his friends, his father and stepmother sit up in bed and listen in on the call from the primary bedroom. When the call ends, Gail turns to her husband. "What has our boy gotten into?" Robert, Sr. is an astute, career politician, but a deer in the headlights when confronted by his wife. "Tell me," she says. "I *demand* to know."

He sighs. "Honey . . ."

"Don't 'honey' me. And don't give me the network news version, either. Give me the behind-closed-doors summary. What kind of danger is Robbie in?"

"As of right now, the threat we're dealing with is local-only, but if it fell into the wrong hands—the Soviets, let's say—this would become real, World War III-type stuff. Thanks to several lucky breaks, some of them provided to us by Robert and his friends, there's a fix, but it's imperative we act tonight. You heard Robert's story; his friend from the arcade knew somebody who knew somebody who knew somebody, that sort of thing. It's *always* that sort of thing. But rest assured, I'll be coordinating from afar and he'll be here. Listening in, yes . . . but safe."

"Do you promise?"

"I promise. I have this chance to start over with him, and I'm not going to blow it."

8

Detective Lieutenant Mayotte sits at the kitchen table of his apartment on Bryn Mawr Avenue. The apartment, a cluttered two-bedroom in up-and-coming Edgewater, is all he can afford on his city detective's salary and is all he really needs. The life-long bachelor's residence is as much of a pigsty as his desk at work, but he seldom has trouble finding anything—a place for everything and everything in its place. What's more, his plus-sized tuxedo cat, Max, loves the mess. So many hiding places!

Mayotte ends his call to Bob and sets the cordless phone on the table. He yawns and makes his way to the tiny kitchen. He rinses out the coffee pot and fills it with fresh water; the sink overflows with piled-up dishes that hinder easy access to the faucet. He opens a tin of Folgers. Empty. "Crap," he mutters. He looks down at the sensation of something slinking around his ankles and finds Max at his feet. "Hey buddy, you finally coming around? Not mad at me anymore?"

Max replies with a single *MEOW* that suggests food is more important than affection.

"Yeah yeah, one track mind." Mayotte picks up Max's food dish. The moist, canned food has been eaten out of the middle of the bowl, but everything along the rim remains untouched. "Max, why do you waste food like this?" Disgusted, he scoops the leftover food into the trash bin, which of course is on the verge of overflowing. He scoops a fresh can into the bowl and sets it on the kitchen floor to Max's immediate delight. "Enjoy, you heifer you." He tosses the empty can in the bin. The liner has inevitably torn from being so overpacked. *Happens all the time,* he thinks, resignedly.

Mayotte grabs the phone again and enters the living room. He kicks off his shoes and parks himself on his hideous, cat-clawed fabric sofa. The glass-topped table between the sofa and the television is permanently ringed with coffee mug stains, and *TV Guides* are stacked three-high. What a slob.

He dials a number and his cousin Trish picks up on the third ring. "Hello?" she answers.

"Hey, it's J.D."

" 'Bout time you return my call, cuz."

"Did you leave a message?"

"Only about a dozen."

Mayotte glances at the answering machine on his kitchen counter—the light flashes red. "So I see. You know I'm bad at checking those."

"On the case again?"

"Yeah. Got a big break, too."

"Good. About the 'Occupation,' I think they're calling it?"

" 'Blockade and Occupation.' And yes. Can't say much more than that. I called to see if you have any coffee I can borrow. Place on the corner's closed . . . although . . . actually . . . will you be home for a while? I'd like to pick your brain about something."

"I was about to head to the laundromat. You have a key, don't forget. Just stop by whenever and help yourself."

"I'll do that. Thanks, Trish."

"Of course. What's on your mind? I need to get over there soon before the good dryers are taken, but I guess I can spare a few minutes."

"What would you do if you knew humankind was doomed to extinction in, say, another 40 years?"

"Wow, that's dark, cuz."

"Humor me, would you?"

"What would I do? Well first of all, I wouldn't be entirely surprised. I'm not as jaded as you, but we humans are greedy, aren't we?"

"We are."

"Can we stop it from happening?"

"I'm not sure."

"Can we slow it down at least?"

"Maybe."

"This is all just a hypothetical, right?"

After a moment: "Let's say it isn't."

. . .

Mayotte's cousin lives in a one-bedroom condo two blocks away. She is a changed person since the disappearance of her son, Jonathan, seven years earlier. She thinks of him—and of her ex-husband, Carl—often. Her shoulder-length hair is accented by a patch of grey above the left side of her forehead; it appeared almost overnight following the funeral for her little boy. She eventually forgave Carl for slapping her. He pays his alimony on time every month without fail but refuses to take her phone calls, except during the days leading up to the anniversary of their child having been declared dead; their phone calls that week are brief, and serve merely to let the other person know what time he or she will be visiting their late son's empty grave so their paths don't cross. Trish can never forgive herself, however, for her stupid playground love affair and the havoc it wreaked. She still has feelings for her ex-husband, and even loved him at the time she was cheating on him—at least she tells herself that—but she knows he doesn't love her in return, and supposes she deserves that.

If Mayotte is a bachelor slob, then Trish is a bachelorette neat freak. She's the one who stops by to feed his cat; who reminds him to pay his bills; who mends the holes in his socks and scrubs the skid-marks out of his underwear. She loathes going to the corner laundromat, but the washer in her condo has been on the fritz for over a month; Mayotte said for the last five weeks he would stop by to fix it himself, but has yet to make an appearance. She gave up waiting and finally scheduled an appointment for a repairman; the guy was supposed to stop by on Monday, but canceled after the city became closed to the outside world.

Trish's name was dragged through the mud during the investigation into Jonathan's disappearance; though she got the house, a starter two-bedroom, in the divorce, she sold it not long afterwards. She found she had trouble sleeping there. Having bricks thrown through the front window with the words HARLOT and SLUT painted on them didn't help. She made a tidy profit on the sale—in a morbid twist, the home's value skyrocketed; funny what salacious gossip will do—but she donated the proceeds to the National Center for Missing and Exploited Children and bought a simple condo near her cousin. Now, she works as an administrative assistant for the neighborhood United Way, and arranges a twice-yearly food drive for Habitat for Humanity. Friends—all new ones, all made over the past few years—tell her she's overqualified for her job with the perennially underfunded non-profit. She nods and tells them they're right, but stays where she is as a way of doing penance.

. . .

"You're scaring me with your non-hypothetical, cuz," Trish says. "But I s'pose I'd answer a question with question: Can we change our lifestyles to delay this from happening? You know, recycle more, consume less, don't vote a straight party ticket, stuff like that?"

"We have to, cuz," Mayotte replies. "We simply have to."

"Is that enough? In your non-hypothetical scenario, is that enough?"

"I don't know. I think as a species we face an uncertain future."

"Absolutely we do! There's a hole in the ozone layer! A giant meteor could wipe us all out tomorrow! Heck, cuz, they're putting in lights at Wrigley! There's always the potential for end times. As a detective, with all the stuff you've seen, you know this better than most."

"Maybe you're right. Maybe we just try to do better, little by little. Be the best stewards we can be with whatever time we have left, and cherish every moment."

"I like that sentiment. But are you *sure* you're okay? It's not like you to wax philosophical."

"I'm okay. Tired and in need of coffee, but excited for the big break. In the longer term, though, send positive vibes."

"Sure, I'll send some your way."

"Not to me. To Mother Earth as a whole."

"Uh, I can do that." Trish half-snickers.

"It's not funny. She's gonna need it."

"Wait, there's not a giant meteor headed toward us, is there?"

"There is, cuz. It's called 'time.' "

"Wow, you really do need coffee."

"I really do. Let me give Max here some attention, then I'll stop by. I'll fix your washer, too."

"I'll believe it when I see it."

"*Touché.*"

"Bye, cuz. Bye, Max!"

Trish grabs her purse from the kitchen table and slings it over her shoulder. On her way to the door, beside which lays a laundry duffel, she passes a kiss from her lips to a framed school picture of Jonathan.

9

Mayotte sets the phone on the coffee table. He looks down at the sound of Max's meow. "You want attention, don't you?"

*MEOW.*

"Alright, I know what you like. Just for a few minutes though." Mayotte lays down on the couch. "C'mon up here." Max jumps up and lands on his stomach. "Oof, you're heavy. Time for Jenny Craig." He strokes Max's fur, and the kitty's motor begins its contented purr.

"You like that, don't you? Yeah, I'll bet you do . . . I know, Maxi Poo . . . I'll be around more soon, I promise. I'll give you less food but more attention . . . yeah . . . yeah . . . yeah . . ."

Mayotte, who has been awake for almost 72 hours, closes his eyes and drifts off. He is asleep within minutes, and his snores are as loud as Max's motor.

It's 10:30 a.m. He won't wake up for another 11 hours—the single slip-up in 16 distinguished years on the force, but one that will change the course of the night's events and cost him his career.

10

Miles Myrick is worried.

The messages he and Christopher Gilman blitzed to Ross remain unread. The messages are essentially interstellar emails sent from a decade before email was a commonplace thing (although Al Gore, Jr., still a first-term United States senator in 1987, might insist otherwise). In them, Miles explained that Wesley is indisposed and that more Loyalist reinforcements are needed in order to meet the quota originally agreed upon. Receiving no response, Miles has little choice but to recall two dozen men from their posts across several of the city's less-important border crossings. Most of them are sent to CGC-Meigs to stand guard, but a few are sent to stake out the Hancock HQ as well. When those soldiers report back that police still aren't letting non-residents enter the building, Miles figures time is just about up. *Lemme make two more round-ups of volunteers for Phase Three,* he reasons. *We'll still miss our quota, but only by a little bit. I'll tidy up here, send Ross's men back, booby-trap the time chamber, and be on my way to a new life. On Mars, they'll call me a hero!*

. . .

The six-foot, three-inch Miles is the product of a broken home. His parents divorced when he was just five, and their joint custody arrangement meant he was shuttled back and forth between two different homes, with each parent trying to turn him against the other. He is still young, just 27, and takes on character traits from both parents. His Catholic mother was a substitute teacher and a chain smoker with a two-pack-a-day habit, and Miles took up the habit himself during his teenage years. His Jewish father, who bore a shaggy beard his mother found irresistible, worked for IBM, and Miles picked up the man's knack for information technology. Physically, Miles has his mother's brown eyes and slender physique, and his father's myopia and height. In terms of facial hair, he opted for a mustache rather than a full beard. The 'stache is not a good look for him, but no one has the heart to say anything.

Miles lost his mother, Estelle, to lung cancer two years ago. She was diagnosed following a coughing fit during a routine Pap smear, and died seven weeks later. "She just gave up," Miles told friends and relatives in the months that followed, and promised he would stop smoking. He cut back but failed to kick the habit entirely. Hindsight is 20/20, however, and he knows that if he *had* quit, he wouldn't have had reason to step outside at the exact instant Bob and company came snooping, thereby staving off the subsequent downward turn of events. He reminds himself once every hour how lucky he was to have not been killed by Wesley for his mistake. While the more logical thing to do now that Wesley has perished is to simply run away, the Catholic guilt complex passed down from his mother demands he stick around to tie up loose ends and see Wesley's original plan through to completion . . . even though his confrontation with Bob and company a few nights prior suggested his boss hadn't told him everything.

11

Miles has tasked Gilman with taking inventory of the weapons closet, and has asked Balthazar to man the workstations while he himself catches some Z's at his desk. Balthazar, who Miles hired six weeks before Phase Two, isn't much for small talk, but caught on quickly to the task at hand. At Wesley's urging, Miles has kept Balthazar somewhat in the dark about certain details, but "B," as Miles calls him, *does* know that people sent forward in time will help save the species in the longer term, despite any protests to the contrary while being dragged, kicking and screaming, to the time chamber. Miles decides to let Balthazar make his own choice about whether to come along or cut and run.

The core functions of the job—basic data entry such as logging dates, times, and cargo—is straightforward, but post-Journey cleanup can be a bit much. (The orientation bays with water-based cleaners in the Mars time chamber to make the job more hygienic are not features of the Chicago equivalent.) Questions posed to Balthazar during his interview included the following: *1) What are the key programming languages? 2) How would you calculate time and distance between two points? 3) Do you have a strong stomach? 4) Do you have a large family? 5) Can you be trusted with sensitive information?*

Balthazar's answers: *1) FORTRAN, LISP, COBOL, BASIC, Pascal, and C.* (Miles was only looking for FORTRAN, COBOL, BASIC, and Pascal, and was thus impressed by Balthazar's answer.) *2) To calculate time, divide distance by speed. To calculate distance, multiply speed by time. 3) Yes—I love roller coasters and horror movies. 4) I have an older brother in California, but we're not close. My parents died in an auto accident when I was 17. 5) Yes—if it's none of my business, it's none of anyone else's, either.*

Miles believes this last question to be the most important. He was intrigued Balthazar didn't ask many questions regarding the time chamber itself. The young trainee, who double-majored in physics and mathematics, was more confused by the mysterious appearance of the City Hall bologna in the chamber than by that of Ross's Loyalist soldiers. *Kid's good,* Miles thinks. *Better than me, even.* "Sure you don't mind working late tonight, B?" he asks his trainee.

"I don't mind," Balthazar replies. "Don't have any plans. Can't really go anywhere, anyway."

"Great. It may get crowded in here later. We'll need to stay alert. Log anything and everything that comes through. And let me know the second you get a blitz back."

"Will do, boss."

Miles's first instinct was to tell his trainees not to call him "boss" or "sir" . . . but later decided he liked it, just as he's sure Wesley liked it when Miles addressed him the same way.

## 12

While Detective Lieutenant Mayotte and Max sleep and while Miles and Balthazar play their waiting game, the five people gathered at the Wilkinson home get ready for dinner. "Smells good, Mrs. W.," Pete yells as he exits the upstairs bathroom and fans the air behind him.

"*Thank you, Pete,*" Gail yells back from downstairs.

Pete sticks his head in the guest bedroom on his way back to Bob's room. "I'd stay out of the bathroom for at least 20 minutes if I were you," he tells Lori.

"*Ewww!*" Her standard reply. She is flipping through a stack of Wilkinson family photo albums.

Pete enters Bob's room. Bob lays in bed and listens to music via his Walkman. Pete starts to talk, but his best friend motions that he can't hear him. Bob removes his headphones and Pete hears Bon Jovi's "Wild in the Streets," tinny but unmistakable. "Roberto, you ever have to shit so bad you pull your pants down and squat, and you're already done shitting by the time your butt touches the seat?"

"Dude! Why'd you wait so long?"

"I like pushing the envelope."

"Gross!"

"So as I was wiping my ass, I started thinking . . ."

"Do I wanna hear this?"

"Maybe. So . . . you know how I told you Josh and Susie may have had a thing for each other?"

"Yeah?" Bob hits the STOP button. "And?"

"So . . . that night in the cave . . . I couldn't sleep, and . . . I looked over, and . . . they were going at it."

"Arguing?"

"No. Doing it."

"Oh . . . In front of you?"

"Well, they sort of stepped away for privacy. And I didn't actually *see* it, but . . ."

"But you knew."

"Yeah."

"Thanks for telling me . . . I guess?"

"I told you in case you were feeling guilty about Lori, since she used to be Josh's girl."

"Why should I feel guilty? As if I don't have enough other shit to worry about?!"

"No. I mean, you shouldn't, but . . . you've got a lot on your mind, and I just . . . I thought you should know."

"Pete, Lori can *never* know. Not because of she and I, but because . . ."

"I wasn't planning on telling her."

"Keep it that way."

"I will. I promise." Pete paces, anxious. "You nervous about tonight?"

"Ready to be done with it."

"Me, too."

"Would you stop pacing?! Go play Sega or something!"

"What the shit, dude? What's your problem?"

"Sorry, I guess I'm just anxious."

"I am, too. Take a chill pill!"

"That's not a bad idea actually." Bob opens the top drawer of his dresser, filled with the pill bottles he stole from Dr. Kirchner's office. He dry-swallows two lorazepam.

"No water?"

"Nah, I've been taking 'em dry for like three years now."

"How long do they take to kick in?"

"I rarely take 'em anymore, so they kick in pretty fast when I do. 'Specially if I take two."

"Hell, maybe *I* should take two."

"No way. Be glad you don't have the stuff running through your head I've got."

Pete shrugs. "I don't know, Roberto. After what I saw up there . . . I may never sleep well again."

"Fair enough. But try nine years' worth of nightmares."

"You're better though, right? I mean, you don't talk much about your real mom anymore, and through this whole thing you've been pretty take-charge, so . . ."

"Maybe."

". . . And now, you and Rain-Rain."

"Until I blow it."

"Look, girls who look like that don't exactly pick losers, okay? Stop being so hard on yourself!"

Bob nods, reluctant. "I s'pose you're right."

"Absolutely I'm right."

"It's scary how much self-confidence you have."

"Well, I lost some after going you-know-where, but, uh, thanks, Roberto."

"I'm just glad you were finally able to remember everything that happened."

"That makes one of us."

The door to Bob's room is ajar, but Lori knocks anyway. "Can I come in?" she asks.

"Sure," Bob replies.

"I'll get out of here so you two can bone," Pete remarks. Bob punches him in the arm. "Owww!"

"Dick," Bob says.

Pete retreats into the upstairs hallway, then comments on his handiwork. "Ah, it's still lingering."

"Dude!" Bob remarks.

"He's so grody sometimes," Lori remarks once Pete is out of earshot.

"To the max," Bob adds, and they giggle. "What's up?" he asks as she presents a photo album.

"I found this on the bookcase at the end of the hall. Is this you?" Lori opens the album to a page with pictures dating back approximately 16 years.

"Oh, God!" Bob is mortified; the picture in question is of two-year-old Bob splashing in the bathtub, clad only in his birthday suit.

"You were so cute! I like this one, too." She turns the album back two pages to pictures celebrating Bob's first birthday. In one image, Bob's tiny hands holds the mushy remains of a piece of birthday cake, the rest of which is smeared across his face and bib.

"Oh, God!"

"Don't be bashful. I'm sure my folks have a photo somewhere of me stuffing my face with birthday cake, too."

"I'll bet it looked better on you than it did on me."

"Awww, thanks, Bobby." She gives him an unexpected peck on the lips and returns her attention to the photo album. She flips forward and comments on a picture of Bob being pushed in a stroller through Brookfield Zoo by a woman in a white tank top and hideous, red-and-white checkerboard pants that went out of style circa 1980. "Is this your birth mother?"

"Yeah. There's a better picture of her on my dresser."

Lori approaches the dresser and studies the framed picture—a Sears Portrait Studio headshot—of Marie Christine

Wilkinson, *nee* Plimpton. "She was very beautiful. You have her eyes."

"You think so?"

"I do. They're kind eyes."

"This was taken in '76, a few months before she got sick. It's the last picture of her before she died, come to think of it."

"I'm sorry." Lori grabs his hand in hers. "I can't imagine losing a parent."

"It's hard. At least she was in good spirits whenever I came to visit, like I said in the hot tub the other day. But when I was a couple years older, Dr. Remus—she was my head-shrinker before Dr. Kirchner—suggested I read a few books on the subject. Based on how they described what she went through, not just during chemo but at the end, when her lungs filled up with water, if I had a choice of dying from leukemia or of dying like we saw in those videos of the time chamber, I think I'd choose the time chamber."

Lori opens her mouth to speak but is interrupted by the sound of squeaky springs. She and Bob peer out the bedroom window, which is open to let in the spring breeze. They look out and see Pete bouncing on the trampoline. He doesn't get much airtime—he takes it easy to protect his sensitive stomach—but he lands funny on one of his jumps and rolls over the side and onto the grass. "He's terrible at that," Lori observes.

"He is indeed," Bob replies. He takes a mental picture to tease Pete about later.

"He's *sooo, sooo* bad." She fails to stifle a giggle.

Bob nods. His expression turns dour after a few moments of levity. The weight of everything they've seen is back, like a regifted Christmas fruitcake.

"*Suppertime!*" Gail's voice beckons from downstairs. Bob snaps out of his stupor.

"It'll be okay, Bobby," Lori says. She places a hand on his shoulder. "Let's enjoy a nice meal, like the detective said."

"You're right," Bob replies. "And I *am* hungry."

13

For a while, dinner is a joyous affair. The meal, served up by Gail, includes baked pork chops, mashed potatoes and gravy, creamed corn, salad, and—of course—applesauce. Her husband and our young heroes compliment her cooking numerous times, and the only early damper is when Gail brings a bottle of white wine to the table but Robert, Sr. abstains so he "can stay 100%." Gail, who has already poured herself a glass, is disconcerted. She offers some to Bob, Pete, and Lori, but they each decline. True to form, Bob opts for his usual Mountain Dew, which prompts comments from the parental units about how Mountain Dew can't possibly complement the taste of pork chops. His response: a shrug, a big swig, and an exaggerated "*Ahhh.*"

Halfway through dinner, Robert, Sr. receives a phone call that casts a pall over the remainder of the meal. He disappears into his study to take the call, and returns with his briefcase. "It's time." As if on cue, the doorbell rings. He opens it to greet the state trooper who will drive him through the safe crossing to the staging point—the parking deck beside Soldier Field.

"Ready when you are, Senator," Trooper Connors says.

"Be right there, Officer." Robert, Sr. returns to the dining room and kisses Gail on the cheek. "Back in several hours. Don't wait up." He hurries to the door and is escorted to the patrol car.

"Good luck, Mr. W.," Pete says.

The glass of wine Gail hastily poured earlier remains untouched. She sits at one end of the table, elbows on the armrests and hands together, pensive.

"Everything's gonna be okay, Mrs. Wilkinson," Lori says.

"I know, dear. Finish your dinner."

Gail and her teen charges finish their meals in silence. They clean their plates, but Gail's cursory offer of desert—chocolate cake, normally Bob's favorite—is declined by all parties. Bob, Pete, and Lori clear the table afterwards, but when Lori asks Gail if she can help with the dishes, Gail dismisses her and says, "I'll take care of them later. Go wait with your friends for your phone call."

Lori takes the hint. She is about to head upstairs when she sees Bob and Pete sitting in the parlor. "Hey," she says, with less than her usual enthusiasm.

"There she is," Pete replies with a smile; it's a solid effort, but less than the boisterous "Rain-Rain!" he would've exuberantly cried out on a normal day.

She takes a seat next to Bob. "What time is it?"

"Almost nine. "He should be calling soon."

"You nervous?"

"Little bit. Honestly, I can't wait for him to tell us it's over."

"Same," Pete adds.

"Me too," Lori fakes her best smile and notices Bob's hand begins to shake. He senses her staring but doesn't bother to control his tremors. She's already seen him at his worst, and she didn't cut and run.

"Damn it, why isn't he calling?" Bob glares at his blue and yellow Swatch watch: 8:57 p.m.

The phone rings and everyone jumps. "I've got it!" Bob leaps out of his seat. "Hello?"

"Robert, it's your father."

"Oh, hi dad. I was expecting the detective."

"He hasn't arrived yet."

"Is everything okay?"

"Everything's fine, but I forgot to grab those weapons and pads you and your friends seized."

"I can bring 'em to y—"

"No no no, stay home. I . . . we'll figure something out. In the meantime, I just wanted you to double-check that the garage door is closed and the workbench is locked."

"Uh, I'll check again, but they should be."

"Perfect. We just got word Chief Barnes's SWAT team is set up at Montrose Harbor and awaiting our go. It'll be radio silence here before long, but I'll have the detective lieutenant follow up as soon as he can. Meanwhile, send your best vibes to Chief Barnes's team."

"Okay dad, will do."

14

A flurry of activity on the upper level of the Waldron Parking Deck suggests the gang's (almost) all here. Robert, Sr. ends the call made from a mobile command phone near the staging area where Hizzoner, Deputy Mayor Orr, Chief Barnes, and Captain Bennett have already gathered. Trooper Connors approaches. "Need us to stay?" he asks.

"Not necessary," Robert, Sr. replies. "You'd be waiting all night. Go on back to *Casa de Wilkinson* and continue to keep an eye out for suspicious vehicles. Black vans in particular."

"I don't wish to overstep, sir, but can I ask what's going on? Is this about the Blockade and Occupation?"

"I'm afraid I can't say."

Barnes approaches and adds his usual, berating two cents. "Take the Drive back, sonny, and radio us if you see anything suspicious along the way. Can you do that?"

"Yessir." Connors returns to his unmarked car, which idles a few yards away.

"We have a good view over here," Barnes tells Robert, Sr. He leads him to a vantage point where their colleagues gaze at CGC-Meigs, on the other side of Burnham Harbor, its eastern docks shuttered since 1984 at the hands of one Wesley Arendt.

"Senator." Mayor Washington extends his hand.

"Long time no see, Your Honor," Robert, Sr. replies. "How are we on time?"

"That's a question for Chief Barnes."

"Thank you, Harry," Barnes replies. He checks his watch. "Our SWAT team should be setting off from Montrose Harbor as we speak. Choppers are ten minutes out, ready to take out anyone on the roof at the first sign of trouble. As for the airstrike further afield, I guess we're waiting on you."

"Thanks for the update, Leslie," Mayor Washington responds. He *hates* being called Harry, but Chief Barnes has been a grade-A prick for years, seldom able to read the room. Why change now?

"Do we have the green light?" Barnes asks.

"I know we're waiting on one or two others, but assuming Senator Wilkinson has no objections, I see no problem in authorizing the airstrike while we wait."

"Senator?" Barnes asks Robert, Sr.

"I have no objections," the senator replies.

"Let's take our goddamn city back," Barnes says. He tunes his radio to the correct frequency and presses the TRANSMIT button. "This is Barnes," he radios. "Air strike approved."

15

Gary/Chicago International Airport—IATA code GYY—sits 25 miles southeast of Chicago's Loop. It has just two runways, and, as such, is often omitted from discussions about Chicagoland airports. Tonight, the airport plays its own small role in history as the departure point for five military strike aircraft— Fairchild Republic A-10 Thunderbolts—that have been cleared for takeoff. Their objective: strafing runs along the perimeters of Chicago's Midway and O'Hare International Airports. Drive-by patrols along Central Avenue, Cicero Avenue, Irving Park

Road, and Mannheim Road—peripheral streets alongside Midway and O'Hare—scouted five CGC vans, and cautious estimates suggested as many as ten Loyalists apiece. There are actually just three Loyalists per van, which makes tonight's strafing runs resounding triumphs.

A total of three rockets are launched from the ground—two by Loyalists at O'Hare and one by a Loyalist at Midway—but none reach their intended targets. On the other hand, nearly every round fired from each Thunderbolt's Avenger autocannon is a direct hit. The five Thunderbolts—two circling Midway and three circling O'Hare—make three flyovers of the target areas. The second and third runs prove unnecessary. The vans are annihilated and 15 corpses are later recovered, several of them so badly torn up they barely resemble bodies. Investigators are stumped to find no matching print or dental records for any of the bodies autopsied; were this the internet age, online trolls would have a field day with conspiracy theories and false flag claims. Fortunately, in the Reagan-era 1980s, capitalism is king and hasty bribes from the Chicago Police Foundation, via monies seized from the now-frozen accounts of the late Wesley Arendt, convince the investigators to focus on what they *do* know—namely, that military-grade rounds made short work of all 15 (Mars-born) goons.

CPD officers on the ground raid the terminals, which have been shuttered since the Prom Night Massacre. They find a few Loyalists in the control towers and a handful of homeless men and women living in the tunnels below. The Loyalists, who witness the strafing runs from their vantage points in the towers, surrender without a fight. The unhoused are sent packing. They do their fair share of grumbling but will never know how lucky they were to have avoided capture by Wesley's team in the early stages of Phase One, when many of their kind were abducted from the city's various parks.

The FAA reclaims control of Midway and O'Hare International Airports before dawn the following morning, and limited ground operations resume within 24 hours. Both airports operate at normal capacity by Labor Day weekend.

16

Bob grows increasingly impatient. "Why isn't he calling?!"

"That's what I'd like to know," Pete remarks. "It's already 9:15."

"I'm paging him again." Bob dials Detective Lieutenant Mayotte's beeper number. Five interminable minutes tick by and the page goes unreturned.

"Maybe he got held up and is still at the station?" Pete suggests.

"I tried there. They said they don't know where he is."

"Call 'em again."

"Fine." Pete and Lori crowd around the receiver. They would normally be too close for comfort, but Bob pays little mind this time.

The precinct must be lightly staffed; it is several rings before the CPD operator picks up. *"Central District. Please hold."*

"Anything?" Pete asks.

"They've got me on hold."

"I'm worried, Bobby," Lori says.

"I am too," Bob replies.

Finally: *"How can I direct your call?"*

"Uh, Detective Lieutenant Mayotte, please."

*"One moment, please."*

The PSA in place of hold music has changed. *"In light of recent events, the Chicago Police Department reminds you that a citywide 8 p.m. curfew is in effect until further notice. All CTA bus and train routes are subject to alternate circuits and frequent service interruptions. Please plan your travels accordingly."*

The operator returns. *"I'm not getting an answer at that extension."*

"This is sort of an emergency. He's supposed to be with the chief and the mayor. Can you connect me remotely to where they are?"

*"I'm sorry, we are unable to do that."*

"Uh, how 'bout at home?" He shrugs, and Pete and Lori nod their encouragement. "Can you put me through to his home number?"

*"We are unable to do that."*

"Can you at least call him for me? It's literally a matter of life and death."

*"One moment, please."*

"No, don't put me on . . . Shit."

"Eight p.m. curfew, huh?" Pete references the PSA and holds up his watch so the others can see how late it is.

"If she comes back and says he's not answering, I say we head there ourselves," Bob suggests.

"How are we gonna get into the city with the curfew?" Lori asks.

"I'll crash through the roadblock, I don't care."

"Take it easy, Bobby."

"I'm serious."

"I know. And I'm on your side. Just—"

The operator returns. *"No answer at his residence."*

"Damn," Pete mutters.

*"His answering machine is full, so I was unable to leave a message. I did page him, however. Is there a message you'd like to pass on when he calls in?"*

"Tell him, 'We went in on our own,' " Bob answers.

*"Is there a name for reference?"*

"He'll know. If he calls, just give him the message."

*"I will relay the message. Thank you for calling the Chicago Police Department."*

The line goes dead. Bob turns to the others. "Are we doing this?"

"My stomach says no, but my mind says yes," Pete replies.

"I'm scared, but ready," Lori decides.

"Pete, help me get the stuff," Bob says. "Lori, we'll meet you in the car."

While Bob unlocks the workbench with Pete at his side, Lori uses the downstairs bathroom. She is a nauseous bundle of nerves. Bob and Pete return to the kitchen, rifles slung over their shoulders and porta-pads stacked in their arms. Bob grabs his keys from the counter and almost drops everything in the process. "Robert Dean," Gail calls from the dining room. She sits in darkness and is on her third glass of wine.

"Mom. Lemme turn the light on for you," Bob says.

"I'll see you in the car, Roberto," Pete says. Bob hands him the keys and Pete makes a hasty exit.

"I know where you're going," Gail remarks. "I wish you wouldn't, but I know I can't stop you. I do ask, though, that you and your friends be careful and stay out of harm's way."

"Always. But mom, we're just doing clean-up. Getting rid of these things once it's safe to do so. Dad forgot to take 'em with when he left." He raises his arms to draw attention to the objects he is holding.

"Finish your clean-up, then, and come straight home. *Straight home*, do you understand?"

"Absolutely. Should be a piece of cake."

Bob heads for the front door. "Goodbye," Gail whispers once he's out of earshot. She hears the toilet flush and gets up. She tiptoes to the bathroom and waits beside the door for Lori to emerge.

Lori rinses her mouth out. "*Lori?*" She hears her name being called from outside the bathroom. She opens the door and almost knocks Gail over.

"Mrs. Wilkinson, you scared me!"

"Sorry, dear. That was not my intention."

"It's okay. Can I help you with something?"

"Take care of Robbie for me."

"Of course!"

"Do you love him?"

"W-wha—"

"Do you love my son?"

"With all my heart."

"Then bring him back to me alive."

"Why are you saying this? Like I said at dinner, everything's gonna be fine."

"I wish I could believe you, dear."

"You're scaring me, Mrs. Wilkinson. Believe me, I'd never let anything happen to Bobby."

"Go then. Go then and hurry back. And be safe."

"Um, okay." Lori flees to the car. Pete sees her coming and immediately slips into the back so Lori can take her rightful place next to her new beau.

"Ready?" Bob asks Pete and Lori buckle up.

"*¡Listo, Roberto!*" Pete replies with what little he remembers from Freshman Spanish.

"I'm ready too," Lori says. "But your stepmom kinda freaked me out back there."

Bob backs out of the driveway. "That may be my fault. I've never really been that nice to her."

"You can work on that when we get back."

"I will." They speed off toward the city.

. . .

With Lakeshore Drive a veritable ghost town after curfew, Bob, Pete, and Lori will make it to Northerly Island in what may be record time. Although they can expect hassle at the roadblock similar to Bob and Lori's awkward crossing two days earlier, when the officers on duty cracked wise about Lori being out of Bob's league, they will ultimately make it across without incident, aside from these uncouth remarks. As it happens, our young heroes will reach their destination at the same moment as the surviving SWAT boat—the other one having been sunk during an open-water ambush.

In all, 13 people will raid the CGC-Meigs location—Bob, Pete, Lori, nine SWAT officers, and one ill-fated squad leader.

But 13 is an unlucky number. Most of them will not make it out of there alive.

## 17

Two open-top boats, filled with 11 SWAT officers and one squad leader apiece, set sail for CGC-Meigs from quiet Montrose Harbor. Each leader, Commander Kaczmarek in boat #1 and Commander Morgan in boat #2, totes a tactical bag, fastened to his person via a cross-chest shoulder strap. Inside each bag: triage kits, spare magazines, and five bricks apiece of C-4. The waning gibbous moon provides sufficient natural light as they motor across the lake, lights off and with minimal wake, toward Northerly Island. Their plan is not unlike the one hatched by Bob, Pete, Lori, and Vinnie on that unfortunate Sunday less than one week earlier: Boat #1 will tie down at 12th Street Beach and boat #2 will moor near the steps between the Shedd Aquarium and the Adler Planetarium. Meanwhile, two CPD police choppers will hover overhead, snipers prepared to take down any Loyalists standing armed watch on the roof. After the rooftop is cleared of any hostiles, Captain Bennett and Detective Lieutenant Mayotte will each drive up the approach road and wait for the all clear from Kaczmarek or Morgan. Once they receive the all clear, Bennett will arrest any surviving Loyalists while Mayotte will give all weaponry and JourneyTech prime placement near a heat source and C-4 brick.

The SWAT watercraft decelerate as they approach a pair of motorboats floating idly in open water. From SWAT's vantage point, the boats appear unoccupied. Kaczmarek shines a light on the easternmost boat and speaks into his megaphone: "Attention on the water. This is Commander Kaczmarek with the Chicago Police Department. If there is anyone inside the craft, please raise your hands and prepare to identify yourselves. I repeat, please identify yourselves!"

Commander Morgan shines the light on the second idle boat and speaks the same warning into his megaphone. After no response from either boat, he radios to Kaczmarek. "Let's check it out."

"10-4," Kaczmarek replies. He kills the motor and pilots his craft toward the easternmost boat. A Loyalist soldier pops up from his hiding place inside the boat and fires AK-47 rounds that take out the light. The soldier is joined by two more, each of whom wield AKs as well. They open fire a split second before Kaczmarek's unit, and their quick action makes all the difference. The SWAT commander is struck in the chest and falls overboard into a moonlit Lake Michigan, taking his tactical bag with him. The weight of the C-4 drags him underwater.

"Shit!" Commander Morgan addresses his team. "Hodgson, Warshawski, Ramirez, Cruz, get their sixes! Everyone else, watch starboard and be ready! That craft may not be empty." There are no signs of activity from the westernmost boat, which continues to float idly. The quick-thinking Warshawski, gamine since childhood and a tough SWAT officer not unlike Rose Martínez, lobs a grenade over Kaczmarek's bullet-ridden craft and into the easternmost boat. Direct hit!

With all SWAT eyes on the explosion, the Loyalists hiding in the westernmost boat make their move. One of them pops his head up and shoots out the light on Morgan's craft. The weapons fire startles the others into action. Morgan loses two men in the subsequent firefight, but his remaining SWAT members make quick work of the three Loyalists inside the boat. "Head count Bravo Team, stat!" Morgan yells.

"Warshawski!"

"Cruz!"

"Brown!"

"Medellín!"

"Burke!"

"Ramirez!"

"Christensen!"

"Akinmade!"

"Hodgson! Sir, they almost kicked our ass!"

"Hodgson, give me a sitrep," Morgan replies. "Anyone need triage?"

"Kalicki and Rutherford are—"

"I know, Hodgson! Anyone else? Any injuries?"

"Don't think so, sir."

"Thank you, Corporal. Akinmade, take the helm."

"Yessir!" Akinmade, the team's other female operative, steers the craft toward the 12$^{th}$ Street Beach landing.

Morgan radios the staging area. "This is SWAT Commander Morgan, reporting a Code 77."

"*Damage report, Commander,*" Chief Barnes's staticky voice crackles.

"Threat neutralized, but I've lost two men and Commander Kaczmarek's team is . . . they're gone, sir. Along with half the C-4."

"*How's your ammo count? Can you reach your objective?*"

"Affirmative, sir. We've discharged quite a few rounds but are still well-stocked. You're gonna wanna send in some divers. Heading to our beach landing now."

"*Take it slow, and stay dark. We're still waiting on the choppers for air support. ETA . . . three minutes.*"

"10-4."

18

"Son-of-a-bitch!" An enraged Chief Barnes slams the radio on the railing along the edge of the upper level of the Soldier Field parking deck.

"Barnes, where are those choppers?" Hizzoner asks.

Captain Bennett peers southward through a pair of binoculars. "I see 'em!"

"Gimme those." Barnes yanks the binoculars from Bennett's hands.

Robert, Sr. peers through a second pair of binoculars and asks, "Where's Detective Lieutenant Mayotte?"

"Where indeed?" Bennett replies. "He's never late. Something must be up." He jogs to his unmarked cruiser and dials Detective Lieutenant Mayotte from the brick-sized car phone mounted to his cruiser's center console.

19

It isn't the ringing of his phone that rouses the detective from sleep. Rather, it's the kneading of Max's paws on his chest—that, and the hungry kitty's reminder *MEOWS*. Mayotte sleepily glances at his Seiko watch and sees it's 9:35 p.m. His entire body springs to attention. A startled Max hisses and leaps off him. "Shit!" He hurriedly puts his shoes on. He notices the light on his answering machine blinking. He presses the PLAYBACK button and takes the leak of a lifetime while the messages unfurl—two apiece from his cousin, his precinct operator, and Captain Bennett.

He finishes urinating and haphazardly pours dry food into Max's bowl with one hand while dialing *Casa de Wilkinson* with the other. Max fusses over the mess as the phone rings. "Hello?" Gail's voice answers on the other end.

"Yes, Robert, please."

"Junior or Senior?"

"Junior."

"I'm sorry, he's not home. He went out with his friends maybe 15 minutes ago. Can I ask who's calling?"

"This is Detective Lieutenant Mayotte. If you see him or if he calls, tell him and his friends . . . tell 'em, 'I messed up, and I'm sorry.' "

"Is everything okay, Detective?"

"Not yet, but it will be." He hangs up without another word, and grabs a foil-sealed packet of Pop-Tarts along with his holster and keys. "Back soon, Max." He hurries out the door and locks it behind him. A ravenous Max has already forgiven his owner for the messy pouring job, and devours his kibble as if there's a race against time.

For Detective Lieutenant Mayotte, there really is.

## 20

The speedometer hovers around 70 as Bob's Trans Am races through North Shore traffic lights and makes its way toward the guarded intersection where Chicago Avenue becomes Clark Street.

"Slow down, Bobby," Lori says.

"Hope they don't give us any shit this time," Bob says as he decelerates.

The street is otherwise deserted, but the same chauvinistic police officers as before—Holowitz, Cherry, and Sanchez—are on duty. Their bookish partner, Brooker, is nowhere to be seen; tired of his colleagues' boorishness, he requested a new posting but didn't give specifics as to why. For one thing,

Brooker knows not to snitch on his fellow deputies. For another, departmental staffing needs during the Blockade and Occupation are of the all-hands-on-deck urgency, and far be it for the career-minded Brooker to want anyone suspended and unavailable for duty.

Bob rolls down his window at the urging of Officer Holowitz. "It's past curfew, kids," the officer condescends. "Road closed."

"We need to get through," Bob insists. "Our names should be on a list."

"The list cuts off at curfew," Holowitz remarks.

Officers Cherry and Sanchez approach. "What's going on?" Cherry asks.

"This kid says they need to get through."

"Officers, when we came through the other day, our names were on a list. Wilkinson . . . Dimkowski . . . Rainsmith? Or maybe just the license plate numbers?"

Cherry turns to his partners. "I remember this car! There's that hot piece of ass again."

Sanchez peers inside and shines his flashlight one-by-one on Bob's, Pete's, and Lori's faces. "She's got two dudes this time!"

Bob is unamused. "There's no time for this! Call Detective Mayotte. He'll clear it up!"

"Easy there, tiger," Cherry replies. He asks his partners what they should do.

"That car legit was on the list when they came through the other day," Sanchez admits. "There were only two people in it last time."

"That's a sweet ride," Holowitz taunts. "I'd hate to have it towed and get it scratched up in impound."

Sanchez gestures with his head in Lori's direction. "Speaking of scratches, I bet she'd scratch us up *real good,* if you know what I mean."

Cherry cranes his neck for another lecherous look. "Yo, you ain't kidding." And with a sigh: "Alright, let 'em through."

"Should we mark the time?" Sanchez asks.

"Brooker would. For whatever that's worth."

"Well in that case, I ain't markin' shit."

"Right." Cherry turns to Bob, Pete, and Lori. "You can go. Don't speed."

"Assholes!" Lori yells out as Bob peels away, but the squealing of his tires drowns out the sound of her cursing. It doesn't drown out the sight, however, of Pete flipping dual birds at the deputies, each of whom will end up in department-mandated sensitivity training at some point in their respective careers.

Cherry turns to his colleagues. "Such a babe."

"You think she's bangin' both of those dudes?" Sanchez asks.

"Totally, she's into hot cars and nerds," Holowitz surmises. "I dated a chick like that once."

"You did not!" Sanchez punches his braggadocious colleague in the arm.

. . .

Bob drives south a few blocks and merges onto Lake Shore Drive, which he takes all the way to the turnoff for CGC-Meigs. The Bonneville driven by Trooper Connors passes them in the opposite direction, but Connors and his partner, Trooper Novak, don't give it a second thought, as Bob is still accelerating when they pass.

"What was up with those cops back there?" Pete asks.

"Bobby and I ran into the same ones when we passed through two days ago," Lori replies.

Bob settles on 80 mph for a cruising speed. "You had an AK in your lap then. I half-thought you were gonna wax 'em."

"Miss Cartwright in P.E. told us freshman year men are nothing but pigs. I'm starting to see what she means." Lori looks at Bob, who drives with the concentration of a Zen master. She takes his hand in hers and rests it on the gearshift. "No offense," she adds.

"None taken," Bob replies. "I know what you mean." Pete, who not so long ago air-humped Lori at Vinnie's Arcade Alley, says nothing.

21

Two police choppers arrive on the scene. They circle overhead and provide air support while the remaining SWAT boat attempts to tie down. Two of the three rooftop Loyalists shoot at the choppers. One of them takes out the lights on the forward chopper. Panic crackles over the radio. "Air support, you have permission to engage," Chief Barnes radios. The forward bird, its snipers now without the benefit of searchlight assist, retreats momentarily to get out of the line of fire. The second chopper's sniper team fires on the CGC rooftop and takes out one of the soldiers almost immediately. The second Loyalist returns fire, but the skilled pilot easily evades the weapons fire. The third Loyalist meanwhile, fires on the approaching SWAT boat, which slows as it nears 12$^{th}$ Street Beach.

Morgan and the nine SWAT officers under his command take cover, and three of them blindly return fire in the general direction of the rooftop. The second chopper fires at the rooftop soldier. From the vantage point of the parking deck staging area, the soldier appears to be hit, and falls backward to what Barnes, Bennett and the others assume—erroneously—is his death. More on that later.

The remaining rooftop Loyalist returns fire at the second chopper. The bird's tail rotor is hit, and the chopper spins out of control. One of the snipers falls from the open hatch and into the drink. "Oh, this is not good," Mayor Washington remarks.

Cries of *"Mayday!"* crackle from the radio. The first chopper returns from its initial retreat and takes out the remaining soldier. It makes haste to avoid getting struck by the second, crashing chopper. Captain Bennett watches through the binoculars as two passengers jump from the chopper a few seconds too late. It crashes into the rocks comprising the shoreline due south of 12th Street Beach. It explodes, and the fireball consumes its fleeing passengers as well.

"Mother of God," Hizzoner says.

"Marshall, where the hell's your detective?!" Barnes asks.

As if on cue, a squeal of tires is heard in the distance. "Maybe that's him," Bennett remarks.

## 22

"Turn left here!" Pete cries out. Bob makes a hard left turn onto the access road that passes between the Field Museum and Soldier Field on its way to Northerly Island.

*BOOM!* The police chopper explodes into a ball of flame in the distance. Lori screams.

"Oh, God!" Bob cries out. He drives faster. The Trans Am turns left onto the connecting thoroughfare at such a high rate of speed its two right wheels lose contact with the asphalt.

"I'm gonna be sick!" Pete cries out. He grabs the *oh, shit* handle for dear life. Bob takes the next right at the same clip, and the tires squeal. "Oh, stop it already!"

Bob slows down as they pass Burnham Harbor to their right via the causeway. He makes a final right turn onto the unnamed access road leading to the rear of CGC-Meigs. He pulls to a halt just past the bulbous outcropping that he recognizes from his last visit as the time chamber. He gets out and makes note of an angled flaw in the asphalt, as if the contractors paving the access road simply unloaded the surplus of hot asphalt over a pile of crushed gravel, then had the courtesy of grating it to a 45-degree slope to keep delivery drivers from backing into the fence beyond. What an odd bit of roadwork!

"Careful Bobby," Lori cautions. "We don't wanna attract the wrong kind of attention."

"I think the helicopter did that already," Bob replies.

"Look, there they are!" Pete points toward the water. The SWAT boat has tied down. Its officers deboard and splash through water's edge onto the beach.

"Put your arms up so they don't think we're a threat." Bob raises his arms as if in surrender, and his friends do the same.

Captain Morgan approaches. He shines his Maglite on our heroes as his colleagues target their chests with red laser sights. "Don't move!" he orders. "State your names!"

"Uh, I'm Bob, and this is Pete and Lori. Did Detective Mayotte not tell you about us?"

"Negative. We haven't heard from him."

"W-w-we were hoping he was with you."

"Negative. This area's restricted. What's your objective?"

"We have some of their technology to destroy."

"Sorry, no civilians."

"Hey, wait a minute—" Pete begins.

"Officers, we're not here to steal your thunder," Bob explains. "We're here to ensure any future tech, or whatever it's called, is melted down when you blow the place up."

"I'm calling this in. Stand by." Morgan directs Ramirez and Warshawski to watch the roof for a possible ambush, then speaks into his radio. "Base, we've got three civilians here who arrived unescorted. Please advise, over."

"*This is Barnes. Can you identify the civilians?*"

"What are your full names?" Morgan asks, and repeats the names as he receives them.

Indecipherable chatter over the radio, and then Robert, Sr.'s voice crackles: *"This is Senator Robert Wilkinson. Put my son on the line."*

Morgan hands the radio to Bob. "Hi dad," Bob says. "Detective Mayotte never called. And since you forget the pads and stuff, we had to come and see this through. Sorry."

*"I know, Robert. And I suppose I'm not surprised. But I want you out of there."*

"No can do, dad. I've seen too much to sit this out."

The radio crackles again, but several seconds elapse before Robert, Sr. replies. Finally: *"Your stepmother will wring my neck if she finds out. Stay safe. Stay in your car and out of sight until you get the signal from SWAT that any threats have been neutralized. Do you understand?"*

"I understand. Where's Detective Mayotte? He was supposed to call at 8:45 with an update." Commander Morgan makes a revolving motion with his hand for Bob to wrap it up.

*"We've had trouble reaching him."*

"You'll check on him, won't you?"

*"That's not top priority, but we'll follow up when this is over. Now please hand the radio back to the team leader."*

"Okay."

Morgan takes over the transmission. "This is Commander Morgan. We've landed; there are ten of us plus your son and his friends. Awaiting your instructions."

*"We're blind to the action on your side, Commander. It's your move, whenever you see the advantage."*

"Yessir. Initiating radio silence."

*"Godspeed, Commander. Keep my boy out of harm's way."*

"10-4." Morgan no sooner switches off his radio and clips it to his belt when a spray of AK rounds startles everyone on the ground. The shooter: the surviving rooftop Loyalist, wounded but apparently still in the fight.

"Get down!" Morgan yells. He turns to Bob, Pete, and Lori. "You three, behind me and lie low!"

Our teen heroes duck beneath an overhanging eave; the Trans Am is too far to make a run for without getting hit. Morgan motions for Ramirez, Warshawski, and the others to return fire, and for Hodgson to secure a grenade to the building's (new) rear door. There is no external handle, only a metal plate where the handle should be. Warshawski makes quick work of the rooftop soldier—or so she thinks. Hodgson uses medical tape from the triage kit to secure the grenade to the plate on the door. With everyone amply warned, he pulls the pin. The grenade explodes after five seconds and blows the metal door open. It hangs by a single hinge.

. . .

Miles has been expecting this and has no need to summon Wesley's goons via the red panic button this time. They are already here—eight instead of the usual four. "Battle stations," he announces.

"Stay down, sir," one of the goons, a time-traveling crack shot named Urquhart who grew up in the same neighborhood on Mars as Lucien Reynolds, orders. Miles nods and flees for the mainframe room. He motions for Balthazar to follow suit, but the tech trainee is too slow, and his hesitation costs him his life.

. . .

A smoke bomb is thrown through the back door to disorient those inside. "Night vision," Morgan orders, and motions the others inside. He, Bob, Pete, and Lori bring up the rear. "Stay down," he says.

"You got it," Pete replies, coughing. "I can't see shit anyhow."

A Loyalist goon fires into the smoke—an AK, not a plasma rifle. Morgan's men target the weapons burst and return fire. The goon flails, firing wildly as he goes down. A dozen stray rounds embed themselves in Balthazar's chest on their way to the workstation behind him. Sparks fly.

"I'm hit!" SWAT Officer Akinmade cries out.

"Everyone down!" Morgan yells.

"Think my vest took the brunt of it," Akinmade adds.

"Sir!" Bob yells over the noise.

"What is it, kid?" Morgan replies.

"Some of those weapons fire concentrated energy. They'll vaporize anything they hit."

"Good intel. Now stay down!" Morgan addresses his team. "You hear that, Bravo Team? Whatever you do, don't get shot!"

"Aww, man!" the cowardly Hodgson cries out. As if on cue, dual plasma bursts fire in their direction. The first burst hits the wall behind them and the second burst hits SWAT Officer Christensen below the knee. He falls to the ground with a pained shriek, *sans* half a limb.

"Engage!" Morgan orders. The firefight lasts for several minutes. The Loyalists, mindful of damaging the time chamber, are especially precise in where they fire. The SWAT officers are reactive rather than proactive, and fire a smelting plant's worth of rounds. Akinmade is all but useless, but the other wounded officer acquits himself valiantly before falling.

After Christensen, Cruz, and Burke fall, Hodgson fires blindly. "This is crazy," he cries out. "Game over, man. Game over!"

"You secure that shit, Hodgson!" Morgan replies without looking back.

"Sir, Hodgson's not wrong," Ramirez says from his kneeling position next to the team commander. "This ain't exactly the walk in the park Barnes said it would be."

"I'm five-by-five, Ramirez, so don't lose faith. There's a lotta weird shit in here, so conserve ammo until you've got a clean shot." With that, Morgan bags an AK-wielding goon.

Pete turns to Bob and Lori. "This is messed up."

"Where's the detective?" Lori asks.

23

The well-rested detective races along Lake Shore Drive. He didn't bother to affix his Kojak light when setting out, and as he exits Lake Shore Drive for Northerly Island and CGC-Meigs, in his haste he fails to notice the homeless woman pushing a shopping cart full of cans through the intersection. And why shouldn't she? She has the WALK sign, after all.

"Shit!" Mayotte says at the last minute. He swerves to avoid hitting her and overcorrects; his car flips over and crashes into the traffic light on the other side. He opens his door from the inside and crawls out. His nose is bloodied and broken. He stands up with considerable effort and brushes broken glass from his hair. The woman continues to push her cart in the opposite direction, clueless about what's been happening in the city. Mayotte quashes the urge to call her a "dumb broad" or something similarly sexist, and limps, desperate, toward the staging area.

24

"Forget him," Bob replies to Lori's inquiry regarding the detective's whereabouts. "We need a weapon. I'll be right back."

"Be careful!" Lori calls after Bob as he scatters across the room during a lull in weapons fire. He exits via the grenade-warped rear door, passing the rock that doubles as a doorstop during Miles's smoke breaks. He removes the plasma rifle from the trunk of his prized Trans Am.

On his way back, he once again notices the outside of the time chamber bulging from the superstructure like a pregnant belly. He also notices a pair of enormous cooling fans at the base, and a generator of sorts between them. The generator is housed inside a lockbox not much different from what you might find on the side of your house to feed an internet service provider's drop cable from the pedestal to the house itself. A lightbulb illuminates in his mind. For all the diligence done by Wesley's team, they neglected to shore up security behind their own building.

Then again . . . Bob is about to step back inside when he is accosted by the seemingly indestructible rooftop Loyalist, who managed to climb down the ladder to ground level despite the bullet wounds in his leg and shoulder. The enemy soldier, whose tag reads HOLSTON, is *sans* firearm; his AK-47 ran out of ammo when he shot at the approaching SWAT team earlier. He compensates by slashing Bob's arm with a tactical knife.

"Ow!" Bob drops his plasma rifle and ducks the second slash. He lunges for Holston's legs and the man falls onto his back. Holston grunts as Bob inadvertently squeezes the gunshot wound in his thigh while pulling his legs out from under him. Bob leaps on top of him and punches him in the face. Holston slices Bob's cheek and Bob elbows him in the chest. While his elbow is planted, Bob propels his arm outward to knock the knife from Holston's hand. It scatters to the ground, out of either person's reach. Bob rolls onto his side toward the rock/doorstop. As Holston reaches for his knife during these two vital seconds, Bob punches him again, knocking him flat on his back. Bob lifts the rock with both hands and brings it down over Holston's face, crushing his skull with a gruesome SPLOOT sound.

Bob picks up the rock with both hands for a proactive second strike, but can only lift it halfway before dropping it. No matter; Holston's face resembles cherry cobbler. Bob wonders why he feels a sudden heaviness in his chest. He looks down to find the tactical knife buried to the hilt in his sternum. Holston's dead hand is clenched tight around the grip. "Uh-oh," Bob says, simply, and needs both hands to pry the man's hand from the knife.

25

Miles sneaks out the front door to flee for his life at precisely the same moment Bob exits the rear door to fetch the plasma rifle. His cowardice escapes everyone's notice during the fire-fight. Although his car, a 1984 Dodge Colt, is parked in the complex's underground garage, sandwiched between two black vans, Miles reasons that going after it isn't worth the risk. Instead, he runs.

He stops along the causeway, halfway to Lake Shore Drive, to catch his breath. With spots dancing before his eyes and his nerves in need of a smoke, he fails to notice Detective Lieutenant Mayotte limping determinedly toward CGC-Meigs. Miles lights a cigarette and takes the last puff of his young life. The detective sees Miles in his lab coat and immediately draws his weapon. "Hold it right there!" he orders. Weapon raised, he half-jogs, half-limps the remaining distance.

Miles exhales and shakes his head to clear his vision. He raises his hands as if in surrender. At the last possible second, he kicks the detective in the knee and takes off running. Mayotte drops to one leg in a howl of pain. "Freeze!" he yells. Miles fails to comply. Mayotte pulls the trigger and hits the bespectacled technician in the back. Miles stumbles to the guardrail and falls over the side, splashing into Lake Michigan. His spinal cord severed from Mayotte's crack shot, he quickly drowns, not far from where Vinnie met a similar fate.

Mayotte prefers a suspect in custody over another dead body. He peers into the water but sees no sign of Miles.

"Dammit!" He limps onward to the staging point, more gingerly than before, and hopes this isn't his last night as a police detective.

## 26

Removing the knife from his sternum is supremely unpleasant, and carries with it the risk of bleeding out. Bob scoots back, applies pressure to his sternum with his left hand, and takes the biggest breath he can manage. His teeth chatter and his legs jerk as he slowly pulls out the knife with his right hand. He tosses the knife aside and lifts his shirt to check the damage. It isn't pretty. The wound contracts and expands with each breath he takes, and he knows he doesn't have much time. He decides to help Pete, Lori, and the remaining SWAT officers inside . . . even if it's the last thing he does. He grabs the plasma weapon and re-enters the building unseen. Once inside, he rests against the wall to catch his breath and await the moment he can deliver at least one kill shot.

. . .

The shootout continues ever on. Burke, Medellín, and Hodgson have fallen. Morgan shows Lori how to hold and unsafety the plasma rifle while taking cover behind a protected wall. "Now, this weapon is lighter than my AK so it won't recoil as much, but it still gave him some kickback when he used it." Morgan refers to a nameless, fallen Loyalist soldier whose anti-matter plasma rifle scattered within Lori's reach. "Be prepared for that and expect a bruised shoulder in the morning. Hold it firm like so, and squeeze the trigger continuously for a steady stream."

"Got it," Lori says. Her hesitant nod suggests otherwise.

"You sure? Just point, keep the sight level with your chin, and shoot."

With a more assured nod: "I can do that."

"I'm right here. And we're still in this." He puts one hand on her shoulder, then turns to Pete. "How 'bout you?"

Pete peeks out from behind the wall to return fire. He wields an AK, not a plasma rifle. He fires a series of rounds, then ducks back behind the wall. "I'm good." He gives a thumb's up. "Got one of 'em in the leg, I think. He went down like he slipped on a banana peel."

"Good shooting. Be sure to finish the job." He removes a magazine from his bag and slides it down the floor to Pete. "Sending you a mag. It's on your right at four o'clock. You're probably running low."

"Yeah," Pete replies after returning another burst of fire, "I'm out now."

"We'll cover you. Change out!"

Pete nods. He and Morgan swap positions and Lori moves closer to the hot zone. Morgan motions for Warshawski to lob a grenade at the goons, and Warshawski complies. She is shot and killed whilst lobbing the grenade, so the toss goes wild and its detonation takes out a stand-alone Loyalist goon instead of the main grouping of four. "Shit!" Morgan says. He turns to Lori. "Okay, we need you now."

She nods in confirmation. Her continued trigger action sends the first flew plasma blasts over the heads of the Loyalist goons, but she corrects course and rips a hole in the stomach of a soldier from the remaining group. His colleagues return fire and she screams her retreat behind the wall. Once safe, she turns and notices Bob crawling toward her. He leaves a bloody route map in his wake. "Bobby!" she cries out. He puts a finger to his lip in a "hush" motion.

"Stay down, Lori!" Pete yells without looking in her direction. He grabs the fallen Burke's weapon and joins Morgan and the other remaining SWAT officer on the front lines, Ramirez. "Let's finish these assholes!"

"Watch for the recoil and wait for Ramirez," Morgan advises. He motions for Ramirez to lay suppressing, low-angle fire toward the soldiers' feet. Ramirez complies and knocks two of the three remaining goons off their feet. Pete jumps up and fires at the third, who is hit in the throat and dies instantly. Ramirez raises his weapon to fire at the remaining, wounded pair, who regroup from their downed position. Ramirez dry fires.

"I'm out!" he exclaims. Pete and Morgan return fire at the soldiers and finish them off. Except for the steady roar of the time chamber's cooling fan, the cacophony has stopped.

Bob crawls toward them. His slow movement catches Pete's eye. "Bob!" he cries out. Morgan turns around at the sound of Pete's voice, and this act proves fatal. One of the goons, down but apparently not out, fires a few rounds. They rip through the back of Morgan's vest, just above the Kevlar. Like García and Johnny on Mars, he dies without knowing what hit him.

Pete and Ramirez whirl around, but it's Bob who takes decisive action. While lying on his stomach, Bob fires into the fallen grouping of Loyalists until his plasma rifle clicks, depleted. The cooling fan shuts down and now, at last, the room is silent.

All eyes are on Bob. The front of his shirt is soaked through with blood, sweat, and dirt, and he has seen better days. Blood seeps from a gash in his arm. A flap of skin hangs from his cheek, cut through almost to the bone. Lori drops her weapon and crawls to Bob's side.

"Dude," Pete says, "you look like shit."

"Like Admiral Ackbar?" Bob's speech is strained but still clear.

"Worse." Pete can't quite manage to smile.

"It's over," Ramirez says, weapon at his side.

"No," Bob shakes his head and struggles to sit up.

"We've gotta destroy the building," Lori says.

"Yep." Bob nods.

Pete turns to Ramirez. "Where's the stuff to blow this place up?"

"Lemme check Morgan's stash." Ramirez swaps out his magazine as a first course of action, then rifles through the contents of Morgan's tactical bag. He retrieves the C-4. "Just five bricks," he says. "And this." He tosses an ACE bandage to Pete, who catches it one-handed.

"Not enough C-4?" Bob asks. Ramirez shakes his head.

"Uh, what if we spread it all around?" Pete asks.

Bob nods. "A-anywhere they have tech," he suggests. "Here, of course . . ."

"The weapons depot," Ramirez adds.

"And the mainframe room," Pete confirms.

"Guys, shouldn't we get him to a hospital first?" Lori asks.

Bob, who takes the bandage from Pete and unfurls it with shaky hands, shakes his head. "There's no time."

"That's not for you to say!" Lori retorts.

Bob lifts his shirt to reveal a grotesque wound, made worse by him crawling across the room. "Oh Bobby!" Lori wails.

"Wrap that around his torso, tight as you can," Ramirez says. "We'll need to dress the wound to prevent infection, but this'll buy us some time."

Lori takes over wrapping the wound. "I hope that's not too tight," she says.

Bob shakes his head and forces a pained smile. "I have an idea. B-but I'll need someone to help me to my car."

"Your car? What are you—"

"H-hear me out. L-let's put a brick right there"—he points to the base of the time chamber—"and o-one there"—he points to Balthazar's workstation, which continues to belch sparks—"a-and another down the corridor . . ."

"Don't forget the mainframe room," Pete points out.

Bob nods. "Yes. P-put one there, then the last one up front. I-if you see any plasma weapons, m-make sure you put 'em by the C-4. Don't leave a-anything the Feds can take outta here."

"Let me radio this in," Ramirez says.

"No!" Bob says. The forcefulness of his voice sends a bolt of pain up and down his spine. "They can never know what's here. Th-they'll take it."

Ramirez considers this. Thought a competent officer, he isn't ready to be in charge. He still sees himself as a grunt, albeit one whose C.O. was killed and who is now taking orders from a bunch of teenagers. He always figured Warshawski would be the next officer among them to get her own command.

Pete turns to the SWAT officer. "Bob's right. You know he's right."

Ramirez nods. " 'K. I'll take care of the C-4, you guys corral the weapons. Here, take this." He tosses Pete a radio from Morgan's tactical bag.

Pete gives the orders this time. "We'll meet out back. Everyone makes it out of here." He turns to Ramirez, then to Lori, and then to Bob. "*Everyone.*"

No one moves, so Pete claps his hands. "Let's go!" Lori and Ramirez jump. With that, Ramirez runs toward the mainframe room, C-4 bricks in his arms. Pete turns to his friend. "Roberto, let's grab the stuff from your trunk. Can you stand?"

Bob shakes his head, not in defiance but in clarification. "It's not enough."

"What's not enough?"

"The C-4. W-we need something more, something w-with fuel a-and real impact to set it off."

Lori runs a comforting hand through Bob's hair. "What are we gonna do?" she asks.

Pete looks on in confusion until Bob sets the stage. "R-remember Mr. Hunt's lectures about inertia? Th-the initial i-mpact—"

Pete takes over. "The initial impact action can lead to a greater reaction depending on environmental factors."

"Like velocity," Bob says. He motions toward the cooling fan.

27

Robert, Sr., Mayor Washington, Deputy Mayor Orr, Chief Barnes, and Captain Bennett stare through binoculars from their collective post atop the parking deck.

"What's going on down there, Senator?" the mayor asks. "I've neither seen nor heard *bupkes* since that chopper went down."

"Harry, let's send in another SWAT team," Chief Barnes suggests. "My men'll make short work of whatever's going on."

"There's nothing left of the damn SWAT teams you *already* sent in!"

"You don't know that!"

"Easy fellas, let give our men on the ground more time and see what they come up with," Robert, Sr. says. "No one's fled the scene. Besides, my boy's down there!"

"I say five more minutes, tops," Chief Barnes remarks.

28

The rear door swings open and Pete emerges, radio clipped to his belt. Lori and Bob follow, arms around each other's shoulders for support as they stumble to his car. "Need a hand?" Pete asks.

"I think we're good."

"Go help the SWAT guy," Bob adds.

"So we're doing this, then?" Pete half-asks, half-states.

Matter-of-factly: "Someone has to."

"We're still meeting here when we're done inside, right?"

"I-I'm not dead yet."

"Don't you say that. Don't you goddamn say that." Pete looks away, ashamed, as his eyes well up with unexpected tears.

Steadfast, Bob replies, "I'll see you soon."

Pete nods, head turned, and hands the radio to Lori. He retreats inside to relocate any stray porta-pads and plasma weapons as close to the C-4 bricks as possible. Lori turns to Bob. "C'mon Bobby." They make their way to his car. She steadies him as she opens the car door. "Careful getting in."

Bob gets behind the driver's seat and winces as his stomach muscles contract. He goes for his seatbelt but is in too much pain to manage the reach-around. Lori hands him the seatbelt. "Thanks," he says. "W-wouldn't want my foot to s-slip as-as-as I floor it."

"No. We wouldn't want that." Lori fights back tears as the belt clicks into place. "All set?" she asks. She hopes he'll say 'no,' and she can't help but wonder if this is all a bad dream.

Instead, he nods. She closes his door and jogs around to the other side. She gets in and stows the radio inside the glove compartment. "Rain-Rain." Bob's words are soft and tender.

Lori shakes her head. "I'm not ready to say goodbye. Please tell me there's another way."

Bob looks down at his ACE bandage, which has soaked through and turned a gangrenous pink. "I'm done for."

"You're not, sweetie, you're not. We can get you to a hospital, there's still time!"

Bob puts his right hand over her mouth just as she did that day at Lover's Leap. "Shhh," he whispers. She nods and ceases talking.

Slowly and romantically, he moves his hand to her neck, to her left shoulder, and down her left arm. Over the bump of her ulna bone as it ends at her wrist. Over her knuckles and the tops of her fingers. Finally, he takes her hand in his. He brings her hand to his lips and kisses both sides, softly and tenderly.

He rests her hand on the center console and looks her in the eye. "I'm glad we both crashed prom."

"Me too." She offers up her best, teary-eyed smile.

They hear a noise and look up to see Pete and Ramirez exit the building. Pete jogs to the car, Ramirez at his heels, toting his automatic weapon and the now-empty tactical bag.

"W-we good?" Bob asks.

"We good," Pete answers. "C-4 in the time chamber, one by the workstations, another one in the front in what looks like a chem lab, one in a closet filled with weapons, and the fifth in the computer room."

"I shot out the mainframe for added measure," Ramirez adds. "The microchips inside it should help fuel the flames. When you hit the generator unit, it should implode the transporter, set off the first charge, and then BOOM! The others go off like dynamite. That's the beauty of *plastique.*"

"Perfect." Bob coughs.

"It's a solid plan," Ramirez says. He withdraws a billfold. "Also, we found a body in one of the holding cells. I had to shoot the lock off the door. I.D. of the departed says 'WESLEY ARENDT.' Is that who we were after?"

Bob and Lori nod.

"Best I can tell, he died of natural causes. Heart attack, maybe?"

"Too many Journeys through the time chamber," Pete surmises. "I only took one round-trip and felt nauseous for hours afterwards in each direction."

"S-serves him right." Bob says. He coughs again.

Ramirez's expression grows dour. "Before you go through with this, know we can still get you to a hospital. I admire your heroism, but I'm sure there's another way. We'll have to move fast, though. You've lost a lot of blood."

Bob shakes his head. "L-let's see this through. I-I hope those fans kick in soon."

"As you wish, then. Be sure to go out at least 50 yards so you can get good acceleration and hit it with maximum impact."

Bob nods. "I've got this."

Ramirez closes the remaining distance to the car door and extends a hand. "It's Bob, right?" Bob nods, weaker this time. "I'm Oscar. It was an honor to know you, Bob." They shake hands and Ramirez retreats into the background. This is not his moment.

Pete approaches the window. "This is kind of exciting, Roberto. I've always wanted to see how fast this baby can go."

"Me too," Bob says with a strained smile.

Pete imitates Doc Brown from *Back to the Future,* possibly the only movie he and Bob like more than *Star Wars:* "Eighty-eight miles per hour!" Bob laughs, but it quickly turns into a coughing fit. "Sorry," Pete adds, knowing the coughing spell was a byproduct of his wisecrack.

Bob is fading fast, and doesn't have much to say to his life-long friend. Or maybe he has lots to say, but neither the time nor the strength to say it.

"I love you, man," Pete says. His lip quivers. He blows the usual lock of hair from his eye as Lori watches from the passenger seat. She wants more alone time with her man, but knows he and Pete need a moment as well.

Bob steels himself. "Hey, tell Gail a-and my d-dad that—"

"I'll tell 'em you were very brave."

Bob gives a thumb's up with one shaky hand. "S-sounds good."

The time chamber's external cooling fans kick on. Everyone jumps.

"Time to go," Pete says. He retreats to where Ramirez waits.

Bob turns to Lori. Despite her tears, she tries to think only of the few happy times she and Bob spent together. "Bobby, that time in the motel when we shared the bed after the hot tub . . . were you not wearing any pants?"

"You're a-asking me this *now?*" he remarks. Lori nods, and Bob shakes his head in response. "I c-couldn't believe it when you e-entered the room and just c-crawled into bed."

"You were a perfect gentleman." Then, after a pause: "I'll tell your dad and stepmom you didn't suffer."

"It's time!" Ramirez yells from a few yards away.

Lori throws an angry nod his way. She brushes her hair from her eyes and gazes longingly at the young man dying beside her. "Your stepmom's real nice. I'm sure she'd have loved to see the great guy you *totally* would've grown up to become . . . as would I."

"Don't cry, Rain-Rain."

"I'm trying not to, it's just . . . before you go, tell me you love me."

"All my life."

"Oh, Bobby." She leans over the console, careful not to touch his chest, his cheek, or his arm. She gives him a kiss on the other cheek, a peck on the lips, and one final, probing kiss. She knows the moment can't last forever, and pulls back. She gets out of the car and gives him one last look. She'll spend the next three months regretting her final word to him, even though it was simple and efficient: "Bye." She runs off to join the others.

"C'mon, let's beat feet," Ramirez says. He jogs toward the causeway and away from the facility itself. Pete and Lori hold hands as they run, but only to support each other from collapsing out of grief and exhaustion.

Bob starts the engine, shifts into gear, and does a U-turn. He passes his friends without a honk or wave. He reaches the end of the roadway. Here, the asphalt is too narrow to make another U-turn. Instead, he shifts into Reverse to turn himself around, then shifts into Park. He looks down at his chest. The ACE bandage, which has come untucked, resembles a putrid, pink sponge. He lowers his visor and lifts the mirror. The left side of his face is a mess. Lori couldn't do much to fix it, and it wouldn't have mattered anyway. *How am I still alive?* he wonders. With all the strength he can muster and all the pain he can withstand, Bob reaches over to the glove compartment and removes the radio. It feels like a ton of bricks. "Do something for me, and do it big," he says, quoting the late Dr. Kirchner.

<h1 style="text-align:center">29</h1>

"Hey, there's some movement," Chief Barnes says. He raises the binoculars for a closer look.

"Who is it?" Mayor Washington asks.

"That's Robert's car!" Bob's father exclaims.

"Looks like one of our SWAT guys and a couple kids," the chief says. "That your boy behind the wheel?"

"That's Robert, alright."

"Why isn't he giving them a ride?"

"I don't know."

"Where are the other SWAT guys?" the deputy mayor asks.

"Where's the all clear?" the mayor adds.

"I don't know, dammit!" Robert, Sr. snaps.

With that, his radio crackles. "*Dad?*" Bob's voice, sounding weak.

Robert, Sr. scrambles for the radio before his colleagues can grab it. "Robert! You sound terrible. What's going on down there?"

"*W-we're good here. The place is secure. Thought you'd wanna know Wesley's dead.*"

"How?"

"*Not our doing. H-he was already dead when we got here.*"

"That's interesting news. Now get outta there so our men can secure the area."

"*I-it's already taken care of. Sending my friends o-o-out of harm's way. Just o-one more thing to do.*"

"We'll pick 'em up." Robert, Sr. motions to Chief Barnes, who radios for a cruiser to collect Pete, Lori, and Ramirez.

"Ask him where the others are," the mayor says.

"Robert, where are the others? We sent two whole units."

*"Th-there were … c-complications. B-but it's a-a-a-alright, dad. J-just one last thing."*

"Robert? Son? You're breaking up! Can you hear me?!"

Some silence, then one final response, the last words Robert, Sr. will ever his son utter: *"I-it's alright. I'm going home."*


Radio silence.


30


Bob switches off the radio. "I love you dad," he whispers. His strength depleted, he lets the radio fall to the floorboards and takes the deepest breath he can muster. He shifts into Drive, places both hands on the wheel, and puts the pedal to the metal. The tires squeal and the car lurches forward, going from 0 to 60 in less than 15 seconds.


31


Detective Lieutenant Mayotte emerges from the Waldron Parking Deck elevator. He limps to the staging area to the sound of all-out confusion. His heart sinks as he deduces things did not go according to plan. *How much of this is on me?* he wonders.

"What the hell's he doing?" he hears Chief Barnes ponder.

"Senator?" he hears Mayor Washington remark.

"Sir?" he hears Deputy Mayor Orr ask, dumbfounded.

*"ROBERT!"* he hears Bob's dad yell into the radio. He watches him fumble and almost drop it. "Robert, is everything alright?! Can you hear me?!"

Radio silence.

32

Pete, Lori, and Ramirez stand back as Bob races past them, his face locked in an intense stare. "Look at him go," Pete marvels.

The needle hovers at 78 when Bob turns into the cement ramp. His Trans Am climbs the concrete hill, angling and achieving lift off, its right and then left tires becoming airborne as the angle and velocity invert the car and propel it upside down into the generator at just shy of 80 miles per hour. Blood from the knife wound on Bob's cheek fills his eyes as the car makes contact, so he doesn't actually witness his own death.

The car, cooling fans, and generator explode as a single fireball, with the bulbous time chamber going next. It sets off the first square of C-4 . . . then the second . . . and so on.

33

"*ROBERT!*" Senator Wilkinson bellows into the radio. "*SON!*"

Chief Barnes immediately radios for EMS and fire as Detective Lieutenant Mayotte takes his tardy place beside a furious Captain Bennett.

"What the hell just happened?!" Mayor Washington asks. His stunned deputy mayor can only shrug.

"I don't know," a shaken Senator Wilkinson replies as the fireballs multiply. He yells into the radio again. "Robert! Do you read me?! Say something!"

Radio silence.

34

Pete, Lori, and Ramirez are blown off their feet by the blast, their faces blackened with soot. Ramirez is first to get back on his feet. He offers his hand to the others. "Are you okay?"

Pete takes Ramirez's hand and staggers to his feet. "I'll live," he says. "You hurt, Lor?"

Lori shakes her head and crumples into a ball of tears. Pete's eyes water from the heat and from the emotion of the evening. He turns to watch the blaze and jumps when another, smaller explosion goes off from within the wreckage. "Burn baby burn."

A procession of cruisers at least five deep races down the access road to their aid. The first cruiser brakes within a few feet of our heroes, and its driver, a burly man whose name-plate reads SGT. WILCOX, steps out and gazes upon the blaze. "Holy shit. What happened here?"

"What needed to happen," Ramirez replies. He looks at Pete, who gives the subtlest of nods. There will be questions. And more questions. And still more questions. Many answers will be given. Some answers will be misinterpreted. Other answers will be ignored.

But not tonight.

# Epilogue

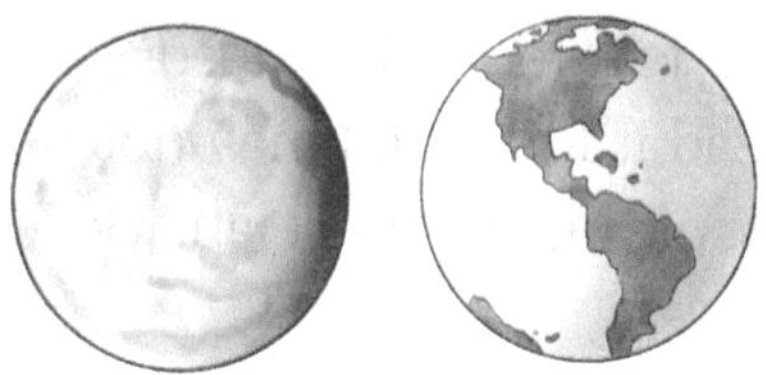

1

Picture it, if you will: As hard as things can be some 228 million kilometers (142 million miles) from the sun, life on Mars goes on. It's ironic that terraforming the Red Planet is the only option to ensure humankind's continued survival. With Earth's ice caps having melted long ago and the moon not having a viable gravity system, Mars—New Earth—has to work . . . it simply *must.*

The civil war over forced labor was a disgusting affair that depleted an already-scarce populace. It's over now; the peace treaty about to be signed will usher in a new age. McCarthy asked Susie to be the planet's new chancellor, but she turned him down. "I'm a fighter, not a politician," she explained, and her query as to why the Old Man himself didn't want the job isn't answered until the formal treaty ceremony, where she at least humors McCarthy by agreeing to sign the treaty document as the event's official witness.

"I'm an old man, Miss Walker," McCarthy says as they walk, McCarthy in front and a disarmed Sauron X following them, reprogrammed not to kill but to surveil. "I'll take the position on an interim basis since no one else wants it, including yourself. My only ask, besides begging you to reconsider, is that you head up the search for a successor. This settlement of ours faces an uncertain future, and it needs someone young and incorruptible to lead it forward. I may not be easily corrupted, but I'm nearly as old as Methuselah. Governing is a young person's game."

"I will be honored to lead the search, sir," Susie says. She already has someone in mind but tells herself she'll try to vet all candidates as objectively as possible, rather than just assume Leonard Debussy is the best person to succeed the Old Man.

They reach the treaty stage and he motions for them to stop. "To tell you the truth, I'm glad you turned down the top job."

"Sir?" she asks, confused.

"You've been an irreplaceable asset to our cause. And we won! Sure, in many ways the hard work hasn't even begun, but we're just three signatures away from real change. Use this victory as a personal motivator—not for you to continue as strategist or fighter or mess cook, but for you to live your life. Find someone. Settle down. Rest. Be happy. I haven't seen you smile in a beater's age."

Susie nods, pensive, and they climb the risers to the stage. Another Sauron patrols from the opposite side of the stage, and two soldiers stand guard. McCarthy turns to her. "Here we go." He takes a seat at the table, Susie on his left and a dethroned Ross on his right.

The treaty stage is set up in the main auditorium of the Ronald Reagan Audience Hall, where attendees are protected from the blustery elements outside. A capacity crowd fills every seat and then some, but aside from a few ne'er-do-wells who failed their pre-admission pat downs, no one is refused entry.

The speechifying before the actual signing is not as nauseating as you may have expected—it's a recap of the timeline of key events in Mars history from colonization through the present, with the briefest acknowledgment of Earth-based research circa "the late 20th Earth Prime-century" that made settlement possible. Ross, no longer Chancellor Ross but now citizen Ross, shakes hands with McCarthy and Susie before the signing, and appears visibly pained to do so. He is signing his death warrant, after all, and knows he has just minutes left to live. McCarthy signs his name near the bottom of the treaty document over a signature line on the left side of the page. After a few seconds of hesitation, Ross does the same, scrawling his name over the right-side signature line. Susie signs below theirs with her remaining hand over the witness signature line on the bottom-center of the page. They stand up, shake hands again, and that's that. The crowd roars its approval. Soldiers take Ross into custody and cuff his hands behind him while futuristic gallows are rolled forward. The soldiers lead Ross to the gallows and up five steps to the platform and the hangman's noose. They place a black sack over Ross's head and tie his feet with rope as he faces the crowd, which quickly grows silent—there is nary a cheer nor a boo to be heard.

McCarthy has one more bit of nasty business to attend to. He grabs a copy of the New Earth Constitution, pages laminated and tear-proof, from the table. He takes two steps forward. "Almost over," he whispers to Susie as one of the soldiers affixes a microphone to the breast of his jacket. The two men nod—the execution is ready to proceed.

The Old Man flips to the correct page of the document and reads the conviction: "As interim chancellor of New Earth, I, Atwood J. McCarthy, bring the condemned, former Chancellor Dorian H. Ross, to the gallows on day 12,319 on the planetary calendar. On the charge of crimes against humanity and at your own confession of guilt, I order you, in accordance with New Earth bylaws, to a sentence of death by hanging, to be carried out forthwith for all to see. Do you understand this charge and this sentence, former Chancellor Ross?"

"I understand," a defanged Ross says from inside the sack.

"Do you have any last words, former Chancellor Ross?"

"I am sorry for what I've done." The apology sounds genuine, but it's too late.

"With that, we close the book on this dark chapter, and dare that the fates may have mercy upon your soul." Chancellor McCarthy nods at the first gallows soldier. The soldier uses a handheld remote to open a trap door on the platform, one meter below Ross's feet. The soldier nods back at McCarthy. The Old Man, in turn, nods at the second soldier, whose right arm is outstretched on the drop lever.

The audience remains silent. People have been through a lot, yet miraculously, no one salivates at the sight of their disgraced former chancellor with his head in a noose. Those in attendance feel as if they *must* be here, to see through to conclusion something brutal, yet necessary. You can hear a pin drop . . . or a rope snap. The second guard returns the nod and pulls the lever. The pedestal beneath Ross's feet is yanked back, and he drops until the rope jerks taut. His neck snaps and he dies almost instantly. Ross's body spasms for a few seconds as he shits and pisses himself, then grows still. The rope sways back and forth for 40 seconds before slowing to a stop.

The crowd, equal parts mesmerized and horrified, lingers for a full minute, then slowly shuffles toward the exits. It's cold and grey, appropriate weather for a hanging perhaps, and transport shuttles wait outside to ferry people to various drop-off points throughout Zones Alpha and Omega.

Aside from McCarthy and the soldiers who now accompany him everywhere, Susie is the last to leave. One of a shrinking number of people to have been conceived and born on Mars, she has outlived nearly everyone she's ever known and loved, starting with her parents and ending with Josh, a tough athlete who was once described as "decent" by a former classmate of his from a different time and place. Susie looks forward to the challenge of finding someone to succeed Interim Chancellor McCarthy, but suspects while there is, finally, a light at the end of the tunnel, that tunnel is very, very long.

"Susie," McCarthy calls out as she trails the crowd heading to the shuttles.

She turns to him. "Yessir?"

"Live your life. That's an order."

She smiles. Just barely, but it's there, and it's a start.

3

Picture it, if you will: Six months have passed since the Blockade and Occupation, and life in Chicagoland has returned to some sense of normalcy. The "L" runs more or less on time, same as before. Traffic on the Dan Ryan is a bitch, same as before. The city's unhoused, many of them veterans, hunker down against the weather on Lower Wacker Drive, same as before. The Chicago Bears go 11-and-4, same as the year before. Vinnie's Arcade Alley is open with the same name as before. A banner above the door reads UNDER NEW OWNERSHIP, but aside from a reduced customer base, little has changed here, too.

It's the day after Thanksgiving, and decorations adorn Michigan Avenue and Equitable Plaza, formerly known as Pioneer Court and so named for the city's French-Haitian settler, Jean-

Baptiste Point DuSable, who built a trading post in this spot in the 1700s. The *Christkindlsmarkt*, a German food and heritage market with a holiday bent, won't debut here until 1996, but a giant Christmas tree and Nativity scene are *de rigueur*. Despite the unseasonably mild weather, the crowd that normally gathers to watch the tree lighting is more subdued than previous years. Similarly, CTA buses, as well as suburban MetraRail, run reduced hours due to lower ridership. When you consider than almost 5,000 residents and commuters are estimated to have disappeared—exact numbers will never be known—is it any wonder those citizens who push for life as we know it to go on find themselves fighting an uphill battle?

A marble monument covered by a tarp sits in one corner of Pioneer Court, opposite the Christmas tree and dwarfed by the adjacent Equitable Building. A quartet of CPD officers, winter coats unzipped on such a mild, late fall day, stand dutiful guard in front of caution tape surrounding the monument while an events crew sets a podium on rafters, arranges folding chairs for the press, and runs wires for the audio system prior to the monument's early afternoon unveiling.

4

If City Hall is its usual hive of activity, then Mayor Washington's office is the center of worker bee bustle. Despite weighing in at 284 pounds and bearing that load on a frame already suffering from hypertension, high cholesterol, and an enlarged heart, few people in the city work as hard, pre-or-post-blockade, as Harold Washington himself.

He stands over his desk and flips through his calendar. His press secretary, the always-on Alton Miller, paces back and forth, stressed over an especially busy day. The mayor's phone, forwarded to his secretary's desk, rings in the next room as it does all day, every day.

"Mr. Mayor, sir, let's table our comments for the school board until after the unveiling. I say we send 'em a memo, not a press release—couple sentences max—and nip the inevitable bad PR in the bud by just not giving it the attention naysayers think it deserves. One or two news cycles and it'll be forgotten." Miller, who clocks in at half of what Hizzoner weighs, is so high-strung he is just as likely to die of a heart attack or stroke as the mayor himself.

Or maybe not. "Your Honor, are you okay?" Miller asks as the mayor struggles to loosen his tie, then grabs his left arm with his right hand.

"Can't . . . breathe," the mayor gasps. He collapses at his desk.

"Jesus . . . Sir? Your Honor?" Miller checks the mayor's pulse in a state of panic and picks up his phone. "Shanelle, this is Alton. Call 911, I think Hizzoner's had a heart attack!"

5

A large crowd has gathered in front of the covered monument. Police flank Robert, Sr., Junior Senator Crisp, Governor Thompson, Deputy Mayor Orr, Police Chief Barnes, and Captain Bennett. Reporters and VIPs fill the folding chairs immediately in front of the monument. Pete, Lori, and Gail are among those gathered in the front row. Others include Lori's parents, Charles and Helen; Corporal Ramirez and his pregnant wife, Lety; the widows of Air Force Captains Hunter and Ramsey; the spouses of Senator Crisp and Governor Thompson; and the requisite military brass.

Notably absent from the dedication: Detective Lieutenant Mayotte.

Police snipers perch atop the Equitable and Wrigley Buildings. Reporters from the local network affiliates and from WGN-AM radio, which conveniently broadcasts from the Tribune Tower next door, round out the crowd. Samara sits in the back row alongside her partner, Jane, who sips coffee from a paper cup with ERNIE'S BAGELS embossed on the outside. Pete scans the crowd and locks eyes with Samara. They exchange strained smiles. *It's good to see a familiar face,* Pete thinks. *I'm glad Samara got a happy ending, but damn, such sad memories otherwise.* He's certain she feels the same way.

One reporter performs an audio check, then steps into the frame and begins to speak. "This is Gretchen Hollingsworth with WFLD, reporting live from Pioneer Court, where Mayor Washington, Governor Thompson, and several members of local, state, and federal government are about to dedicate a memorial to the heroes of last May's blockade. It's been six months since those days darkened this great city by the lake, and millions mourn the passing of friends and associates who perished or simply disappeared during the Blockade and Occupation, many through acts of heroism and many more by simply being in the wrong place at the wrong time. We're just moments away from the unveiling and from the mayor's remarks."

A police cruiser, siren off, pulls into the plaza, as far from the press cameras as possible. Chief Barnes trots over to the cruiser, which has its window rolled down while the officer riding shotgun breaks the news of the mayor's passing. Chief Barnes nods and jogs back to the others. He fails to keep a straight face as he whispers the news to his fellow government officials. The hubbub does not escape the notice of the crowd, which erupts in what-could-it-be murmurs. There is a general air of disagreement over who will address the press corps that has gathered, until, finally, Robert, Sr. is overheard saying to his colleagues, "Oh, for crying out loud, I'll say something!"

The deputy mayor slips away as Robert, Sr. approaches the podium, stern-faced. "Is this on?" he asks into the mic and gets the requisite feedback squeal in response. "Perfect. Ladies and gentlemen of the press, residents of Chicago and of the State of Illinois, concerned citizens, we'd like to begin with an unexpected announcement. We apologize for the late start, but we just received news that Mayor Washington, who was supposed to kick off today's dedication, was pronounced dead, we believe of a heart attack, earlier this afternoon. His press secretary, Alton Miller, was present at the time of the late mayor's passing, and will make his own announcement as well as provide succession information from City Hall at four o'clock today. We don't have any additional information at this time, but on behalf of both branches of Congress and of those other governmental bodies gathered here today, I would like to extend our condolences to the mayor's family."

Gasps and murmurs overtake the crowd, but Robert, Sr. is determined to get through the dedication. He thumbs through his cue cards with leather gloves on as he waits for the gossip to down. Once the crowd stills, he proceeds with his original address and barely references the cards. "We came here today not to announce death, but to celebrate life. With that, I'd like to proceed with our original agenda, however soured though the hour may have become. Six months ago, the scourge known as the Blockade and Occupation of Chicago came to an end, and today we pay tribute to those who helped make this momentous victory possible. Frankly, there are too many heroes to name, and if you believe what you read, more are alive but forever separated from us, millions of miles and hundreds of years away."

He pauses and makes eye contact with Gail, Pete, and Lori. Gail wears a simple pantsuit. Pete wears a dark wool suit that is two sizes too big and that he can't wait to change out of.

Lori wears a black dress that would be called stunning were the occasion less somber.

"But let's stick with what we *do* know," Robert, Sr. continues. "We know that on May 25th, a raid was made on the Chicago Genetics Center operations facility on Northerly Island, over the site of the former Merrill C. Meigs Field, and that an explosion detonated the convertor believed to have made time and location displacement possible. We know that this explosion set off a chain reaction which disabled laboratories and holding bays inside the CGC facilities themselves. We know also that company CEO Wesley Mannfred Arendt perished in the explosion, and that no unusual activity has since been reported in the vicinity of Northerly Island. Finally, we know that elsewhere that same evening, bombing runs were conducted along the property lines surrounding Chicago Midway and O'Hare Airports, and that several dozen terrorist suspects —also known as Loyalists—remain in custody, awaiting trial alongside the two dozen former CGC administrative employees we successfully tracked down. All of this information was made available in the Pentagon Papers published just three weeks ago.

"Today is the day after Thanksgiving. As such, before we unveil our memorial to the Heroes of the 1987 Blockade and Occupation, I'd like to share a few thoughts that lend perspective to the many moving parts of the greater operation. Who are these heroes we should be thankful for? Who ran sorties from Washington to Midway and O'Hare while the airports were under siege? Who gathered intel detailing how citizens were transported, by molecular de-composition technology, from their homes and businesses to the CGC operations facility and beyond? Who struck the fatal—"

Robert, Sr. pauses to compose himself. In the audience, Pete, Lori, and Gail do the same. Lori holds her mom's gloved hand in her left hand and Pete's in her right. She squeezes his hand and fights back tears. Robert, Sr. continues his dedication. "Who struck the fatal blow that disabled the CGC convertor? I was privileged to know several of these people—these pilots, these police officers, these impromptu crusaders for the Windy City, these . . . American teenagers. It is my honor . . . m-my most humble honor . . . to memorialize them here today. You owe them. I owe them. *We* owe them . . . everything." His voice squeaks with the last word. He motions toward the sculptor, who pulls a drawstring that raises the tarp.

"Ladies and gentlemen," Robert, Sr. concludes, "May I present 'Selflessness,' by Hyde Park sculptor Mabel Greene."

He vacates the podium, overcome with emotion. His colleagues console him with pats on the back and nods of the head. There is no applause in this somber moment, just the sound of press camera flashes lighting up the memorial, a vertical slab of marble sculpted in the shape of the Sears Tower, featuring a raised fist on one side and a Lockheed cargo jet above the fist. Molded into the base of the tower are three figures standing upright, noble, gazing up at a flag of the city, blazed into the forearm of the raised fist.

Below, the base of the monument reads, THE SELFLESS: HEROES OF THE BLOCKADE AND OCCUPATION, and is followed in smaller letters by a list of names in two columns. Some names, such as Bob's, are preceded by an asterisk. Below the columns, in the same size and lettering, are the words, AND THE MISSING. Below and to the right, in smaller lettering, is an asterisk and a single word: DECEASED.

After the initial barrage of press photos, spectators line up in twos to read the names up close. Pete and Lori approach alongside Gail, Helen, and Charles. Helen immediately spots Lori's name (which does not have an asterisk), and Lori searches for Bob's. She bursts into tears at the sight of it. Helen rests a hand on her shoulder. Pete traces first, his name (no asterisk), then Bob's. His lip quivers with bottled-up emotion as Gail turns to him. "Thank you, Pete. Thank you for being a friend to my son."

That's all it takes. "I'm sorry, Mrs. W.," Pete says, barely able to get the words out. "I, um, I can't be here right now. I just . . . I'm sorry." He runs off.

"Pete!" Lori exclaims.

She turns to run after him, but Gail restrains her. "It's okay Lori, let him go."

"He'll be alright, sweetheart," Helen adds.

The WFLD reporter continues her coverage of the event. "An emotional dedication this Friday after Thanksgiving as you can see, and a surprising one as well," she reports. "In a moment we'll return to the studio for more words on the life and career of the late Mayor Washington, who was the city's first Black mayor, who was widely praised on both sides of the aisle for his swift response to the Blockade and Occupation, and who, as we just learned, has died unexpectedly. We'll be bringing you coverage of his press secretary's address later this afternoon as well, so be sure to stay tuned. As for the dedication itself, to echo the words of Senator Wilkinson, we owe a debt to those citizens and good Samaritans who played a part in bringing last May's events to a swift conclusion. The monument behind me, by local artist Mabel Greene, is called 'Selflessness,' and that seems a fitting name indeed. This is Gretchen Hollingsworth with WFLD, reporting live from a stirring and somber scene."

6

Picture it, if you will: A soft coat of new fallen snow marks Christmas Day, 1987. The temperature is a peaceful 36 degrees, so the snow sticks around a few days but doesn't prevent much of a skidding hazard for those long-haul truckers unfortunate enough to be spending the holiday on the road.

A Jaguar XJ6 pulls into the Wilkinson driveway. Charles, Helen, and Lorraine Rainsmith emerge from the car, Charles holding a bottle of dessert wine and Helen carrying a Christmas ham. Last but not least, Molly hops out of the back and makes yellow snow. They walk to the front door. The door opens before Lori has a chance to ring the bell. "Merry Christmas," Gail exclaims from the other side. She opens the screen door, reinforced with storm glass for the season, and admits her guests. Molly jumps excitedly at Gail, who finds herself far from overjoyed. "Oh my, aren't you a sweet girl?" she says, putting on a fake smile as only a politician's spouse can do.

"Down, Molly May," Lori commands. The dog obeys, although her tail continues to wag with the enthusiasm of a kid in a candy store.

Robert, Sr. waves at the guests from halfway down the stairs. "Merry Christmas, friends." Molly runs up to greet him and he gives her a much-sought-after scratch on the chin. This makes her whole year.

"Merry Christmas," Helen replies, as chipper and folksy as ever.

"Merry Christmas, Mr. and Mrs. Wilkinson," Lori says.

"We brought foodstuffs and libations," Charles adds. He tucks the wine bottle under one arm so he can unzip his coat.

Gail relieves Charles and Helen of the ham and wine. "Let me get that for you. Pete's around here somewhere; he can take your coats."

"On my way," Pete says from an oversized chair in the parlor. He gets up and extends an arm for everyone to drape their coats over. "These'll be right in there." He sets them atop the grand piano that takes pride of place in the large but sterile room.

"Bless you, Peter," Helen says. "Merry Christmas."

"Merry Christmas, Lori's mom," he replies.

"You can call me 'Mrs. Rainsmith,' how 'bout that?" Helen instructs, always so prim and proper.

"Yes, Mrs. Rainsmith."

"It'll be another 30 minutes for dinner, I'm afraid," Gail says. "You're early."

"The early bird gets the worm," Charles explains.

"I suppose that's true. Anyway, the ham was not expected. Helen, if you'd like to follow Lori, she'll show you where the kitchen is. I'm sure we can find a platter to warm that up. We otherwise are just waiting on the turkey."

"Certainly," Helen says. "Lorraine, dear, show me the way."

"It's just over here, mom," Lori says. Molly, whose wet nose kicks into overdrive at the smell of turkey and brown and serve rolls, leads the way.

Gail turns to the three males loitering in the foyer. "Charles, if you want to follow my husband, I believe he was about to watch that dreadful Jimmy Stewart movie in the family room. Right now, I need to speak with Pete here."

"Not a fan?" Charles asks. "It's a classic!" He is referring, of course, to *It's a Wonderful Life*.

"Oh, she loves it," Robert, Sr. says.

"Not every year, broadcast back-to-back-to-back for 12 straight hours, I don't," Gail corrects him.

"It's in the public domain, honey." Robert, Sr. cups his hand and whispers in Charles' direction, "She loves it."

Gail looks at Pete, who wears baggy corduroy pants and an ugly Christmas sweater featuring Han Solo and Chewbacca in Santa hats. Yes, ugly Christmas sweaters have been around since the 1980s.

"Come with me." She leads Pete into the parlor. A six-foot, artificial Christmas tree is illuminated in one corner of the room, but it pales in comparison to the much larger tree in the family room, which boasts a vaulted ceiling and simply begs for a 12-foot, real Douglas fir. "Have a seat."

"What's up, Mrs. W.?"

"Have you spoken with your parents today? Or your sister?"

"Uh, yeah, I called and spoke to my mom this morning. Becky's working through New Year's. Well, not today, obviously. Uh, the store offered her and mom both seasonal overtime. After that, they're gonna try and make it up here for, like, a delayed Christmas or something. It would only be for a few days though; ma said Becky's already enrolled down there for next semester and wants to finish out the school year. I guess she really likes it there."

"And she'll be a senior next fall?"

"Uh, that's right." Pete has no clue where this line of questioning is going.

"That's what we wanted to talk with you about." Gail purses her lips in thoughtful consideration of what she's about to say. "Pete, dear, you know you can stay here as long as you'd like, right?"

Pete nods. "I know. You and Mr. W. have been very kind that way."

"We're happy to have you. And Pete, Robert and I discussed this, and thought with today being Christmas, it would be . . . well . . . Pete, we know you're 18, but all the same . . . we would like to adopt you."

Pete says nothing. He stares at the carpet, astonished and more confused than ever.

Gail continues. "You don't have to give us your answer right away. We don't want you feeling pressured. I know you've been having a rough time with everything. It's been difficult for us, too. But things are different now. The senator's stepped down from the science committee and cut back his travel schedule. And as you know, I've stopped accompanying him on every trip. So it wouldn't be like it was with Robbie, where we were just never around. Besides—and don't take this the wrong way

—we're starting to wonder if your parents are ever even coming back."

Pete's lip quivers like it did at the dedication. He opens his mouth and takes in air as if to speak . . . but remains silent.

"Pete, I'm sure your sister has adjusted by now to her new school. If she completes the spring semester down there, do you *really* think she's going to want to return here for just one more year of high school? You said yourself a lot of her friends died, too." She is quick to wipe away a single, runaway tear. "I apologize for being so direct. It's just . . . It doesn't sound like your sister wants to come back. Or your mom or your dad, for that matter. Just last month you said your dad found work outside Tampa as a shift supervisor, and I have it on good authority that the place he worked here closed its doors a few months ago. And your mom has a job now, too? Pete . . . son . . . your family abandoned you!"

Tears pour down Pete's face. Gail steps forward to give him a hug. He raises an arm like a defensive shield and wards her off. A look of devastation washes across her face—but only for a second. She is the wife of a politician, after all. She steels herself and retreats to the kitchen.

Pete crumples in his chair, hands clasped, as his whole body shakes. It takes him several minutes to get his emotions under control as seven months' worth of trauma—and a few, too-brief moments of levity—bowl him over. Earth's destruction as witnessed during the Journey. The horror of the Pit. Humping motions at Vinnie's. Getting snapped by Josh's towel in the locker room. The belly beater attack. The shootout in the time chamber. He and Bob laughing over something only they would find amusing. Bob speeding past him, Lori, and Corporal Ramirez. The memorial sculpture being unveiled.

He is the oldest 18 year old in the world.

A gentle snow falls outside as the Wilkinson and Rainsmith families relax in the family room after Christmas dinner. A fire blazes in the stone hearth on one end while the giant tree provides mood lighting on the other end. Molly sleeps on her side in front of the fireplace, her belly stuffed with people food. That timeless classic, *A Charlie Brown Christmas,* airs on a massive projection TV, the sound muted. A Fisher audio system circa 1980 plays Christmas music at a comfortable level—background noise, really. Dessert wine has been consumed by all, including Lori, although when Robert, Sr. tops off everyone's glasses, Helen covers Lori's with her hand—one glass is enough for her little girl, thank you very much.

Notably absent from the fireside chat: Pete.

"Gail," Charles says, with a slight slur to his words, "let me once again say what a splendid meal that was." Either Charles started drinking before they left for the Wilkinson home, or this dessert wine is some strong stuff. Or both.

"There's always a bounty on Jesus's birthday," Helen, the insufferable optimist, points out.

"Where's Peter?" Robert, Sr. asks.

"Where *is* that boy?" Helen remarks. "He just disappeared right after dinner, didn't he?" She turns to Lori. "Sweetheart, did you see where he ran off to?"

"No, mom."

"Today was a tough day for him," Gail explains. "It's a tough day for us all."

"Amen," Helen adds.

"I'll go look for him," Lori says. She places her empty wine glass on the kitchen counter on her way upstairs to Grandma Ruth's old room. Making heads or tails of the dishes piled around the sink will prove a formidable chore in the morning for whomever tackles them.

. . .

Pete lays on his back like a stargazer in the bedroom once occupied by Grandma Ruth. Headphones cover his ears as he listens to *The Joshua Tree* by U2. Lori knocks on his door, and he lowers the headphones to his neck. The spiritual rock eulogy "One Tree Hill" echoes from the Walkman. "What's up?" he asks.

"They were looking for you downstairs. You okay?"

Pete shrugs. "Apparently, my family's abandoned me."

"They'll be back. Besides . . . Christmas in Florida? Can you blame 'em?"

"I guess not." After a few beats: "I miss him."

"Bobby?" He nods. "I miss him too. Every day." Lori sits at the edge of the bed.

Pete is quick to change the subject. "How's college?"

"Fine, I guess," Lori says with a shrug. "Just Gen Ed's mostly. Poli sci, psychology, stuff like that."

"Sounds boring."

"Psych's pretty interesting. It's a 101 so we're just studying theory, but, like, to learn how to help someone discover what's inside their own head could be cool, I guess. Like . . . I never would've thought about it until . . . you know."

"I know."

"You should try it, Pete. I mean, not psychology necessarily, but college in general. I don't know if it's too late to enroll for spring semester, but there's always next fall. Maybe think about it?"

"Maybe. Not so sure it's for me anymore."

"So what *is* for you?"

"Dunno. Think I might join the Peace Corps. Like Tom Hanks in *Volunteers.*"

Lori nods. "I can see you doing that. You'd get to make a difference in people's lives."

Pete shrugs. "For what little time they have left. For what little time we *all* have left."

"Hey, you totally don't know that. We might change the future for the better. Um, with what we know now? People are capable of amazing things!"

"I hope you're right, Lor."

"Call me 'Rain-Rain.' "

"Nah, that was yours and Bob's thing."

Fighting back tears, Lori steels herself and walks over to the door. "It was good seeing you."

Pete nods, lips pursed. He, too, struggles to hold back tears, and can no longer look Rain-Rain in the eyes.

. . .

Lori crosses the hall and opens the door to Bob's old bedroom. She enters the room and takes a long, slow scan of everything in it. The wallpaper trim of antique cars over a cadmium green background. The electric razor on Bob's dresser. The *Back to the Future,* Samantha Fox, and Alyssa Milano posters. The framed picture of his birth mother. A Chicago Bears pennant. His hairbrush. A *Peanuts* lunchbox, not eaten out of for years but kept, perhaps, as a nostalgia item. A retro White Sox baseball cap, emblazoned with the team's classic, 1919 logo. A Lego prop plane. The Pinewood Derby race car carved out of balsa wood during Bob's Cub Scout years. A bulletin board with merit badges thumbtacked to it. A Rubik's Cube, midway to being solved. A bottle of English Leather cologne (*Who told him to buy that?* Lori wonders). A pint-sized Statue of Liberty, a gift from Grandma Ruth for Bob's ninth birthday. Grimlock and Slug, a pair of *Dinobot* Transformers. His Snoopy stuffed animal, much loved as a child and currently in need of a bath and some stuffing. Dual stacks of Atari 2600 and Sega Master System cartridges in side-by-side towers next to his 19-inch Zenith television. VCR and game consoles on a stand below the TV. An adjacent milk crate, overflowing with LPs. On his headboard, a record player, its turntable covered with dust. Above that, a yellow CAUTION sign. His pillow, of which Lori takes a long, mournful sniff, savoring Bob's musk.

She peeks in his top dresser drawer, sees neatly folded socks and underwear, and decides snooping through his unmentionables is a bit too invasive. She walks over to his closet instead. His backpack hangs from one of the doorknobs. Inside the closet sits a skateboard in one corner and a tennis racket in another corner, cobwebs running across the strings. In the opposite corners sit a pair of black loafers, worn only once, to a dreadful Career Day event, and a Darth Vader-shaped carrying case for *Star Wars* action figures. The rod is lined with clothes on hangers, and she brushes the back of her hand against the clothes. She closes the door and the backpack falls from the knob. She carries it to his waterbed. After steadying herself, she opens the pack and removes its contents, one item at a time. His Trapper Keeper, a ruler, a spiral notebook, a trigonometry calculator, a paperback of *The Catcher in the Rye*, and two textbooks, each one wrapped in a book jacket fashioned from a brown paper grocery bag. The second book catches her eye—it is Bob's physics text, with I LOVE LORI scribbled on the jacket in red ink and shaded with pencil. "Oh, Bobby," she whispers, and hugs the book to her chest for dear life.

Like Pete, she, too, is overcome with memories. Hers, though, are only happy ones. One she has returned to many times in her mind, as she does now, is of a moment that, if the technology still existed for her to travel back in time, she would not dare revisit in person, because it was perfect just as it was: she and Bob at Lover's Leap, sitting on a blanket as she turns to kiss him and he retreats, then moves in for a second try . . . and a third . . . and a fourth. This fourth kiss, long and sweet and real, is the kiss all others in her life will be compared to, and found wanting. Bob and Lori made love afterwards, but it was the kiss itself Lori will never forget, a moment suspended in time and forever in her heart.

# Author Note

Thank you for not roasting me too hard after reading Part One and throwing up your hands in frustration over my decision to send Pete and Dana on their Journeys without immediately revealing their fates. For Part Two, I figured the least I could do was resolve that nasty cliffhanger in the sequel's opening pages.

Young Savannah, who somehow survived an interstellar Journey *in utero*, is a fighter, much like Dana, Susie, and Rose. Together, these remarkable women will work with Interim Chancellor McCarthy and his successor (Leonard?) to heal a divided civilization and vie for a safe and equitable future.

Dana made the conscious choice to remain on New Earth for the sake of her child, and of course it was the right one. She has much to learn about motherhood, and about life in the 24th century.

As for Susie and Rose, they were lucky to walk away with their lives, although their survival came at a heavy cost. Hopefully, time will ease Rose's bitterness over the death of her friend Dixon, and Susie will heed the Old Man's advice to live a happy life. She certainly deserves one.

Our heroes in Chicagoland face similarly uncertain futures. If Pete joins the Peace Corps, will the small difference he makes in that capacity be enough to assuage the dark cloud that hangs over him with the knowledge of Earth Prime's ultimate fate?

Lori is still undeclared at the end of *Displaced – Part Two*, but something tells me she'll take out double majors in psychology and political science next fall. Was she right when she posited that maybe, just maybe, humankind will work in harmony, not opposition, to delay its own extinction? Only time will tell, but whatever happens, methinks Lori will enjoy a full, fruitful life, and will never stop fighting the good fight.

But what about the novel's men and women of law enforcement? To whom will Captain Bennett assign the disgraced Detective Lieutenant Mayotte's casework? Detective Heinbrenner seems as good a candidate as any. Mayotte clamors to know the backstory of the bright-eyed Heinbrenner, an *émigré* from behind the Iron Curtain. Frankly, so do I.

For purposes of genre classification, *Displaced – Part Two* is science fiction/time travel. At its core, however, it's a tragedy that deals not just with time and location displacement, but with suicide and mental illness as well. If you struggle with feelings of self-harm, I encourage you to reach out to the **988 Suicide & Crisis Lifeline** (formerly the National Suicide Prevention Lifeline) for 24/7 support. Simply dial or text 988 from your cell phone. All calls are confidential and free. Remember: You are not alone.

Thank you to my illustrators, Zoe Price (Instagram: *@_Art.ificer_*) and Stephanie Tunnell (Instagram: *@bright_abyss_miss*; portfolio: *https://stephanieltunnell.crevado.com/*). Thank you as well to my original beta readers, Tessa Brown, Jorge López, and Nan Richards.

Last but not least, thank you to everyone for reading!